I was out of my league—I just didn't want the bad guy to know it...

"Look, the stuff is in London," I said. "That's all I'm telling you now. But I need time to make arrangements to turn it over to you."

"Why don't we just go and get it right now?"

"It's not that simple. I have to do things to make it work. The girls are involved in this thing, too, I told you that. And I have to protect myself, don't I? You may not trust me, but I don't have a hell of a lot of trust in you, either. You know where I am, you know where the girls live. I don't know anything about you. So in one way you've got the upper hand. But on the other side, I've got what you want, so you have to deal with me. You hear what I'm saying Mr...what's your name anyway?"

His face twisted in anger. His eyes had sparks in them. "Fuck you! You don't need my name. Tell me what you got in mind."

"Tomorrow morning, 10 a.m. Meet me in front of the Tate."

"What's that?"

"It's a museum, asshole. The one you're going to meet me at is called the Tate Modern. Just ask any taxi driver. They'll take you right there."

"What'd you do, park it in a museum?"

"Don't strain yourself trying to figure it out. Meet me there and you'll get your stuff. Guaranteed. If not, you know where to find me."

He shook another cigarette out of a pack and lit it with a gold lighter. He blew some smoke through his nose and gave me another of his cold, blue looks, trying to show me how tough he was. If the look was meant to scare me, it did, a little, but I wasn't about to let him know it.

And then, with a loud grunt, he pounded his fist into the middle of my belly. It felt like I'd been kicked by a horse. The breath shot out of me like an erupting volcano. I bent over, grabbing at my middle. Pain. Lots of pain. My eyes filled, my knees buckled. While I was gasping for air I heard him say: "Just so you don't get any ideas."

KUDOS for *Deadly Secrets*

In Deadly Secrets by Robert Boris Riskin, Jake Wanderman is a retired teacher/amateur detective, who volunteers to help a friend's long lost daughter when she is accused of murder. Jake follows the girl to London where he uncovers some dark secrets about the victim and makes himself a target, inadvertently, of the killer. Although I had a little trouble comprehending why a Shakespeare-spouting, retired teacher would make a good detective, once I got into the story, I quickly overcame that. Deadly Secrets has a strong plot and some very interesting characters. – *Taylor Jones, Reviewer*

Deadly Secrets by Robert Boris Riskin is an amateur detective story along the lines of Agatha Christy's Miss Marpel. The main character is a retired teacher who plays detective for a friend when his daughter is accused of murder. Other than a sharp mind and some friends on the police force, Jake doesn't have much to recommend him as a detective. But he makes an interesting character, nonetheless. I like the fact that he continually quotes Shakespeare and never seems to notice that no one else gets the joke. It reminds me of some of the nerds I knew in college. Along with quite a few intriguing characters, Riskin has given us a strong storyline, some very tense edge-of-the-seat moments, and a lot of fast-paced action. It is not a book that you can read once and forget. – *Regan Murphy, Reviewer*

Jake Wanderman is not your average retired teacher and Shake-speare maven. He has tangled with the Russian Mafia in Moscow and assassins in Jerusalem and always come out on top. Now his childhood friend's long-lost daughter is a suspect in a murder investigation and Jake's help is needed. The daughter flees to London and he follows, searching for clues. Instead, he uncovers rape, suicide, and secret identities. And falling in love with the female detective on the case only complicates the issue.

Like Sam Spade phoning in his reports to Effie, Jake Wander-man talks us through this corkscrew case in his own inimitable, Brooklyn-wise-guy style while quoting Shakespeare at every opportunity.

ACKNOWLEDGEMENTS

As always, I'm not sure where to begin because there have been so many people who have helped me in the process of writing this manuscript. I'll try to remember to include everyone, but if, inevitably, I've left someone out, please forgive me.

First, and foremost, to my writing brethren, The Ashawagh Hall Writers Workshop, led by the indomitable and brilliant Marijane Meaker (aka M.E. Kerr). Their incredible insightfulness, criticism and suggestions, gave me the knowledge, inspiration, and desire to be able to do this work.

To Dr. Estelle S. Gellman, my best friend and motivator. Faith Spink and Hal Riskin, my daughter and son; Gloria Beckerman, poet and friend; Stephen Grossman, most knowledgeable lawyer for legal information and advice; Sag Harbor Village Police Chief, Tom Fabiano for his time and knowledge, Detective Sergeant Vincent Posillico, formerly of Suffolk County Homicide Squad, who answered dozens of questions about police procedure; and numerous others with whom I've discussed various issues that came up while writing this book.

Thank you!

DEADLY SECRETS

By

Robert Boris Riskin

A Black Opal Books Publication

DEADLY SECRETS
Copyright © 2014 by Robert Boris Riskin
Cover Design by Jackson Cover Designs
All cover art copyright © 2014
All Rights Reserved
Print ISBN: 978-1-626941-19-9

First Publication: MARCH 2014

Published by Black Opal Books **http://www.blackopalbooks.com**

DEDICATION

This work is dedicated to all those whom I loved, still love, cherished and still cherish: my wife, mother, father, uncles, aunts, cousins, my children, grandchildren and great grandchildren, my nieces and nephews, and my friends. And the woman who has become my loving companion.

My parents and their siblings fled the pogroms and forced conscriptions to come to America. They had no English, few resources. But they were determined to survive. And by dint of hard work and effort, they did indeed do more than survive. They made good lives for themselves and their children.

My wife was stricken with polio at the age of twenty-three. She spent the rest of her life in pain but never let that deter her from her great art and ability to live her life to the fullest.

My memories of them are my inheritance. My love for them and their love in return has given me the strength to endure all that life had in store for me in the past and to look forward with great expectations to the years that lie ahead.

CHAPTER 1

This is art?" I said. "For this, you dragged me out of the house?"

Morty Adler shrugged. "What can I tell you? She's famous. World-class famous."

We were at an art opening in East Hampton in August. This was like saying there was snow in the Arctic. Southampton, East Hampton, Water Mill, Wainscot, Montauk, all had professional artists who came for the summer or lived there year round. In addition to well over sixty galleries, they displayed their art in banks, book stores, real estate agencies, in fact, almost any place that would have them. On any given weekend in season there were dozens of openings. The crowds showed up for the more famous, of course. The one we were at was crowded, but not with the usual hangers on. These folks were all well-heeled and well-dressed because it was for charity.

The particular "art" I was referring to was an installation, set up in the Valerie Venable gallery. It consisted of a living room, bedroom, and kitchen. The colors were uninteresting, the furnishings right out of a 1950 *House Beautiful* magazine, complete with a reproduction of a Norman Rockwell Saturday Evening Post cover. What made this a work of art, I didn't know, but maybe that was the point. A brochure claimed that the artist, Sarajane Relda, had created dozens of these apartments and furthermore, they could be found in museums and private collections all over the world. The brochure also explained that visitors were invited to use the apartment as if it were their own. You could cook something for yourself or your friends in the kitchen. You could party in the living room, or even take a nap in the bedroom.

The whole thing struck me as pure bullshit but Morty had asked me to come as a favor and since he was my best friend I couldn't say no. But I couldn't help remembering that the last time he'd asked me to do him a favor I got mixed up with the Russian Mafia, the KGB, the FBI, and the NYPD. Not only mixed up but locked in a Lubyanka prison and almost killed. I could do without that happening again.

What I really wanted was to be alone. I was not in good shape, mentally or physically. The past year had been a rough one. The murder of a friend. A beating that put me in the hospital. These I'd dealt with. In the long run your brain accepts, your body accommodates. But the one thing I had not been able to accept was the sudden, unexpected death of Rosalind, my loving wife, just about one year ago. I was still a long way from dealing with its consequences.

"I could be home having an agreeable vodka on the rocks," I said. "Instead, I'm here with you, surrounded by blue blazers and diamond earrings."

"What can I say?" Morty said. "You're a pal. I really didn't want to go by myself."

"Why didn't Sherri come with you?"

Sherri was Morty's spouse. I thought of her that way, a spouse, not a wife, because I'd never liked her.

"She went to visit her mother. Actually, I'm glad she did. It's a little easier without her."

"Why? You and she not getting along?"

"Nothing like that. It's just better without her."

I was about to question him further but I could tell he wanted to get off that subject. "I'll take your word for it," I said. "*A friend should bear his friend's infirmities*." I was quoting Shakespeare, a habit I'd developed after teaching it for thirty years. Morty didn't blink. He'd heard me do this a zillion times.

"At least you'll get some good food. They brought in a famous chef. Tickets for this are five hundred bucks."

"Well, that's a change from the usual suspects in search of free wine. But why are *you* here? And for this kind of money? I don't recall you ever being interested in the fine arts. Your direction is more in the line of golf, tits, and ass."

I can speak the King's English as well as anyone, but when I'm with Morty my Brooklyn roots tend to take over.

Morty looked away from me. "I didn't pay anything. The artist e-mailed me from London—that's where she lives. She said she's doing a show in East Hampton in July and would I like to come to the opening. She arranged for free tickets."

Servers had begun circulating through the crowded room with trays of glasses filled with champagne and others containing elaborate looking hors d'oeuvres.

"Who is this artist? And why would she comp you a thousand dollars' worth of freebies?"

Morty reached for two glasses. "Just a minute. I need this." He managed to get the first glass down in one gulp and began drinking the second, but at a slower rate.

"What's with you and the champagne? You never drink."

"It looks like good stuff. Don't worry. I can handle it."

"Okay. Then I may as well join you," I said. I took the champagne and reached for a canapé.

"Tuna ceviche with edamame puree on a wonton chip," said the girl holding the tray. She held out a sheaf of napkins and smiled at me, obviously proud that she'd said it correctly.

"Thanks." I popped it into my mouth. It was good. I appreciated an unusual hors d'oeuvre but I was equally happy with pigs in a blanket, deli mustard, and potato knishes—soul food. Hot dogs always managed to bring back memories of being young and biting hungrily into one at Nathan's in Coney Island. Morty and I had done that on hot summer days, getting there by subway at first and then, when we were old enough to drive, taking dates on cold winter nights. It was cheap and fun and usually led to parking in one of the rest areas on the Belt Parkway where we would spend a while necking and getting both hot and frustrated. Unlike now, when teenage sex was taken for granted, in those days the girls we knew insisted on virginity.

"Another blue ball night," we'd say afterward.

A server came by. I couldn't help asking, "What've you got?"

"Peppercorn crusted filet mignon on daikon."

Morty and I each took one.

"This chef has talent," I said. "Now how about answering my question."

He grabbed my arm. "There she is."

Two young women had come into the room accompanied by an older woman in a long-sleeved, red dress down to her ankles. Shining on her neck were a trio of necklaces studded with red stones. Her high spiked heels were red, as were her nails, of course, as well as her lipstick. For all I knew, her bra and panties may have been red, too. Happily her eyes were not, but their dark pupils glittered as they took note of who was in the room. This woman had to be Valerie Venable, owner of the gallery. Red was known to be her signature color. A good choice if you wanted to make sure you were noticed.

Morty took a deep breath. "Time to bite the bullet. Come with me, okay? I need you."

The two younger women were complete opposites in looks, build, and just about everything else. The one that drew my attention as we got closer was, of course, the better looking one. She was about five eight and wore her low cut black dress with an air of elegance. Silver rings adorned all the fingers of her right hand while the other was bare. One ear had four tiny diamonds stitched into it. I looked at her mouth. When I meet a woman, what I most want to examine is her mouth, then her eyes. Rosalind's mouth was incredible. I could never take my eyes off it.

I never really understood why some women's mouths are attractive to me and some not. This young woman's mouth was lovely, with a narrow upper lip, and a full lower one. Kissable, you might say. Her eyes were dark and appeared to be almost black, probably because of her thick black eyebrows.

The other girl had a body like my friend Morty, bulky and round, wore her hair in a page boy that reminded me of an old Barbara Stanwyck movie, and was dressed in a blue polo shirt and jeans. Her mouth was thin and she had a jaw like a bulldog.

The three of them looked at us and for a moment. No one spoke. Then the one in the black dress held out her hand, a serious expression on her face. Morty shook her hand. I could see that he was trembling. Obviously something powerful was going on here. I was getting more and more curious.

"I'm so glad you could be here," she said.

"Thanks for inviting me." He turned toward me. "This is my friend, Jake Wanderman. I asked him to come along. My wife's out of town. I hope you don't mind."

She held out her hand to me. "I'm Sarajane Relda, and I'm very pleased to meet you." Her accent was definitely American but there was also a touch of upper crust English in it. "This is my friend, Margo Staller, and this is Valerie Venable. It's her doing that I'm here."

The gallery owner was a small woman, with auburn hair, eyes encircled with black eyeliner, and mascara'd lashes. She managed a nod at me then began searching the room for more important people.

Margo shook both our hands. "I'm very pleased to meet you." Her accent was all English, but not the plummy kind, you know, where the sounds seem to come from the bowels.

There was an awkward silence. I attempted to break it. "Is this your first visit to New York?"

"No," Sarajane said. "But it's the first time I've been in The Hamptons."

"It's my first visit," Margo said.

"How long are you going to be in East Hampton?" Morty said.

"We haven't made definite plans. Several days certainly."

"I hope we can get together at some point."

"I'd like that," Sarajane said. "Valerie has arranged for the gallery to be open twenty-four hours a day. The idea, of course, is the allusion to real life. But I'm quite sure I can get away for an hour or two sometime."

"That would be great," Morty said.

"Speaking of food," Valerie said. "We are in for a treat tonight."

"I know what you mean," I said. "We've already had some of the hors d'ouevres. And they were excellent."

Valerie continued as if I hadn't spoken. "I was supremely lucky to get this fabulous chef to participate. He's just opened the trendiest new restaurant in New York. *Sylvia*, it's called. He's had one in London for some years and one in Paris. It's said they're named after his mistresses. Isn't that amusing?"

I noticed that, upon hearing this, Sarajane's face showed a brief moment of something I couldn't quite identify. Shock? Dismay? I wasn't sure, but it was gone almost instantly. She said, derisively, "I don't find it at all amusing."

"I think you should circulate," Valerie said, ignoring her remark just as she'd ignored mine. "Give people a chance to meet you."

Sarajane looked at us and shrugged. "I suppose I should. Hopefully, we can talk later. All right?"

Once we were alone, I said, "Okay. Now give."

"Fine," Morty said. "But first, another glass of champagne is required."

"You're gonna fall on your face."

We tried to find a quiet place to talk but there was none.

"Why don't we step outside?" I said, "It'll be less noisy."

We showed our tickets to a security guard at the entrance so that we'd have no hassle getting back in. Outside, some smokers were gathered, puffing away. We went a few yards farther and I waited for Morty to explain what was going on.

"You remember after I graduated NYU I went to college in Philadelphia?"

"I remember, you said it was the best osteopathic college in the country."

"And I didn't come home?"

"You wrote that you liked it there and wanted to set up a practice. I thought you were nuts. Who would want to be in Philadelphia?"

"I didn't want to be there. They made me stay."

"Who made you stay?" I said. "Your family?"

"Not my family. The girl's family. The girl I knocked up."

The light clicked on. Relda? The name had sounded odd to me originally. Suddenly it became clear. The artist's name—Relda—Adler spelled backward.

"Holy shit," I said. "Sarajane is your daughter?"

He nodded. "And this is the first time I've seen her since she was 11 months old."

CHAPTER 2

I had a million questions. "Why now? Why here? What made her get in touch with you?"

"I don't really know," Morty said. "Like I told you, she called me from London. Explained who she was and said she wanted to meet me. Then she e-mailed me her picture. Can you imagine how I felt? After all these years? I was a total mess. I couldn't think of what to say."

"How come you didn't first set up a private meeting somewhere? Wouldn't that have been better?"

"This is what she wanted. I wasn't about to argue."

I turned away from cigarette smoke that had drifted over. "Amazing that you kept this secret all these years. Wait a minute. Is it possible that Sherri didn't know anything about this either?"

"She still doesn't. I never told her I'd ever been married."

"Are you kidding me? How do you keep something like that from your wife?"

"It just never seemed like the right time to bring it up."

"I don't know. I can't understand why you kept it a secret. You didn't run out on the mother and baby, did you?" I answered my own question. "Nah! Not you."

"I didn't run out exactly. But I did leave them." His eyes went behind me.

"I've been searching for you." It was Sarajane, looking more beautiful than before. "They're doing an interview with me for television. I thought you might like to watch it."

We went back inside and found Valerie and Margo. "The Food Channel people are here" Valerie said. "They're getting ready to interview Tony and Sarajane. I arranged the whole thing."

"Tony? You're sure that's the chef's name?" Sarajane asked.

"Yes. Tony Oakhurst. Why? Have you heard of him?"

Sarajane didn't answer.

A young woman came in wearing a headset. "Are you Ms. Relda? I'm Gillian Hanson, the producer. I'll be asking you and Mr. Oakhurst a few questions. Don't worry. The questions are quite straightforward and won't give you any problems." She clipped a small microphone to Sarajane's blouse. "We're ready to begin."

Margo looked at Sarajane, studying her. "Is something wrong, SJ?"

"Give me a minute," Sarajane said, not moving. She clasped her hands together and closed her eyes.

"What's the matter? You're not ill, are you?"

"I feel a little faint, that's all."

"If you're nervous about the cameras, don't be," Margo said. "Just be yourself, charming and lovely. It will be over before you know it."

One area of the living room had been set up for the interview. Powerful lights focused on a platform for the participants to stand on. Behind them, the wall had been blanked out with dark cloth so the background wouldn't compete with the people being filmed. The invited guests had been moved to the back of the room allowing the camera crew to operate.

Morty whispered to me. "Something's upset Sarajane. I get the feeling she doesn't want to do this."

"Maybe its just nerves."

"Where's Mr. Oakhurst?" a voice behind the camera said.

The door from the kitchen opened and a man came out wearing a white apron and white chef's toque. He was tall, broad shouldered, and walked with an air of *Hey*! *Look at me*! *I'm hot stuff*! "Excuse me, please," he said, pushing past people in his way. He smiled when he saw Sarajane and held out his hand. "Sarajane Relda. I'm delighted to see you again."

Sarajane did not answer him nor did she take his hand. I couldn't be sure if it was because she was nervous or if it was a deliberate insult, but it was obvious that Oakhurst took it as an insult.

"This is not live," the producer Gillian said, clipping a microphone to his shirt. "So don't worry if you flub something. We'll be able to edit it out. Okay?"

"Sure," Tony said.

"Then shall we begin?" the producer said.

"No!" Sarajane shouted. She stepped back. "I can't do it."

Her eyes seemed to grow larger. The pupils became black, rolled up, and vanished. Then her eyes closed and she fell slowly and quite gracefully to the floor.

CHAPTER 3

I rushed forward with Margo and Morty right behind me. Sarajane lay quietly, unmoving, her face peaceful, as if she were sleeping. I could see her chest rise and fall so I knew she was breathing. I couldn't help a flashback to the night Rosalind died. We'd just come back from dinner. I opened the front door. As I followed her inside she stopped for a moment, then without a sound, she fell slowly to the floor. I stooped down to see what had happened. She was in the same position as Sarajane, partially stretched out, knees bent beneath her, eyes closed, seemingly asleep. I don't know how I knew she was dead, but I did.

Now my face was very close to Sarajane's, perhaps an inch or two away. "Sarajane," I said.

She opened an eye, winked at me, and quickly closed it.

I heard Margo say, "Can't you do something?"

"We want to get blood flowing to the brain," Morty said. "We need to elevate her legs."

"Get some pillows, would you?" I said to Margo.

Morty put his ear next to Sarajane's mouth to check her breathing, then turned her head to the side, took hold of her wrist, and felt for a pulse. Margo came back and handed me a couple of pillows. "Is she going to be all right?"

I stuffed the pillows under Sarajane's ankles so that her legs were off the floor, took off my blazer, folded it, and put it under her head. I wanted to tell Morty she was all right but there was no way to do it with everyone nearby.

"She's okay," Morty said. "Her pulse is fairly rapid but not abnormal and her breathing is clear. She fainted, that's all."

"Should we get her to a hospital?" Margo said.

"That won't be necessary," Morty said. "It's hot in here. She was nervous, probably hadn't eaten for a while. Fainting in such a situation is not surprising."

"I can't believe this is happening," Valerie snapped.

Tony Oakhurst stood next to Valerie. "I'm sure she's going to be fine. Probably too much excitement. Women..." He didn't finish.

Sarajane's eyes opened. She blinked a few times, apparently trying to focus, then said, "I think I must have fainted."

Morty smiled. "Yes, you fainted. Now lie there a while longer, then we'll move you into the bedroom where you can be more comfortable."

"Thank God you're all right," Margo said.

Sarajane tried to sit up.

I put my hand on her shoulder. I'd decided to play along. "Not just yet. Give your body time to revive itself."

I looked up because I sensed the crowd closing in on us. "Hey people. Would you please move back and give the lady a chance to breathe? Thank you very much."

Sarajane shook her head. "I think I'm able to stand up."

Morty and I both helped her up with me wondering what the hell this young woman was up to.

"Don't try to walk yet," Morty said. "Are you a little dizzy?"

"No. I'm fine."

"Then let's go into the other room away from the crowd. You can sit there for a while and rest. I don't want you doing anything else, just yet."

"Is that absolutely necessary?" she asked.

"Do what the doctor says," Margo said. "You've had a nasty shock."

We went into the bedroom which had a queen size bed, night tables on either side, a dresser, and two upholstered armchairs. Sarajane sat in one of the chairs, Margo in the other. Valerie sat on the bed. Morty and I were both standing.

"Would you like something to drink?" Margo asked her.

Sarajane shook her head. "I feel all right. Really, I do."

There was a loud knock at the door. Before anyone could respond, it opened and the chef came into the room. He went directly to Sarajane. "What is all this? I say hello and you act like you never saw me before in your life?"

Sarajane didn't answer.

"Hey," I said. "Give her a break. She's just getting over a faint."

He glared at me. "Who are you?"

"A friend. And I think you ought to back off a little here."

"I'm sorry. I'm upset. I haven't seen Sarajane in a long time. I was looking forward to this. I wanted to congratulate her on her success as an artist. I wanted to celebrate that we've both become successful in our fields. And then she treats me like I'm a piece of shit."

"I couldn't have described you better myself," Sarajane said.

"Whoa," Oakhurst said, stepping back and holding up his hands. "You're not going to start *that* all over again."

She closed her eyes and wrapped her arms around her shoulders, as if shielding herself from him. "Please get him out of here."

I took hold of his arm. "Time to go, friend."

The chef tried to wrench his arm away, but I didn't let go. Then I squeezed his bicep, which was as soft as a banana, I knew it had to hurt.

"Hey!" he yelled. "What the hell do you think you're doing?"

"Getting you the hell out of here."

I pushed him out and shut the door behind him.

Morty and the two women were staring at Sarajane, waiting for her to say something. The only sound in the room was breathing.

Sarajane was pale, but seemed composed.

"What's this all about?" Margo said.

"We'd certainly like to know," Valerie added unnecessarily.

It's something—" Sarajane hesitated, shook her head. "It's difficult to talk about."

"Then don't," I said. "Maybe you ought to take a break. Go back to your hotel and get some rest."

"SJ," Margo said. "I think now would be an excellent time to go back to the hotel."

Sarajane nodded.

"Okay," I said. "Let's go. I'll take a look and see what's happening out there. There might be an army wanting to see how you are."

I opened the door a crack and peered out. The TV lady producer was there and right next to her was Oakhurst. I nodded at the woman. "She's okay. Not to worry."

"What about the interview? Will she still do it?"

"No way." To Oakhurst, I said, "I thought I told you to get lost."

"Who are you to tell me what to do? I need to speak to Sarajane."

I closed the door. "He's still out there," I told her. "I don't know if you heard but he insists on talking to you."

Sarajane shook her head. "No. Not now. I can't."

"All right. I'll run interference for you."

"Please. I don't want anything bad to happen."

"Nothing will happen unless he makes a nuisance out of himself."

"Jake," Morty said. "The guy's not a criminal. I'm sure Sarajane doesn't want any violence."

"Violence?" I was surprised to hear Morty say that. But then it struck me he'd sensed what I hadn't realized myself, that I was not only ready but wanting to hit someone. A lousy way of dealing with my own *mishegoss*. I took a deep breath to calm myself. "Sure. No problem. I'm not going to do anything rough. You know me. I'm a peace now person. *'I feel within me a peace above all earthly dignities…'*"

"Don't mind him," Morty said. "Shakespeare pops out of him in the most unlikely circumstances."

I took Sarajane's arm and marched her quickly toward the exit.

Tony Oakhurst called out: "Sarajane, we have to talk. It's important."

"Keep moving," I said.

"At least tell me where you're staying. Let me call you."

And then we were outside.

CHAPTER 4

There was still daylight when I got home but I went through my security check anyway to make sure there'd been no break-in and that no one was hiding in the shrubbery. I'd been ambushed once by goons and that had been more than enough to motivate my installing a security system. It wasn't foolproof, but it was a deterrent.

I punched the code on the alarm, went in, and headed directly to the liquor cabinet where I knew I'd find my magnum of Luksusowa. It was Polish vodka which gave me subliminal feelings of uneasiness because I hated Poland and its people for what they'd done to Jews in the WWII era. They'd helped capture and kill them during the German occupation. And when the war was over and some of the few Jews still alive managed to return to their hometowns, they were then massacred for daring to reclaim their homes and businesses. Of course, I knew there'd been good Poles just as there'd been good Germans. The bad feeling remained but I made compromises. One of the compromises had to do with their excellent vodka. And how long can one sustain hate, after all? *Thou art so possessed with murderous hate, that 'gainst thyself thou stick'st not to conspire.* In other words, hatred wears you out. Better to forgive—and drink good vodka.

I filled a highball glass with ice, cut a slice of lime, and poured the vodka until the liquid rose to the top of the ice. I let it run down my throat and waited for the result. A warm glow began in my stomach and spread slowly through my body, finally coming to rest in my brain. Alcohol was good. A wonderful pain killer. Shakespeare was well aware of the pleasure of alcohol...*A* *cup of wine that's brisk and fine...*But it had to be controlled. Shortly after Rosalind died, I'd lost the ability to manage my drinking, or much of anything else. There were countless nights when I'd lost track of how many glasses I'd had and found myself stumbling into bed half unconscious.

Then, for a while, I thought I'd gotten through it. I stopped drinking, went back to weight lifting, taking long bike rides, playing tennis, gardening. I even got into martial arts, taking classes in judo. I was careening toward sixty but my hair had no gray in it and my body began to show signs of getting back to the excellent shape it had been in before.

I went into the kitchen. I'd begun to cook again, something I loved to do. I was especially fond of Julia Child recipes like *Crepes Farcies et Roulées* and *Filet de Boeuf Braisé Prince Albert*, time-consuming but fun to prepare and very good to eat. Once in a while I'd invite Morty and Sherri to share some of my cooking, but mostly I was alone.

During that brief period I'd gotten pulled into another murder. It had the beneficial result of forcing me stop thinking about myself. I spent all my time and energy on that case and almost got killed for it.

But the good stuff didn't last.

CHAPTER 5

The phone woke me. The clock read 5 a.m. Caller ID told me it was Morty.

"What's going on? I had enough excitement for one night."

"You won't believe this," Morty said. "Sarajane just called me. She and Margo are in the police station in East Hampton."

"What happened?"

"I don't know. She said she really couldn't talk. Just that something terrible had happened. They were letting her make this phone call and that was about it."

"She didn't say anything about why they were there?"

"No. Just that I should come right away. I thought you might want to go with me."

"I'll be right there."

❧❧❧

I'd known Morty since we were five years old. I was outside my house throwing a ball against our garage door and this kid came along and asked if he could play.

"Sure," I said, and we began tossing the ball to each other, softly at first, testing each other out. The throws kept getting harder and harder with the intent being to see who could throw it the hardest. When it appeared to be a draw, we thought about something else to do. I don't remember which one of us came up with the idea but we decided to throw stones as far as we could.

Morty was first. He reached for a stone and let it go.

We watched it and almost immediately knew trouble lay ahead. The stone sailed into a window of the house across the street.

We ran like crazy into my house where I blurted out the story to my mother. A few minutes later the neighbor knocked on the door. My mother told the neighbor not to worry, she would pay for the damage. Then she gave us cookies and milk.

We'd been close as brothers ever since.

***

Morty's house was off Noyac Road, same as mine, but that was the only similarity. I lived in a Cape Cod, with small rooms upstairs and down. Rosalind had removed some walls to make the rooms larger. Our short driveway was just wide enough for two cars. No garage.

Morty lived on three acres. His driveway of crushed blue gravel lined with Belgian block wound one way and then another for some two hundred yards before circling around to a parking area near the front entrance. The house itself was more of the same: enormous rooms furnished by a New York City decorator with a connection to ABC Carpet and Home. There were two Remington bronzes—Morty's taste—a collection of Venetian glass—Sherri's and the decorator's taste—and a series of colorful abstract paintings signifying nobody's taste. Morty had done well in his practice, but it hadn't hurt that Sherri had come from a family solidly embedded in Wall Street.

I parked Rosalind's Cabrio near the front door. I'd never liked the VW but ever since her death I'd felt compelled to use it. Morty's Mercedes was in the garage, of course, next to Sherri's Jaguar convertible. I wondered if Sherri had come back from her visit to her sister.

Before I could knock Morty opened the door. His usual half smile was now a scowl.

"When did you hear about this?" I asked.

"Maybe a half-hour ago."

He went toward the kitchen and I followed him.

"Did Sherri get back yet?"

"No. She's due back later today. I made coffee. Want some?"

"No thanks. Let's get over there. I'll drive. Splash some water on your face. You look like hell."

The East Hampton Village police department was on Cedar Street near North Main right next to the fire department. It was a twenty minute ride down Route 114 to Stephen Hands Path then onto Cedar, a well-known speed trap. A cop often hid in the bushes waiting for the unwary to go over the limit. I drove carefully and watched the speedometer.

"You know you're going to have to tell Sherri about Sarajane," I said.

"I know. I have to figure out how to do it."

"Open your mouth and let the words come out."

"You're a big help."

"You were going to tell me why you kept this whole thing a secret, remember?"

"Yeah, okay." He took a deep breath. "It was all about the marriage. It was doomed from the start. We got married, but we didn't have any money so we lived with her parents. I went to school and she stayed home waiting for the baby. She was born almost the same time I graduated. I got a job with a group of chiropractors and after a while I was making enough for us to move into our own place."

I had questions but didn't want to interrupt him.

"We just couldn't get along. Marybeth was a kid who'd never had to do anything. She didn't know how to cook or care for the baby. I was out working like a dog all day trying to make a living. Her mother came over a lot but that didn't help."

"I'm not surprised."

"It just kept getting worse and worse until I couldn't take it anymore. I had to get out. But Marybeth didn't want me to go. Even though I said I'd help support the baby, it didn't make any difference. Her mother and father were also furious. Looking back on it later, I realized it wasn't all her fault. We were both kids, both know-nothings. A couple of hot nights together and no thought of the consequences."

"I think it took a lot of guts on your part, to do what you did."

"It didn't seem that way at the time. But I kept my promise. I sent her a check every month without fail. Even when I could barely make my rent. When I got my own practice going, I increased the support without being asked. And that included everything, even art school in Paris."

I was still watching the speedometer. "Why didn't you go back and see the kid?"

"They wouldn't let me."

"Why the hell not?"

"Marybeth never forgave me for leaving her. She said I'd abandoned her and the baby and so I didn't have any rights. And my being in another state was no help. I spoke to lawyers about it. They said I could go to court but she could always find a way to obstruct me. I didn't have the strength to fight her."

"Just the same, you have nothing to be ashamed of."

"You're wrong. I am ashamed. I should have fought harder but I didn't have the guts. I took the easy way out. Maybe that's why I never told anyone."

CHAPTER 6

The police station was a brick building with glass windows set back from the street. Black letters above the windows spelled out, *East Hampton Village Police*. There was a small lawn in front with low growing evergreens around the foundation. It might have had a country-cozy look in the daytime but at this hour it seemed forbidding.

When we walked in, the uniformed officer at the front desk said, "Dr. Adler. What're you doing here?"

"Hi, John. My daughter called me. Can you tell me what's going on?"

"One of those girls brought in is your daughter? Jesus."

"What happened?" I said.

"This gentleman is a friend," Morty said. "Jake Wanderman."

"Hang on a minute, guys." The officer spoke some words I couldn't hear into a phone. "Someone'll be out in a minute."

I glanced at Morty for an explanation of how he and the cop knew each other. "John's a patient of mine," he said.

"He's a great doctor," the cop said. "Saved me from becoming a cripple."

The front room of the police station was sparse: a desk for the policeman, a couple of benches, a few framed photographs of East Hampton on the walls, a New York State flag, an American flag.

We waited a while, then a door at the side opened and someone appeared that made my eyes open wide. I knew her. Oh yes, I knew her. And seeing her again brought a rush of con-

flicting memories. Detective Sienna Nolan. That she was a Suffolk County homicide cop was not a good sign.

"Hello, Detective," I said. "Nice to see you again." I put out
my hand and she put hers into it. Her hand was warm, the touch,
friendly.

"Good to see you too, Jake. Sorry it has to be under these
circumstances."

"Are we dealing with a homicide here? And is Dr. Adler's
daughter involved?"

Without answering me she held out her hand to Morty. "I
remember you, Dr. Adler."

"What's going on?" Morty asked.

"Come inside," she said.

We followed her into a corridor and then into a room with a
table and four chairs—period. The bare walls were painted a
pale gray.

I'd first come in contact with Detective Nolan a while back
when a friend of mine was murdered. She was put in charge of
the case. I was involved because my friend's daughter asked me
to be. Sienna and I had disagreements and arguments along the
way to finding the murderer. In spite of that, or maybe because
of it, our relationship grew close. Maybe too close. At any rate
she was beautiful and ruthlessly efficient. She'd also saved my
life.

Sienna closed the door and sat down putting a notebook
and pen on the table. "There was a 911 call from the Venable
gallery about 2:30 this morning. The call was made by a security
guard. He reported a dead body and two women at the scene.
When the local uniform got there he found your daughter, Dr.
Adler, her friend, and a body."

"Whose body was it?" I asked.

"The victim's name is Tony Oakhurst. I understand he's a
famous chef."

"Was," I said. I looked at Morty. He looked at me. "And he
was murdered?"

"Correct."

"You don't think my daughter had anything to do with this,
do you?" Morty said.

She didn't answer his question. "Do either of you have any explanation for the two women to be in the gallery at that hour?"

Morty shook his head.

"No," I said. "But you must have asked them that already. What did they say?"

Again she didn't answer. She was good at that.

"When can I see her?" Morty said.

"In a little while. We understand you were both at the gallery last night. I'd like to get your version of what happened there. My partner will talk with you, Dr. Adler, and I'll interview Jake. It won't take long."

"Why can't I see my daughter now?"

"Because we need to do this first."

"Then can I see her?"

"Of course."

I felt bad for my poor friend. Here he was with his new-found daughter in this sticky situation and he was all but helpless. I wished there was something I could do to help him.

The door opened and a man came in. He was in his forties, dressed in a suit and tie. He had wide shoulders and over-developed, weight-lifter muscles that threatened to rip the seams of his suit jacket. "What's up?" he said.

"My partner," she said, "Detective Battle."

"Josh. This is Dr. Adler. He's the father of the artist. And this is Jake Wanderman, a friend of his. You can use the other interview room, okay. I'll be with Mr. Wanderman."

When they left, Sienna leaned forward and adjusted her notebook, not looking at me. "Tell me what happened last night, Jake. Start from the beginning."

"Don't you want to ask me how I am? I can see you're looking good."

"You look fine. As for the rest of it, this is not a social visit."

"You still with that same guy?

"Maybe this was not a good idea—my doing this interview."

"Does he know anything? About us, I mean?"

"No. Nobody does. Remember what I said afterward? It was a one-time thing. She shook her head. "I made a mistake. I'm going to let my partner do your interview."

"Don't do that. I'm sorry. I'll try to keep the past out of this. Your private life is none of my business, anyway. What do you want to know?"

"Can I count on you now?"

"Absolutely. *Mine honor is my life*. I'll be good."

"All right. Tell me what last night was all about. What you did, what you saw, any interaction between Oakhurst and anyone else. Did anything occur that was out of the ordinary?"

I tried to think about how much I should tell her. She was, after all, a cop, and at this point an adversary. Because Sarajane was Morty's daughter I felt it was my duty to protect her. I decided to be cautious. "Nothing very unusual, I'd say."

"All right, just tell me your version of the evening."

"Well, it was an art opening. Big deal charity event. Morty was invited by his daughter. She's the artist, but he didn't want to go alone. He asked me to go with him. I went. Reluctantly. Art openings are not my thing."

"He's married, isn't he? Why didn't he go with his wife?"

"She was out of town."

"What time did you get there?"

"About five, five-thirty."

"Then what?"

"Nothing much. There was food. The show itself."

"I understand there was to be an interview for TV."

"That's right."

"But it was canceled. Do you know why?"

I was trying to guess how much she knew and how much she was fishing for. "Sarajane fainted and couldn't do it."

"Was she ill?"

"Too much excitement, I guess."

I didn't see any reason to tell her that Sarajane had faked it.

"Did you ever meet her before last night?"

"I never even knew she existed."

"You didn't know Dr. Adler had a daughter? I thought you were close friends."

"Not close enough, I guess. I only found out last night when he decided to tell me. That's when I figured out her name is Adler spelled backward."

"Do you know why she did that, not use her real name?"

"Don't have a clue. But he told me he hadn't seen her since she was a baby. When she called it came as a total surprise. She said she had this show scheduled here and would like to meet him. Morty was nervous as hell but everything went smoothly."

I didn't know why but I was sorry I'd given that information away.

"Why hadn't he seen his daughter in all this time?"

"You'll have to ask him."

She made a note. "Did you meet Oakhurst?"

"Don't be tricky, okay? If you spoke to Sarajane, you know I met him. He was doing the catering for the affair."

"It's not a trick. Why are you so defensive? I'm just asking questions as I think of them."

"Sorry. I'm a little tense. I think you can guess why."

"I'll ignore that. What happened after she fainted?"

"We did some first aid, took her into the bedroom. After a while she felt better but not enough to do the TV interview. Then she and her friend went back to their hotel and I went home."

"Wasn't there some kind of confrontation between Ms. Relda and Mr. Oakhurst?"

So she knew that much. "Oh yeah. I forgot about that."

"It was only a few hours ago. What's happening, Jake, your memory going bad?"

"It wasn't that big a deal. He wanted to talk to her and she didn't want to talk to him. She asked me to get him to leave her alone, which I did."

"How did you do that?"

"I asked him to leave the room and when he resisted I kind of pushed him out the door."

"You assaulted him?"

"I didn't do anything of the kind."

"Weren't there words back and forth between them?"

"Only that he wanted to talk and she said she didn't want to."

"What time was this?"

"I'm not sure. Maybe around seven thirty, eight o'clock."

"Was that the last time you saw Mr. Oakhurst?"

"Yes."

"What about Ms. Relda? Did you see her later that night?"

"No. I went home. I haven't seen her since." There was a moment of silence. "By the way," I said. "How was the guy murdered?"

"He was stabbed. We believe it was with one of his own knives."

CHAPTER 7

We were done. Sienna led me to another room where I found Morty along with Sarajane, Margo, and the other detective. The young women both had the same appearance: red eyes, limp hair, body language suggesting they had not an ounce of energy left.

"For the moment, you're now all free to go," Sienna said. "Of course, we'll want you to remain available for further questioning."

When we were outside the sun was shining brightly. I was tired and my eyes felt as if they had sand in them but it was a beautiful day and the air was good to breathe. "What do you want to do, Morty? About the girls?"

"What do you mean?"

"Are you kidding me? Don't you want to talk to them, find out what happened?"

Morty slapped the side of his head. "Of course. I wasn't thinking."

"Then let's tell them you'd like to take them back to your house. We can give them coffee, something to eat, whatever, get the story, and let them crash."

"You think that's a good idea? Sherri is coming back sometime this morning."

"Great. You can tell her everything. *Confess yourself to heaven.*"

Sarajane and Margo had no objection. In fact, I think they were glad to have some comfort offered to them. But first they wanted to go to their hotel and freshen up. We drove them back to the Hunting Inn and waited in my car.

"You don't think they had anything to do with this, do you?" Morty said.

"No, of course not."

I didn't want him to get more upset than he already was. But I wasn't as sure about their innocence as I tried to sound. Sarajane had faked that fainting spell which showed there were other aspects to her. I hadn't mentioned that yet to Morty and didn't think now was the right time. And it wasn't good that the victim was Oakhurst, considering what had happened between them at the gallery. Obviously, there was something in the past that was bad, bad enough that just seeing him could have that effect on her. Was it possible that she could have killed him? Or maybe she and her friend together? I didn't know anything about this girl, her background, her life, her personality, except for the little I'd seen just those few hours ago. I guessed it was possible for the two women to have found the chef temporarily alone. They might have had an argument that got out of hand and killed him. Or, they might have planned to do it all along.

When Sarajane and Margo finally came out of the hotel they were not the same tired, worn-out-looking women they had been before. Now they seemed refreshed, vibrant, apparently having done whatever women do, seemingly without effort, that results in remarkable transformations.

We drove without talking as if an unspoken pact had been made that we would wait until later before they told us whatever they were going to tell us.

Morty's house was empty. Sherri wasn't back yet.

Coffee for us, tea for Sarajane and Margo, and toast. That was the extent of Morty's abilities in the kitchen. But I was hungry. "Do you have any eggs?"

"Take a look. Be my guest."

There were a dozen eggs, not the kind I used, from uncaged chickens that lived on fresh veggies, but white supermarket eggs that had probably been in cold storage for months if not years. I asked the young ladies if they'd like me to cook something and they nodded yes. I found butter, mushrooms, and onions. In a few minutes I'd sautéed the onions and mushrooms, whipped up the whole dozen, added pepper and dried parsley, and made four not bad omelettes. After we'd eaten and I'd had my hunger satisfied, I said, "Okay ladies. What do you say? We'd like to hear what you told the police."

They glanced at each other, expressions of doubt clearly visible.

"You know, about what happened last night."

"Can I say something?" Morty said. "About my friend Jake, I mean. It might sound to you like he's a bit pushy. That's because he is. But in a good way. He's trying to help me and to help you. I'm not good in this kind of situation and he is. He's been in two murder investigations already. And helped find the murderer in both of them. In fact, he's known locally as the 'Sam Spade of Sag Harbor.' He's had a lot of experience and knows what he's doing. What I'm trying to say is that it's to your benefit to tell him everything you can."

"That's very nice of you, Morty. I really appreciate that. The 'Sam Spade of Sag Harbor.'" I didn't reveal that the rabbi of the synagogue in Sag Harbor had once told me the same thing when he'd asked me to help him out with an enraged member of the congregation. "But I'll bet these ladies have no idea who the hell 'Sam Spade' is."

Sarajane laughed. "You're wrong. He was the detective in *The Maltese Falcon*, one of my all-time favorite films."

"SJ has watched that movie at least a dozen times that I know of," Margo said, "although I must say, it's not my cup of tea. Anyway," she said, turning to Sarajane. "Why don't you tell them. It's your story, not mine."

Sarajane put her cup down. "Very well. I'll tell you exactly what I told that woman detective. When I do a show like this, I mean, where the work is kept open twenty-four hours a day, I always make it a point to go back in the middle of the night to see what, if anything, is happening. I've always done this. And Margo, more often than not, comes along. We walk in, see who is doing what. Its usually quite enjoyable, even entertaining. I've seen people dancing, listening to music, playing card games, or just sitting and talking.

"But last night was different. We could sense it the moment we got there. Firstly, there was no guard at the entrance. I wasn't happy about that but I assumed he was in another room. We called out. There was no answer. There were no people at all. Not a sound except for music playing in the background.

"That was the living room. We went into the bedroom to see if anyone was there. What we saw was the guard, fast asleep on the bed. We tried to wake him. I smelled liquor on his breath and guessed he'd had some of the leftover wine. He mumbled something about no one being there and that he'd only just fallen asleep. We left him to get himself together and wandered back to the only other room we hadn't been in. That was the kitchen. And that's where we found...the body."

She lowered her head.

"What exactly did you see?"

Sarajane shook her head. Margo answered for her. "Oakhurst was lying on the floor. He was on his side. It seemed as if he were trying to crawl away from his attacker. The handle of a knife was clearly visible in his back. There was a considerable amount of blood."

"Jesus Christ," Morty said.

"Did you go near the body? Touch anything?"

"Neither one of us moved. We were in shock, I think. We stood in the doorway and didn't budge. There was blood all over. At that moment the guard came, looked over our shoulders, and yelled, 'What the fuck!' Then he called 911."

"That's it? You're sure?"

"Absolutely sure."

"Well, at least there are no fingerprints or anything like that," I said. "But you realize you're under suspicion, don't you? Both of you."

"Not really," Sarajane said, recovering. "Why should we be? All we did was discover the body."

"You were there in the middle of the night," I said. "That alone would make them suspicious."

"I thought I'd just explained that."

"Come on," I said. "Get real. I believe you, but that doesn't mean the cops believe you. Now let me get to something else. How much did you tell the cops about Oakhurst? And about how you were upset at seeing him?"

"I told them that I'd known him when I was going to art school in Paris. And that I hadn't liked him, that's all."

"Did you tell them you fainted? And because of that canceled the TV interview?"

"I told them I didn't feel well."

"I told them you fainted, but I didn't tell them you faked it."

"What?" Morty said.

Margo didn't look surprised.

"How do you know that?" Morty said.

"I know," I said.

"He's right," Sarajane said. "I felt it was the only way I could get out of doing the interview."

"Your history with this guy Oakhurst is going to come up," I said. "Obviously, something happened that made you upset at seeing him. If it impinges on this case, the cops will find out about it. They're going to dig into every aspect of your life. Your lawyer will want to know, as well."

"Lawyer? You think I need a lawyer?"

"Definitely. So far you're in the clear, but who knows what'll happen next? You need protection that only a lawyer can give you. Do you want to fill us in on Oakhurst? Maybe it'll help us to help you."

"Do you really think they can find out what happened in Paris six years ago?"

"If they dig deep enough, yes."

Sarajane turned to Margo, who nodded at her. "Up to this point, Margo is the only one I've ever told." She sipped from her cup. "Back in Paris I was enrolled at the Ecôle des Beaux-Arts. Tony was going to the Cordon Bleu. We met at a bar where students used to hang out. He was handsome, charismatic. I was nineteen and quite innocent. In no time at all I fell madly in love with him." She stopped, struggling a bit. It was clear that what she was bringing back from memory was not pleasant.

We waited until she went on.

"He was not interested in me. He seemed to be with a different girl all the time. Then one day he asked me out. Just like that. I was thrilled.

"It was a fantastic night. We went for a walk along the Seine. We had dinner in a bistro. We drank wine. We talked and talked. We walked all over Paris until it was almost daylight. We had croissants and coffee for breakfast. And then we went back to my room."

She stopped again. This time the pause was longer.

"And…" I prompted.

She said something. Her voice had been clear before. Now the words came out so softly I couldn't hear them.

"I'm sorry, Sarajane, I couldn't hear what you said."

Instead of answering, she hid her face in her hands and turned away.

Margo spoke for her. "What SJ is trying to tell you is that the son of a bitch raped her."

CHAPTER 8

I heard a hoarse animal-like sound from Morty.

"Jesus," I said. "I'm sorry. I can't imagine how you must've felt. Nineteen and alone in a foreign city. Did you have any friends who could help?"

"Not really. I wasn't particularly close with anyone. I decided it was best to say nothing about it."

"Why was that?"

"I was ashamed. And he was convinced he'd done nothing wrong, that I'd been just doing the "girl" thing. That I'd been saying no but what I'd really meant was yes. I tried my best to avoid being anywhere he might be. But that didn't disturb him. He'd approach me when I was out with friends. He'd come by and leave notes for me. He couldn't understand my attitude."

"So you managed to stay away from him? You haven't seen him since you left Paris? You've had no contact with him at all?"

"That's correct. That's what I told the detective."

"But you didn't tell her about the rape."

"No."

"Did anyone else know about it?"

"They wouldn't have heard about it from me. It's possible, perhaps even likely, he told friends he'd slept with me. But if he told them anything beyond that, I wouldn't know."

"The cops are going to talk to a lot of people. I doubt they'll go as far as Paris. Still, it's possible."

"We definitely need a lawyer," Morty said.

"Yes," I said. "And then you'll both have to decide, how much should he be told?"

The gravel driveway crunched under the wheels of a car. That had to be Sherri returning home. I glanced at Morty to see his reaction. He had the same distressed look on his face that he'd had since early that morning.

"This is going to be interesting," he said.

I wasn't sure that was the right word. "You know what?" I said. "Maybe it would be best if I went home. You and Sherri and your daughter need to work all this out in private."

"Maybe I should go, too," Sarajane said.

"And me, as well," Margo added.

"No," Morty said. "Please don't go, any of you. I want you to stay. I don't know how Sherri's going to take this. I'll need all the help I can get."

I was doubtful we'd be much help. Sherri was a no-nonsense person, used to having her own way. She ran both the house and Morty's life. Sometimes he'd complain to me, saying he wished he had bigger balls so he could stand up to her, but for the most part he seemed to be content. At any rate, there was an awful lot to tell her, and not any part of that could be considered good news.

We heard her come in through the back door, an entrance that led to a mud room and then the kitchen.

"Maybe you ought to go and let her know we're here," I said to Morty.

"Good idea." He went into the kitchen shutting the door behind him.

We could hear their voices but the sound was muffled so that it was impossible to tell what was being said. I looked at Sarajane and Margo to see if their hearing was better than mine. They each shrugged, indicating they couldn't make out anything either.

They were behind the door a long time before it finally opened. Sherri came into the room followed by Morty. His former troubled expression had changed to one I couldn't read. Sherri, on the other hand, was clearly smiling. She didn't look at all like someone who'd driven a long way. Her blonde hair was pulled back into a ponytail. Full makeup and wearing a tailored black shirt, black jeans, and silver jewelry. She went directly to Sarajane who rose to her feet.

"You must be Sarajane. I can see the resemblance." She held out her hand. "I'm delighted to meet you. Welcome."

"Thank you," said Sarajane.

"I've just heard what happened last night. I can't imagine how you must be feeling. Can I get you anything?"

"No thank you. We've just had breakfast. Mr. Wanderman made us delectable omelettes."

"Of course." She smiled at me. "Our wonderful friend Jake, the great cook and the great detective. Thanks for taking care of them, Jake."

"Sure."

The words sounded genuine, not the sarcasm I might have expected. This wasn't the Sherri I was familiar with. Something weird was going on. Now I understood what the changed expression on Morty's face had meant: it was puzzlement. No wonder. If Morty had just told her everything, why would she be so calm? And not only that, but friendly, as well?

"Why don't we all sit down and discuss what to do next?" Sherri said.

The two girls and I were already sitting. I knew I should've been calling them *women* but they were so much younger that I couldn't help thinking of them as girls. Sherri and Morty joined us. For a while nobody spoke. I didn't want to be the buttinsky anymore so I waited for Sherri and sure enough she came in on cue.

"Morty said you all were talking about a lawyer. Do you know any, Jake?"

"Not really. I've heard good things about a criminal lawyer in Sag Harbor, name of Longwood, but I don't know him."

"Jeremiah Longwood," Sherri said. "I do know something about him, as a matter of fact. He defended the son of a friend of mine. The boy'd been caught with heroin or cocaine, or some kind of drug, and he got him off. My friend was very impressed. She couldn't stop raving."

"I never heard anything about that," Morty said. "What friend was this?"

"You don't know her. Julia Lattanzio. She's in my bridge game."

"Funny. I thought I knew all your friends. Wait a minute, is she the one with long hair and great looking—" he stopped.

"Tits?" Sherri finished for him.

He nodded, blushing.

My friend had never before shown shyness when discussing the female body. He was an avid looker, along with every other male I'd ever known except those who preferred men to women. I guessed his newly found daughter's presence had something to do with his current state.

"No. That's someone else. I told you, you don't know her. At any rate, I think, if Sarajane and her friend have no objection, we ought to call this lawyer right away and set up an appointment. I don't think there's time to go searching for anyone else."

"Yes, that's fine with us," Sarajane said. "Agreed, Margo?"

Margo nodded but didn't look happy. I didn't blame her. They were being driven by circumstances over which they had no control.

Sherri went to the local Yellow Book and found the number. "Sarajane, perhaps you'd like to speak with him."

"I suppose I should," she said, sounding as if it was the last thing she wanted to do.

"Poor thing, you must be exhausted. Would you prefer that I do it for you?"

"That would be so kind."

Sherri got on the phone and without giving anything away made an appointment for four o'clock in the afternoon. "He could have made it earlier but I wanted to give you both time to rest."

"Thank you. We do need some sleep."

"Why don't you stay here? We have plenty of room."

"I appreciate the offer, but I'd prefer to go back to the hotel. I'm sure Margo would, too. We'll at least be able to change our clothes."

"Whatever you wish. My husband will drive you back, won't you Morty?"

"Sure thing."

"Why don't I take them?" I said. "It's practically on my way home."

"I hate to put you to all this trouble," Sarajane said.

"He's so sweet, isn't he?" Sherri quipped.

Long after I dropped them at the Inn, I was still trying to figure out the new Sherri.

CHAPTER 9

I got home too tired to do anything but close my eyes. I woke up before noon, which meant I'd slept less than two hours. I was bummed out. Ever since Rosalind's death there'd been occasions when I'd suddenly found myself depressed, so I wasn't surprised. During my fitful sleep, I'd had a series of dreams involving women disappearing behind closed doors, which hadn't helped. I gulped a double espresso and tried to get my head together.

It was a warm day, a good one for the garden or the bike. My body was demanding activity. The garden hadn't been looked at in a while so I chose that. I was soon out there, hard at work, yanking the many weeds that loved my place. It wasn't long before my hands were dirty and sweat was rolling off my forehead into my eyes. I stopped for a minute, sat back, and rubbed my eyes with the back of my hand. I remembered the summers Rosalind and I had been in the garden together, working side by side and complaining about the weeds and how they took over no matter how much we tried to keep them out. I suddenly found it hard to breathe. I sucked air and said out loud, "Rosalind, where the hell are you when I need you?" I dropped flat out on the grass and shut my eyes. I wanted to cry. I willed myself to cry. But nothing happened.

After a while, I sat up and went back to the weeding but there was no longer any pleasure in it. I returned to the house, drank a tall glass of ice water.

I remembered that I hadn't spoken to my father in a long time. I usually phoned him once a week, not that I was obliged to. I did it because I loved the guy.

He rarely called me. "Too busy living," he explained.

He lived in a majestic old apartment building on Central Park West with his girlfriend, Zeena. I'd first met Zeena at an engagement party given for her and my father in a Brighton Beach restaurant owned by her dad. There was a big crowd. My father—who looked more like my brother—came in, his arm around a girl with hair the color of summer corn. He was a lot taller than the people around him. Zeena appeared to be in her twenties. Her extreme youth surprised me, but not that much. The older Dad got the younger his women got. What attracted them, I didn't know, but whatever it was, he had it.

She wore a sleeveless red dress that clung to her body, which was itself a steeplechase course of winding curves, hills, and valleys. A gold circle sliced through one nostril. A diamond stud glittered in her bottom lip. On her right arm at the shoulder was a tattoo of a bird. Later, when we were alone, she saw me looking at it. "It's the dove of peace," she said.

My father had always had a woman in his life and in his bed. I became aware of that not long after my mother died. I was nine years old. It wasn't long before there was an "Aunt" in the house who became my surrogate mother, the first of many. I think there were five before I was thirteen. I stopped counting after that. I remembered they were all very nice to me and I was always sorry to see them go. When I was older and asked for an explanation, the answer was: "I can't help it, sonny. I wasn't meant to be alone."

In that way he and I were very different. After Rosalind there'd been only one woman, Sienna, and that had been anything but a love affair.

He was the cool man of the world type. It blended with his manner of dress, which was custom tailored everything: bespoke suits, bench made H. Smith shoes crafted in London, Jimmie Li of Hong Kong shirts, even his underwear, which came from a contractor he found on the Lower East Side who ran a sweat shop for Calvin Klein and had my father measured personally by his sixteen year old niece.

My father didn't start out that way. His lifestyle had evolved slowly through the years as he went from being a seller of life insurance to the middle class to being the high flying operator of Central Park West, who traded oil leases, real estate, odd lots of anything that could be bought cheap and sold high.

Zeena turned out to be a remarkable girl. The fact that she and my father, in spite of their age differences, were still together, amazed me. The additional fact that they'd never married didn't seem to bother her.

Zeena answered. This was odd because my father was the one who always got to the phone first. There was something else. Her tone of voice didn't have the spark and tingle it usually had.

"What's up? Everything okay?"

"No," she said. "Nothing's okay."

"What is it? What's going on?"

"I'll let Harold tell you all about it. He's heading this way."

Then my father came on. "Hello, sonny. How's it going, my boy?" He sounded just the way he always did.

"What did Zeena mean when she said nothing's okay?"

"Did she say that?"

"Yes."

"She shouldn't have. It's a little disagreement, that's all. We're going to work it out. I'm sure of that."

"She sounded awfully upset."

"Don't worry about it. You've got your own *tsuris*. You still haven't gotten over Rosalind. But I know you will, sonny. Deep down, you're tough."

"We're not going to work it out," Zeena said. She'd picked up an extension phone. "I'm leaving you and that's final." There was a decisive click.

"Hey!" I said. "This is serious. What the hell happened?"

"It wasn't anything. We were at a party. I got smashed and was doing a little flirting, that's all. Zeena took it the wrong way."

"You call what you were doing, flirting?" She was back. "You had one hand on her ass. And the other under her dress."

"I was smashed, I told you. I didn't know what I was doing."

"Bullshit! And it's not like it's the first time."

"I never did anything more than that," my father said. "Never. I never betrayed you in word or deed. Not with anyone. And believe me, I had plenty of opportunities. But we shouldn't be talking like this with my son on the phone."

"He's my son, too," she said. Loud, this time. The energy was back in her voice, "I'm glad he's on the phone. I'm glad he's hearing this. I want him to know what a shit he has for a father."

"That's cruel," my father said. "Sonny and I have always had a great relationship. Do you think he'd turn on me now?"

"I just want him to know you're not the wonderful human being he thinks you are."

"Hey guys. Don't put me in the middle of this. I love you both and want you to stay together. Zeena, you're the best thing that's happened to my dad in a long time. Please reconsider. When he says he was smashed and didn't know what he was doing, you can believe it." I was figuratively crossing my fingers behind my back. "I've seen him that way many times."

"See?" My father said. "See? I don't know what I'm doing when I drink too much. My base instincts kind of take over. They take control of everything, especially my hands."

"This is too much," Zeena said. "Now the both of you are ganging up on me."

I could hear a change in her tone. "Think about it," I said. "That's all. Just don't make any hasty decisions. That's not so much to ask."

"You hear that?" my father said. "Sonny knows what he's talking about. He's always been smart. What else do you expect from a professor?"

"I've never been a professor. I was just a teacher."

"Don't get technical on me. You're smart. You know a lot about what's in books. You don't know shit from shinola about making money but that's another story."

CHAPTER 10

Because of the brouhaha with Zeena I was able to get off the phone without telling my father anything about the previous night. He'd learn about it soon enough. Then, of course, I'd get an earful of *How come you didn't tell me? I had to find out about it from the TV.* In addition, because he was the original know-it-all, he would demand to hear all the details from me and that would, in turn, elicit all sorts of editorial advice and comments. But that was in the future and I'd be better able to deal with it.

I'd no sooner put the phone on its cradle when it rang.

Morty. "You won't believe this, Jake. The girls are at the station again. For fingerprints. The cops also came to their hotel room and took the clothes they'd worn yesterday."

"When was this?"

"Not long ago. Maybe in the last hour or two."

I looked at my watch. It was 2:45. Their appointment with the lawyer was at 4:00. "I think you better call the lawyer and tell him what's happening. He'll know what to do. Then call me back."

I hung up and prepared to wait. After less than thirty seconds I knew I couldn't. I tried Morty but the phone kept ringing which meant he was probably talking and not picking up the waiting call. I was sweaty and dirty and badly needed a shower but there was no time for that. I got in the car and headed for the East Hampton police station. I didn't know what good I could do there but I wanted to be where the action was.

The shortest way to get to East Hampton from Sag Harbor was to take Route 114. This was a more or less direct road without many curves but with a distinct "no passing" double yellow line for its entire length. The speed limit had recently been reduced from 55 MPH to 45 MPH. If you got behind a diddler doing 30 MPH, you were stuck. Stuck that is, unless you were a red neck in a pickup or a yuppie in a Range Rover, in which case you made your own rules and passed whenever you felt like it.

Of course, because I was in a hurry, I found myself behind a driver doing 40 MPH. So I broke the law in my own way and called Morty while driving. This time the call went through.

"The lawyer's going over there," Morty said.

"What else did he say?"

"Nothing."

"I'm on my way now. I couldn't wait. You're coming, too, right?"

"Check. And Sherri, too, I guess."

"Great," I said, making sure to keep my tone neutral.

I went to the same police station I'd been to before but when I asked about the girls the cop didn't know anything about them.

"They must be over on Pantigo Road," he said. "East Hampton Town police. This is the Village station."

I didn't know the reason, what's more, I didn't care. But I wondered if Morty knew this. Either he knew or he didn't, and if he didn't, he would find out.

The Town police station was behind the East Hampton Town Hall and next to the Justice Court building. When I got there I found the driveway partially blocked. An arrow directed me around a huge construction site. I remembered reading that Adelaide De Menil, one of the old time multi-millionaires had donated a bunch of historic buildings to the town so they could not only be preserved but used for offices. They sat there, above ground, waiting for foundations. In the meantime there was a lot of mud.

The police station itself was an unpretentious—no, ugly— one-story cinderblock building with a couple of parking spaces in front. There wasn't much to see at the entrance, just a desk with a cop behind it. I was told by the officer at the desk there was nothing he could do for me. "All I can tell you is their lawyer got here a little while ago. You'll just have to wait."

I had no authority to say or do anything so that's what I did—nothing. At least it was a good sign that the lawyer had showed up. I went outside and waited for Morty to show. If I were still smoking it would've been the perfect time to light up but I'd given up that weed twenty years ago. Not the other weed though. I didn't use it much but I liked to keep some of it around in case of emergency. When I was really down it added a great boost to the vodka.

I saw Sherri's Jaguar come up the driveway and park. Morty and Sherri got out and waved at me. "What's happening?" Morty said.

"*Nada.* The lawyer's here. That's all they'd tell me. Maybe, since you're her father, you can get somewhere."

We went inside. Morty told the cop who he was and that he wanted to see his daughter.

"Sorry," the cop said. "You'll have to wait."

"What do you mean, we have to wait?" Sherri said. "My husband's daughter is here. And her lawyer as well. He has every right to see her."

Sherri's voice and attitude hit the cop like a couple of bricks. It didn't surprise me because I'd seen her angry before, but it sure took the wind out of him. "Take it easy, lady. I'm just doin' my job."

"Well, do it right. Call someone if you have to. But we want to see her right now."

He looked down, hiding from her glare, and picked up the phone. Before he could say anything, Sarajane and Margo appeared, followed by an extremely tall, thin man dressed in a dark suit and looking like an undertaker with a mission. This could only be lawyer Longwood. I wondered if Sienna would appear but she didn't.

"There you are," Morty said. He rushed forward and put his arms around Sarajane.

She responded by burying her face in his chest. I was glad to see this happen. It was the first time I'd seen real emotion from either of them. I knew Morty'd been feeling it but until now, maybe because of it having been a long held secret, it seemed he'd been reluctant to let it show.

We all introduced ourselves to the lawyer and then went outside. "Let's go back to my office," Jeremiah Longwood said. "We can talk leisurely there and I'll explain everything as much as I'm able."

We drove back to Sag Harbor. His office turned out to be above a bank on Main Street. We followed him up a flight of stairs to the second floor, through a small waiting room to an interior office where a middle-aged woman with red eyeglasses sat at a desk.

"Jackie, we'll be going into my office for a while. Don't put any calls through until I say it's all right."

His office had a comfortable feel to it. The room was not especially large but had enough space to hold his desk, a table piled high with files. At the other end were an armchair and a couch. Framed degrees, photos, and art work decorated the walls as well as bookshelves filled with lawyerly looking books.

"We need more chairs," he said, picking up a phone. "Jackie, would you be kind enough to bring in three folding chairs?"

In a moment, the good secretary appeared, shlepping the chairs by dragging them along the floor. I went over to help. Sarajane and Margo sat in front of the desk, Sherri, Morty, and I behind them.

Longwood's funereal face cracked open to let a hint of a smile out. "Welcome. When you called for an appointment this morning, I didn't expect this." Every one seemed to relax a bit, which is what I guessed he'd intended. He leaned back. "Let me review what's occurred so far. When Dr. Adler called and told me Ms. Relda and Ms.Staller were at the police station I was not officially the attorney of record so I had to ask you, Dr. Adler, to state to me that I was, or I could not act. You understand that, don't you, that I wasn't trying to force myself into this case?"

"Of course," Morty said.

"Good. It's important you understand because I don't take every case that's offered to me." He paused. "Although there have been times when I regretted turning someone down. We had a high profile murder out here a few years ago. I didn't want any part of it because I'd become acquainted with one of the principals. However…" He let the rest of the sentence go as if he now regretted having mentioned it in the first place. "Let's get to the present. I learned a few facts from the police. They informed me of how Ms. Relda and Ms. Staller are connected to the murder of this man Oakhurst. Today they took clothing from Ms. Relda and Ms. Staller and also took their fingerprints. It was good you called me when you did because it enabled me to arrive at the police station in time to inform the police that for the time being these young ladies were not going to answer any questions. And in the future if questions were going to be asked, I would have to be present."

"You can do that?" Morty said.

"Yes. Keeping one's mouth closed at the right time is quite important." He pointed to a picture on the wall. It was a drawing of a trout under which was written, *If I'd kept my mouth shut, I wouldn't be in this frame.*

"Now let's get our house in order. First, there's the matter of a retainer. My usual fee for a criminal case is twenty-five thousand dollars. However, since no one has been charged yet we don't know if there will be a case. I'll therefore accept ten thousand. If nothing further develops, you'll be charged only for my time. My hourly fee is $400 dollars." He paused for a few moments, letting this sink in. "Are there any questions?"

For a while nobody spoke. Then Sherri said, "That's fine." She addressed Sarajane and Margo. "Don't worry about the finances. We'll work everything out."

"Good." He put his palms together and held them under his chin as if he were thinking deep thoughts. In my opinion, he was either a bonafide ham or the most lugubrious individual I'd ever met. "Next," he went on, "I'll need to have an in depth discussion with these two young women, as well as with you, Dr. Adler, and you, Mr. Wanderman. I was told that both of you were at the gallery the night of the murder. It's important you give me your impressions of what happened. Are we agreed?"

No argument. He wanted to talk to each of us in private, beginning with Sarajane. He told us he didn't expect us to wait because the length of each interview could not be predicted. He would call us to make appointments but he wanted to do this as quickly as possible.

Margo said she would wait. Morty and Sherri said they would, too, wanting to get it over and done with. I elected to go home.

CHAPTER 11

I tried to think about the entire affair in order to get a clear picture. It was complex. A weird art opening. A found daughter. A murder. The murder victim a rapist. So far the police knew nothing about that event in Sarajane's past but how long before they found out? Sarajane said she'd told no one but memory was fallible. Now there was a lawyer in charge. He'd get all the information he could from each of us and go from there. We had to hope he was good.

I changed into shorts and a tee shirt and went down to the basement. I had a punching bag and a speed bag. I worked the speed bag for about fifteen minutes, starting slowly and building up to a rapid crescendo, my hands beginning to tingle. The morning sweat had dried on my body. Now I could feel the new and more satisfying layer of perspiration begin to appear. I put gloves on and turned to the heavy bag. I pounded it with jabs, left, rights, combinations. The hits sent shock waves through my arms as far as my shoulders. Endorphins began whizzing inside me and I got the high I'd been hoping for. After a few more minutes of pummeling the bag, it was time for a shower and a drink.

Luksusowa vodka in hand, my thoughts turned to Sienna Nolan. The very beautiful Sienna Nolan. I said her name out loud, rolling it around my tongue the way you might with something that tasted extremely fine. I remembered in vivid detail the one night we'd spent together. I also remembered the disappointment I'd felt when she'd made it clear there wasn't going to be another. Not exactly the truth. I'd felt much more than disappointment. Her taking it as a one-night stand had left me bruised and battered. I wasn't a bad guy. I thought I deserved better. At the same time it helped diminish some of the guilt I'd felt even though I'd tried to tell myself there was no good reason for guilt.

What was Sienna doing at this moment? And what was she after, taking the girls' fingerprints and clothing? They'd been there a long time which meant their fingerprints had to be all over that gallery. So what was she looking for? Was it possible the cops had found prints at the murder scene itself? Maybe on the knife? Or something on or near the body? But even if they had found something, how could that have anything to do with Sarajane and Margo? The girls said they'd seen the body from the doorway, that they hadn't gone anywhere near it. In which case it was probably Sienna being her usual, professional self. At least I hoped so. But I also thought it might be a good idea to try to find out.

I called the police station. She wasn't there. Next call was to her office in Hauppauge. They told me she wasn't in. I asked for her cell phone but they wouldn't give it to me. My only option was to leave a message and hope she'd return my call. I wasn't optimistic about that but there was no other choice.

Soon enough it was time for dinner. Did I want to just eat or did I want to treat myself by making something special? I didn't know. I was floating a bit even though the endorphin effect had faded away. I knew my good feelings were due to Polish potatoes but who cared? I peered into the refrigerator and freezer to see what was there.

As it turned out, not much. Home-made hummus, cheese, herring, eggs, and an assortment of salad stuff. The freezer had chicken thighs, pork chops, peas, cauliflower, and a couple of bagels. The pantry had cans of tomatoes and a variety of pasta. That last decided me. A simple dinner of linguini with a light tomato sauce. Not much trouble to make but eminently satisfying, especially with the accompaniment of a pleasurable glass of Sangiovese.

I set about chopping onions and garlic, sautéing them in olive oil and, when the onions were translucent, adding the can of plum tomatoes, breaking them up first. All I had to do was toss in some oregano, boil the pasta, and I'd be in clover.

O happiness, enjoy'd but of a few!

When the phone rang I was holding a glass of wine and savoring the taste as it combined with the rich sauce and the linguini. Sienna's voice in my ear made my hand shake. I put the glass down.

"Hi," I said. "I'm glad you called me back."

"I'm glad you're glad. What's your problem?"

"Why do you think I have a problem? I wanted to talk to you, that's all."

"About what?"

At the station she'd seemed tense and ready to take offense at any remark that struck her as off. She still sounded that way, which made it imperative that I be very careful choosing my words. "I was wondering if you might want to have a cup of coffee with me."

"Why would I want to do that?"

"I thought we were friends. Isn't that what friends sometimes do?"

"Jake—Jake—I don't know—why do I have the feeling that with you there's always something underneath the surface? Am I wrong?"

"You are so wrong." I put one hand on my heart proving my honesty. "So wrong. When I saw you at the police station, I realized we hadn't seen each other for a long time. I thought it would be nice to touch base with you again." Touch you again, I couldn't help thinking.

Instead of the snappy comeback I'd expected, there was a long silence. I thought I could hear her breathing.

I didn't wait. "What do you say? It'll be nice. I promise."

She sighed. "You know what? It's against my better judgment but you are very persuasive."

"That's wonderful," I said, and I meant it. "When can we do this? How about tomorrow morning? Are you available?" Available. Why was it that with her I was always thinking in double entendres?

"I'm not sure about the time. I'll be out East doing interviews. We're tracking down all the people who were at the Venable gallery. Suppose I call you when I have a minute."

"Did you talk to Valerie Venable yet? The gallery owner? She should have a lot of info on the chef. She's the one who arranged for him to be there."

"How do you know that?"

"She told us. Bragged about it as a matter of fact. How she got this fabulous chef to pitch in for the charity."

"Thanks. Good to know. Anyway, I'll get in touch when I'm free."

"Great. How about giving me your cell phone number so I can reach you if I have something important?"

"I don't give out my cell phone number, Jake. Sorry."

"I won't abuse it."

"Nope. I cherish my privacy."

I almost said what came immediately to mind, which was, *Does the guy you're seeing have it?* But I wasn't that dumb. "Okay, then. I'll give you mine, though, in case I'm not home when you call."

After we'd hung up I looked at my caller ID. The number was the same one I'd called. I got in touch with Morty to see how things had gone with the lawyer.

"Fine," he said. "Told him all the same stuff I told the detective. He'll probably get to you tomorrow."

"How're SJ and Margo?"

"They seemed quite subdued. They're obviously concerned, worried even, I'd say. And I can't blame them. Here they are, trapped more or less. I feel sorry for them."

"Of course, you do. And you should. What do you think about the lawyer?"

"I like him. I think he's smart and knows what he's doing. He told us he has a private investigator who works for him and that he's available, if needed."

"I thought I was your private investigator."

"You are, Jake. But this guy is a pro. Licensed, I mean. Not to say that you aren't terrific, too."

"Very kind of you."

"You know what I mean, Jake. Right now there doesn't seem to be anything a private investigator can do, anyway, so we don't have to discuss it."

"Fine," I said. "Talk to you later."

CHAPTER 12

The next morning I waited for Sienna to call but I didn't hear from her. I did get a call from Longwood's secretary. She wanted to set up an appointment. I said I'd get back to her because I didn't want to tie myself up. Sienna finally called just before noon.

"Sorry it took this long," she said. "It's been pretty hectic."

"Not a problem. Since it's so late, how about lunch?"

"I don't have time for a long lunch. Too much to do."

"You have to eat, don't you? I wasn't thinking about a restaurant. They're all too crowded anyway. East Hampton is a zoo in the summer. Why don't I get us some sandwiches and we have a picnic somewhere? How does that sound?"

"Okay, I guess."

Not what I'd call enthusiastic, but I pressed on. "Where are you?"

"I'm sitting in my car across from Town Hall."

"Stay there. I'll pick you up and we can go together, or you can follow me. The place I have in mind is not far from there. What do you like to eat?"

"Oh, I don't know. Anything."

"Fine. Coffee, tea?"

"Apple juice."

"See you in fifteen minutes."

After I hung up I realized she must have called from her cell phone. I checked my caller ID again and saved the number. Good. I was one up on her.

I got sandwiches and drinks at the IGA in Sag Harbor. I had to wait in line a half hour. In winter there might have been one or two people ahead of me but summer changed everything. I'd driven down Main Street on the chance that someone might pull out and give me a space but no such luck. I had to go around behind the stores to the big lot and even there it was not easy.

Once again to Route 114. I was lucky this time. No slow poke in front of me. Still it took fifteen minutes to Stephen Hands Path, another ten taking the Cedar Street back route to avoid going through the nightmare of East Hampton village, which was considerably worse than Sag Harbor. Cars were required to stop for anyone in the pedestrian crosswalks. Sag Harbor had two but East Hampton had a lot more as well as more people. There seemed to be a constant stream of pedestrians moving from one side to the other, half of them sucking on ice cream cones and strolling as if they were on a boardwalk.

I finally pulled up behind Sienna's red Mitsubishi Eclipse. It seemed to me that mostly women drove cars that looked like toys. I couldn't imagine why. To me they were dangerous. I got out and went to her window.

She gave me a disgruntled look. "I didn't think you'd ever get here."

"Hey. I came from Sag Harbor. You don't know what traffic is like in the summer."

"Sure, I do. But let's not discuss it."

She got out of her car and locked it. I had in mind to hold open my car door for her thinking it might soften her up if I acted like a gentleman, but she moved too fast and opened the door herself. Nothing was going right.

"I'm taking you to the duck pond," I said. "It's the only place in town that's quiet. There'll be people but we can find a bench and have some privacy."

"Umm," she said.

Whatever that meant.

The duck pond was actually a stream. It was part of a nature preserve located in the heart of East Hampton village. It stretched across several residential blocks. The pond itself was narrow and surrounded by natural wetlands with an incredible variety of moss, shrubs, vines, and wildflowers. Dirt paths meandered on either side with an occasional bench for those who wanted to sit.

Only two cars were in the small parking area. Most people were probably at the beach. We strolled for a while without talking. It was a hot day and the air was heavy. There was no one near. It was silent and peaceful. It felt as if we were alone on the planet. I hoped the atmosphere would get to her, do something to un-charge her. When I saw an empty bench I suggested we sit. She agreed. At last something positive.

We unwrapped the sandwiches and ate without talking. I couldn't concentrate on the food because I was thinking about how to get the conversation started. Obviously, I couldn't begin by immediately asking her questions about fingerprints and clothing. I had to get at that obliquely if I was going to get there at all.

"How's your sandwich?" I said. Duh!

"The tuna has a little too much mayo but otherwise not bad."

Well thank you very much. It cost me nine bucks and it has too much mayo. How about that? "Tastes pretty good to me." I tried to keep the annoyance out of my voice.

"Oh, it's good. I didn't mean it isn't a good sandwich. And thanks for getting it, by the way. The apple juice is delicious."

"You don't have to say it's a good sandwich if you don't think so. You won't be hurting my feelings. I didn't make it, after all."

She turned to look directly at me. "You're funny."

"Funny? How? Funny, strange? Funny, funny?"

"It's a perfectly good sandwich," she said. "And I like being here with you."

"I like being here with you, too. I was looking forward to it all day."

A woman wearing short shorts and a bathing suit bra top appeared, holding a little boy by the hand. She looked condescendingly at the sandwiches on our laps but otherwise didn't acknowledge our presence. This, as well as her manner of dress, indicated she was from the city. City people did not make eye contact with locals. "Don't worry, Henry," she said. "We'll see the duckies soon. They're probably just taking a nap."

I didn't speak until she was out of sight while secretly wishing she would trip and fall into the water.

"I'm really glad you're here," I said.

"I'm glad, too. But I want to be honest with you, Jake. If you have something personal in mind, you should forget about it."

Personal? Was she referring to the information I was hoping to get or to me? I decided to stay away from what I really wanted. Then again, what did I really want? "Because you're involved with someone?"

She hesitated. "I'm not sure I should tell you this—"

"Tell me what?"

She shrugged. "I'm not really involved anymore."

So she'd been talking about us! Now that was interesting! "Not really? Or just not?"

"Not."

"What happened? No, never mind. I don't want to know. I'm sorry. I'm sure it can't be easy to break up with someone. Especially, when it's the second time."

She sighed. "No, it isn't easy."

"I don't understand something," I said. "Why are you telling me not to think about you in a personal way when at the same time you're telling me you're no longer involved with anyone?"

"Simple. Because I don't think we have any kind of future together."

"Oh." I blinked. "Well, that's pretty direct."

"I'm sorry. But that's how I see it."

I wasn't surprised by what she'd said. I hadn't given myself much of a chance to begin anything with her again. Still, I couldn't help feeling as if I'd been shot down.

Then her hand sneaked over and covered mine. "You know I'm attracted to you. It happened right from the first day we met."

"Not as much as I was attracted to you."

"But if you remember, I was the one who made a move. Not you."

"True," I said. "And I'm still glad you did."

She withdrew her hand, finished the last of her sandwich, and looked at my lap. Not for anything sexy, I realized, remembering her voracious appetite. The few times we'd eaten together she'd consumed her food as if she'd been starved. She was looking at my lunch, or what remained of it. I'd eaten less than a half of my sandwich. "Are you going to finish that?" she said.

I held out the sandwich. "Go ahead. It's all yours."

As she chewed heartily, I tried to think how I could possibly turn any of what had happened into something positive.

"Did you get to talk to Valerie Venable?"

"I spent most of the morning with her. She's the one who provided me with a list of names of all the guests."

"Did she tell you anything else that might help?" Would Valerie have known anything about Oakhurst's past? Did he have a reputation as a ladies man?

"At this point I don't know. Homicide cases take time and effort. You should know that. There's a lot of grunt work. Talking to witnesses, family, friends, and so on. We're at the beginning."

I couldn't think of anything else except to go for broke. *Things done well and with a care, exempt themselves from fear.*

"Would it be breaking any rules if I asked you something about Sarajane and Margo?"

She didn't answer while she continued to chew. Finally, she swallowed. "Depends."

"You took their fingerprints and clothing. Why?"

She smiled and shook her head. "Sorry, Jake."

"How about I guess? You found prints on the knife or something near the body. You've got a piece of clothing, or fibers."

"No comment."

"Am I close? Can you tell me that?"

"No comment."

We put the remains of the lunch in a receptacle and headed back to my car. Again, we were the only people on the path. I felt a very strong urge to kiss her. I wondered how she'd react.

So I kissed her.

She opened her mouth and our tongues met. I tasted the tuna fish along with other flavors. Delicious.

I hadn't learned anything about the case but it seemed to me that under the circumstances it hadn't been a wasted afternoon.

CHAPTER 13

When I dropped Sienna back at her car, she went off without another word. What was I supposed to make of that? As usual, where she was concerned, I was a little dazed and a lot confused. But there was always hope. Shakespeare had it right: *The miserable have no other medicine but...hope.*

Shakespeare—there seemed to be something written about him almost every day in the week. Currently, I was into a book about his earlier life, *The Lodger Shakespeare*, by Charles Nicholl. He'd been a lodger in a house where a family dispute had come about, bringing with it a lawsuit. The suit had to do with a dowry that hadn't been paid and William was called to testify on behalf of the plaintiff. Shakespeare himself says little when he testifies but another witness speaks about the couple and of Shakespeare's "giving each other's hand to the hand." This suggests that Shakespeare had something to do with their getting married, that he was in some ways a facilitator. Shakespeare never explains this but a servant says that "Mr. Shakespeare laye in the house." In Elizabethan times that meant he was living there. Shakespeare did a riff on this word in Othello when Desdemona asks the Clown where Cassio lies. The response is: *I know not where he lodges...and for me to...say he lies here or he lies there, were to lie in mine own throat.* Lies and more lies. They came up a lot in Shakespeare, just as they did in the present.

I'd read at home but not for long. I had too many other things to do: the garden, where pulling weeds, transplanting, pruning, fertilizing, and other chores never ended. Then there was the house itself, a fifty year old former bungalow that Rosalind and I had remodeled, time after time and room after room, doing most of the work ourselves: designing, constructing, painting, wallpapering, and so on, until it had the comfort level we'd been looking for. But something was always breaking down, or wearing out, or otherwise in need of repair. Currently, there was the recent appearance of a leak in a section of the roof. I was having a problem because the leak only happened when the rain came down a certain way and when the wind was blowing in a special direction. I hadn't yet been able to figure out which type of rain or which wind direction—some detective—the result being that whenever it rained, I spent a lot of frustrating time tramping around the house looking up at ceilings. Then there was shopping and marketing for food and planning what to eat as well as doing the cooking. All required more time than there was in a day. How had Rosalind and I managed all this when we were both working?

I was about to head home when I realized I was close to the Huntting Inn where Sarajane and Margo were staying. I thought it might be a good idea as well as friendly to drop by and see them. And if by chance I happened to glean a few kernels of information, that wouldn't be bad either.

I decided to call first since they might not like my just dropping in on them. I used free information on the cell to get the number. A male voice said, "They checked out."

What? "Checked out? When was this?"

"I don't know. I came on this morning. I only just now saw that they'd gone."

"I'll be right over," I said.

The Huntting Inn shared its premises with the Palm restaurant. The reservation desk for the restaurant stood just inside the hotel entrance. The lunch hour was still going strong. Loud voices emanated from the dining area. The maitre d' nodded at me as if he thought I might want to join the affluent gourmands. No thank you, not in season. Too crowded. Too noisy. Too filled with upward strivers ordering five-pound lobsters. I smiled, shook my head indicating I wasn't interested, and went over to the hotel desk. There was a young guy staffing it, probably a college kid working for the summer.

"Hi. I'm the guy just called you about Ms. Relda. I'm a friend of hers. Can you tell me when she left?"

"It was yesterday."

"What time yesterday?"

"You'd have to speak to the person who was on duty. It could've been anytime."

"Did you happen to hear anything about why they left?"

"No. But I'm only on a couple days a week."

"Okay. Not really important I guess. Did they leave any messages, or a forwarding address?"

He looked through some papers on his desk. "Nope. Nothing I can see."

I thanked him and went outside to think. What did this mean? Where'd they go? Why did they go? Did they tell anyone? If they had told anyone, the only person I thought it could be was Morty.

I called him at his office. Zelda, who had replaced the motherly Sylvia, was a Gorgon posing as a receptionist. Her apparent goal in life was to protect him from the public: salesmen, patients, friends, relatives, it didn't matter.

I tried to make my voice sound as urgent as I felt. "Zelda. This is his friend, Jake Wanderman. I need to speak to him. It's an emergency."

"What kind of emergency?"

"Never mind. It's important, okay? Put me through."

"Just a minute."

I could just about hear her teeth grinding. She'd never liked me and she hated to give in. I felt nothing would've pleased her more than to cut my balls off with a hatchet.

Morty picked up. "What is it, Jake? I'm busy with a patient."

"Did your daughter call you last night?"

"No. We went to bed early. Why are you asking?"

"Because she and her friend are gone."

"Whaddya mean, gone?"

"Gone, as in gone away. I was in East Hampton so I went over to the hotel to talk to them. They checked out. No forwarding address. No nothing."

"I don't believe it. Where would they go?"

"I don't have a clue."

"Why would they do this?"

"I can only think of one reason, but I'd rather not say it."

"Look. I can't talk now. I'm booked solid until four. Can you come over here then?"

I said I would and headed for home.

Did they really skip? It sure looked like it. I hazarded a guess that it might have had something to do with the police taking their fingerprints and clothing. And if that was the real reason, it would have to mean that there was something fishy in the story they'd told about discovering the body. It struck me now that it was entirely possible that something else had happened, that they'd invented a fable. Something that could lead to fingerprints and clothing evidence.

...for me to...say he lies here or he lies there, were to lie in mine own throat.

Were there lies told by Sarajane about what happened at the gallery? Were lies told about other events? My God. Could it be they were actually murderers? That they'd thought they could get away with it by telling that fake story and when they saw they couldn't, they decided to take off? No. I was shaking my head. I found that scenario hard to believe. My instincts told me they could not have committed a murder. They were liars, possibly. I remembered that wink Sarajane had given me when she'd supposedly fainted. But that wasn't enough to convince me they were killers.

Still, I was shaken. Sarajane and her friend Margo hadn't existed for me a few days ago. And now they were gone. I'd liked SJ right away, just as I'd liked Zeena, my father's girlfriend, the instant I met her. Some kind of bonding had taken place. I felt sorry for Morty. SJ wasn't my daughter but she could've been. Up to this point I was sure that Sienna knew nothing about their departure. I wondered if I should call her, see what kind of reaction she had, hear how she felt. I'd especially like to know what she'd do about it.

I decided to wait.

CHAPTER 14

When I got home I found one of my alarm systems flashing. I'd had two systems installed after I'd been beaten in my driveway by a couple of Russians, beaten badly enough to be hospitalized. This happened a year ago, after I'd gotten involved with the Russian Mafia and some stolen Fabergé eggs. It was an interesting introduction to what could happen to someone taking on the job of a PI.

One system was standard: wired windows and doors and 24/7 monitoring. The other was a concealed motion detector at the head of my driveway. I'd had it tweaked so that it recorded any entry above the height of three feet. I shut it off and went outside. I walked all around the house looking for signs of an attempt to break in. I didn't see any. If anyone tried, sirens would have gone off loud enough to be heard a mile away. The same thing would happen if they attempted to cut off the power source.

At the front of the house I looked up and down the street. All was familiar: The twenty year old Volvo station wagon parked three doors down, the Silverado pickup in the driveway across the street. There were no strange cars. If all this sounds somewhat paranoid, I don't deny it. Getting pounded into unconsciousness has a way of doing that to you.

I went next door and rang my neighbor's bell. Marge Goodly was a handsome, fortyish woman married to a guy who looked like John Wayne.

"Hey, Marge," I said, when she opened the door. "Notice anyone looking around my house recently?"

"Why? Those bad guys after you again?"

"I hope not. Just wondering, because one of my alarms was flashing."

"As a matter of fact, there was a black Escalade in your driveway a short while ago. I happened to glance out my window and noticed it. I don't know how long he was there."

"One guy?"

"Right."

"What did he look like?"

"I couldn't tell, really. The windows were tinted. Pretty dark.

"Thanks, Marge."

"No problem. Anything you want me to do?"

"Just keep your eyes peeled."

"I always do."

Who was this guy in my driveway? I didn't know who he was or what he was, but it made me uneasy. Salesman? Possible, but not likely if he was driving an Escalade. But he could've been a real estate sightseer. There were lots of those. In fact, Rosalind and I used to do it all the time. We'd drive into strange neighborhoods to look at houses, and often into the driveways too, sometimes long curving ones where the house was hidden until near the end. I was usually nervous but not Rosie.

"What're they going to do, arrest us?"

It was fun, and even exciting, especially when we'd come across a fabulous landscape, or a sculpture sitting on a lawn, or an odd gazebo. Educational, too, because we'd sometimes get ideas about how we could improve the look of our own house.

Inside, my answering machine was blinking.

Morty: "Jake, Sorry, I have to change the time and place. I won't be able to see you in the office. Too damn busy. Can you come to the house around five? Don't bother to call. I'll expect you."

That gave me two hours. I was no longer in the mood to do any reading or anything else for that matter. I was still bummed out by the guy in my driveway. But it was summer and it was hot and I was sweating. I put on trunks and biked the short distance to Long Beach. The beach was situated on Noyac Bay and as beautiful as any on the Mediterranean. Whenever I came back from a trip I looked forward to what I knew I'd see driving back from the airport. At a certain point I had to make a turn that took me to the beginning of the beach. And there it would be, spread out before me, the long stretch of sand and the bay, the water blue or green or battleship gray, depending on the weather and the sun or lack of it. And I would *kvell*. I'd sigh with delight at having the opportunity to experience the pleasure of this wonderful sight again. It meant I was home.

I spread my towel and went directly into the water. There wasn't too much of a shock. In less than a minute my body responded and I began to relax. I swam in the cool water for a while and floated on my back, looking up at the few clouds in the sky. When I'd had enough, I stretched out on the sand to let the sun dry me and, in short order, fell asleep.

By the time I got to Morty's house, the good vibes from the beach had disappeared. Sherri and Morty greeted me with worried looks. We went into their kitchen, a high-ceilinged room with lots of windows looking out to their garden and pool.

"Tell us what happened," Morty said.

I told them about my going to the hotel and related what the hotel clerk had said.

"And that's it?"

"I'm afraid so. That's all I know. And you haven't heard anything at all?"

"Nothing. What do you think is going on? Didn't you say you had an idea?"

"It's just speculation. I don't want to upset you."

"You can't upset us more than we already are."

"I'm not so sure about that."

"Go ahead, Jake," Sherri said.

"Okay." I took a deep breath. "I think they took off because they're afraid."

"Afraid of what?"

"Afraid of being arrested for murder."

"You're out of your mind," Morty said.

"Just a minute," Sherri said. "Why do you say that, Jake? You must have a reason."

"I do." I went on to explain my theory about the girl's fingerprints and clothing fibers: that if one or the other or both of them should turn out to be discovered at the scene, that would make their discovering-the-body story a lie. It would also tie them ever more closely to the murder itself. "Maybe they didn't want to wait and find out. They might have felt that running away was their only option."

"Wow." Morty was staring at the table and shaking his head. "I don't believe it. Those girls couldn't murder anyone."

·   "How do you know?" Sherri said. "You only just met them. Anything is possible."

"Don't forget the possible motive," I said. "The police don't know it yet but I don't see how they wouldn't find out."

"What's this about a motive?"

"You didn't get to hear about it," Morty said. "Sarajane was raped by the guy who was murdered. It happened a while ago when they were both students in Paris."

There was a sharp intake of breath from Sherri. "My God."

"I've been laying out a "worst-case" scenario," I said. "It's all just speculation."

"What do you think about calling the lawyer?" Sherri said.

"Right now, I wouldn't call anybody. Anyhow, what good would it do? He wouldn't be able to help, would he? Unless you want him to send his own investigator out on it."

They looked at each other. "That's one of the things we were discussing before you got here, Jake. We had an idea about asking you to look into it."

"Look into it, how?"

"We don't exactly know," Sherri said. "You're the guy who's done all this detective work. You tell us."

"Let me get this straight. What exactly are you asking me to do?"

"I would guess the first thing would be to find out where they went. Then go and talk to them and hear what they have to say. That would be a start, wouldn't it?"

I was a little surprised. At the same time I felt a jolt of pride that my friends had enough confidence in me to ask me to do this. They could have used the lawyer's PI. But not, of course, without having to give him all kinds of information. This way it was strictly unofficial and between us. I didn't hesitate. "I'll be glad to do it."

"Great," Morty said. "And don't worry about expenses. Just let me know what you need."

"Fine," I said. "How about a hundred bucks for dinner at the Palm?"

CHAPTER 15

I was kidding about the Palm but that's where I was headed. Not to the restaurant, but back to the hotel. Now it was the height of the dinner hour. Couples waiting for a table were standing around outside, in the lobby, and drinking at the bar. The maitre'd was too busy to even look my way.

A girl was behind the hotel desk. She looked like another college kid on a summer job. So young, so pretty, so naïve, I hoped.

"I wonder if you can help me," I said. I handed her the business card that identified me as a PI. I'd had them made the previous year shortly after I'd helped catch a murderer. Rosalind and I thought it would be a great idea for me to become a private investigator, so the first thing I did was order business cards. Then I learned that I'd have to put in three years working for a licensed PI in order to get my own license. So much for that great idea. Still, I wasn't about to throw the cards out even though they didn't cost all that much. In the end they'd turned out to be quite useful.

She studied the card. "You're a private detective?"

"That's right."

"Cool. I never met one before. What can I do for you?"

"Just answer a few questions, if you can. I'd really appreciate it." I gave her my most sincere, I'm-just-like-your-dad smile. "Were you on duty yesterday when Ms. Relda and her friend checked out?"

"Gee, yeah. I was."

"Do you remember the time?"

"About three o'clock."

"Could you tell me if they said anything to indicate why they were leaving?"

"Not to me."

"Did they seem nervous, or upset?"

She frowned, thinking. "I didn't notice. Is anything wrong?"

"No. Not to worry. Ms. Relda's father wanted me to ask. He didn't know she was leaving, that's all." I reached out and took my card back. It wasn't legal and I didn't want it to fall into the wrong hands, such as Sienna's. She'd once threatened to have me arrested for using it. "By the way, did they have any visitors yesterday?"

"Visitors?" She frowned again. I imagined it helped her thought process. "I don't know if you'd call him a visitor. A man came in and asked for Ms. Relda. I called their room and he spoke on the phone. Ms. Relda came down and they went outside. She came back alone."

"What did this man look like?"

She shrugged. "Average looking guy."

"Was he tall? Short? Anything unusual about him? You know, did he have a scar, a tattoo?"

"Wow!" she said. "This is just like *Law & Order*."

"Yeah. Almost like the real thing. Well, did he? Was he unusual in any way?"

She shook her head. "No. Well, maybe. His head was shaved. That's not unusual anymore, but he had a big head, with like a roll of fat at the back of his neck."

"How about when they left? They used a taxi, right?"

Before she could answer an older man approached. I didn't know who he was but he spoke with an air of authority. "Sally? What's going on here?"

She was flustered. "This man is asking about Ms. Relda."

"I thought that's what I heard. You should know we don't give out any information about our guests."

"I wasn't asking anything personal," I said. "Her father was worried that she seemed to have left in a hurry and asked me if I could find out why she left, that's all."

I was glad I'd taken my card back. Now I had to hope Sally didn't tell him I'd claimed to be a PI.

"I'm afraid that's none of our business," he said.

"Okay, I understand."

"Now if there's nothing else..." He was making it evident that I was to leave the premises.

"Of course," I said, thinking furiously at how I could get one more piece of information. "Umm...just one thing, would it be possible for you to call a taxi for me? I don't have my car. A friend dropped me off."

"I'm afraid you'll have to do that on your own, sir. There's a public telephone in the bar."

"Fine. Who would I call?"

He sighed. I knew he wanted to tell me to get lost but his job required him to be polite. He went around behind the desk, reluctantly pulled open a drawer, and looked down at something. Then he read out some names.

"Could I write those down?" I said. "You're going too fast for me."

"Do you have something to write on?" He was clearly annoyed.

I shrugged, enjoying his discomfort. "I forgot my notebook."

"Sally, give him a pen and some scrap paper." He looked at her then at me. "And that's it!" He came back around the desk and returned to wherever he'd come from.

"I'm sorry," she whispered, when he'd gone. "Don't bother writing anything down. Call this guy. He's the one who drove them." She handed me a card.

She'd figured out what I wanted. It made me glad that she wasn't as dumb as I'd thought. "Sally, I want to thank you. You've been a great help. I hope I didn't get you into any trouble." I put a twenty dollar bill in her hand. "Have a coke on me."

Her wide-eyed expression of surprise and wonder at all that had just taken place, made my day.

The guy at the Inn, the Escalade guy in my driveway—had to be same guy. Shortly after he talks to Sarajane, she and Margo leave. Coincidence? I didn't think so. But what could he have done or said that would cause them to go?

Outside I looked at the card. "Harry's Taxi." I called from my car. "Detective J. B. Vandervogel of the East End Task Force. I need some information."

"The what? Who did you say this was?"

He sounded old and was probably hard of hearing.

I repeated my Task Force thing.

"Uh, okay. What sort of information you looking for?"

"I understand you made a pickup yesterday at the Huntting Inn."

"I surely did. I was there."

"Can you tell me who you picked up?"

"Why would you want to be knowing that?"

"Never mind why. Just tell me who the fare was."

"I don't like to give out information if I don't know why I'm giving it."

Who did this yutz think he was, talking to a cop like that? "Listen mister. I don't know who the hell you think you are. But if you don't want to be arrested and charged with obstruction, you damn well better give me an answer, and I mean right now."

"Okay, okay. No need to get all riled up. Let's see. I'll just check my book here." After a pause, he said, "It was 3:10 p.m. Two ladies."

"And where did you take them?"

"Kennedy airport. JFK. That's a damn long ride."

"What terminal did you take them to?"

"International."

"Okay, Mr...what is your name?"

"Hugo Peterson. And if you're going to ask why my business is called Harry's Taxi it's because I bought it from a guy named Harry."

I decided to be magnanimous. "Hugo, you've been a big help. Thanks very much. If I need anything else, I'll get back to you."

It was pretty clear where they'd gone. But I wanted to be sure. I went home, first checking to see if any alarm had been breached. Thankfully, no. I got on the computer and looked up flights to London. There were plenty. And the timing was right.

From 5 p.m. on there were more than half a dozen. I would have been very surprised if they'd gone anywhere else.

I poured vodka over rocks, swallowed some of it, and called Morty. "I'm pretty sure they're in London."

"You found out already? So fast?"

"I was lucky."

"Hold on a second." I heard him call out to Sherri to pick up the phone. When she did, he said, "Go on. Tell her what you told me."

"The girls are in London. They flew back last night. Wait a minute. I amend that. It looks like they flew back to London. They were at the airport at the right time. Of course, they may have gone somewhere else. And even if I'm right and they did go to London, it doesn't mean they stayed there. If they're running, anything is possible."

"How'd you find out so fast?" Sherri said.

I told how I'd gotten the information, leaving out the part where I'd identified myself as a detective. I also left out the guy at the hotel and in my driveway. They didn't need to be upset more than they already were.

"So now what?" Morty said.

"I'm not sure. Let's talk about it in the morning."

After I hung up I thought about Sienna again. I needed to talk to her. I needed to find out what she knew relating to the girls. She had that information and most likely might not want to give it to me. But I had knowledge, too, information that she didn't have. I felt there was a good chance for a trade. Images and the feel of her tongue with its taste of tuna fish came flooding back to me. I picked up the phone.

She answered almost immediately. "Okay, Jake. So you have my number. What are you trying to prove?"

"Ouch! I haven't said a word yet and you're already jumping down my throat."

"I'm sorry. You called at a bad time."

"No, *I'm* sorry. I'm not out to get you upset. But I have something important to tell you. When can we talk?" There was a period of silence, then a loud sigh. I said, "Hey, girl. Forget it. You sound low. It's nothing that can't wait. Is there anything I can do to help?"

"Not really. I have to—" Her voice broke. "I have to work it out myself."

"Sienna. What's going on? Are you crying?"

"I guess I am. Life sucks sometimes."

"I know about that. Would you like me to come over? You can tell me about it."

"That's nice of you, Jake. But no."

"Why not? I could hold your hand. You'd definitely feel better."

"I don't think that would be a good idea."

"You're sure?"

"I'm sure. Sorry, Jake. But I'm hanging up now."

And she did.

More confusion when it came to Sienna. True, I'd known her less than a year but we'd been through a lot together. Yet I'd never seen her even close to tears before. I decided to call her again the next day.

With all the excitement I expected to have a difficult time falling asleep. What I didn't expect was to be woken up just after three in the morning. I hoped it was Sienna but it was Morty on the phone.

"I'm sorry, Jake. I know what time it is. But I had to tell you what just happened."

"And what was that?" I mumbled.

"I just got a phone call from Sarajane. You were right. She's in London. It's eight o'clock in the morning over there. She apologized for waking me up but she said she knew I must be worried."

"What else did she say?"

"Not much. She told me she had to leave New York. That she had a very good reason. When I tried to get her to explain, she said she wouldn't tell me over the phone. She sounded very upset."

"I'm not surprised."

"At least I know where she is."

"Right."

"Now I feel dumb for calling you at this ungodly hour. I'm sorry."

"Don't be. We'll talk in a few hours. Okay?"

He hung up and I tried to get back to sleep. It wasn't easy but I finally managed. Not for long. At 6 a.m. the phone rang again. It was my Dad. This was not a surprise. He'd always been an early riser, as well as a late-stayer-upper.

"Hey, sonny, I hope I didn't wake you, but if you were asleep it's time to get up. I got news, my boy. Very interesting news."

"I'm sure. What is it?"

"There was a story in the paper yesterday and on TV about a murder in your neck of the woods. I meant to call you as soon as I saw it, but I got involved in a new project and more or less forgot about it. Until this morning. Did you see it?"

"No."

"It mentions an artist and a chef. I thought you might be interested."

"I know about it."

"You do? How come?"

"I was there."

"Why am I not surprised? I had a feeling you'd be involved. What's the scoop?"

"Dad, I'm still half-asleep. I'll call you later and tell you all about it."

"Just a minute, big shot, I'll tell *you* something I'll bet you don't know." He paused. "The murdered guy's name was Oakhurst, right? Anthony Oakhurst?"

"That's right. What about him?"

"A girl was found murdered last night. It seems this guy Oakhurst had been subletting a place on East Sixty-Seventh Street. Someone slugged the doorman, went up to his apartment, got in, and murdered this girl. Whoever it was also trashed the place."

"This was on the news this morning?"

"The Early Show. Channel 2. Check it out."

"I will. Thanks, Dad. Talk to you later."

I was no longer sleepy.

CHAPTER 16

Now I really needed to call Sienna. I waited until 7 a.m., figuring it was early enough to make an impression but not so early that she might think, *Omigod, what could this be*?

"How're you feeling?" I asked her. "Better, I hope."

"I'm fine. Thanks for asking. But you're not calling at this hour to ask me that. What's on your mind?"

I tried being subtle even thought I knew I wasn't any good at it. "I was wondering if you'd heard about a woman's body being found in Tony Oakhurst's New York apartment."

"The answer is yes."

"Do you think there's any connection?"

"Too early to tell. But I don't like coincidences."

"Who was the victim? Do you know?"

"Her name was Anna Lombardi. She was a bartender at his restaurant in the city. The detective I spoke to said the doorman told him she'd been staying overnight on a fairly regular basis which leads to the conclusion she was his girlfriend."

"Any idea why she was killed?"

"NYPD thinks it's one of those wrong place-wrong time situations. The way the place was trashed, it looked like the killer was searching for something. Or maybe he was a burglar looking for loot. We don't know."

"How was she killed?"

"Stabbed and strangled."

"Whew! I appreciate your telling me all this. I know you don't have to."

"Nothing secret about it."

"But you have some other information that I'd appreciate your telling me. I hope you will."

"And what's that?"

"The other day you took the girls' shoes and some clothing. I assume you sent them to the crime lab. I'd like to know what turned up, if anything."

"Uh-uh, Jake. I don't see any reason for you to know that."

"How about if I tell you something you don't know? Would you consider that a fair trade?"

"And what could that be?"

"Not so fast. I'll make a deal with you. If what I tell you is significant, and I think I can count on you to be honest about it, will you give up your info?"

There was a moment of silence. "Deal."

"Here it is: the young ladies are gone. They're no longer in this country. In fact, they're back in London."

"You're kidding me."

"Not."

"When did they leave?"

"Night before last. They checked out of the hotel in the afternoon, went to the airport, and caught an evening flight out. And something else. A man paid a visit to them just before they checked out. He spoke to Sarajane for a few minutes. I think he might've paid me a visit, too. But I'm not sure."

"Shit! Pardon my French. Why didn't I put somebody on them?"

"I wondered about that myself. I thought you'd at least take away their passports."

"Not so simple. I'd've had to charge them with a crime to get their passports. I wasn't ready to do that."

"So you didn't find anything?"

"I didn't say that."

"What are you saying?"

"I'm not saying anything right now."

"I thought we made a deal."

"Sorry. I have to give some thought whether or not to clear it with my boss first. Is that okay with you?"

"No it isn't. A deal is a deal. I gave you some really important news. And now you're welshing on me?"

A moment of silence. "Give me a little time. I'll meet you in two hours."

"Where?"

"Name a place."

"I don't know where you live. How far up island are you?"

"Don't worry about where I am. Just pick a place to meet and a time. I'll be there. I promise."

I chose the diner in Bellport, just off the Sunrise Highway. It was strictly a hunch that it was a middle point between us. For me it was less than an hour. When I drove into the parking lot I saw her red Mitsubishi Eclipse.

The breakfast rush was over. I had no problem spotting her in a booth. She was forking eggs, bacon, and hash-browns into her mouth as I sat down.

She looked up at me. "I hope you don't mind my eating. I didn't have breakfast."

"Not at all. I like to watch you eat. You're so good at it."

"Of course you mean that as a complement."

"What else could I mean?"

I signaled for the waitress and ordered coffee. While I drank I watched in silent admiration as she went about eradicating every trace of the bacon, eggs, and potatoes. It reminded me that the first time we'd ever gotten together to talk, it had also been in a diner. I remembered watching in astonished amusement as she wolfed down enough food to satisfy a lumberjack. Then as now she finished by scouring the plate clean.

I raised my cup to her. "Well done."

"Thanks for being so patient."

"Sure. And now can we talk? Or rather, will you talk?"

"Okay. The lab found clothing fibers from the victim on Relda's dress. We also found her fingerprint on the knife that killed him."

"That sounds pretty serious. How come you didn't arrest them?"

"Because it's not enough."

"Why not? I don't understand."

She smiled sweetly. "I'll give you a short course on evidence. There's such a thing called "innocent access." In regard to fingerprints, for example, a print can remain on an object for a long period of time after it was handled. So finding a finger-print at the scene of a crime isn't, of itself, significant enough proof. What that means is that the investigator has to think of how the print could have gotten there by other means than the commission of a crime. Follow?"

Before I could speak, she went on. "A defense lawyer could claim that the knife had been handled previously by the suspect. Now if there'd been a bloody fingerprint, that would've been a lot better."

"And what about the clothing?"

"Same difference. She could have brushed against him ear-lier in the evening, or something like that. Anyhow, the bottom line is that if I make an arrest on only that kind of evidence, I'd be a fool because the odds are she'd get off. A good defense lawyer? Her youth and looks? No way. And then if the case gets dismissed 'with prejudice' she can never be prosecuted again, even if I find incontrovertible evidence. What I want is a slam dunk and for that I need a lot more. Background. Motivation. Witnesses. You know the process, Jake."

"Yeah. Lots of hard work. Are you going to follow up, even though she's in London?"

"Damn right. I get what I need, I can always bring her back."

"You can extradite from there?"

"From England? Absolutely."

I drained my cup. "So now what?"

"I'm going back to work."

"Thanks for telling me all this. I guess your boss said it was okay?"

"I never asked him. I'm not a welsher."

"I never thought you would be." I reached across the table for her hand. "Will you tell me what's up with you? Why you were so upset yesterday?"

She allowed her hand to rest in mine for a moment before she gently withdrew it. "I'm sorry, Jake. I'm just not ready to share that with you—or anyone else, for that matter."

She slid out of the booth, picked up her handbag, and left.

CHAPTER 17

One more time, Sienna had left me in a state of confusion and frustration. The only thing clear was that I knew I wanted to see her again. And it had nothing to do with murder.

Then almost before I knew what was happening, I found myself trying to relax in the forward cabin of a Virgin Atlantic plane. I was on my way to London. Morty had wanted me to talk to Sarajane in person, believing it was the only way to get the true story of why they ran from East Hampton.

"Jake. I need you to do this. I'd go myself but I can't. It's my busiest time of year. I can't leave my practice. And Sherri can't do it. She's all booked up with her charity work. Besides, she wouldn't get anywhere with them."

He was right on all counts. He had a large practice, and as for Sherri's personality, let's be charitable and say she had a way with people that caused many to prefer a root canal over time with her.

Morty said they'd pay all expenses and I'd go in style. It struck me as a little extravagant until I remembered that Sherri's parents had left her, along with two siblings, something like fifty million dollars. Morty had continued to work. He told me he would have felt ball-less if he lived on Sherri's money. But at the same time he didn't mind having it available whenever he might need it.

Virgin Upper Class was impressive. But I almost didn't make it. When the announcement was made for first class passengers to board I headed for the gate only to trip over a bag.

Instinctively, I reached out to keep myself from falling, and what I found was someone's arm.

"Sorry," I said.

The arm was attached to a hard looking guy with a shaved head who glared at me. "Watch where you're going, asshole," he said.

I righted myself. "What's with you, buddy? You think I grabbed you on purpose? You should be so lucky."

"Asshole," he repeated.

I gave him my most withering look and left it at that.

Anyhow, Virgin Upper Class was very much that. The seat was covered in soft leather and with the push of a button would convert to a full size bed. There was a separate bar area, soft lighting and smiling attendants offering me everything but their bodies and souls. I declined the bar, preferring to stay in my delightful nook while sipping my Stoli, chomping on an assortment of nuts, and awaiting my order of filet mignon.

When Morty put the proposition to me I was conflicted. Sure I wanted to get the true story from Sarajane, if I could. But there were still things to do here in regard to the murder, now two murders. I was convinced they were connected. I wanted to talk to Valerie Venable. I needed to find out what she knew about Tony Oakhurst. She must have vetted him carefully before choosing him to be the chef at the opening. I also wanted to talk to the doorman at Oakhurst's building where the second murder had occurred.

Also, a lot of other things were going on in my head. One was my house with its various problems. Maybe it wasn't a big deal but it bothered me when I didn't take care of things. More important was that even though more than a year had passed I was still grieving over Rosalind's death. At the same time I was trying to deal with the guilt that my desire for women in general, and Sienna in particular, had stirred up. Rosalind and I had had a great sex life. We fit neatly into the category known as "sexually active." It had taken a while after Rosalind died for sexual feelings to return. But once they came back they were powerful and as months passed they intensified. I'd never acted on those longings, perhaps because whenever I'd felt the urge to go to bed with a woman, a feeling of remorse immediately surfaced. That was enough to slow me down, but it wasn't enough to get rid of the urges altogether.

There'd been one exception, Sienna, but that had been her doing not mine. And there'd been plenty of guilt attached. Still, the memory of pleasure remained.

CHAPTER 18

The hotel Morty booked me into was a Hilton. Luxurious by my standards. Rosalind and I had always traveled as economically as possible. We'd go off season and stay in moderate hotels or B and B's. Sometimes, toward the end of a trip, we might splurge, book into one of the famous old grand hotels, and have dinner in a three star restaurant, but that was rare.

The hotel was in a convenient location. It overlooked Hyde Park and was not far from where Sarajane lived. My room wasn't ready because I'd arrived before checkout. I left my one piece of luggage with the desk clerk and went for a walk. It was a warm day, hazy but pleasant. I tried to concentrate on how I was going to approach Sarajane. It wasn't going to be easy. Morty had called and told her I was coming. When I'd asked how she sounded he said she did not seem exactly thrilled.

"What do you mean?"

"Umm," he said, or maybe it was "Uhhh."

"Are you suggesting she doesn't want to see me?"

"I wouldn't say that exactly."

"What would you say, exactly?"

He scratched himself as if he had poison ivy. "All right, the truth is she said she'd changed her mind. She doesn't want to talk about it at all."

"So why am I going?"

"Because I know you can do it. If anybody can get her to talk, you can."

"Come on, Morty. She hardly knows me."

"Not true. You made a great impression on her. She told me that. You were very helpful to her all the time she was here."

"She apparently couldn't care less. Now I think my going there is ridiculous. A miracle man, I'm not."

"I can't deny that on the surface it might seem a waste. But listen, she's my only child. She's been out of my life for so long and now she's back. I'm her father. Don't I have the right to know what's going on? I think I do. In fact, I know I do. And I really don't give a damn how much it costs to find out."

I strolled over to Hyde Park and just meandered, looking at beautiful flowerbeds, people, dogs, and children. There was the Serpentine, a beautiful body of water with a couple of swans. Altogether it wasn't much different from Central Park. Everyone looked the same now: jeans, shorts, T-shirts, sandals, a more or less slobby look, not what I would have expected from the uptight Brits. Maybe they weren't so uptight anymore. I'd heard they even had decent food to eat as long as you avoided the kidney and mutton pie.

I sat on a bench and closed my eyes for a second or two. I could feel jet lag creeping up on me. When I opened my eyes again, I noticed a man standing some distance away. He looked familiar. I had the feeling I'd seen him before. I tried to think where—and when. Then I remembered the tripping incident at JFK. I was not sure it was him. The man at the airport had been wearing a suit. This guy wore jeans and a shirt. But he had the same, big, shaved head. That suddenly caused the bulb to light up. The hotel clerk at Sarajane's hotel had said the guy who came to see her had a shaved head. It couldn't be the same guy, could it? And why would he be following me?

I told myself to calm down. Maybe it was jet lag bringing on paranoia. When I looked again the guy had moved on and was no longer in sight. I walked slowly back to the hotel. Before entering, just to be sure, I glanced back to see if the same man was nearby. Of course he wasn't.

The room was ready for me and I for it. I showered and even though I knew it was not a good idea, stretched out on the bed and quickly fell asleep. After a couple of hours I forced myself to wake up. It was time to call Sarajane.

"Of course I remember you, Mr. Wanderman. It wasn't that long ago." Polite but cool. "I'm sorry you've made this long trip for nothing."

I couldn't help noticing that since she'd returned to England her accent had become more English than it had been in East Hampton. "It won't be for nothing if I get to see you and report back to your father that you're well and in good spirits. That in itself will be worth a lot." I was lying, of course. Somehow I had to find a way to pry the information I wanted out of her.

"So long as you're not expecting anything more."

"Not a thing. When can we get together?"

"I'm not sure. I'm really quite busy."

"I've got plenty of time. Just tell me when you're *not* busy."

"It's difficult. I have lots of appointments."

"You have to eat, don't you? Why don't we have lunch?"

In the end, she invited me to her apartment. After lunch. The time was set for early afternoon.

That was actually fine with me. I went to sleep, knowing that I had a free morning and the opportunity to see the famous Globe Theater, the reproduction of the theater where many of Shakespeare's plays were performed. Shakespeare was not only a great poet and dramatist, he also had an excellent business sense. He eventually became a part owner of the theater and accumulated quite a bit of dough.

After breakfast, surprisingly good, with real croissants, I got into a taxi and headed for the Globe. The theater was in Southwark on the Thames. It turned out to be a fabulous treat. From the outside, it rose white walled, pennants flying, striped in black in Tudor fashion with a black cowl around the roof, making it look like something out of a dream. There were tourists everywhere. Old, young, short, tall, loads of children. I heard dozens of languages.

I walked around, soaking in the atmosphere, and then I thought I spotted the guy from the park again. One minute I saw him, the next minute I didn't. I hurried through the crowds searching for him. A guy with a bald head. Pretty dumb. After a while it seemed like half the men there were bald. I gave up and went into the theater.

It was huge, as it was in Shakespeare's time when it could accommodate between 2000 and 3000 people. For a penny you could stand in the pit, the space directly in front of the stage. I stood there and tried to imagine thousands of people around me. I could hear their murmuring, their voices. I could feel the excitement of the crowd as the play began. I also couldn't help feeling that I was being watched.

I closed my eyes and tried to think of Macbeth approaching the witches.

When shall we three meet again
In thunder, lightning, or in rain?

I opened my eyes and swiveled around, wondering if I might see my guy. I saw only unfamiliar faces.

For an additional penny you could sit in one of the galleries that encircled the stage. For yet another penny you could avoid the hard seat with a cushion. Outside the theater was a bustling market. During pauses in the play, vendors from the market would circulate so the theatergoers could get something to eat and drink.

I left the Globe with the uneasy feeling that I was being spied on. I took a taxi back to Sarajane's. In the taxi, I looked through the back window. If someone was following me, I couldn't tell.

It was plain to see that Sarajane lived in a posh neighborhood much like the upper East Side. The American embassy was there, Berkeley Square, and a number of beautiful townhouses. Her apartment was in one of those townhouses. I suddenly remembered I'd never come up with any kind of plan to get Sarajane to talk.

There were four nameplates at the door. Hers had two names on it: Relda and Staller. That was a bit of a surprise. Back in Easthampton she'd introduced Margo as her friend, not her roommate. I couldn't help wondering what kind of roommates they were.

I pushed the button.

Her voice came over a speaker. "Who is it, please?"

I told her.

Her voice informed me her apartment was the first one near the stairs on the second floor. The buzzer sounded. I pushed the door open. And then, just like that, it hit me. I had my strategy.

I bounded up the stairs two at a time, eager to meet the challenge ahead.

CHAPTER 19

Margo opened the door, eyes unnaturally bright and glittering. She looked different, even though she was wearing the same kind of clothing she'd worn in East Hampton, a polo shirt and jeans. She smiled at me in a curious way, as if she were amused by my being there.

"Hello, Mr. Wanderman. Come in, won't you?"

I got what was different. She'd cut her hair. The page boy was gone. In its place was a short boyish cut, almost military in style, but it didn't look bad. In fact, it was attractive because it had a softening effect on her features.

I followed her from the entrance through a foyer into the living room. It was elegant but not grand. I could all but taste the money it must have cost to own this place. Muted colors, paintings, sculpture. The room was just large enough to hold a sofa, a couple of armchairs, tables, and bookcases. The style was modern but not sleek. It was not a room that made you feel comfortable. I knew Rosalind wouldn't have liked it one bit. Warmth and friendliness was what Rosalind aimed for when she decorated a room. She tried to make an impression, yes, but also to make the visitor feel immediately at home.

Sarajane rose from the couch and greeted me with a cool handshake. Some things had not changed: the tiny diamond studs were in one ear, the silver rings were on every finger of her left hand. I searched her face looking for a sign of stress. I didn't see anything but her usual serene beauty.

"So nice to see you again, Mr. Wanderman."

"Please call me Jake. Okay? I'm not comfortable being called mister."

"Of course. Won't you sit down? Can I get you something to drink?"

"I'm fine, thanks."

I sat on the couch. They sat in chairs across from me. There was a strained silence as I tried to think of something to say. I came up with a lame, "You have a beautiful apartment. Do you have a studio here, too?"

"Thank you. We like it. It's a good location. As for my studio, that's in another part of London altogether."

Okay, I thought, *enough already.* "I know you told your dad you didn't want to talk but a lot has happened since you left. Things that I'm sure you don't know about. I'm hoping you'll change your mind when I tell what they are."

"I won't promise anything," Sarajane said. "But I'm willing to listen."

"First, I know that before you left the hotel you had a visit from a man. I don't know what he was after. I don't know what he said to you. But the fact that you left the hotel shortly afterward, made me think. It made me think about what it was he could've said to you."

"What makes you think he said anything?"

Her answer told me something important. She'd confirmed what the desk clerk at the Huntting Inn had told me. "You went outside with him. I know it wasn't for a cigarette. You don't smoke. I have a suspicion that he said something that frightened you. Am I right?"

"I'm still listening."

I sensed a quickening of interest from her. "There's more. Oakhurst was shacking up with a woman who worked for him as a bartender. She was living in his apartment in New York. She was murdered not long after this man paid you a visit."

Margo abruptly stood and went out of the room. After a while she came back.

"That's terrible," Sarajane said. "But I don't see how that has anything to do with me."

"I think it does," I said. "It's logical that the murders are connected. It's also possible that the guy who came to see you is the same one who murdered the girl in New York."

A whimpering sound came out of Margo. Her eyes were closed. Her arms were wrapped around her, holding herself together. She seemed as if she was about to explode into a million pieces.

"I don't think it's logical at all," Sarajane said. "You're putting things together that don't necessarily go together."

"What if I tell you this guy is now in London? Would that make it more logical? He might be outside your apartment as we speak."

Margo sprung to her feet, went to the window, and looked out.

Sarajane didn't blink. She was cool, all right. "How would you know this? You've never seen him, have you?"

"I got a pretty good description from the desk clerk at the Huntting Inn."

"And you just happened to come across him? Pardon me, but I find that difficult to swallow."

"I saw someone in Hyde Park yesterday who looked familiar. He was the same guy I'd seen at JFK when I was waiting to board. He also fit the description I'd gotten. I don't believe in coincidences."

"Neither do I. But let's assume you're correct, that you did see this man in London. Perhaps he's following *you*. There's no reason I can think of for this man to seek me out, much less to murder me. I don't have what he wants." A look of dismay came and went in a flash. She knew she'd let something slip out that she shouldn't have.

"What was it he wanted?"

She didn't answer.

"You just said he wanted something. Why not tell me what it was? It's for your own good."

Margo left the window to come over and glare down at me. Her eyes were wide and rimmed with red, her face contorted. "Why are you doing this? There's no one out there. Who are you anyway? Why don't you leave us alone?"

She was more than angry. Her eyes, her body language, indicated she was almost out of control. I was no expert but I was pretty sure she was on something,

Sarajane got up and put an arm around her shoulders. "Calm down, baby. Nothing to get so upset about." She led her away. "Sit down now, won't you? Please?"

Margo sat, her arms gripping the sides of the chair, her body rigid.

It was clear to me now that Sarajane and Margo were more to each other than artist and friend. "I'm sorry. I didn't mean to cause such an upset," I said. "Believe it or not that's the last thing in the world I want to do."

"I appreciate that," Sarajane said. "But under the circumstances, I think you should go now."

"Please don't say that. Your father's my best friend. He sent me here to help you in any way I can."

"I'm sorry."

"I'm sorry, too. But I hope you'll let me come again."

"Perhaps."

I wrote the name of my hotel and room number on my card. "If you need me for anything, don't hesitate. I'm not very far." As I was leaving I asked if I could phone the next day.

"It might be better if you didn't. I'll call you if need be."

Great. I thought. It was like those job interviews I had when I was a kid looking for my first job. "Don't call us. We'll call you."

Outside, I realized I'd done a lousy job of interviewing. I'd learned a little: they were upset by the guy in East Hampton, if not scared. Margo was possibly a druggie. But essentially I'd screwed up. I had no choice but to call Morty and tell him of my abysmal failure.

I once more looked in all directions. Once again, I saw nothing unusual. The sun was shining and it was a beautiful day. But I headed back to my hotel, feeling as if I were enveloped in a heavy London fog.

CHAPTER 20

When I reached Morty I was apologetic.

"That's too bad, but give her time. You only just got there."

"It's not going to work."

"How about I call her again? Maybe I can get somewhere."

"Sure. Try it. You're her father. Maybe she'll relent."

"I'll do it. And I'll let you know what happened."

"There's something else I have to tell you." I was sick of secrets. I'd decided to come clean about everything. I proceeded to tell him about the man in East Hampton and in my driveway. I also told him about the possibility that he was in London, but emphasized that I might be seeing things. "At any rate, something's going on. I don't what it is, But Sarajane's right in the middle of it."

"That sounds serious. Who do you think this guy is? And what could he want from Sarajane?"

"I honestly don't have a clue."

"I'm going to call her right away."

"There's more. You remember the cops took the girl's fingerprints and some clothing? Well, they found stuff. Sarajane's fingerprint was on the knife that was used to kill Oakhurst."

"What?"

"You heard me. And fibers from her clothes were also found on his body."

"My God. How come they didn't arrest her?"

"Because she could've touched the knife some other time, and as for the clothing, that's more or less the same thing."

"Well, that's something, anyway. What a mess. How come you didn't tell me all this before?"

"I was trying to keep you from worrying."

"That's a laugh."

"I apologize. But now we have to move on. If you can get her to talk to me, that would be a big help."

"I'm gonna try my best, Jake." There was a pause. "One more thing, is there anything else you haven't told me?"

"Yes."

A groan. "What is it?"

"The food here ain't so bad."

At least I got him to laugh.

CHAPTER 21

Morty called me back an hour later. The news was grim. Sarajane said I'd upset Margo so much she was spending all her time trying to calm her down. He asked her about the man. She denied there was one. Said I'd made the whole thing up. He was as disheartened as I'd ever heard him.

"I'm really sorry, Morty. I hate to say I told you so but I told you so."

"I know, but I had hope. And I still do. Wait it out. Maybe she'll change her mind."

"I'm willing to give it a day or two."

"Don't set up any time frames. Wait and see what happens. In the meantime, why not enjoy London? It's on my dime."

It was nice of my friend to make that offer. London was a city offering as much sightseeing as anyone could manage. But I'd done all that with Rosalind years before. We'd been to Westminster Abbey, Houses of Parliament, Old Bailey, the Royal Gardens, the Tower, and the Tower Bridge, watched the changing of the guard at Buckingham Palace, and so on. I had no desire to see any of those again, and certainly not without Rosalind.

But good theater, that was a thought, something I might manage. I found a day-old *Evening Standard* in the hotel lobby and looked to see what was available. There were a couple of plays I knew I'd like, especially a revival of one by Pinter called *The Homecoming* that Rosalind and I had seen in New York. *Okay*, I thought. *I'll do it.* I went to the concierge to ask about tickets. There was someone already at his desk. After waiting a few minutes I left. Who was I kidding? There was no way I could sit in one place for a couple of hours.

Ironic, wasn't it? I was given the keys to the kingdom and couldn't find the lock in the door. Instead of theater and sightseeing, I went to my room and watched British TV. There was the BBC and ITV. I listened to people ostensibly speaking English and most of the time couldn't understand what they were saying. In addition to incomprehensible language the programs were as boring as ours: sitcoms, soaps, game shows, reality and talk shows, crime shows, even an old Poirot, and of course, programs about endangered animals in Africa.

What made me actually laugh were the weather reports. They featured a weather person who showed a map with drawings of clouds, or sun, or sprinkles. Talk about incomprehensible. The icons moved rapidly across the screen and disappeared in seconds so that I never could figure out what the forecast was.

I gave up and sat in the lobby, which was somewhat more interesting. The hotel attracted visitors from all over the world. There were some Americans—how did I know they were Americans? Their voices of course, but also, there's always something about the way our tourists dress that give them away. I can't explain exactly what it is, the sneakers, the tee shirts, the baseball caps, I'm not sure. But there was no way I couldn't tell they were Americans. At this hotel, the Americans were in the minority. There were many more Asians, Africans, Indians, as well as other Europeans. I heard a number of languages I didn't recognize. All this was fascinating and held my interest for a while, but then I'd had enough. I needed action, any kind, even a walk would help.

Since Hyde Park was so close, I decided to go back. I had a faint hope that I might spot that guy again. Actually, I wasn't sure about him anymore. My suspicions were fading. Even if the guy in the park was the same one from the airport, what did that prove? He could've been strolling in the park just like I was.

I went to Hyde Park Corner where the public orators were and listened for a while to a guy who was wearing a clown costume. There was an audience of ten, one of whom was sleeping peacefully in a carriage. The orator had a loud voice but as with the English on TV I couldn't understand more than a few words.

I left the park and walked up one street and down another, looking back every once in a while, seeing nobody and feeling foolish.

At certain times my stomach told me it was time to eat. Normally, I would've tried to find a good restaurant but I was so out of sorts all I wanted to do was fill my stomach, go back to my room and hope for Sarajane to call, even though I doubted she would. I found a fast food sandwich shop where "egg roll" was among the choices and thought I'd give it a try. When they called my number I went to the counter but what I saw was a sandwich.

"This isn't mine," I said.

"You ordered egg roll, didn't you? That's what this is, a fried egg on a roll."

Ah, the English.

But it was edible.

The next morning I was ready to go home. I hadn't slept well, waking every two hours, going to the bathroom, having bad dreams. I didn't think I could stand another day of this. I decided I'd call Sarajane. And if she didn't want to see me, so be it.

After breakfast, I was heading back to my room prepared to make the ultimate call. As I passed the front desk I heard my name called. The man behind the desk was holding up an envelope.

No, I thought. This was too much like a scene from an old movie. Sure enough, the message was to call Sarajane as soon as possible.

Her voice was no longer the cool dispassionate one I'd heard before. "Thanks for returning my call so promptly."

"What's up?"

"He's here. The man you talked about. He tried to get into my building."

Crazy, but that bad news made me feel good. It proved I wasn't imagining the whole thing. "How'd he do that?"

"The buzzer sounded and when I asked who it was, he said it was a delivery. When I asked from whom, he said FedEx from the Venable Gallery.

"I almost let him in but something was bothering me. I thought what could Valerie be sending me without my knowing about it? I decided I'd call Valerie and confirm this. I told him to come back another time. He insisted the delivery be made today or it would be returned.

"I told him to wait a minute and went to the window and looked out. There was no FedEx truck in the street. I knew something was wrong. He pushed the bell again but I didn't answer. When I looked out I saw him walk away. I'm sure it was the same man who came to see me in East Hampton."

"When did this happen?"

"Last evening."

"Why didn't you call me right away?"

"Margo didn't want me to. We were both very upset. We stayed up all night, discussing the situation."

"What was there to discuss? Is there something more than what you've told me so far?"

"Yes."

"I'll be there in five minutes," I said.

CHAPTER 22

This time it was Sarajane who opened the door. She wore a simple white linen blouse that looked as if it had been made of cream, a slim black skirt, and white low-heeled shoes. It was clear she hadn't had much sleep. Dark shadows under her eyes, red streaks in them, no makeup. But still beautiful. I looked for Margo but didn't see her.

"She's in her room," Sarajane said, reading my mind.

"Tell me again what happened."

She went through the account of the man ringing the bell claiming to be FedEx.

"Did you call Venable to see if she'd sent anything?"

"No. I was so sure he was the same man I'd seen in East Hampton that I didn't bother."

"I think you should call her anyway. I didn't see a FedEx tag on the front door, but I think we should be absolutely sure that it wasn't legitimate."

"And if I'm right, then what?"

"Then you're going to tell me everything. And I mean everything."

"I'll call now."

There was a small desk in one corner of the room with a phone. She picked up a business card, studied it, and dialed. The conversation was brief. She put the phone down, looked at me, and shook her head.

Margo came into the room. "I heard what you said." She looked at Sarajane. "Do you have to? Tell him everything?"

"Yes, baby. We can't run away from it any longer."

There was a long silence. While waiting for Sarajane to speak, I told myself to stay focused on her face. I wanted to be able to decide whether she was telling the truth or not. Judging from past performance, I couldn't be sure.

"All this," Sarajane finally said. "The man, I mean, his coming to see us in East Hampton and now here. It's all because of what occurred the night of Tony's murder."

"Go on," I said. "Tell me what happened that night."

She closed her eyes for a brief moment, leaned forward in her chair, and began to speak.

"Margo and I were walking toward Valerie's gallery. It was about two in the morning. I'd done this kind of thing before. It was always interesting for me to see who came to my installations in the middle of the night. When we got to the gallery, Margo pushed open the door. The air was filled with stale cigarette smoke and the distinct smell of marijuana. The floor was littered with empty bottles of wine and beer, cigarette butts and ashes, paper cups, and what looked like candy wrappers. We didn't see anyone and there wasn't a sound.

"'The place is filthy. And so much for the no smoking rules,' Margo said.

"'It's strange. There's no one here.'

"'Not like the last time in London. That installation was full of people all night long,' Margo said.

"'Perhaps The Hamptons crowd doesn't care about art.'

"But they apparently like to party. Isn't there supposed to be a guard on duty?'

"'Yes, of course. I don't understand any of this.'

"We went through the main room and found the door to the bedroom closed. When we opened it, we discovered the uniformed guard asleep on the bed, a bottle in his hand.

"'Pig!' Margo muttered. 'I'm going to wake him up.'

"'Wait a minute,' I said. 'I heard something.'

"'What?'

"'I thought I heard a noise. I think it came from the kitchen.'

"'I didn't hear anything.'

"'I'm sure I heard something. I think we should see what it is.'

"'Shouldn't we wake him up first?'

"'Why? What good would he be?'

"I closed the bedroom door and we headed for the kitchen. All signs of a party were gone except for some items on the kitchen counter and two bottles of wine on a table, both of which were lying sideways, obviously empty. Tony Oakhurst, shirt pulled out of his pants, still wearing his chef's toque, was leaning over the counter holding a straw to his nostrils.

He said something that sounded like "Ahh" and straightened up, the straw in his hand. He turned around and saw us. His face contorted into a combination of a smile and a leer. 'Welcome, ladies. Can I offer you a hit? As you can see, I've got plenty.' He pointed to a plastic bag on the counter. The contents of the bag were visible because the front of the bag had been pulled back so that a large white object inside was exposed. Now we could see a smattering of white powder on the counter

"'My God,' Margo said. 'That's a kilo of coke. It must be worth a fortune.'

"'Indeed it is,' Tony said, the word 'is' coming out like 'ish'. 'And it's all mine.'

"'Where'd you get it?' Margo said.

"'Never you mind where I got it. Do you want some or not? I can't offer you any wine. Big Mike and myself, we polished it all off.' He began to giggle. 'Polished it. That's good.' His shoulders shook as he continued giggling. 'Big Mike had too much. He missed the best part.' He pointed to the coke.

"'What are you doing here at this hour?' I asked.

"'I might ask you the same thing. In fact, I will ask you. What are *you* doing here at this hour?'

"'My installations are open 24/7. I always go in the middle of the night to see how things are.'

"'Is that so? Well, I'm here cleaning up last minute details. Can't you see?'

"'I do see that, yes. Perhaps you can tell me why it is that you're here alone, except for the drunk who passed out in the bedroom? I presume that's Big Mike?'

"He laughed loudly. 'You want to know about people? Is that what you mean? Thrill seekers? Free-loaders? There was a whole bunch of them before. They brought their own booze. They were drinking, singing, smoking pot. Making a lot of noise. I got hold of Mike. He had a bottle of scotch. "Mike," I said, "let's throw these cocksuckers out. They're making too much noise." So that's what we did. We chased them away. Mike and me, we threw 'em out. Every single one of them. After they left we went to work on the booze.'

"'You had no right to do that. This is my show, not yours.'

"Oakhurst reacted with mock horror. He stuck the straw between his teeth and held up both hands, palms facing out. 'Oh, the great artist is insulted? *This is my show, Tony, not yours.* Well, isn't that too bad. It was my name and my food that brought the crowds. Not your shit. You call what you do art? What a joke. It's nothing more than a mock-up of an apartment. Anybody could do it. It doesn't take a stitch of talent.'

"Margo had moved over to the counter where the coke was. She picked up a spoon and began to scrape some cocaine off the brick and onto the counter. 'Is there another straw?'

"'Be my guest.' Tony handed her his straw.

"'Margo, for god's sake,' I said. 'What on earth are you doing?'

"'Having a hit. Why not?'

"'You promised.'

"'I know.'

"'Atta girl,' Tony said. 'You only go around once.'

"'Tony,' I said. 'Will you please shut up and mind your own business?'

"'That's no way to talk to your former lover. Remember that great time we had? As a matter of fact, I had in mind that we might do the beast with two backs again Wouldn't you like that? You sure did the last time.'

"'I didn't think it was possible to sink any lower than you already are.'

"'Is that right? You should be grateful I fucked you at all. Why don't you take your butch girl friend and get the hell out of here?'

"'This gallery is for my show. You were invited for the opening and that's all. It's you who should get the hell out of here.'

"'Is that so. Well, I don't feel like it. So what're you going to do? Throw me out?' He walked toward me with his arms in front of him, his hands reaching for me. 'I put you down once and I can do it again.'

"Margo came up behind him and pushed him so that he stumbled. He regained his balance and began to laugh.

"'The two of you want to take me on, is that it?' He went into a crouch and began moving his hands and arms as if he were going to do karate or some form of martial arts. 'Okay, come on. Let's see what you can do.'

"I don't know what I was thinking but I was so angry I lost control of myself. I ran to the counter and picked up a chef's knife. 'Get out.'

"'Not likely.'

"Then I might just have to do something drastic with this knife."

"'What, are you threatening to cut my balls off?'

"'That might be a good idea. It's exactly what you deserve. Emasculation is the only remedy for vile people like you.'

"'You miserable cunt!'

"He suddenly ran straight toward me. Before he could get to me, Margo reached out and pushed him again. This time he fell. He went over awkwardly, one arm and leg beneath him. His head collided with the base of the kitchen counter. The chef's hat rolled to one side and blood began oozing from the top of his head.

"'My god, Margo,' I cried. 'He's bleeding.'

"'All I did was push him. I didn't know what he was going to do to you.'

"'He doesn't look good.' The knife slipped from my hand, making a clanking sound as it hit the tile floor.

"Oakhurst's eyes were closed and saliva was leaking from the side of his mouth. He was breathing heavily and moaning. In spite of the sound coming from him, he appeared to be unconscious.

"'What should we do?' I said.

"'Let's get the hell out of here,' Margo said. 'We don't need to be a part of this.'

"'But we just can't leave him.'

"'Yes, we can,' Margo said.

"She took my arm and pulled me along until we were out the door and onto the street. 'We're going back to the hotel and pretend none of this ever happened.'

"We began walking back to the Huntting Inn.

"'I don't feel good about this,' I said.

"'You'd feel worse if someone came in and found us with that bastard. Especially with him on the floor and bleeding. Hopefully, when he wakes up he won't remember a thing.'

"We continued walking, Margo trying to get me to walk faster. We were within a half block of the Inn when I stopped.

"'I can't do it. I have to go back. What if he dies because we left him like that?'

"'You didn't do anything. I was the one who pushed him. Besides, it was an accident. I certainly didn't expect him to fall and crack his head open.'

"'It doesn't matter. I have to go back. If you don't want to come with me, that's all right, too.'

"'Don't be ridiculous. Of course I'll come with you. But I think you're making a big mistake.'

"'If I am, it won't be the first time.'

"We began walking back to the gallery. This time I was the one walking quickly with Margo lagging behind.

"I gingerly pushed open the door. All seemed the same, the odor of smoke, the absence of sound. We walked slowly to the kitchen and opened the door. Tony was still on the floor. But his position had changed. He now lay sprawled flat on his face, arms stretched out in front of him. His white coat was stained with blood. The knife I'd dropped on the floor was now stuck in the middle of his back, the handle straight up.

"For a moment we were frozen. Then Margo went to the counter, stepping carefully around the blood. She picked up the bag of cocaine and put it into her purse.

"'My god, Margo. Are you insane?'

"'He won't need it anymore.'

"'You're out of your mind. What are you going to do with that much? How will you be able to keep it?'

"'I'll figure something out. Meanwhile, as I said before, we'd better get the hell out of here.'

"'This time, I couldn't agree more.'

"We turned to leave but the security guard stood in the doorway, one hand supporting himself against the jamb. He looked as if he were still half asleep. Then he saw the body on the floor and his sleepy eyes suddenly opened wide. 'Hold it right there,' he said."

CHAPTER 23

That's a hell of a story," I said.

For one thing, I wasn't sure I believed it. I'd never forgotten the incident the opening night at the Valerie Venable Gallery when I'd thought she'd fainted only to have her wink at me when I rushed to help her. If she was that adept at faking a faint, she might be equally adept at inventing a yarn.

"It's the truth."

"I'll take your word for it. But a few things disturb me. You said that just after you found the body, that's when Margo stole the coke. Which means she had it in her purse at the police station, right? How come the cops didn't find it?"

"They didn't look. You were there, don't you remember? We were treated as witnesses, nothing more. Later, of course, they took our fingerprints and clothing. I suppose they might have found some residue of cocaine but they probably wouldn't have been surprised by that. Artists, you know."

"And when they interviewed you, you just made up that story about finding the body?"

"Yes."

"How did you manage to get your stories in line? Didn't they interview you separately?"

"Yes. But we had time before the police arrived to sort it out. The security guard didn't stop us from speaking to each other. He was so groggy he could barely stand."

"Okay, so you went back to the hotel. What did you do with the coke then?"

"Nothing. Margo put it in her suitcase."

"And where is it now? Let me guess. You brought it with you."

"Rather. It's worth a bloody fortune," Margo said. "What would you have me do, leave it behind?"

"God forbid. That would make life too simple. What about the airline? How'd you manage to get it through customs?"

Margo smiled. It was a surprisingly beautiful smile. I hadn't seen it before, but at that moment I wasn't in the mood to admire it. "I'm rather proud of how I managed it," she said.

"Tell me. I'd love to know in case I ever have the opportunity to do it myself."

"In spite of your sarcasm, I'll be pleased to explain it to you."

I leaned back. "I'm all ears."

She looked at Sarajane and smiled again. "You weren't too pleased about my doing it, were you?"

Sarajane looked anything but pleased, even now. "Hardly. If the customs people had examined the box we'd be in jail right now." Her tone was decidedly not that of a happy camper

"But they didn't, did they? And they never had, in the past, had they?"

Sarajane nodded her head in agreement but that did nothing to change the look of disapproval on her face.

Margo directed her attention back to me. "I took full advantage of Sarajane's fame as an artist. When she travels on business she always hauls a large box full of art supplies—paints, brushes, tools of all kinds. We've been through customs in many parts of the world. Rarely has the box ever been opened. I've been toting along my drug of choice for years. A few grams, though. Nothing like this time."

"But it has been inspected in the past?" I said.

"Once, in Greece. A cursory inspection, I assure you. They opened it, glanced inside, and closed it up again."

"Lucky. So how did you do it?"

"I'll show you," she said.

She went out of the room and came back with a pint sized glass jar, the kind used for canning. It was filled with what looked like blue paint.

"This is it," she said. "Looks like a jar of paint, doesn't it?"

"Sure does. You've got the coke inside that jar?"

"Exactly. In a glassine bag. The bag is completely sealed, and the jar is tight. No odor either. If they opened the box at all they'd see jars of paint. Nothing more."

"Unbelievable," I said. "Can I see it?"

Margo brought the jar over to me and screwed off the top. I looked inside and saw nothing but liquid. "What kind of paint is this? I don't smell anything."

"It's acrylic. Water based. Noncombustible."

"Amazing."

"I thought it was quite brilliant," Margo said.

"Except for the possibility that they might have opened a jar and poked inside."

"Of course, there was always that chance. But why would they? They never had in the past."

"Okay, you did it. You got the stuff here, for your own personal use, I imagine. But you apparently didn't think about possible consequences."

Sarajane suddenly spoke. "Such as?"

"Maybe that coke didn't belong to Oakhurst," I said. "Maybe someone else owned it or had a share in it. It's worth a lot of money, isn't it?"

"About 100,000 pounds I'd guess," Margo said.

"What's that in dollars? About a hundred and fifty thousand? That's a lot of money to some people. Did you think you could just walk away with something like that and nobody would notice?"

Neither one of them answered. They were staring at me now as if they knew what I was going to say next. "It doesn't take much imagination to connect it to the guy who came to see you at the hotel in East Hampton."

"You're right," Sarajane said. She stood up and paced back and forth. In her creamy white blouse, black skirt, impeccable makeup, she looked more like an upper class society type than a working artist. "When he came to the hotel he asked if I had it. I should have given it to him right then and there. But I didn't know who he was. I denied knowing anything about it. He told me I'd better be telling the truth. He said if he found out I'd been lying, I'd regret it the rest of my life. And that life wouldn't last long. He never once raised his voice. His eyes were a pale blue. I felt as if he were looking into my soul. After he left, I told Margo what had happened and we both agreed the best thing to do was leave East Hampton as quickly as possible."

"It would've saved a lot of trouble if you'd just given the stuff to him then," I said.

"I'm quite aware of that. The question is, what are we going to do now? Can you help us?"

"I'll try my best. But it's not going to be easy. I'm guessing that this guy wasn't able to locate the coke in The Hamptons so he must have concluded that you had it. That's why he's here. And he wants it back. I'm assuming that now you're willing to give it to him. Is that right?"

"Of course," Sarajane said, returning to her seat.

"Why should we?" Margo said. "We aren't absolutely certain that it's his."

"At this point I couldn't care less," Sarajane said, the anger in her voice barely contained.

"You're kidding, right?" I demanded. "You want to keep it and find yourself dead? Besides, the coke might be his. Maybe that's who Oakhurst got it from."

"What do you mean?" Sarajane said.

"Maybe they were in business together."

"Oh." Margo sighed. "I never thought about that."

"Or anything else, except where the next hit was coming from," I snapped.

"You see!" Margo turned to Sarajane. "You may be angry with me but I have a right to be angry, as well. He has no respect for us at all."

"Mr. Wanderman, could you at least try to be civil?" Sarajane growled.

"Civil, shmivil." These women were getting under my skin. I didn't care about their relationship with each other, which didn't seem to be going to well at the moment. It was their seeming ignorance about the danger they were in that was getting to me. "You're in a lot of trouble, the both of you. Don't you understand that?" There was a long silence. "Before we go any further, are we in agreement that you're giving the coke back?"

Sarajane spoke sharply. "Margo?"

Margo nodded. "I suppose so. But how disappointing after all that ingenuity."

"Tough." I leaned back in my chair and tried to think. I glanced around the room, taking in the modern furniture, the muted colors, the whole feeling of the place, and suddenly wondered what Rosalind would've thought about the way it was furnished and decorated.

This thinking about my late wife happened all the time, often at the oddest moments. I knew Rosalind wouldn't have liked the austere feeling, a sharp contrast to the way she would've done it. I also knew she would have hated the painting on the wall opposite me. It was huge, maybe eight feet across and five or six feet in height, an abstract, with jagged streaks of color on a black background. Rosalind loved color and contrast, but not the kind that broadcast harshness and stridency. In the short time I'd known Sarajane, this kind of painting didn't seem to me something she would've liked either, but that only reminded me again how little I really knew this young woman.

The silence continued. I tried to make eye contact but neither one of them would look at me. I wasn't sure what to do next. Finally, in a more or less desperate attempt to get a conversation going again, I said, "This is a dilemma Shakespeare would've loved."

"What does Shakespeare have to do with anything?" Sarajane asked.

"Nothing. My mind is a cluttered Shakespeare attic, that's all. Real life often triggers a reaction that recalls something he wrote."

"What would he have to say about this problem?"

"Good question. Give me a minute." I rummaged around in my attic. "How about, *The miserable have no medicine. But only hope.*"

A grunt came from Margo. "Bloody awful. Is that the best you can do?"

"You're right," I said. "It stinks. How about...*Prayers and wishes are all I can return.*"

"Never mind all that," Sarajane said. "It would be more to the point if Shakespeare could tell us what to do."

I stared at the painting on the wall again, not really seeing it, and an idea came to me. Suppose I was right and Oakhurst and Shaved Head were in a partnership. Shaved Head delivers the coke to Oakhurst who brings it out to East Hampton to distribute or to give it to someone else to distribute. Oakhurst decides to keep it for himself and rip off Shaved Head. He gets a call that it hasn't been delivered so he comes out to see what's going on. He might be the one who killed the girl in Oakhurst's apartment in New York. The place was trashed as if someone were looking for something. Maybe he kills Oakhurst too, or else he learns that Oakhurst is dead, finds out about the girls and pays them a visit. He then discovers they skipped and traces them to London. That all made some sort of sense. But what I didn't get was why he'd be following me. The answer to that was that maybe he wasn't. Maybe it was just a coincidence I'd run into him in the park. I'd never really seen him anywhere else.

Assuming all that was on target, and I had to admit that took a lot of assuming, the next question was how to get the coke back to Shaved Head without being killed or maimed in the process.

"Okay," I said. "Let's talk about how we're going to give the drugs back. Any ideas?"

I looked at them and saw frowns and their heads moving negatively from side to side. Even while frowning, Sarajane was beautiful. Her skin luminous, her body voluptuous, her aura, Mona Lisa. I couldn't say the same for Margo. I had no idea what attraction she held for Sarajane but there was none for me. True, she had a beautiful smile, but her body was square, without softness, about as alluring as a fire hydrant and, on top of all, that she might be a cokehead.

In spite of the fact that the room was large, I began to feel as if the walls were pressing in on me. I stood up, stretched, and went over to the window. Not much to see. A London street that was surprisingly similar to the streets in the West Village but without the charm. Brick townhouses, cars parked endlessly one behind the other, some leafy trees providing a touch of green in contrast to the bricks and stone. Other than that, the only difference was that the cars had the steering wheel on the wrong side.

I was about to turn away when I saw something move behind one of the trees farther down the block. I stared at the spot, waiting to see if I was right. A few moments later I saw what looked like cigarette smoke. I had a funny feeling. Was someone watching the apartment? Could it be that our man, Mr. Shaved Head himself, was actually hanging around waiting to see what he could see?

On a sudden impulse, I decided to go downstairs and find out. "I'll be right back." I headed for the door.

"Where are you going?"

"I think our guy is outside watching this place. I'm going to have a talk with him."

Margo's eyes opened wide. "What? Are you insane?"

"Keep the door locked and don't let anyone in unless I say it's all right. And I want you to watch me from the window. If it looks like I might be in trouble, call the cops."

"I'm not sure this is a clever thing to do," Sarajane said.

"Neither am I."

I went down the stairs, through the front door, and onto the sidewalk. I walked slowly down the street, trying to look casual. It struck me then that this was not like the Village at all. It was too neat, too tidy. The buildings looked as if they'd been scrubbed. Iron railings, orderly little shrubs and plants, nothing out of place, not even a scrap of litter. Definitely not New York.

I headed in his direction, sort of strolling and staying on my side of the street. When I was opposite him, I stopped. For a minute it crossed my mind that I might be doing something very dumb. I could possibly be letting myself in for a whole lot of trouble. But hell, I'd promised Morty to look after his daughter and, at the moment, this seemed like the best way to do it.

I checked to see if there were any cars heading my way then I crossed the street.

He watched me coming and took a drag on his cigarette. I could see blue veins criss-crossing the top of his gleaming skull like railroad tracks. He gave me a cold stare and blew smoke in my direction.

"How are you today?" I said.

He was about my height and had a good fifty pounds on me. He had a gut that drooped over his belly, but even with the flab I could see he was a tough cookie and could probably put me away without too much trouble. His eyes were pale blue marbles just as Sarajane had described them.

"You're a wise guy?" He sounded American but I heard a trace of an accent.

"Just trying to be friendly, that's all. But I have a question for you. What're you trying to accomplish by following me and the young ladies all over London?"

"What am I trying to *accomplish*?" He mimicked me. "That's a good one."

"Let me put it another way. What do you want?"

"You know what I want."

"I think I know but I'd like to be sure. Why don't you tell me in plain English? Then we'll both know."

Hearing his voice again, I was sure of an accent, maybe a hint of Russian? I wasn't sure. He might have lived in the States for a long time. That would help account for his sounding a lot like an American. Even so, it was all but impossible to speak American without being born in the U.S. or growing up there at a very early age. Anyhow, this hint of an accent that might be Russian made him seem more dangerous. I'd been beaten badly by Russian mobsters in the past and had no desire for a recurrence.

His pale eyes were small, set deep into a fleshy face. He stared intently at me. He seemed to be trying to figure out if I was conning him or not.

"I'm not bull-shitting you," I said. "I'm here to look out for the girls. I'll do whatever I can to get you off their backs."

He looked up and down the street. There was no one within twenty yards of us. "Are you recording this?"

"No. Why would I? You've been watching too many movies. " I held out my arms. "Search me if you want."

"Never mind. It makes no difference. And don't tell me you don't know what I'm doing. Those cunts stole something that belongs to me. I want it back."

He stared at me again watching for my reaction.

I tried to show him my best poker face. I wasn't sure how to go with this. I had to admit to him that the girls had the coke but also had to keep him from doing anything about it right then and there.

I looked up at the window of the apartment and saw the two of them watching us. That made me slightly less nervous. "They're willing to give the stuff back."

"Good. Let us go get it." He dropped the cigarette on the pavement and stepped on it.

"Hold it," I said. I wasn't about to let him upstairs. "It's not here. When I found out what was going on I took it out of their apartment. I didn't want them getting into more trouble."

"So *you* have it?"

"Let's say I know where it is."

"Where is it?"

My mind was feverish. I was trying to stay one step ahead of him. "Not so fast. I have to think about this. I don't want anything happening to the girls but I also want to make sure nothing happens to me either. I said I'd give it to you but I have to figure out a way to get it back to you at the right time and the right place."

"Maybe I should kick the shit out of you right now and then you give it to me?"

This was easier to deal with. "You could try. And you might be able to do it. But if you look up you'll see we're being watched. You lay a hand on me and they'll call the cops. Then where'll you be? I don't think that's what you want, is it?"

He looked up at the apartment window—I hoped they were still there—then directed his pale blue eyes back at me. "I'm listening."

Now what? I had to get away from him in order to find a way to work things out. I had to find a way to slow him down, convince him that if he'd be patient he'd get everything he wanted. How to do that?

"Wait here. I'll go upstairs and talk to them. I'll be right back."

I started to walk away from him but he grabbed my arm. His fingers dug into me as if he were trying to rip out a vein. "Where do you think you're going?"

It wasn't easy but I managed to get out of his iron grip. My arm already felt black and blue. "I told you, I have to talk to the girls."

"What about?"

"What do you think? They're a part of this, too, you know."

I was getting desperate. He wasn't going to let me walk away without giving him something positive. I needed to think what that could be. I'd already told him I'd taken the drugs away. What could I tell him that would hold him off? I had to convince him I'd put them someplace. Where could I have put the coke that would be difficult to get to at that moment? Where could I have stashed it that would be safe, and how could I then arrange to meet him and turn the stuff over without getting killed or damaged in the process?

Then it hit me. Left Luggage. Of course, that would do it. Left Luggage was what the English called the baggage check-room. They were at the airports and in railway stations. All I'd have to do is give him the ticket and he could pick it up without my being there. But of course I didn't have a ticket because I hadn't done it yet.

"Look, the stuff is in London," I said. "That's all I'm telling you now. But I need time to make arrangements to turn it over to you."

"Why don't we just go and get it right now?"

"It's not that simple. I have to do things to make it work. The girls are involved in this thing, too, I told you that. And I have to protect myself, don't I? You may not trust me, but I don't have a hell of a lot of trust in you, either. You know where I am, you know where the girls live. I don't know anything about you. So in one way you've got the upper hand. But on the other side, I've got what you want, so you have to deal with me. You hear what I'm saying Mr...what's your name anyway?"

His face twisted in anger. His eyes had sparks in them. "Fuck you! You don't need my name. Tell me what you got in mind."

"Tomorrow morning, 10 a.m. Meet me in front of the Tate."

"What's that?"

"It's a museum, asshole. The one you're going to meet me at is called the Tate Modern. Just ask any taxi driver. They'll take you right there."

"What'd you do, park it in a museum?"

"Don't strain yourself trying to figure it out. Meet me there and you'll get your stuff. Guaranteed. If not, you know where to find me."

He shook another cigarette out of a pack and lit it with a gold lighter. He blew some smoke through his nose and gave me another of his cold, blue looks, trying to show me how tough he was. If the look was meant to scare me, it did, a little, but I wasn't about to let him know it.

And then, with a loud grunt, he pounded his fist into the middle of my belly. It felt like I'd been kicked by a horse. The breath shot out of me like an erupting volcano. I bent over, grabbing at my middle. Pain. Lots of pain. My eyes filled, my knees buckled. While I was gasping for air I heard him say: "Just so you don't get any ideas."

He walked away, leaving me frozen in place, twisted like a wind-blown umbrella.

CHAPTER 24

I didn't know how much time passed before I heard footsteps. I was still a tree in a petrified forest, eyes squeezed shut, and trying to deal with the pain in my gut. I inhaled the musky odor of perfume and thought salvation had arrived.

"You poor thing," I heard Sarajane say. The sound of her voice was like the music of angels. I felt her arm go around my back, supporting me. "Are you all right?"

I was about as all right as a fly on flypaper but I wasn't about to admit that I wasn't. "Just had the air knocked out of me, that's all." My voice sounded like a crow's mating call.

With all the effort I could manage I straightened myself. My knees were a bit wobbly but at least I was standing. I saw then that Margo was there, too.

"That murderous bastard," she said. "He ought to be shot for that."

"Maybe for other things," I managed to say. "But not for a sneak punch in my gut."

We went back upstairs, walking slowly and deliberately, the two of them on each side holding me as if I were an invalid. I sure felt like one. With every step I took, my stomach muscles screamed at me.

When we were finally back in the apartment, they made me sit on their most comfortable chair. I closed my eyes and tried to relax but they wouldn't let me. They were like vultures on road kill with one question on top of another.

"What happened?"

"Why did he hit you like that?"

"Did you provoke him?"

"It looked like you were having quite an argument down there."

"Hey," I said. "Back off a minute, would you? I'm still trying to learn how to breathe again."

"I'm so sorry," Sarajane said. "I apologize for the both of us. Subjecting you to all these questions when you've just been through such an ordeal. Would you like something to drink?"

"I would. Vodka, if you have it."

"With tonic?"

"With nothing. Just pour it over ice."

Sarajane went into the kitchen and came back with a bowl filled with ice cubes. She took it to the far end of the room where there was a small bar. She returned and handed me a brimming glass.

That son of a bitch had done quite a number on me. Reaching for the glass, I could feel my hand shaking so I held it with both hands, not wanting to spill any of it. Even so, it took some effort to hold the glass steady. "Am I drinking alone?"

"Not at all," Margo said. "It wouldn't be hospitable to let Mr. Wanderman drink alone." She got up and made a drink for herself then looked at Sarajane. "Are you joining us?"

"Fine," came the grudging reply. "I'll have something, too."

Apparently, the tension between them that I'd observed before still persisted. I waited for them to prepare their drinks and raised the glass to my lips, still holding on with both hands. Before drinking, I said, "Many thanks for helping me. *'I have half a dozen healths to drink to these fair ladies.'*"

"Shakespeare again?" said Sarajane.

"What else? I've got a million of 'em."

"We'd prefer to hear what happened outside, if you don't mind."

I swallowed a large amount of vodka and waited for it to do its job. It did it well, slowly warming my stomach and allowing the pain to ease. After a few moments of this, I swallowed the rest of the drink and put the glass down on the table beside me.

I then proceeded to tell them everything, up to and including my idea about meeting Shaved Head at the Tate. Originally, I'd been pleased with that idea. Actually, there are two Tates, the Britain and the Modern. I'd seen a brochure that showed they ran a boat between the two museums. It had suddenly struck me that all I had to do was persuade the ugly mug to go on the boat. I didn't see why he'd turn me down. He was there to get possession of the drugs, so at that point he'd have to be following my instructions.

Now, even though I had the proof he could be vicious—that sucker punch still resonated—I thought I'd be safe on a boat filled with tourists. What was he going to do, shoot me in front of a crowd? I didn't think so, but who knew with this guy? I didn't see that I had much choice except to take a chance that he wouldn't. But I thought the best part was that I wouldn't even have to get off the boat. When we got to the other end, I'd just hand him the ticket to the luggage storage, wish him good luck, *adieu*, and then stay where I was. I could just see the look on his face. He'd be mad as hell, but then he'd realize there was nothing he could do about it. He wanted the coke and he'd have the ticket for it. So off he'd go and that would be the end of that. I hoped.

While I was telling them all this, I sort of floated above the scene, watching myself and listening to what I was saying. I didn't sound like a victim of laryngitis anymore, but as I went on describing my plan, I became less than pleased. What I'd thought was a great idea before now appeared to be full of holes. Shaved Head might have his own ideas about dealing with me that I had no clue about. This guy was no amateur. And he'd made sure that I knew it.

I retrieved my glass but there was nothing left in it but ice cubes. Having no choice, I chewed on an ice cube and waited to hear what they had to say.

Neither one said anything at first. They sipped their drinks. I thought about asking for a refill then decided against it. I didn't want them to think I was dependent on alcohol, even though I'd gone through a phase when I was. After Rosalind died I'd used alcohol as a form of salvation. But I'd eventually managed to work through that.

Sarajane spoke first. "I think what you've planned here is nothing short of brilliant."

"You do?"

"Absolutely. I think you've solved all our problems. That monster will get back what he wants and we'll be free once again without any more to worry about."

"I hope you're right," I said. Once again, I had to wonder if I really believed her. But what would her motive be for lying?

"I'm not so sure," Margo said. "A lot can go wrong."

"Probably," I said. Now, I thought I knew what *her* motive might be. She wanted me to go through with my plan because I'd be the one in danger, not either one of them. "I can think of something right off the bat."

"What's that?"

"Well, for one thing, I have to take the package to a train station and deposit it in Left Luggage. Suppose he's still hanging around outside when I leave here and sees me carrying a parcel. Then what?"

"So let him have it," Margo said. "Why go through all this rigamarole? Let him have it and be done with it."

I watched as she swallowed more from her glass. I swallowed along with her but since there was nothing to swallow except my own spit, it wasn't satisfying. "You still don't get it," I said." This guy might be the guy who killed Tony Oakhurst. He might also be the one who killed a girl in Oakhurst's New York apartment."

"When was that?" Sarajane said. "We heard nothing about that."

"You were already gone, that's why. Someone searched his apartment and killed this girl who was apparently living there. Bad luck for her. At any rate, if he is the killer, he might just decide to do me as well. I can identify him, can't I? Getting rid of me would take one of his problems away."

"He's right," Sarajane said. "We all have to keep away from this man."

"All right then," Margo said. "If it comes to that, there's another way out of the building,"

"Of course," Sarjane said. "There's a small garden at the rear for the use of the tenants. We've never used it because it's so uninviting. No place to sit. It's just for looking at. But I believe you'll be able to climb over the fence. You'll then find yourself on the next street over. I can't imagine he'd be expecting you to leave that way."

"You're sure about this?"

"Absolutely," Margo said. "And you won't have to climb over the fence. There's a gate. It's locked, of course. All we have to do is get the key from our janitor. He has a flat on the ground floor."

I smiled. Good news, for a change. Now I felt able to ask, "Do you think I might have another drink?"

CHAPTER 25

I no longer needed two hands to hold my glass. I sipped my vodka like a gentleman.

"Margo," I said. "I think now would be a good time for you to get the box ready for me."

"You mean, immediately?"

"If you don't mind. I should get going ASAP."

She stood up. "Very well."

"Before you do this," I said. "I need to ask you something. I want an honest answer."

"Oh?"

"I think you know what I'm about to ask."

"I can guess. You want to know if I've been indulging a little from the stash, is that it? Well, the answer is that I have. You don't think I brought it all this way just to look at it, do you? Like a painting on a wall?"

"How much?"

"Not that much. I sniffed a line here, a line there. I'm not consumed by it, you know. I can handle it."

"You used to be able to handle it," Sarajane said. "Lately, I'm not so sure."

"How dare you say that!" Margo said. "You don't see me sneaking out of the room at odd hours, do you? Have I ever done a break night? Have you ever seen me cabbaged? No. I'm at the computer and on the phone all day long, doing work for you. I like the stuff. I admit it. But I sniff only when I want to. I'm not a cokehead. I dare you to call me a cokehead."

"In that case, I can only say that I'm delighted you're not," Sarajane said.

"I'm delighted that you're delighted."

It was obvious Margo was agitated. I looked at her eyes to see if they were as bright and glittering the way they'd been when I first came to their apartment. I was pretty sure then that she'd been using, but now she seemed under control. Still, I wondered if her over-the-top-reaction to Sarajane's comment was honest or due to her really being a cokehead. You know...*thou doth protest too much.*

"Ladies, ladies," I said. "Let's keep to the business at hand. I asked only because I don't want this guy to examine the stuff and say we cheated him."

"How could he?" Margo said. "The package wasn't sealed. This man who's been stalking us must have had a suspicion that Oakhurst had already broken into it. Which, in point of fact, he had."

"That makes sense."

"I'm so glad you think so," Margo said, sounding not glad at all. She strode out of the room, leaving behind an uncomfortable silence.

Sarajane tapped her foot on the floor. I tried to think of something to say but came up empty. I swirled the ice in my glass. Without warning, Morty popped up in my head. Like Hamlet's ghost.

"I know I told you this before," I said. "But I think it's worth repeating. I came here because of your father."

"I know that."

"He couldn't come himself, of course. You understand that he has a busy practice. So he sent me. I have some experience, not much, but some. And I'm his best friend. But his not being here doesn't mean he isn't worried about you, or that he cares any less about you. He's worried and frankly, I'm worried, too. I have to tell him something about what's happening and I don't have a clue what I should say to him."

"Why can't you just tell him the truth?"

I stared hard at her, trying to see past her expressionless demeanor, behind the eyes that gave nothing away. Did she really mean that? Did she really want me to tell him everything, her story of finding the body of Oakhurst, her partner stealing drugs, the very real threat to their lives? I was trying to get some impression of who this woman was and what she wanted. But I wasn't getting anywhere.

"The truth isn't always the answer," I said. "Somehow I think you already know that."

"I have no idea what you mean."

I wasn't sure what I meant, either. *Is not the truth the truth?* Not always. It's not just the opposite of lying. There's also the matter of being forthcoming, the matter of being honest about things. In that respect, I had a lot to answer for, as well. As far as Sarajane was concerned, I'd been less than truthful. I hadn't told her what was happening in New York...that Sienna had found evidence of her contact with the murdered man....the fibers of her clothing, the fingerprint on the knife. She didn't know that she was considered a prime suspect and that the Homicide cops were working hard to find enough evidence to have her extradited so she could be tried for murder.

I'd told her father that part of the story and I was very sorry I'd told him. There was no need for Morty to be so burdened. Now if I told Sarajane, would it do any good? I didn't know. I didn't know because I wasn't sure about how much she was involved. Suppose her story wasn't all that she'd said? I didn't like to think so, but it was possible, wasn't it, that she'd actually killed Oakhurst? Perhaps not with premeditation, but in a fit of anger, or self-protection? That would explain why she ran from East Hampton back to London. Because she knew they'd find something. Anything was possible at this point.

Quandaries, quandaries. I was struggling with these thoughts when Margo came back with the box neatly taped and tied with cord. I looked hard to see if there was any white powder under her nose but I didn't see any.

"Okay," I said. "Let's find the janitor so I can get out of here."

"It won't be a problem," Margo said. "The man is like a mole. He never seems to leave the building."

The three of us went down one flight of stairs, reversed along a corridor until we came to the end of it. A door with a narrow nameplate spelled out, "Mr. Hedwig." Margo knocked twice. After a few moments, we heard the sound of a key being turned and then the door opened.

Mr. Hedwig was not much taller than five feet with a head as large as a honeydew melon. His skin had a greenish cast and was filled with tiny pockmarks that made it look like the surface of the moon. Set into this moonscape were small dark eyes sunk so deep into their sockets it seemed as if he were peering at us out of a cave.

"Aye?" he said.

"I'm so sorry to disturb you, Mr. Hedwig, but it's quite important," Margo said.

He replied by grunting.

"We have a very large favor to ask of you."

He said nothing, waiting. Not much of a conversationalist.

"Yes. My friend here—" She gestured toward me. "—is trying to avoid someone. There's a person in front of the building who has been quite obstreperous to him in the past. My friend has no wish to confront him again and so I suggested he could leave through the garden. Would you mind providing the key for the gate?"

Mr. Hedwig took this in, silent as the grave. He looked at me. I smiled as pleasantly as I could. He looked at the girls. He scratched his head. Then he spoke words, real words that could be understood. "I am not allowed to give out the key, Miss. 'Tis against the rules of the landlord."

"We won't keep it very long, Mr. Hedwig," Sarajane said in a voice so sweet it all but dripped syrup. "Just enough to open the gate. We'll return it immediately."

The melon head moved from side to side, slowly and negatively.

"Can'at be done, y'see. 'Tis against the rules of the landlord."

"Yes, you already said that," Margo snapped.

I could hear her voice getting testy and didn't think that would do us any good. I decided to butt in. "Suppose," I said, reaching into my pocket with my free hand, searching, and finding what I was looking for—a ten-pound note. I handed it to him. "Suppose you come along with us and open the gate yourself. How would that be? No rules broken, right? Everything hunky dory?"

His eyes blinked rapidly a few times. He reached out and took the tenner, slipping it deftly into a pocket. "Wait here. I'll be back in a jiff."

He returned in a few moments, holding an enormous ring of keys. A few of them looked large enough to open a jail in the Château d'If. He closed his door, carefully locked it with one of the keys on the ring, escorted us to another locked door. He opened that and led us down a few more steps to the garden. There was a single light outside which enabled us to walk along a narrow path not more than a couple of yards long. We followed him, listening to the keys jangling and tinkling in his hand like a tambourine. He inserted one of the keys and gave it a turn. The lock opened easily. He removed it and pushed the gate open.

I stepped through it. "Thank you, Mr. Hedwig," I said. "And goodnight to you all."

Holding the box under one arm, I waved at the three of them with the other and headed away as quickly as I could.

CHAPTER 26

I walked to the nearest corner, clutching the box and looking back to see if anyone was following me. Nobody. I breathed easier but I still had a lot to be nervous about. For one, my friend, Mr. Shaved Head, who might be lurking somewhere in the darkness. And two, this box full of dope I was cradling in my arms as if it were a precious newborn babe.

The next street over appeared to have traffic so I headed in that direction in the hope of finding a taxi. It didn't take long before one came along. I got in and asked the driver to take me to the nearest train station.

"Do y'mean the Underground, or the main railway?"

"A railroad station. Where they have trains. You know, choo choo?"

"Railway then. The nearest is Victoria, guv."

"Good. Victoria it is," I said.

He put the meter on. I sat back in the seat, and a most comfortable seat it was, too. The London taxis were so much roomier than the ones in New York. That was a major difference but some things were apparently not very different. He'd only just begun to drive when he spoke. I had a sense that this guy was going to be much like some cabbies I'd come across in New York. He wanted to talk.

"American, are you?"

"That's right."

"I was sure of it."

I, on the other hand, didn't want to talk. I needed to think about what I had to do and how I was going to do it. The last thing I wanted to do was chitchat with a taxi driver. I'd thought if I made my answer brief it might give him a hint. No such luck.

I knew I shouldn't respond but I did. "How could you tell?"

"Your manner of dress," he said. "I knew you were a Yank before you'd said a word."

I was wearing jeans, a polo shirt, and sneakers. Apparently that was enough. "Very perceptive," I said. "I guess we're as obvious as a neon sign."

He laughed. "You might say that."

We went on driving for what may have been all of another thirty seconds before he was at it again. "Going on a trip, are you? A rail trip? I like the rails. I have to say one thing about the British railway system. It's the best in the world. I have a cousin who's a conductor on the Brighton line."

"Is that so?"

I felt like asking, as kids do when you take them for a long ride, *Are we there yet*? Then I mentally shrugged my shoulders and gave up, keeping the conversation moving along. "The New York City Subway used to have a Brighton Line. It took you to Brighton Beach on the ocean. I went there a lot when I was a boy."

"Our Brighton is on the ocean, as well. Small world, isn't it?"

What else could I do but agree?

And with that, he pulled into the front of Victoria Station and opened my door with one hand, without having to get out of his cab.

I paid him and gave him some of the change without counting it.

"Ta, Yank," he said and drove away.

The station loomed high in front of me. Behind me was a parking lot filled with buses. The station entrance at street level had crowds moving this way and that, jostling me on the sidewalk. Above the entrance was a huge building of old red brick, a clock tower in the center and arches on either side. I stood there for a few minutes, trying to think. After the relative quiet of the taxi, the immensity of the building, combined with the intense movement of the people around me, was startling. I hesitated, unsure of myself. Then I reminded myself why I was there. I had come to do a job. So do it, already, schmuck.

I walked into the station, the package bulky under one arm, and found an enormous space, larger than Grand Central. The floor was marble, offset with intricate colored squares, which made arresting patterns. All around me was everything I expected to find in an airport but somehow, not in a railroad station: stores, restaurants, signs and arrows indicating facilities of all kinds, and people. Masses of them. It seemed as if half of London must have decided they had to go to Victoria Station that day.

I walked gingerly through the throngs. I was not happy schlepping this dangerous box around. Ridiculous scenarios played in my head. Suppose I tripped and fell and all the contents spilled out. Suppose I'd been followed by Shaved Head without my realizing it. I looked behind me and around me and happily did not see anyone that looked like him. I told myself to stop acting like a rube with green ears and go about my business. The first thing I had to do was locate the Left Luggage Department. I spotted an information booth and found a woman staring off into space. When I moved into her range of vision, she gave me a disgruntled look, suggesting that I'd interrupted her daydream and she was damned annoyed about it.

"May I assist you?"

"Could you tell me where Left Luggage is?" I asked.

"It's between platform seven and eight."

"Thank you. And where would that be?"

She pointed over to my left then asked, "Is there anything else?" in a tone of voice that suggested there'd better not be.

So much for the polite-English myth. I told her there wasn't and let her go back to her daydream.

The short interview had not gotten rid of my tension. I walked toward the platforms where the Left Luggage Department was, hoping there wouldn't be any problem leaving a package. Why should there be? Isn't that what the department was for? Besides, I was obviously a Yank and would probably come across as a tourist, so what did I have to worry about? Hah!

There was an older man at the counter. His eyes were half closed and his head tilted to the side as if he had difficulty holding it up. He'd apparently had a long day, but he was polite when I asked about leaving the box.

"May I see identification and your ticket please?"

"Ticket?"

"Yes, sir. You must possess a ticket in order to deposit a parcel."

"Oh?" I expected to be asked for ID but the ticket was a surprise I didn't need. I did a quick bit of mental juggling. "Oh yes, of course. I was going to buy my ticket after I left here. I didn't know you needed a ticket before you could leave a parcel."

"Indeed sir, a ticket is necessary."

"Right then. I'll get one and be right back."

I went in search of the ticket booths. Now I had to decide on where to go. I looked at the signboard listing destinations and remembered that the cabbie and I had talked about Brighton. The name reminded me of an old movie made from a Graham Greene story called Brighton Rock, the rock being drugs. Convinced that it was an omen of some sort, I bought a round trip ticket to Brighton and went back to Left Luggage, hoping there weren't going to be any more surprises.

A different agent was there when I got back. He asked for the same, identification and my ticket. I handed both to him, hoping that Brighton was okay, that it didn't have to be a ticket to Timbuktu, or some other place. He glanced at it and took the package from me. "Does this belong to you, sir?"

"Yes, of course."

"No one gave you anything to put in there?"

"No."

"Anything hazardous, such as explosives, firearms. Any food, plants, animals, or fish?"

"No." I remained *shtum*. I was abiding by TV lawyers advice not to offer information other than what was asked for.

"We're going to have to scan it, sir."

My stomach did a somersault. Oy! "By all means," I said as casually as I could.

I stopped breathing altogether as I watched him disappear behind a curtain. Suppose they discovered what was in there? I'd probably be arrested. They'd throw me in the jug like they did that kid in Afghanistan or Turkey or wherever it was. He was sentenced to ten years, wasn't he? Great. That's just what I needed, to be tossed into an English jail and have to eat porridge for the rest of my life. But I'd known about the risk before. It was too late to do anything about it now except to pray that Margo's trick of hiding the stuff in paint would work.

After a few minutes he came back without the parcel and handed me a ticket. "This is your receipt, sir."

Good old Margo. Knew what she was doing. I was able to breathe again. I took the ticket and walked away slowly. No more box. No more anxiety. I couldn't help smiling. I felt as if I'd just climbed Everest and planted a flag on top.

CHAPTER 27

Outside I inhaled deeply of the night air and almost choked. It was full of gasoline and diesel fumes from all the cars and busses. I didn't care. The box was safe. I had the receipt, which I'd give to Shaved Head in the morning and that part of the affair would be over. I had no idea what I'd do after that but it didn't matter. I didn't even want to think about it.

My stomach told me I was hungry. There were dozens of restaurants in the station but I was now outside and wanted no part of going back inside. I began to walk and almost immediately saw a pub called "Shakespeare's Tavern." How serendipitous was that? Perfect. I'd treat myself to some pub food and a beer and then head back to the hotel for a good night's sleep.

The place was jammed. It was Victoria Station all over again. The noise level from patrons running their mouths pounded my eardrums. In addition, loud music was backing it up. I guessed the proximity to the station and the Underground made this pub a convenient place for a meal or a drink. My first instinct was to go somewhere else, but since I was already there, I decided to give it a try. Still, I knew it was not going to be easy to find a table in this mad house so I looked to the bar to see if there was anything available. What I saw gave me a distinctly unpleasant shock. I didn't have to look twice to know who it was. The light from above bounced off his gleaming head like crystal rays. Maybe he had followed me, after all. No. I was being paranoid. If he had, he would've tried to get it from me in the station.

He was busy talking to a woman with long black hair. Their heads were together in what appeared to be earnest conversation. I had the feeling it was more a business conversation than a lovers'. Of course, I had a prejudiced viewpoint where he was concerned. No way could I imagine this guy ever being a lover. If he fucked at all, it was most likely wham-bam-and-no-thank-you-ma'am.

I moved a little to try and see what the woman looked like. At that moment she turned to survey the place. Her eyes traveled by me and I was able to get a good look at her. She was beautiful. The sultry type, olive skin, eyes enhanced with dark makeup. I guessed her age at late twenties to mid-thirties.

I'd seen enough. The last thing I wanted was for Shaved Head to turn around and spot me. The guy was capable of anything. Who knew what he'd do? I could still feel the effects of his big fist in my belly. I left the "Shakespeare Tavern" in a hurry.

I kept walking and found myself near Buckingham Palace. Even at that hour of the night there were tourists hanging about. Did they do the changing of the guard at that hour? I had no idea. I wandered on, enjoying the feeling of freedom the ticket in my pocket gave me. After about a half hour, I came across a pub called "The Bag O' Nails." Somehow, that sounded appropriate. The place was quiet, clean, and just what I needed. I had low-down pub food: fish and chips and a Guinness. The fish and chips, delivered in greasy newspapers and served without ketchup, was fine. The beer was first rate.

I took a cab back to my hotel. I'd thought I'd be ready for bed, but when I tried to sleep my mind began to race. A kaleidoscope of thoughts zigzagged through my brain.

I missed Rosalind. Of course, I did. I couldn't imagine ever not missing her. The feeling would overtake me unexpectedly, sometimes so strong my eyes would fill at the thought of her. But that wasn't unusual. I'd loved her deeply. And yet, whenever I had one of those thoughts, along with them would come a flash of guilt because I would then immediately think of Sienna. That tough but intensely feminine red-haired detective had managed to get into my system. And, truth be told, I was glad she was there. I was intrigued by her. I had been from the first time I'd met her when she'd come barging into my house, flashing my fake Private Eye ID at me and threatening to have me arrested. The attraction had been mutual. But other than one night, now long past, the only romantic moment we'd ever had was when I'd kissed her at the pond In East Hampton shortly before Sarajane and Margo flew the coop.

Another thought stuck. Me. My life. What had become of it? Was I just...*a poor player that struts and frets his hour on the stage And then is heard no more?* Or was I...*a piece of work...noble in reason, infinite in faculty*? I remembered asking myself those kinds of questions when I was a twenty-year-old. And again as a thirty-year-old. What difference was there in questioning ourselves at any age? What did it matter? We all had a right at any time to look deep into our souls and try to find out who we were.

I even thought about calling Morty to fill him in on the latest news and decided it could wait. It would be better to call him when the whole thing was over and done with. Praise the lord I'd never gotten fully into computers. Morty'd wanted me to take one to London so we could keep in touch by email but I only had a desktop at home. He'd offered his own laptop but I'd vetoed it. I didn't want to be bothered. I knew if I'd taken a computer, my life would be even more frantic that it was right now.

I began to think of the next day and how I would handle Shaved Head at the Tate. I didn't get very far. The next thing I knew it was morning. Sunlight streamed in through the windows.

I'd soon find out.

CHAPTER 28

The taxi took me across the Thames via the Southwark Bridge. I remembered being in this neighborhood before. The Globe Theater was around here. I looked out the window and sure enough, there it was, a great white structure with its thatched roof towering over us. The driver dropped me off a block away from the museum. He couldn't get any closer because the Millennium Bridge, a pedestrian's only area, was just ahead.

I stepped out of the taxi and crossed the road to gaze at the Thames. The Tower Bridge was nearby, a fantastic sight. I looked for the Tate's boat ramp but didn't see it. I hoped my plan to get Shaved Head on that boat was going to work.

The guidebooks said that the Tate Modern was an architectural triumph. They'd made it out of an abandoned utility building called the Bankside Power Station. As I looked at it I could understand what they meant. What appeared to be the main building rose up in front of me some ten stories high. A sharpened crease jutted forward, forcing the two sides to flare out. Each side had irregular horizontal slashes of glass in the concrete for light. It felt as if I were standing in front of a cruise ship. The building adjacent had a tall tower climbing above a flat roof. In front of both buildings were paths leading to a plaza. Around this space were fences and behind the fencing were lawns and small groves of birches providing shade. At the center of the plaza was a median of grass and more clumps of birches.

It was a warm and sunny day. The lovely weather had brought an abundance of people outdoors. They were everywhere: couples, women pushing baby strollers, young folks stretched out on the grass, the usual clutch of tourists, easy to spot because of their baseball caps, tee shirts proclaiming "I Love London" and other tries at amusing phrases, and of course, the inevitable white running shoes.

I scanned the crowds trying to locate Shaved Head. There were so many bodies around that it took a while. When I did finally spot his gleaming skull in the center median near a clump of trees, I was surprised to see he was not alone. He was surrounded by a small group. I counted four. Three men and a woman. I backed up, making sure I couldn't be seen. I didn't know what to make of this. Who were these people and why were they there? Was it on my account? Had he told them about me and were they planning something? If so, I didn't think it would be a benefit to my health. In fact, I began to think it might be a good idea if I took off and dealt with the consequences later.

I turned to leave when an idea came to me that there might be another explanation for those people being there. Maybe they were tourists who had stopped to ask him directions or questions. That was certainly a possibility, wasn't it? I had to smile, thinking that if that were the case, I was pretty sure they'd be disappointed. I could just picture Shaved Head saying, "Yes, indeed, just go to the end of the street and turn left. You'll be sure to find what you want there." More than likely, if anyone asked him for help he'd probably tell them to fuck off.

In any event, I thought I'd just wait a few more minutes and see what happened.

Almost immediately whatever discussion had been going on ended. The people around him dispersed. Apparently they weren't all together because two of the men went off in different directions. The other man and woman began walking toward me. I now headed toward Shaved Head, trying to look casual and also to see what these people looked like. As we passed each other, I was startled to recognize the woman as the same one who'd been with Shaved Head in the pub the previous night. She was wearing a sleeveless top, revealing quite broad shoulders and slim arms. One ear was pierced with an assortment of glittering diamonds studs. She was speaking rapidly to the man, intent on what she was saying, but her eyes grazed over me as we passed. I could hear what she said quite clearly but I couldn't understand a word of it. She was speaking in French.

Shaved Head was still under the tree. As I got closer, I could see that he was leaning against it. I stepped onto the grass and was about to call out to him when suddenly his knees gave way and he began to slide down the trunk. Before I could take another step, he crumpled to the ground.

I ran over to him. His eyes were wide open, staring at me. But he wasn't acknowledging my presence. In fact, it soon became clear he could no longer acknowledge anything. He was dead. I was certain of it. Shakespeare, of course, came to mind: *He is dead and gone, lady. He is dead and gone.*

CHAPTER 29

It didn't take long for a mob to gather. There were people all around me, crowding closer to see what was going on. I yelled for someone to call an ambulance. "Hurry," I said and suddenly caught a glimpse of the face I'd seen only a few minutes before, the woman from the bar who'd spoken French. She'd come back. I looked away quickly to break the contact but I sensed that there'd been some sort of recognition. I feared that somehow she might have identified me as the person she'd just passed moments before. Or maybe, without my knowing it, she'd seen me in the tavern the previous night. I couldn't be sure but if she'd made a connection, she'd have to know I wasn't there by accident.

But why was Frenchie there? It could only be because she wanted to see what had happened to Shaved Head. And if that were the case, it was clear she'd known he was supposed to die and had come back to confirm that he had. What that meant, of course, was that she and/or her cohorts had somehow managed to kill him.

I had to get away from there, and fast. As the crowd came closer, I stood up and eased into the middle of it. I slowly made my way through the mass of people and eventually got to the main path I'd come in on. I walked as quickly as I could, trying not to attract attention. When I was almost out of the area altogether, I glanced back. I didn't see Frenchie but a man was walking hurriedly in my direction. He had a beard and was hatless. I recognized him. He was one of the men who'd been standing near Shaved Head. I remembered him because he was wearing a suit when everyone else had on light clothing. Was he wearing a suit jacket to conceal a gun? I didn't know but I didn't wait to find out.

I got to a street that led away from the museum and began to jog. I looked back and now saw the same man standing on the street corner. He started toward me. That gave me a jolt of adrenaline. I changed my jog to a run. I didn't know where I was heading but it didn't matter. I was pretty sure I was running for my life.

I raced around the corner. There were pedestrians everywhere. It wasn't easy to get past without bumping into someone. "Watch it, you bloody idiot," I heard, as well as a few other nasty comments. The sidewalks were crowded so I headed into the street. It was all cobblestones, which slowed me down a little but I kept on. I had to keep going and hope to find some place to hide. I was in good shape. I'd always worked out and participated in sports. I biked, played golf and tennis, but a marathon man I wasn't. I'd never run for exercise or for pleasure. Now I was sorry but sorry wasn't going to help. I needed to get away from this guy and soon. I was running as fast as I could but I knew I couldn't keep up this pace for very long.

The street I was now on was commercial, an attractive area, with stores, office buildings, restaurants. I thought about ducking into one of the stores but the idea that I might be trapped inside stopped me. The next street had row after row of neat brick houses with entryways at street level. I didn't have the time to knock on a door and ask to be let in. I was already sucking air. My legs were beginning to feel heavy.

Then I saw a familiar sight in the distance, the Globe Museum and beyond it, rising high, the Globe Theater. The sight of the theater gave me hope. *True hope is swift and flies with swallow's wings.* If I could get that far, I'd be safe.

There were more people here. Lots more. Tourists, God bless them. Halfway down the block a bunch of them were gathered on the sidewalk next to a bright red double-decker bus. As I ran toward them I saw a sign on the bus: *WORLDWIDE TOURS.* This might be my chance. I didn't know how far behind me the guy was. I had no idea if he could see me as I neared the crowd. I didn't dare waste a second by turning around. At that moment it didn't seem to matter. My legs were lifeless. My lungs had all but shut down. I was finished as far as running was concerned. I had no choice but to try to lose myself in that crowd. Even if he spotted me, I didn't think he'd try to kill me with a group of tourists watching.

I squeezed into the middle of the throng as they boarded the bus, trying to make myself as inconspicuous as possible. I got onto the bus and went toward the back. The rows all had two seats on each side of the center aisle. I came to a row that had one empty seat, the other occupied by a woman. I sat down next to her and tried to get my breathing back to normal.

"Hello," she greeted me. "You seem to be all out of breath. Afraid of missing the bus, were you?" She spoke with a twang that sounded like the guy in the commercial who threw shrimp on the barbie and drank Foster's *beeah*. I was pleased to see that she was wearing a rather low cut something or other that revealed two lovely globes attempting to push themselves out of their confinement. She had silky blonde hair that reached down to her neck.

"Yes," I said and took a deep breath. "That's exactly it. And you sound like you're from another part of the world. Am I right?"

"Aren't you the clever one? I'm from Australia. Sydney. My husband died and I'm treating myself to a holiday. He wouldn't go anywhere, the old penguin. Now he's gone, I can do what I want. Are you on your own, by the way?" She smiled sweetly and touched my hand with hers.

For a brief moment, visions of sugar plums danced in my head. But I quickly dismissed them as inappropriate. This was no time to be thinking of that sort of thing, pleasurable as it may have been. I had more important things to do. "I wish I was on my own," I said. "But alas, I'm not."

"Oh." Disappointment colored her voice.

I looked toward the front of the bus, intent on each person climbing up the steps, hoping I wouldn't see anyone wearing a suit.

A man with a large badge on his chest came down the aisle and stopped when he reached my seat. The writing on the badge was in old English script and spelled out *Tour Leader*. He sported a walrus moustache. "Pardon me, sir," he said loudly, at the same time spraying me with spittle. "I believe you're not a bonafide member of this tour?"

I admired that he could recognize a stranger in the midst of forty or so people he'd never seen before.

The lovely blonde next to me said, "I thought you'd said you'd been on the tour."

"Did I say that?" I turned to the tour guide. "Can I buy a seat now?"

"I don't see why not." He smiled, revealing gapped front teeth that went well with his walrus moustache. "That will be twenty pounds."

I gave him the money and looked over his shoulder to where more people were continuing to come on board.

He handed me a red button. "Put that on, sir, if you will. It's your ticket."

Okay. That explained how he'd known I wasn't in the group.

"You're a strange one," the woman said, turning away from me. Her disappointment in me was now complete.

The bus appeared to be full. It looked like I'd gotten away. I began to feel somewhat relieved when suddenly, up popped the guy at the front of the bus. There was no mistaking the suit and the beard. Now what?

"There's another man who hasn't bought a ticket," I said to the guide, nodding my head toward the front. I didn't know what this would accomplish but I hoped it might buy me some time. Maybe if the chaser was French, he wouldn't understand what the tour guide wanted from him. That could possibly cause a scene, maybe one that would end with his being thrown off the bus altogether.

"So I see," said the guide. He left me and went back down the aisle. "Yes sir," I heard him say. "Did you want to join our tour?"

The man didn't respond. He was looking toward the back of the bus in an attempt to see if I was on it. I hunched over as if I were tying my shoelaces, getting my head below the back of the seat in front of me.

I heard the tour leader repeat his query as to whether this man wanted to join the tour but I didn't hear an answer. Then I heard, "Hear now. What do you think you're doing?"

I looked up and saw my chaser pushing the tour leader in an attempt to get around him. I knew I had to do something. I had a chance to get away by exiting the rear door of the bus while they were struggling. But there was no doubt he'd see me and continue the chase. I couldn't run all day. It was now or never I thought.

I jumped up and rushed down the aisle toward them. The tour leader had his arms around the guy and was holding his own for the moment but I didn't think he could do it for long. I was sure this guy had a weapon on him and was capable of using it. I had no idea if I could do anything about the situation but I was desperate.

I squeezed around the guide and got to where I was able to grab hold of a wrist of the guy who was after me. For whatever reason, I recalled the judo lessons we'd gotten a few times those many years ago in James Madison High's gym class. Our teacher, Mr. Friedman, a lanky guy who wore eyeglasses with black rims, used to repeat over and over that the basis of judo was to learn how to use "leverage." He'd grasp my wrist and the next thing I knew I'd find myself on the floor. That's what I remembered as I pulled hard at my chaser's wrist. I was able to get his arm behind him so that it extended from his body. Then I bent it at the elbow and leaning against him, shoved it upward as hard I could. He let out a howl and a stream of French curses. But he was helpless. And in a lot of pain.

I did it, I thought. I actually did it. I said, "Listen, fucker, I can break your arm, so stop moving."

He was half bent over and grimacing but he'd apparently understood what I'd said because he gave up.

"Call a cop," I said. "This guy might be dangerous."

"I hardly think that's necessary," said the tour leader.

I moved my free hand over the guy's chest and felt a hard shape near one armpit. "This man's carrying a gun. Would that make it necessary?"

"A gun? My Gawd!" He whipped out a cell phone, punched in a number, and spoke. Then he said, "I had no idea. They're on the way. Can you keep him restrained until they get here?"

I gave the Frenchman's arm a slight shove upward and heard a gasp. I smiled for the first time that day. "Restrained? Don't you worry. *I'll screw my courage to the sticking place and will not fail.*"

I relished the curious look I got.

The police came in a car with a siren that sounded like hee haw, hee haw. I remembered reading that the police in London didn't carry guns so I made sure to tell them that this man had one. They removed it, handcuffed him, and took him off the bus. One of them came back with a notebook. He asked for my ID. That took away the idea I'd had of giving a fake name and address. He wanted to know the circumstances of what had happened. The tour guide told his version. I told mine, which was essentially the same story. I certainly wasn't going to say anything more.

And that was that.

When the cops were gone, the bus resumed its journey with everyone chattering away. I sat back down and kept repeating "Yes, thank you, yes, thank you," to those who asked if I was all right.

"Well done," my blonde seatmate said, friendly again. "You look like you're an expert in the martial arts."

Apparently excited by my exploits, she was ready to resume where she'd left off. "I am," I said. "My hands are classified as deadly weapons."

"How thrilling," she cooed and moved closer so that her breasts were nuzzling my arm.

The next stop turned out to be Westminster Abbey. Everyone exited the bus, the blonde in front of me. As they prepared to go inside, I said to her, "You're very charming and I wish I could spend some time with you, but I really have to go."

I didn't wait for a reply and began to walk away when I heard the tour guide call out. "Are you leaving us, sir?"

Instead of answering, I waved back and kept walking.

CHAPTER 30

I was beat. And glad to be back in my hotel room. I'd never really had time to appreciate the overstuffed lounge chair, the Jacuzzi bathtub, the flat screen TV, the well stocked mini-bar, all of which Morty was paying for. I'd been a bit uncomfortable about all that when I first arrived, but now I was glad to have it. Luxury had its good points, after all.

Before doing anything, I called the front desk and told them to notify me at once if anyone came asking about me and not give out any information. I didn't know what Shaved Head had told Frenchie, or even what he knew, but I wasn't taking any chances.

Then I opened the mini-bar and pulled out one of those diminutive bottles of vodka. I saw that it was Absolut, but at that point I didn't give a damn what brand I was drinking. On further consideration, I opened a second bottle and poured the contents of both into a glass. Not wanting to wait for ice to be delivered. I swallowed it in one gulp.

A cup of wine that's brisk and fine,
And drink unto the leman mine.

Yes, indeed.

Then I sat down and closed my eyes.

My body was aching and sore and needed a rest, but that didn't keep my mind from skating along at warp speed. I felt feverish. I was high from the excitement of the encounter on the bus and still a bit frightened. Elation and fear. Fear of being attacked again by this murderous gang and elation that I'd beaten them so far. But how long would that last?

I stretched out in the soft chair that faced the television. The remote was there but I didn't use it. I needed to think. There were too many questions for which I didn't have any answers. Who was this beautiful, pierced Frenchie who'd had Shaved Head killed? Could she be part of a drug ring that had owned the missing kilo? Maybe he'd told them the story of what happened and they didn't believe him. Maybe they thought he'd stolen it and, for that, death was the payoff.

The warmth of the vodka began to assert itself. My eyes were beginning to tear, a sign of fatigue. I rubbed them with the back of my hand and thought about my little house back in Sag Harbor. I missed being there. I missed the beauty of Long Beach and the many times I'd walked its length, in winter as well as summer, watching the sunsets, breathing deeply of the salted air. I missed my old life and its routines, even if it was lonely and often monotonous. I missed Sienna Nolan, her green eyes, her smile. She was a serious woman and didn't smile much, but when she directed one at me, it never failed to make my heart flutter. Even though there was no longer a *relationship*, as the current vogue word would have it, I'd felt that there had been something happening between us the last time I'd seen her. That lovely kiss at the Duck Pond.

London was an exciting city, and a Shakespeare lover's delight, what with the Globe Theater and all that. But I felt as if I'd reached a dead end. What more could I do here? I couldn't be the girl's watchdog forever. And now that Shaved Head was out of the picture, maybe the entire affair was over. The tension that had been driving me all day began to flow outward. I felt myself falling asleep. Grateful, I let it happen and, as I drifted off, the thought came to me that maybe it was time to go home.

CHAPTER 31

The phone next to my chair was chirping. I looked at my watch and saw that I'd slept almost an hour. I heard Morty's voice, loud and clear.

"How you doing?" he said.

"Fine."

"How's it going?"

"It's going."

"What does that mean?"

"I mean there's stuff going on."

"Like what?"

"I don't know. Or I should say, I'm not sure."

"You're being cryptic. Maybe you could explain it a little better?"

"I'm not cryptic. I'm just confused. Hey, how long have I been here, anyway?"

"You don't know? You left here on Tuesday, I think. That means you've been in London four days."

"That's all? It feels like I've been here most of my life."

"C'mon, Jake. What's going on?"

"There's plenty to tell you but I can't do it right now."

"What do you mean? Why not?"

"Because there's so much that's happened I can't get it straight in my own mind."

"That's bullshit. You've always been right on the ball when you needed to be."

"I know. I know. But do me a favor. I need to think. I'll tell you what I'll do. I'll call you back in a little while. What time is it there?"

"7:15 in the morning."

"Okay. I'll call you back in an hour. Then you'll get the whole shebang."

I clicked off, not wanting to keep the debate going.

Suddenly, I was hungry. There was a menu for room service on the desk. I ordered eggs, bacon, toast, and coffee. I needed good old-fashioned comfort food, food I could rely on. When it came, I ravished it all, including the broiled tomato the English always seem to serve with eggs. It was satisfying, as was the exceptionally good coffee, rich and strong, the way I like it. When I'd digested the food and felt satisfied, I called Morty back. I told him everything, including the recent feelings I had about returning home.

"You can't do that!" he said. "Certainly not now. Not with these new people in the picture."

"You weren't listening. There's nothing I can do here any more. I don't have a clue who these people are and no way of finding out. What do you want me to do? Babysit? I'm sure Sarajane would just love to have me hanging around day after day. Not to mention her girlfriend who hates my guts."

I could hear Morty taking a deep breath, probably to get himself calmed down. "Jake, listen to me. Everything you told me leads me to one conclusion. Sarajane is still in a lot of hot water. These new people in the picture are scary. They're killers. What makes you think they won't come after her?"

"How can they, if they don't know she exists?"

"But you yourself said you don't know what they know and what they don't know. What if this guy, Shaved Head, you called him, told them about you? And also about her? It's possible, isn't it? Maybe that's why that guy was chasing you."

"Sure it's possible. Anything's possible. What I don't see is what I can do about it."

"That doesn't sound like the Jake Wanderman I know. If there's a way to do something, you've always been the guy to figure it out."

"At this moment I can't figure anything out."

"You know what. You've got me thinking. Maybe I should go over there. I'm getting *shpilkes* sitting around here doing nothing."

Oy! That was the last thing I needed.

"Why would you want to do that? What about Sherri? What would she say? What about your practice?"

"Right now, I'm thinking about Sarajane. And about how I feel you're quitting on me. You helped me out, I don't know how many times. Ever since we've been little kids. You even saved me from drowning once. Remember? And you promised after that, you'd always be there for me. You remember that, don't you?"

"Shit! Did you have to bring that up?" Now it was my turn to take a deep breath. I didn't want him in London, that's for sure. I wouldn't know what to do with him. He'd be on my ass every second. But he was right about my promises and our friendship. "Let me think it over, okay? Sure, we're still buddies. I won't let you down. I'll think of something."

I hung up the phone. Brave talk, but what could I do to back it up?

I tried to get my brain to work through all that had happened in a logical way but I was having trouble concentrating. I couldn't get that Frenchwoman out of my mind. She was stunningly beautiful and looked nothing like a killer. Why was she there? And, did she kill Shaved Head? Then the obvious suddenly hit me. She was French. That meant something, didn't it? Of course, dummy. It meant there was a French connection. Sarajane had lived in Paris, had studied art there. It was there she'd met Tony Oakhurst. It was there she'd been raped. Could that have anything to do with what had happened back in East Hampton, or here in London?

I needed to speak to Sarajane. Maybe if we talked about the events back then, something would pop up. I decided I'd go over there without bothering to call.

I went down to the front desk and asked if anyone had been asking about me. The answer was no. That was good news. There was a taxi stand just outside the hotel's entrance. Before I got in, I looked around for a character who might be a watcher. I had no idea what that might be. A guy slouching against a light pole smoking a cigarette, like an actor in an old black and white movie? Happily, I didn't see anyone looking the least bit suspicious. I grabbed a taxi and went over to the apartment. When I rang the bell I heard Margo's voice on the intercom. She didn't say a word, just pressed the buzzer to let me in.

It was obvious they were not happy to see me. Their bodies were stiff as poles. No smiles, no greetings, no offer of something to drink. Sarajane wouldn't even make eye contact with me. But they were polite. They asked me to sit down.

I told them that Shaved Head was dead and that a Frenchwoman was involved. Then I asked Sarajane, "When you went to school in Paris, were you ever friends with a woman who had pierced ears?"

"That's funny. Half the girls I knew had piercings, tongue studs, nipple rings, as well as even more intimate ones. And of course, tattoos."

"Well, that won't help then."

"I don't think it makes any difference. I knew these girls but I wasn't that close to any of them. They were all studying art but none of them were any good."

"It doesn't matter whether they were good or not. Do you think you might have made an enemy of one of them?"

"I don't think I made any enemies while I was there, except for Tony."

"There's got to be a connection. And I'm sure it has to do with the drugs. When you knew Oakhurst in Paris, was he using drugs then?"

"Yes. Marijuana, cocaine. I think heroin, too, sometimes. But it wasn't uncommon in that crowd."

"Did you do them, too?"

She nodded. "I was an occasional user, not heroin, though."

"Who was his source? Did you know?"

"Not really. There was so much of it around. Besides, I wasn't interested."

"I think Tony got to be more than a user. I think he got caught up with the buying and selling. And then he became a dealer. Next, you're involved with Tony. It's too much of a coincidence to be an accident."

"Perhaps you're right."

"Are you still in touch with any of the people you knew in Paris?"

"A few people I still see when I go over."

"Good. I want you to give me their names. I want to talk to them and see if I can find anything out. It might be a wild goose chase but I think it's something I have to do."

"Fine," Margo said. "But where does that leave us? Are we safe here or not?"

"To tell you the truth," I said. "I don't know. I think you still have to be very careful. Until I come back, I think you should stick to the routine we've established. Don't go out. Have food delivered." Then I had an idea. "I'll get a bodyguard for you while I'm gone. I'm sure your father will pay for it. Would that help your frame of mind?"

"It would mine," Margo said.

"How long can this go on?" Sarajane said. "We're going stir-crazy. I can't get any work done."

"I don't expect to be gone long. A couple of days, maybe. Try and hold out until then. I'll get myself a mobile phone so we can stay in touch. As soon as I get it, I'll give you the number. Okay?"

"I suppose it will have to be," Sarajane said.

As I was leaving, Margo piped up. "By the way, how is our package?"

"Safe and sound. Not to worry."

I'd almost forgotten about the coke I'd deposited in Left Luggage. One more problem to worry about.

CHAPTER 32

I looked up security firms in the phonebook and called the one that had the biggest ad. I was disturbed to learn that having a guard outside the girls' building as a deterrent wasn't an option. They told me the security person had to have access to a toilet, the ability to make coffee or tea as well as other amenities, unnamed. Also, and this really got me, the guard had no authority to interfere with anyone trying to do harm. All he could do was inform the police. In other words, this could be the scenario: someone breaks in and attempts to do bodily harm to the girls. The security guard observes what's going on, gets out his mobile—as the British call it—and notifies the cops. They eventually come over and find the girls dead or kidnapped or whatever, and maybe they've taken out the guard, too. Terrific!

I called the girls and asked if they would allow a guy inside their apartment. The answer was what I expected.

"Okay then. Follow the rules we talked about. Be very cautious and don't go out until I get back."

I found a phone store in the vicinity, bought a mobile phone that would work in Paris, then called Sarajane with the number. She'd given me the name of a hotel she used when she visited Paris. It was called Moulin Rouge and was located in the 4th *arrondisement*, the *Marais*. That suited me fine. I knew from past visits there were good Jewish restaurants in that neighborhood. I remembered having a corned beef sandwich in one, but I couldn't remember the name of the restaurant. It was nowhere as good as the Carnegie Deli's or even Goldberg's in East Hampton but just the thought of one of those sandwiches, on good rye bread with mustard and pickles, made my mouth water. I booked a flight for the following morning and by noon I was checked in.

The hotel turned out to be small, only about twenty or thirty rooms. My room was more feminine than I was used to: flowered wallpaper, ruffles, curtains, and drapes. But the bed was roomy and comfortable and the bathroom sparkling. What more did I need? How about Rosalind being there with me? We'd made a bunch of trips to Paris and loved every minute we were there. But then I told myself I was being maudlin. I needed to concentrate on why I was there. It wasn't for reminiscing.

After I unpacked, I went out to a stationer and bought a map of Paris that showed streets, Metro and bus stops, museums, cemeteries, parks, and other points of interest.

I took out the notes I'd made of the people Sarajane had given me. There were four names. Three women and one man. Rachel Garnier. Chantal Badeau. Haley Sanford, Florian Legard. She hadn't told me much about her past relationships with them, just that they were the few with whom she was still in touch.

Rachel and Haley were American girls. Rachel had married a Frenchman, had two children, did not work. Haley had remained in Paris after studying. She'd gotten jobs in galleries and eventually opened a gallery of her own. Chantal Badeau was a Parisienne. She'd married a guy from a banking family who was loaded and now led the very comfortable life of the French upper class, far different from her days as an art student. Florian, also French, was gay and lived alone. He had been at the *Cordon Bleu* with Oakhurst and was now a working chef.

Sarajane had said she would call them to ease my way. That was fine with me, but I'd told her not to go into detail, just say that I was a private investigator working for her father. If they asked what it was about, she was to tell them that I would explain when I saw them. My reasoning was simple. Sarajane had told me these were old friends but she'd been reticent about how much any of them knew about her relationship with Tony Oakhurst. I also didn't know if they were even aware of his death. It had no doubt been in the papers over here because he'd been something of a celebrity. But it would probably have been buried in a small column somewhere, certainly not worthy of a splash. At any rate, I thought it might be to my advantage to see their reactions when I spoke to them.

My first call was to Rachel Garnier. I introduced myself and asked about seeing her. She said she had nothing planned for the day, that she was waiting for her children to come home from school. She sounded friendly and was quite willing to see me right away.

Rachel lived in the 13th *arrondissement* on a street called Rue du Banquier, just off the Avenue des Gobelins. It was a fairly short walk from the Metro stop Campo-Formio and not difficult to find.

The neighborhood was bland, the buildings not old and not new. In fact, the entire area seemed a bit rundown. I rang the bell and was let in by a buzzer. Rachel had said there was a concierge, but that I was not to respond if she accosted me, just go right on up the stairs. As it happened, no one paid any attention to me.

Her apartment was on the second floor. Walking up the staircase was something like going back in time to when I was a teenager and visited my Uncle Morris in Brooklyn. He'd lived near Prospect Park on a street of six-story apartment houses. His building was old, the walls thickened with layers of paint, the elevator scratched and rattling when it rose. What I remembered most vividly were the smells of stale cooking everywhere. The same smells were here, as well as the feeling of old dirt hidden away in corners.

Rachel greeted me in a friendly manner and shook my hand with a firm grip. She was a small woman, wore no makeup, was dressed simply in a gray sweater and skirt, and gave the impression she didn't much care how she looked.

The apartment was the opposite of its owner. It was modern, bright, adorned with colorful paintings, patterned rugs, a couple of large bookcases filled with books and interesting tchotchkes.

She asked if I'd like some tea or coffee. I opted for coffee and she went out of the room to get it or make it. She came back with a small cup and saucer and handed it to me.

"Aren't you having any?"

"I've already had mine."

I sipped it slowly. It was good French coffee. I leaned back in my chair and let the taste fill my mouth. It was so good I almost forgot why I was there.

Rachel brought me back. "Sarajane said you were a private investigator and working for her father. What's this all about?"

"I need to get some background on Sarajane's time in Paris when she went to school here. You were in the same school with her, right?"

"Yes."

"Studying art?"

"Of course. It was an art school. What does that have to do with anything?"

"Did you also know Tony Oakhurst?"

The benign expression on her face changed a little. "Sort of."

"Have you been in touch with him recently?"

"I haven't seen him in years. Before I had children, my husband and I went to his restaurant once. Too expensive for us now."

"Did you ever go out with him?"

"Aren't you getting a bit personal here?"

"That wasn't a very personal question. I was just trying to understand what you meant when you said you *sort of* knew him."

"Before I answer that I need to know why you're asking me these questions."

"Okay, I'll tell you. Oakhurst is dead. He was murdered." I watched closely to see her reaction.

Her eyes widened and her mouth dropped open. She was either shocked or a very good actress. "My god. I don't believe it. When did this happen?"

"Just about a week ago. In New York. He was doing a demo at an art show in The Hamptons. Someone stuck a knife in his back."

"That's terrible."

"How well did you know him?"

"Not that well. He liked to hang around with artists. He said people who cooked were boring. There were lots of parties and things like that. He always seemed to be there."

"Did you ever go out with him?"

"Yes. And since I know you're going to ask, the answer is we had a fling. It didn't last long."

"Why not?"

"Because Tony was always on the prowl. One woman wasn't enough."

"How did you feel about that?"

"How do you think I felt?"

"Do you know anything about his relationship with Sarajane?"

"Not much. I think she went out with him a few times."

"Did she ever tell you anything about him?"

"I heard that she told people he tried to rape her."

"*Tried* to rape her? Not that he did rape her?"

"She said he'd raped her but Tony denied it. He told me he'd tried to make love to her but when she said she didn't want to, he'd left her alone."

"And you believed him?"

"Yes. Why wouldn't I?"

"I thought Sarajane was your friend."

"She was. And she still is. But I think she was over reacting. She was young, naïve. I think she led him on and then didn't realize that she'd let him go too far. But as for actual rape, no. I was convinced that Tony was innocent. He was a charmer, yes. And he chased women, yes. But he succeeded more often than he failed. He had all he wanted. Why would he have to rape anyone when he had all the women at his feet anyway?"

"Did Tony use drugs back then?"

"Not to my knowledge. Or at least, he didn't use them when he was with me."

"You're sure about that?"

"Absolutely."

"Do you have any idea who might have wanted to kill him?"

"Not at all."

I couldn't think of anything else to ask her, so I thanked her and left. I went back to the hotel and wrote down as much as I could remember of what she'd told me. I was using one of the books with a black cover and white dots, exactly the same as the ones I'd used when I was a schoolboy. Some things didn't change. Too bad I didn't have a tape recorder.

Of course, the main thing was that I now had reason to question Sarajane's veracity again. Had she lied about the rape? And if so, why? She'd been less than truthful before in her stories and in her behavior, so that was certainly a possibility. But who knew if Rachel Garnier was telling the truth either?

CHAPTER 33

I went back to the hotel and made more calls. Chantal Badeau agreed to see me in the morning at her apartment in Passy. Haley Sanford said it would be fine to meet at her gallery later in the afternoon. Florian Legard told me that he was occupied at the restaurant where he worked but that he'd be happy to give me a few minutes at a cafe nearby before he began the dinner hour. We agreed to meet at les éditeurs on the Boulevard St. Germain des Pres.

I spent some time thinking about my interview with Rachel Garnier. I read the notes I'd made. I found it disconcerting that she had not believed Sarajane's story. What kind of friend was that?

When the time came to meet Florian Legard, I decided to walk instead of taking the Metro. I had no worries here about anyone being after me so it made it easy to stroll along and enjoy the sights and sounds of Paris. The streets were alive with people rushing home from work. It was well into October but the weather was still warm enough for the tables at the sidewalk cafes to be filled. I looked at the patrons as I passed and they looked at me, altogether a pleasant diversion. I thought it would be great if I saw Frenchie at one of those tables. I knew I'd recognize her in a minute, even without that row of diamonds in her ears. I wondered if she'd recognize me.

It didn't take long to reach the Pont Henry IV and cross the Seine onto the Boulevard St. Germain. A few blocks more and I saw the red awning of les éditeurs. Most of the tables were occupied. I had not discussed with Legard how we would know each other but as I approached, I saw a hand waving at me from a table off to the side. The man waving was obviously a chef because he was wearing his work clothes, white shirt, white pants, white apron, and a blue and white checkered do-rag on his head.

"How'd you know it was me?" I said, sitting down.

He shrugged. "For whatever reason it's simple to spot an American." His English was very good, with just enough of a French accent to be charming.

"I'll take that for what it's worth and not as an insult," I said.

"No insult intended."

"Where'd you learn to speak such good English?"

"I worked in the States for a few years." He had a cup of coffee in front of him. "Would you like something?"

"I'll have what you're having."

He waved at a waiter and pointed at his cup. A moment later it arrived.

He held out his hand. "Florian Legard."

I shook it. He had a good strong grip. Chopping away with a knife all day will do that for you, I guess. "Jake Wanderman. Thanks for seeing me at such short notice."

"*Pas de problem*? What can I do for you?"

"I wonder if I might ask you a few questions about Tony Oakhurst."

"Are you investigating his death?"

"You know he's dead?"

"It was in the newspapers. The report said he was murdered but that there were no suspects."

"Unfortunately, that's not quite true. The police in New York consider that Sarajane and Margo are suspects."

"Truly? Is that possible?"

"Quite possible. Not that I think they did it, but the police are not as convinced as I am. That's why I'm here."

"Sarajane is a friend of mine. I'll do whatever I can to help."

"Thanks. I'm trying to find out if there's anything here in Paris that connects with Oakhurst's murder."

He gave me another Gallic shrug. "Fishing expedition?"

"You bet. I'm in deep water and I know it. But let me ask you about Oakhurst. Were you friendly with him?"

"Tony? Friends? Not at all. Tony was out for himself and made no bones about it. If you partied with him, then you were okay. If he thought you were a loser in any way, you were out."

"Did he do a lot of drugs?"

He looked around to see if anyone might be listening to our conversation. The table nearest to us was unoccupied. The next one had a couple making out as if they were alone on a beach.

"Yes." He had lowered his voice. "But he wasn't the only one."

I spoke in a lower voice, too. "How about dealing? Did he sell any?"

"Sometimes. But that wasn't unusual. Whoever scored some would sell it to the rest of us."

"So you don't know if he was dealing in a big way."

"He always had drugs available, coke, grass, sometimes heroin. But I can't say whether or not he was a dealer."

"Where did you stand with him?"

"A bunch of us studying the culinary arts liked hanging out with artists more than with cooks. Why? Because the artists loved to party. Sex was abundant, all kinds, which suited me just fine. I grew up in a small town in Normandy. So it was great to be young and to be here in Paris. Tony was just one of the guys from my group. But as it happened, we did spend a lot of time together."

"And Sarajane, how did she fit in?"

"I became quite fond of Sarajane and she of me. I think my being gay may have had something to do with it. She wasn't a fag hag but we did like each other's company."

"What did you think of her relationship with Tony?"

"I didn't like it. I tried to warn her about him but she was infatuated."

"Do you know what happened between them?"

He hesitated and looked around again before he spoke. "What did she tell you?"

"Sarajane told me he raped her. Did she tell you that?"

"Yes. She only told a few people. Said she didn't want to talk about it. I think she blamed herself."

"You have no doubt it happened?"

"None whatsoever. Why would I? She wasn't the only one."

"What do you mean? He raped more than one girl?"

Florian drained his cup and put it down. "Tony would not be denied anything he wanted. He had women falling all over him, but if he saw one who didn't respond to his charms, he went after her. He wouldn't take no for an answer."

"Who were these other girls he raped? Do you know their names?"

"No. There were stories, rumors. Even one about a girl committing suicide because of him. But I have no proof. It's just that knowing Tony I believed those rumors." Florian looked at his watch, pushed back his chair and stood. "I've got to go. My boss'll have my head if I'm late." He reached inside his pocket.

"I'll take care of that," I said. "And I want to say you've been really helpful. Sarajane is lucky to have you for a friend."

He started to leave.

"One more question. "Do you have any idea who might have wanted Tony Oakhurst dead?"

"Probably a lot of people, but I can't give you a name. Give Sarajane my best, will you?" He waved and left.

I sat there for a while, trying to digest all he'd told me. It was quite different from Rachel's version of events. Even more surprising was that Sarajane had never said anything about other girls. How was I to know who was telling the truth and who wasn't?

I drank the last of the coffee. It was cold.

CHAPTER 34

It was obvious that Rachel Garnier and Florian Legard were complete opposites in their view of Tony. Rachel didn't think Tony was an ego-driven prick while Florian did. Florian said Oakhurst was a user, the other said he wasn't. Rachel denied there was ever a rape, while Florian said there were rumors that he'd actually raped others as well as Sarajane.

I looked at my watch and decided I had time to go see Haley Sanford. It was going to be interesting to hear what she had to say about all this.

I got out of the Metro, at Madeleine, and found myself at the corner of rue Royale and rue du Faubourg Saint-Honoré. The gallery was on Saint-Honoré, farther along past some of the most exclusive shops in Paris. I thought the Sanford gal must have done all right for herself if she could afford the rent in this neighborhood.

I walked slowly, admiring the stores and the famous names: Hermes, Christian La Croix, Versace, Yves St. Laurent. I was looking so closely at the displays in the store windows that it was only after the person was long past that I realized I'd seen someone I knew out of the corner of my eye. It was Valerie Venable, the owner of the art gallery in East Hampton where Sarajane had had her opening and where Oakhurst had been killed. At the same moment that I asked myself what she was doing here, I answered that it was probably business. Certainly art was big in Paris. There were no doubt as many galleries here as in New York, maybe more. For all I knew, she might have just come out of Haley Sanford's place.

When I finally got to the gallery, I found it as extraordinary as the street it was on. The space was large and sleek, an open expanse of gleaming white wood floors, a minimum of ultra-modern metal furniture, a few desks, and some chairs. The art-work was displayed with subtle lighting that brought out the richness of its colors. There was sculpture, as well. All in all, it made a statement that this was a wealthy and successful estab-lishment.

A young woman was seated in front of a computer. She was impeccably dressed and made up. I told her who I was and why I was there.

"Just a moment." She picked up a phone, spoke a few words, then gestured toward a staircase at the back of the gal-lery. "Go right up there, please. Miss Sanford's expecting you."

I went up the stairs and found the second floor set up as an office. There were desks, computers, file cabinets, shelves stacked with books, boxes. It was a vast open space, except for one part where there was a room with an open door.

There was one woman in sight, studiously at her computer. She paid no attention to me. Another woman appeared at the doorway of the room I'd seen. She smiled at me. "You're Jake?"

"You're Haley?"

We both laughed.

"Well, we've figured that much out, anyway," I said.

"Why don't you come in and have a seat?"

I went inside and, predictably, found the office to be fur-nished in ultra-modern, polished wood and chrome without a trace of clutter. She closed the door. I was glad for the privacy.

"Would you like something to drink?"

I shook my head. "Just had lunch, thanks."

I had assumed she was the same age as Sarajane, late twen-ties, but she looked older. Her hair was pulled back firmly in a ponytail. No makeup, a black power suit. Her nails were mani-cured with clear polish.

"This is quite a place you have here."

"I'm glad you like it."

"I'm impressed. You must be a very smart woman."

"I'm not so sure about 'smart' but hard working, yes. And speaking of that, I don't have all that much time to talk. SJ called and said something about you, but she was especially vague. Not like her at all. Could we get to why you're here?"

I didn't bother to go through the same routine as with the others. Something led me to believe that she knew Oakhurst was dead and most likely knew a lot of other things as well. I told her about the murder, the New York cops suspicions of Sarajane, and my feeling that drugs were involved. Just as I never mentioned Margo's involvement before, I didn't mention it now either.

"What is it you specifically want to ask me about?"

"I'd like to get a picture of what life was like here then. I understand there was a lot of partying. A lot of booze, drugs, sex, etcetera."

"All true, but not unusual."

"Were you ever involved with Tony Oakhurst?"

"I was more interested in women."

"Sarajane?"

"Not her thing, then. Although we did become close some years later. Unfortunately, it didn't last."

"Then you were good friends with her at the time you were all students?"

"Yes."

"And did she confide in you about what she said Oakhurst did to her?"

"Just what are you referring to?"

"You don't know?"

She hesitated. "Yes. I know what you're getting at. It's a delicate subject. Tony denied it."

"And you believed him?"

"I didn't know what to believe. Sarajane was very naïve. She could have thought more happened than actually did."

"You mean a woman wouldn't know she'd been raped?"

"No. Of course, that's not what I mean. But she might have exaggerated the fact. It may have been consensual. Or that Tony thought it was anyhow."

"I see. Now what about drugs? Was there a lot of that going on?

"I wouldn't say a lot. There was weed, sometimes a little coke. Mostly it was wine."

"How about Oakhurst?"

"How would I know? I didn't spend that much time with him."

"Did he ever sell any, that you know of?"

"I wouldn't have the slightest idea."

"Did you ever hear a rumor that Tony raped other women?" Her body stiffened. "No."

"Did you ever hear of a girl killing herself because of Oakhurst?"

She stood up. "No, I didn't. I'm sorry, Mr. Wanderman. I'd like to help but I really am very busy. I have a huge opening coming up. There's a ton of work to do."

"Can I talk to you again?"

"I've told you all I know."

"Look, Haley. Sarajane thinks of you as a good friend. She needs your help. Please."

She looked down at her desk. I followed her gaze and saw that she was looking at an appointment book. "All right. I can give you a few minutes around noon tomorrow."

"Great. Thanks a lot. I really appreciate it."

As I walked back to the Metro, I no longer paid any attention to the elegant street I was on. All I could think of was that Haley had been more than evasive. She wouldn't confirm the rape. She denied hearing rumors about Oakhurst or that he dealt drugs. I didn't know if what she'd told me was true or not, but I was sure she knew a lot more than she'd told me. In any case I was left with having to figure out a way of getting her to tell me more. It was not going to be easy. That was okay with me. Whoever said life was a picnic? Certainly not Shakespeare, who had much to say about everything. *Reason thus with life: If I do lose thee, I do lose a thing that none but fools would keep.*

CHAPTER 35

I felt in need of a good dinner. I treated myself to sole *meunière* at a bistro near my hotel. The sole was drenched in brown butter and as I chewed and swallowed I pictured my arteries clogging like a blocked drain in a sink. I solved that problem by drinking two glasses of chilled *Sauvignon Blanc.*

The next morning, after a breakfast of buttery croissants and coffee—more cholesterol but who cared—I went to see Chantal Badeau. She lived in the 16th *arrondissement,* an area that reeked of the green stuff. Euros, dollars, Swiss francs, that kind of green. Her building was on the Quai Passy overlooking the Seine.

A maid opened the door, wearing a uniform complete with lace collar. It looked like she was auditioning for a part in a drawing room comedy. I followed her down a long hallway which led into an immense space. A huge wall of glass overlooked the river.

Chantal was as glamorous as her apartment. She was tall, slim, with dark eyes outlined in black and a face that was a perfect oval. She wore some kind of silky top with matching pants. The color was somewhere between pink and rose and matched the décor of the room. The hand which took mine was soft and pliable. The other hand had a ruby the size of a Bing cherry on one finger. Several additional but smaller stones dangled from her earlobes and sparkled around her neck. No piercings or studs for this elegant lady.

No sooner had I sat down than the maid came in with a tray of coffee and pastries.

I was offered both and happy to accept. I munched on a lemon tart that dissolved so blissfully in my mouth it created a longing for another. But I resisted. I needed to concentrate on the task at hand, not food.

"Sarajane said you were a private investigator." Chantal's voice was heavily accented but as smooth and silky as the rest of her.

"That's right. I was hired by her father to see what I could do to help her."

"I had not realized she needed help."

"Do you know that Tony Oakhurst is dead?"

She didn't blink. "*Vraiment*? No. I did not know that."

"You don't seem surprised."

"I am not. I more or less expected he would die young. He was a very careless man."

"I suppose you're right. He was careless enough to get himself murdered."

"Murdered? Now that is a surprise. Who murdered him?"

"That we don't know yet. My aim is to try and find out. When you knew him was he a heavy drug user?"

"I would not say that."

"Were you in that crowd that partied together?"

She laughed. "Are you suggesting that we all used drugs? The answer is yes, but not to a great extent. I was young and foolish once. I admit it." She opened a purse and took out a pack of Marlboros. "Is it all right if I smoke?"

"It's your apartment."

"Indeed. But I do not like to smoke if there is an objection."

"Go right ahead."

She lit her cigarette with a gold lighter and blew a plume of smoke into the air.

"How about Rachel Garnier? Was she in the crowd that did drugs?"

"That bitch? I doubt it. It was, as you say, she looked through her nose at us."

"Did you know she had a thing with Tony Oakhurst?"

"No. Really? *Quelle hypocrite*."

"How well did you know Oakhurst?"

"Ah. Now we are getting even more personal, aren't we?"

"That's why I'm here, Madame Badeau, to gather information."

"What does my relationship with Tony have to do with anything?"

"I'm looking for a pattern, that's all. Rachel Garnier said Tony was misunderstood."

"She would. A middle class prude trying to be something she was not. But, of course, she was smitten by Tony. She would believe anything he told her."

"But not you. What did you think of him?"

She tipped some ash into a porcelain ashtray. "He was a bastard. *Mais il était charmant.* He was Depardieu, Delon, and Olivier Martinez rolled into one. A combination very hard to resist."

"Did you resist?"

She gave me her version of the Gallic shrug. "I don't deny it. As I said, I was young and foolish. It was all a game. Luckily, I came to my senses." She gestured with one hand. "As you can see."

"Had you heard anything about his relationship with Sarajane?"

"You mean, did he rape her? *Mais oui.* I knew Sarajane quite well, although we were not that close. I didn't hear it directly from her, but I heard about it."

"And did you believe it?"

"Yes. I did not think she would make up something like that."

"But Oakhurst denied it, didn't he?"

"*Naturellement.* What would you expect?"

"Did that change your opinion of him?"

"*Pas du tout.* I'd already had enough of him. It was over."

"Did you ever hear any rumors that he'd raped anyone else?"

She thought a while then shook her head. "*Non.*"

"Did you ever hear anything about a girl committing suicide because of him?"

"*Vraiment*? Really? I never heard such a thing. There was a girl in our class who killed herself. No one knew why."

"What was the girls' name?"

"It was a long time ago. I'm not sure I remember."

"Can you think of anyone who might have wanted to kill Tony Oakhurst?"

She leaned forward and crushed her cigarette in the ashtray. "I'm sorry, but that question is ridiculous. I have not seen him in years. I have no idea who his friends are now, or his enemies."

CHAPTER 36

After I left Chantal I had enough time to get to Haley Sandford's gallery by noon. I was once more back in her office.

Before I could say a word, she said, "I want to apologize for my behavior yesterday. I realized I was rude."

I shook my head. "Absolutely no need. I understand you're a busy woman."

"Well, then," she said. "Good."

"Have you thought anymore about what I asked yesterday?"

"I'm sorry, I didn't. What was it you wanted to know?"

"Are you sure Tony wasn't into dealing drugs? Some other people I've spoken to thought he was."

"Who might they be?"

"I'd rather not mention their names. Everything told to me was strictly confidential. Just as anything you tell me will be."

She shook her head. "Maybe they know more than me. That's entirely possible. I don't have any recollection of that."

"Do you know Valerie Venable?"

"Yes. Why do you ask?"

"I saw her on my way over here yesterday. I just guessed that she'd probably been here to see you."

"As a matter of fact, she left shortly before you arrived."

"Just friends, or business?"

"Business, mostly. We do quite a lot of it together. We trade painters, paintings, sculpture. Sometimes a work will sell better in The States than here and vice-versa. She comes to Paris. I go to New York."

"How often is that?"

"Two or three times a year."

"That's nice. Obviously, it works well for both of you."

"Yes, it does." She stood up. "I'm sorry, but once again, you'll have to excuse me. It can't be helped. I must get back to work. The opening I told you about is tomorrow night. There's still quite a lot to do."

"Did you know someone in your class who died under suspicious circumstances??"

"Why do you ask?"

"I understand she committed suicide."

"I don't know anything about that."

"But you knew her?"

"She was in the class, yes."

"What was she like?"

"I don't know." Her hands were clenched into fists. "Mr. Wanderman, I really don't have any more time for this."

I didn't want this to end. It was obvious she was holding back. But I didn't see what I could do about it. Then I thought of something. "I understand, Miss Sanford. I can see you've got a lot on your mind. Would you mind if I came to the opening tomorrow?"

She didn't speak for a moment. I thought I could hear the wheels turning but I'd trapped her. How could she refuse?

"Of course. It begins at six."

"Great. Thanks." And Valerie was sure to be there, too.

Fortune brings in some boats that are not steer'd. But in this case, I'd done a little steering of my own.

CHAPTER 37

I went away, wondering what Haley Sanford was trying to hide. If a girl in her class had killed herself, she would have to know about it. Maybe she didn't know the girl but she obviously hadn't wanted to talk about it at all.

Back at my hotel I thought it would be a good idea to call Sarajane and ask what she knew about it and also to see how things were back in London.

Margo answered the phone. When I asked how they were, she said, "We are going out of our minds staying inside all day. Do you think it's still quite necessary?"

"I don't know. Have you been checking to see if anyone is watching you?"

"Constantly. And we haven't seen anyone looking even vaguely suspicious."

"Well, that's good."

"Hold on, SJ wants to speak to you."

Sarajane came on. "Mr. Wanderman, I think it's time you let us out of jail."

"Look, I'll be back there very soon. Can you hold out a day or two longer?"

"We can't live like this."

"Just be patient a bit more. Okay?"

I heard a sigh. "I know you're thinking of our safety but I think you're overdoing it."

"Maybe I am. But I'd rather overdo it than risk something bad happening."

"When will you be back?"

"Very soon. Day after tomorrow, most likely. I've been to see all the people you told me about. And I've learned a lot. I'll tell you everything when I see you. Haley Sanford has been most interesting. I'm going to an opening she's having tomorrow night. Valerie Venable is going to be there."

"How nice."

"Did you know they do a lot of business together?"

"Oh yes. For a long time. I saw Haley in New York when I was there."

"You did? When was that?"

"She came to see me just before my opening. She was out to see Valerie on business, and while she was there, stopped by to say hello."

"She was there at your opening?"

"I saw her before. She said she couldn't stay because she had appointments in the city."

"Is that right? Funny, she didn't mention it."

"Probably didn't consider it important."

"Probably not. One more thing. Your friend Florian told me there was a rumor that Oakhurst had raped other girls and that one of them committed suicide. Do you know anything about that?"

There was a long silence. "There was a girl who killed herself. I don't know if it has anything to do with Tony. She was in my art class."

"What was her name?"

"Madeline Vincent."

"Do you know if Tony had any connection with her?"

"No. I stayed away from Tony completely after what happened."

"What about Haley? Did she know Madeline?"

"You know Haley's gay, don't you?"

"Yes. She more or less didn't keep it a secret."

"Well, it wasn't ever confirmed, but some of the crowd thought she and Madeline were having an affair."

"So even if that wasn't true, she knew this Vincent girl quite well, I guess. Right?"

"I'm not sure how to answer that. I really don't know." There was silence for a moment. "I'm trying to remember something else about Madeline but I can't."

"Good enough for now." After once more asking her to remain patient and safe, I hung up.

I wasn't sure what to make of this. A girl in the art class had killed herself. Nobody knew why. Rumors at the time suggested that Oakhurst may have had something to do with it. Haley claimed to know nothing about any of this. She had also been in East Hampton the night before Tony Oakhurst was murdered and somehow never bothered to mention it to me. She'd told SJ she had to leave but what was to have prevented her from not leaving, or from going back to kill our esteemed chef? But why would she want to kill him? For that I had no answer.

That night I had a strange dream. I was in a cemetery looking for a grave. I searched everywhere but couldn't find it. In the morning the dream was still vivid. I realized, of course, that it had to be connected with the story about the girl who'd killed herself. It was only a dream but I had this kind of urgent feeling that I ought to do something about it. I decided that I would find Madeline Vincent's grave.

I called Haley.

There was a sigh. "It's you again?"

"About Madeline Vincent. Would you happen to know where she's buried?"

"Why do you want to know that?"

"I'd like to visit her grave."

"Why on earth would you want to do that?"

I wasn't going to tell her about my dream. "Just something I want to do."

"I'm sorry. I can't help you. I have no idea." There was a click.

Okay. I'd just have to find it on my own, assuming she was buried in Paris. If she wasn't, I'd be out of luck. I got out the little red guide book I'd bought. It was called *Plan Taride* and had a list of all the cemeteries in Paris and its suburbs. There were more than a dozen. I didn't have enough French to do it by telephone. The only way I could find the grave was to go to each cemetery and see if she was there.

I decided to do the famous one first. I'd read that one in Montparnasse was famous because so many well-known artists and politicians were buried there. I found the metro stop for Le Cimitier de Monparnasse and was on my way. I took the number 6 line and got off at Raspail. From there I walked on the Boulevard Quinet until I reached rue Emile Richard. There were two entrances on either side of the road. I went to the one on my right and found a small building. An old man with gray hair sat at a desk. In my limited French I managed to make known what I was looking for.

He opened a huge ledger and began turning pages. After a while he stopped with his finger on a page. He grunted. "*Aha. C'est ici.*"

He opened a drawer and pulled a sheaf of paper from it. It was a map of the cemetery. He marked on it where Madeline's Vincent's grave was. Then he pointed and made motions with his hands that I understood meant for me to go back to the other side of the street. Delighted with my luck in finding her so quickly, I crossed over the rue Emile Richard and entered the cemetery.

A glance at the map did not prepare me for its size. That alone wasn't the surprise. The cemetery was not only large but was also filled with an astounding amount of statuary. There were fantastic sculptures, ranging from heads to full figures, some standing, some lying down, some gazing into space with eyes open, others with eyes closed. There were angels, of course, all sorts, some larger than life size, others much smaller, often hovering over another figure. There were intermittent framed photographs of the dead.

This was nothing like the cemeteries I'd been in back home. The one my parents were in was somewhere in Queens, an area full of cemeteries, each one crowded with tombstones, one next to another, some graves with shrubbery and grass, others unattended, some even falling in. Rosalind had chosen cremation. She'd never liked those hundreds upon hundreds of tombstones that she said were more like clutter than memorial.

I was far from the only visitor. There were a number of men and women, as well as couples, even some with small children, wandering around with maps in their hands. They didn't look like mourners, more like tourists searching for the famous people buried here.

I couldn't imagine wanting to be a tourist in a cemetery. It was too creepy. I hurried along the paths suddenly feeling that I was being watched. Maybe it was because of all those eyes in the sculptures around me.

When I finally came to Madeline Vincent's grave, I saw that it was a simple one, marked only with a small stone. The inscription on it read, *Madeline Vincent, Girl-child, Her spirit will live forever.* Underneath were the dates *November 7, 1972 – January 4, 1993.*

She was only twenty-one when she died. The inscription was touching, but what affected me more was that there was a huge amount of pink roses covering her grave. There were so many you could hardly see the grave at all. They didn't look as if they'd been there a long time. I picked up a rose and sniffed. There was a sweet aroma. The rose was as fresh as if it had just come from the florist.

I looked around to make sure some flower-loving character hadn't been putting roses all over the place. This was the only grave that had them.

Madeline Vincent had been dead for seven years. Who had brought the flowers? And why now? It wasn't the anniversary of her death. It was summer and she'd died in January. I wondered if it was a one-time event or did someone do it regularly? One thing was certain: whoever left the roses had to be someone who knew Madeline Vincent or knew of her. Perhaps that someone also knew her history as well, including why she'd killed herself.

Where was I going with this? I wasn't sure, but if the person who left the flowers also knew the whole story, finding that person might answer a whole lot of questions, including those about rape and suicide and possibly Tony Oakhurst as well.

I wondered how Detective Sienna Nolan would handle a situation like this. What would she do? It would've been nice to have that beautiful redhead around to get some feedback and maybe some professional instruction. It would've been nice to have her there for other reasons, too. I had a flashback remembering our lunch at the duck pond in Sag Harbor and the kiss that followed. A promise of something more to come? Unfortunately, there'd been no possibility of anything further because that was when Sarajane and Margo flew to London and I was sent after them. In any event I was on my own here and had to figure things out for myself.

CHAPTER 38

O ther than that in France an opening was called a *vernis-sage*, it was not unlike most of the ones I'd been to in The Hamptons. Lots of people standing around, holding glasses of wine, air-kissing hellos while searching the crowd for celebrities or for other friends and acquaintances. Just to be different, a few were actually looking at the art.

The dress code was a bit more formal here than back home. The women sparkled in dresses, pant outfits, makeup, and jewelry. The men wore suits, or blazers, open shirted or with ties. There was a feeling of sophistication and money, the kind of group Haley needed to keep her gallery successful.

The show was devoted to one artist. The brochure at the entrance said his name was Anton Tobachniki, from Warsaw. It meant nothing to me. That wasn't surprising, since I was hardly a devotee of the art world, but he apparently was well known. Inside the brochure was a long list of museums and galleries where he'd exhibited.

I looked for Haley and saw her surrounded by several people. I wanted to talk to her about what I'd seen at the cemetery but I needed to get her alone in order to be able to do that. To kill some time, I wandered about, looking at the paintings. The work was colorful, with primary colors of bright reds and yellows. There were figures, outlined in black. They were not realistic, more like cartoons, but they were identifiable. Women, mostly nude, in varying erotic positions but without partners.

I eased my way into the crowd and found the bar. I was happy to see this was a real bar with a bartender, not the pour-your-own-out-of-magnum-sized-bottles-of-cheap-red-and-white-wine-with-plastic-glasses kind of bar I was used to. Here were branded bottles of liquor and individual bottles of wine, even chilled champagne. And the glasses were crystal.

As I sipped my Grey Goose and surveyed the scene, a waiter came by with a tray of puffed pastries. I tasted one and had to admit it was apetizing. Reminded me of Oakhurst's hors d'ouevres at Sarajane's opening. Tony. *Death...hath sucked the honey of thy breath...*Although it was pretty clear that honey and sweetness were never a big part of him.

I spotted Haley again. She was talking to a guy at least a foot shorter than she was. It looked as if she was with a little kid, except this little kid was wearing a tux and had white hair cascading down over his shoulders. He had a broad forehead and, in contrast to his white head of hair, sported a black handlebar moustache.

If he wasn't Tobachniki the artist, I was Little Red Riding Hood.

Haley's eye caught mine. Surprisingly, she gave me a sort of smile waved for me to join them.

"Anton, meet Mr. Wanderman. He's a private detective so you better watch yourself."

Anton gave me a firm handshake and apparently didn't understand a word of what Haley said. "Do you like show?" His accent was as thick as sludge.

I hated that kind of question. It was like someone showing me a picture of a baby that looked like every other baby in the world and then waiting for me to say something wonderful. *That's a baby, all right. That's a real baby.*

I gave him my most sincere, hypocritical answer: "Yes. Extremely interesting."

As it happened, it didn't matter what I said, because he was already chatting with someone else. *Okay, Anton, it was great fun talking to you.*

"Have you got a minute?" I said to Haley. "I know you're busy but I've got something to tell you that I think you'll find very interesting."

"Oh?"

"In private? Could we get out of this noise?"

She shrugged. "I'm afraid not. This is an important open-ing. I've got a great many people I have to speak to. Can't it wait? I assume it's not a life or death issue."

I wasn't so sure about that. "I guess it'll have to."

"In the meantime you might want to talk to Valerie. Unless you've spoken to her already."

"I haven't seen her."

She pointed across the room. "There she is. Wearing her signature red, as usual."

And so she was. Red dress, red heels, red jewelry, lots of makeup and quite attractive, if you liked women who looked as if they were made of plastic.

"I'll do that," I said. "Let me know when you have some time for me."

"I'm afraid it'll be a while before I'm free."

"I can wait."

I made my way over to Valerie. She was in the middle of a conversation with a woman wearing black and made up like Morticia of the Addams family. The combination of all black and all red made for an interesting composition. I waited until the other person went away, then said, "Hello."

Her eyebrows elevated and she gave me a look that said *I don't really want to know but who are you?*

"Remember me? Jake Wanderman? Friend of Dr. Adler, fa-ther of Sarajane Relda?"

It took a while before the light bulb went on. And then her reaction was barely polite. "Oh yes, the man who almost broke Tony's arm pushing him away from Sarajane. What are you do-ing here?"

"I'm happy to see you, too. I'm here on business."

"Are you now in the arts instead of being a private detec-tive?"

So it was an act. She'd known who I was right away. "Not exactly. I'm investigating Tony Oakhurst's murder."

"I thought that's what the police are for."

"In this case, the police are after the wrong person."

"And who might that be?"

"I think you know as well as I do that the police think Sarajane and Margo are involved."

"Why would I know that?"

This was an irritating woman. "Ms. Venable. You've been
out in The Hamptons a long time. You know a lot of very important people. And if anything is happening that might affect
your personal or business life, they would be most happy to let
you know about it. Am I wrong?"

There was a hint of a smug smile. "What brings you to Paris?"

"Sarajane's background. I'm trying to find out if anything
connects."

"Good for you. I wish you well in your endeavor. Now if
you'll excuse me..." She began to walk away from me.

"You don't want to know if I found anything?"

"It has nothing to do with me, despite the fact that the murder happened in my gallery. I'm sorry but I have business to
attend to."

"Speaking of business, I understand that you and Ms. Sanford do a lot with each other."

"That's true. What of it?"

"I understand she was in New York for Sarajane's opening."

"So?"

"She told me she was out there before the show opened.
Did you spend much time together?"

"We concluded our business and she left." Once again she
began to walk away.

"What about Tony Oakhurst? Did you introduce her to
him?"

She stopped. "Not that I recall."

"You don't remember if they met?"

"It was rather a busy time. There was so much to do, I barely remember anything but working like a maniac night and day
to get ready for the opening. Besides, why is it important whether or not Haley met Tony?"

"I'm just trying to put together information. I'm hoping if I
get enough background, something will point to the killer."

"So you don't believe Sarajane did it?"

"No," I said. "Do you?"

"Of course not. Although anything is possible, I suppose."

"Why would she want to do such a thing? Did she have a reason?"

"I don't know the answer to either of those questions. I only know human beings are bizarre and no one knows what any of them are capable of doing."

"Do you know if Tony Oakhurst had anything to do with drugs?"

"Certainly not."

"He didn't?" I asked. "Or you don't know."

"I wouldn't have the slightest idea."

Now she did walk away, leaving me with an empty glass in my hand and more questions. But at least Valerie confirmed what Sarajane had told me about Haley being in New York at the time of the murder.

I looked for a waiter carrying a tray but didn't see one so I headed back in the direction of the bar for another shot of Grey Goose. I got my drink and moved around for a view of Haley. I didn't expect to see her alone but thought it worth a try. When I finally did see her, she was indeed with another person. What was unexpected was that the other person was a young woman, a young woman I couldn't fail to recognize at that distance, or almost any distance. The row of diamonds stitched in her left ear told me in no uncertain terms who she was—the assassin, Frenchie.

CHAPTER 39

For a moment, I froze. This was the girl I was sure had killed Shaved Head and then sent someone after me. Maybe the most prudent thing to do would be to get out of there. Sure, but if there was one thing in life I'd never been, it was prudent.

I moved briskly through the crowd until I was within range of Haley and Frenchie. I greeted them with the happy smile of a man who'd just stumbled across old friends "Hey there, you two. How's it going?"

I expected to see confusion. I was disappointed.

"Oh, it's you," Haley said.

"Right. Would you like to introduce me to your beautiful friend?"

Frenchie had given me a glance then looked back at Haley. She said something in rapid French that I couldn't understand, smiled at me, and walked away.

"Did I say something wrong?" I said.

"Not that I know of. Only that woman you just referred to is not a friend. In fact, I don't know her at all. She just came over to tell me how much she liked the show."

I was sure she was lying. Then again, I couldn't be sure.

"She's very attractive."

"I suppose, if you like the type."

"What's not to like? Young, beautiful, great body."

Her smile was not pleasant. "You're not really that revolting, are you?"

"Only when I try to be."

She made to move away, but I got hold of her arm to stop her. "Let go of me," she said, in a low voice.

"Just a few words before you go. I went to a cemetery today. I found Madeline Vincent's grave."

"Big deal. You told me you were going. Now take your hands off me."

I removed my hand and she began to walk away. First Valerie, now Haley. It seemed as if everyone was trying to get away from me. "I found something unusual there."

That made her pause. "Really? And what could that be?"

I told her.

Her eyes widened for a moment, then returned to normal. "So? What's unusual about flowers?"

"I don't know. It just seemed strange finding flowers there now when she'd died in January."

She shrugged. "You're sure it was Madeline's grave?"

"Positive. No doubt about it. Dozens of pink roses. And not there very long. A day or two maybe."

"I suppose someone is remembering her. What does that have to do with me?"

"I thought it might've been you who left the flowers."

"You're being ridiculous."

I decided to go for broke. What did I have to lose? "I've been told that you and Madeline Vincent were lovers."

This time her eyes opened wide and stayed there. "Who told you that?"

"Sarajane."

It was a while before she spoke. "How could she possibly have known?"

"It's true, then?"

"Yes. What of it?"

"What was the point of keeping it secret?"

"It's too complicated to explain. It's also none of your business."

"So it wasn't you who brought the roses. Do you have any idea who it might have been?"

"No. As far as I know I'm the only person who's ever been to the grave. I was the one who ordered the stone for her."

"Well, that's pretty interesting. Don't you think?"

She glared at me. "What do you mean by that?"

"I mean, obviously someone else mourns Madeline Vincent besides you, that's all."

"Maybe someone made a mistake."

"You don't really believe that."

She didn't answer.

"It certainly would be interesting to know who that person is."

She looked at me but continued to remain silent.

"I wonder if there's any way to find out. I imagine, with your contacts, you might be able to."

"I don't see how. I also don't see why it's of any importance."

"Maybe you're right. But I don't think you are. I think it might be very important."

"Why?"

"I asked you about the possibility that Oakhurst may have raped other women. Also that one of them may have committed suicide because of that rape. Might it be that Madeline was that woman? In which case, someone else might know more about it than we do."

There was another moment of silence. "You may be right, but I don't see there's anything I can do about it."

"Are you sure?"

"Quite sure." She surveyed the room. People were moving around the gallery. There was the constant murmur of conversations in the background. "I must get back to my clients."

"Before you go," I said. "I have a question."

"You seem to have a fistful of them."

"How is it you didn't bother to tell me you were in East Hampton for Sarajane's opening?"

"I don't have time for this. There are people I must speak to."

"But you were there, weren't you?"

"Yes, but I wasn't there for the opening. I was back in Manhattan at the time."

"And while you were there you made no attempt to see Tony Oakhurst?"

She threw her head back and laughed. "Give me a break, would you? I detested the very thought of him."

"Enough to want to kill him?"

"Don't be ridiculous. Goodbye, Mr. Wanderman."

"Why didn't you stay out there and go to the opening of your dear friend?"

"You don't give up, do you?"

"Just answer the question."

"I don't have to answer any of your questions. Who are you anyway? You're not the police."

"I'm in Sarajane's corner. And I thought you were, too."

She sighed. "All right. I did spend some time with Sarajane. You can ask her. It was the day before the opening. I couldn't stay because when I go to New York, I make appointments for almost every minute I'm there. I don't sightsee and I don't waste time. My appointment book, hotel and restaurant receipts show where I was at all times."

"They don't really prove anything. You could easily have gone back to East Hampton with no one knowing."

She took a quick look around. "You're wasting your time if you think I killed him. I didn't."

I took my fake PI card out of my wallet, unclipped my pen from the inside pocket of my blazer and wrote my mobile phone number on the back. "Here. Just in case you think of something else."

Before I had a chance to say anything more, she was gone and I was looking at her back. A nice one it was, too, I thought, before she disappeared into the crowd.

CHAPTER 40

I wanted to find Frenchie. Haley claimed she was just a visitor but I couldn't help thinking that her being here was too much of a coincidence. I worked my way around the gallery on the lookout for her, but after a good fifteen minutes of searching, without result, I had to conclude she'd left the premises. I didn't see any point in hanging around so I left, too.

I walked back along the rue du Faubourg Saint-Honoré. The street was quiet. It was past nine o'clock, the stores were closed, the shoppers were gone. All that remained were a few people looking in the still lighted windows, a sharp contrast from the numerous pedestrians thronging the sidewalks earlier. I was thinking about all that had happened in the past few days, especially the past few hours. Haley's story, was it true? And what was Frenchie doing there? I realized there was a lot to absorb. I needed to get it straight in my head and the best way to do that was to get back to my hotel and write it all down in my black schoolbook.

I was concentrating so hard I didn't notice the man until he came up to me. He was holding an unlit cigarette and saying something to me in French. I didn't understand the words but I guessed he wanted a light. I shook my head, hoping he'd understand I couldn't help him. I looked to see if there was anyone else who might have a light for him but there was nobody near us.

Instead of turning away, he suddenly dropped the cigarette, grabbed my arm with both hands, and began shoving me across the sidewalk. I had no time to react. He pushed me into a narrow alley between two buildings and then shoved me so hard I went down on my hands and knees. The next thing I felt was a kick in the side. I rolled over to get away from him. He kicked me again. Luckily, this one didn't go directly into my ribs, but it still hurt like hell. I scrambled around and managed to get to my feet. I was dizzy and the pain had all but immobilized me. It was dark in the alley, only a bit of light coming in from the street. The attacker had stopped moving. I could see him standing in front of me blocking the way back to the safety of the public sidewalk. I shook my head to clear away the wooziness and hoped my body would start working again.

I heard a click. In spite of the blackness there was light enough to see the shining steel of a knife blade in his hand. He moved the knife back and forth from one hand to another and began to come toward me.

"What do you want?" I said. "Money? I've got money. You can have it. No problem."

I'd been mugged before. On 12th Street in the West Village. Back in the seventies, the bad old days when New York was the city of street crime. And I'd been beaten up, too, just a couple of years ago in my own front yard by a couple of Russian Mafia goons. Both the mugging and the beating happened so fast I couldn't do anything about either one of them.

This was not happening fast. In fact it seemed to be occurring in slow motion. The attacker came toward me slowly, the knife moving back and forth from one hand to the other. I watched it carefully. It was mesmerizing, like watching a cobra. I didn't know if he'd understood what I'd said about the money or not, but I got the feeling it didn't matter. The shifting of the knife from one hand to the other told me this guy was a pro. It was done to distract the prey. He could strike with either hand. It looked like what he had in mind was to do something really bad to me.

The dizziness was gone and I forgot about my aching body. I crouched into a defensive position, getting myself ready to move in any direction as fast as I could. I had to be able to go right or left, forward or back. It was a little like tennis, waiting for the next ball, only instead of a ball coming at me it was a blade.

He made a move toward me and I jumped backward, away from the steel. He made a sound like a grunt and lunged forward again, the knife aimed at the center of my body. As I leaped away I felt something. It stung. I didn't know how much I'd been cut but I didn't have time to worry about it. He lunged again. I jumped again. I didn't feel anything this time but I knew he'd come close. I was getting desperate. I had to do something. As a schoolboy I'd been in a lot of fights. An argument would break out in the middle of a game and there'd be some scuffling and fighting. There was always one guy who was bigger and stronger than the others and one guy who was smarter.

The attacker came rushing toward me again. I held my breath and waited until the last possible second. This time I didn't leap aside. Instead, I kicked out with my right leg and got the point of my shoe to hit him exactly where I'd aimed it, directly into his crotch.

The attacker let out a howl. He dropped the knife. I heard the sound of the blade hitting the cement. He fell to the ground, clutching himself. Screams and a long string of French words, that I was sure were curses, came out of him.

Any man knows that his balls are the most sensitive part of his body. A simple wrong move on a bicycle seat can cause pain, a hard squeeze can cause really severe pain, but a kick in the balls is the ultimate. If you're up against the wall in a fight, *hit him where he breathes.*

I got out of the alley as fast as I could and hurried along rue du Faubourg Saint-Honoré until I got to the Metro. When the train came into the station, I got on with a sense of relief. On the train I noticed some strange looks directed at me. I looked down at myself and saw blood on the front of my shirt. It seemed to have dried, which meant that the knife hadn't gone in very far. I felt some pain but it wasn't bad. My blazer had some cuts in it, too. That meant I'd have to buy a new one. I wasn't upset about that. I was just glad to be alive.

When I got back to my room, I took off my damaged blazer and shirt to look at my wound. I realized I'd been very lucky. The cut was about an inch long. It had scratched the surface of the skin, making it more like a scrape. The blood had dried but when I began to wash it with soap and water it began flowing again. I stopped the bleeding by putting pressure on the wound with a wad of toilet paper and then managed to get a Band-Aid over it.

I poured myself a double shot of vodka and thought about the guy who'd attacked me. He'd seemed more intent on getting me with his knife than taking my wallet. Was he a mugger with a sadistic streak? I had to wonder about that. It was entirely possible that he wasn't. In fact, the more I thought about it, the more it seemed to me that he was not a mugger at all. I tossed back the vodka. Yes. Now I was sure of it. The guy was there to kill me and who else could have sent him but Frenchie?

I got up and made sure the door was locked. For additional security I pushed a chair under the door knob.

Then I tried to sleep.

CHAPTER 41

Of course, I couldn't sleep. I lay there, staring at the ceiling, and listened. Every few minutes I got out of bed and crept to the door, whether I heard anything or not, put my ear against it, and strained to hear. I was listening for footsteps—for anything, really.

The fact of the matter was, I was scared. I realized how close I'd come to being forcibly ejected from this world. I wasn't ready for death. I wanted more than anything to stay alive. There was still so much to do: like breathe. I wanted to smell flowers, swim in the ocean. There was food to cook and enjoy, vodka to drink, women to love.

I was no Superman or any kind of super hero. To stay where I was and take on those who were out to get me made no sense. I decided that I had to get out of Paris, *toute suite*. If Frenchie had sent the assassin she might already know where I was staying. If she didn't know yet, it wouldn't take her long to find out.

The clock on the night table showed it was almost one o'clock in the morning. I dialed the hotel operator and asked her to connect me with Air France. They told me there was a flight leaving for London at 6 a.m. I booked it, called the hotel operator again, and asked for a taxi. I'd made up my mind to go home but there was unfinished business in London I had to take care of before I went back to New York.

I got dressed, packed my suitcase, and stayed in the room waiting for the call to tell me the taxi had arrived. At the airport it was easier. I was there three hours before the flight so there were few people around. I made sure to sit near the desks that were open. If anybody came after me I could yell for help.

The knifer from the alley didn't show—I looked at every man who came into view—and neither did Frenchie, or anyone else who looked the slightest bit suspicious. That made me feel a little better.

I must have dozed off because my phone rang, waking me up. I didn't recognize the number. It was Haley.

"How are you?" she said.

"I'm fine." I looked at my watch. It was a little after five. "You didn't call me at this hour to ask how I am."

"That's right. I couldn't sleep. I've been thinking about what you said. I didn't tell you everything."

"Are you going to tell me now?"

"Madeline and I were lovers, yes. But it was not a two-way street."

"What does that mean?"

"I loved her but she didn't love me. She was satisfied, I guess, with our relationship but she wanted more. She wanted other women, and men, too. Tony Oakhurst was one of the men."

"She told you that?"

"No. Tony told me. He knew we were lovers. He just wanted to brag that he could have anyone he wanted, even a lesbian."

"So I guess if they were lovers, he didn't rape her."

"Not necessarily. Married men rape their wives, don't they?"

"But you don't know if he raped her."

"No."

"How come you're telling me this now?"

"I was thinking about what you said. Your suspicion of a connection between Madeline's suicide and Tony's murder. I don't know if there is one or not. I can't say Madeline killed herself because of Tony. She was a mixed up girl. In fact, she'd tried to kill herself at least once before, that I know of. She had a terrible history, grew up in an orphanage somewhere on the outskirts of Paris. Never knew her mother, or her father. She learned later on that her mother wasn't married. She tried to locate her but never did. The woman may have left the country or died. All she knew was that she'd been abandoned and nobody had ever given a shit about her."

"A rotten story."

"But not an unusual one. At least, I did one good thing for her. I gave her a proper funeral and burial. If I hadn't done it, she would have ended up in an unknown grave somewhere."

"That must have given you some consolation."

There was dead air. Then, "Well, that's it. I hope it's of some help."

Before I could say anything, she'd hung up. I had a lot to think about. Why was she calling me at this early hour? Her first words had been to ask how I was. Was it possible that she and Frenchie were a team and they'd arranged for me to be attacked? And now she was checking to see if I was still alive? Giving me that information about Madeline and Tony might have been her back up for calling me. I had no proof of that, but I couldn't help thinking it.

When the plane took off, I took a deep breath and began to relax. But there was no feeling of complacency. I thought I might be safe in London because nobody knew that I'd left Paris. At least, I hoped nobody knew. I also didn't look forward to what I had to do in London.

The problem of the kilo of cocaine had not gone away. It still sat in Left Luggage at Victoria Station where it couldn't be left indefinitely.

After some point—I was pretty sure it was thirty days—they'd open it up, discover the coke and start looking for me. They'd know who I was because I'd had to provide ID.

That meant I had to get the stuff out of there. Then what? What was I going to do with it? I also had to tell SJ and Margo that I was going home. They'd be on their own. I wasn't sure how they'd react—happy or sorry.

I guessed they'd be glad to get rid of me but they might worry about being without anyone to lean on. I expected to tell them if anything looked bad to call the police, but I was pretty sure they wanted nothing to do with cops.

Another complication was that Margo would want the coke back. It was my job to tell her she wasn't going to get it. My reasoning was simple: if they didn't have it in their possession, nobody would do anything to them. At least, that was my theory and hope. And with that thought, I suddenly knew what I was going to do with the coke.

CHAPTER 42

I was back in my London hotel by 9 a.m. While riding in the taxi from the airport, I was struck by how much different it felt to be in London as opposed to Paris. All around me was a sense of order, of neatness. Traffic was heavy, maybe even worse than Paris, but there was no feeling of urgency, of people rushing to get past you, or honking horns for you to get out of their way. The air was warm, very warm. I realized with something of a shock that while I'd been in Europe August had vanished. I wasn't sure when Labor day was, but the fact that it was now September all but confirmed for me that it was time to go home.

My hotel room was the same because I hadn't checked out. It wasn't worth the trouble to check out and then have to check in again. The expense bothered me. I'd been brought up to be sensible about money.

My father was a big spender, but only when he had a lot to spend. When he was short, he was careful. "Blow it when you can, sonny," he'd say. "But hang on to it when you can't."

Morty was paying the bill, after all, and he had plenty of money. *There is money, spend it, spend it, spend more,* was Ford's advice to Falstaff. So I convinced myself there was nothing to feel guilty about.

I went into my wallet to make sure I still had the Left Luggage receipt. I showered and changed my clothes, called room service and ordered the hotel's good English breakfast. Eggs, bacon, sausage, grilled tomato, hash browns, toast. It made my mouth water just ordering it. I hadn't eaten at the airport and, of course, nothing was served on the plane except lukewarm, taste-less coffee.

I went through the food like a starving homeless man, leav-ing the plate almost as clean as if it had been washed. My moth-er would've been proud of me. Satisfied, I went down to the lobby and out the front entrance. There was usually a lineup of taxis waiting. I was glad to see they were still there. I took the first one in line and went directly to Victoria Station. While in the taxi, I had the feeling I was being followed. I kept looking through the back window to make sure no one was in pursuit. I didn't see any vehicle—car, taxi, or motorcycle—that stayed with us. That was a good sign. When I got out of the taxi, I looked around again, just to make sure, but I still felt nervous.

I went into the station and walked at a good pace through the crowds that apparently were always there. I went straight to the Left Luggage department. No problem retrieving my pack-age. I paid the fee and went back outside, the box gripped firmly under my arm. I kept swiveling my head around to make sure I was still alone. Then I retraced my steps as fast as possible and was shortly back in my room.

Now I had to go through with my new plan. The old plan had been to find a way to get the package to Shaved Head, the idea being it would get him out of the picture and leave Sarajane and Margo safe. Now that Shaved Head was dead and other vil-lains were around, I felt there was no choice but to get rid of the stuff altogether. I hoped that I was doing the right thing. At the same time I felt there was no choice.

I undid the wrapping and exposed the white powder wrapped in its plastic cover. I took it into the bathroom and emptied half of it into the toilet. I flushed and watched the stuff go down smoothly, disappearing in the whirlpool. When the tank refilled, I did the same thing again, emptying the rest into the toilet bowl and flushing. It was exactly the same procedure I followed when using root killer for the septic tank back home in Sag Harbor.

When it was all gone, I washed off the bits of powder that remained on the plastic case. I put the case on the floor and stepped on it to break it up, then wrapped it again and tied it with the string. I planned to toss it in a wastebasket in the lobby.

My next step was to call Sarajane and tell her I was coming over.

"Hold on," she said. "Someone wants to talk to you."

A few seconds went by. "It's about time you called." It was Morty and he sounded angry.

This was a surprise, Morty coming to London, and, I had to admit, not altogether a pleasant one. The last thing I needed was having Morty here, possibly complicating things just by his presence.

"Hello, old buddy." I said, as calmly as I could. "How are you?"

"Mad as hell. And I'm not going to take it anymore."

"You won't have to."

"Are you coming over here? Or do I have to go over there to get some info?"

"I'll be there in a few minutes."

Another taxi. More looking through the back window. On the way I tried to think of how much to tell them. I wasn't comfortable withholding information. It struck me as a form of lying. I'd done it before and didn't like it. And I still felt the same way. But I knew it wouldn't be wise to tell the girl's about the knife attack. It would only cause worry and possibly panic. I was the object of the attack, not them. And I truly believed they were not in danger so it wasn't at all necessary to frighten them. As for the rest, I saw no harm in telling them everything I'd found. I could tell Morty the rest of the story, but later.

Morty didn't give me his usual hug, shaking my hand instead. We went into the living room. The sun was glaring through the windows, making the room so bright it hurt my eyes. This hadn't happened before. I guessed the sun must have moved its position or maybe it was the time of day.

I sat down and tried to smooth Morty's edges with banal conversation. "How are you?"

"Great. Just great."

"When did you get here?"

"Yesterday. I didn't hear anything from you for a long time. Like forever. So I decided to come over and see what's going on."

"I'm sorry about that. I was over in Paris and just didn't give any thought to calling you. Besides, I was pretty busy."

"I assume you went there for a reason," Morty said. He was pacing back in forth in front of me.

"A good reason."

Sarajane was sitting on the couch with Margo next to her. Neither one of them spoke. It felt like they were sitting there, watching a guy being taken apart on a reality TV show. And I was the unhappy subject. Or was it, object?

"I'm glad to hear it," Morty said. "I came over here for a reason, too."

"I know. You just told me."

He gave me a wicked smile. "That's not the whole explanation."

"What is then?"

"I'll tell you, but first, you tell us what you got in Paris."

"You sound like you used to when we were little kids. *You go first, then I'll go.* Okay, I'll go first."

I tried to give them everything while carefully leaving out the knife attack. Mainly, I told them what I'd learned from my interviews with Sarajane's friends. When I'd finished telling them about Haley, the gallery owner, including all she'd known about Madeline Vincent and Tony, Sarajane spoke up.

"I just remembered something else I can tell you about Madeline. One night we found ourselves alone together. I don't remember how it came about. The whole night is fuzzy. We'd been drinking wine, too much I suppose. Maybe it was the hour or the wine, or perhaps she was on something—we all knew she was a heavy drug user—she said something about her mother."

"What?"

"I wish I could remember what it was but I can't. I do remember being surprised to hear anything from her because she'd never really told us anything personal about herself before. For example, she'd never told us about being raised in a home. We heard about it somehow. You know how these things are."

"You can't remember what it was she said?"

She frowned and shook her head.

"Try."

"It's no use. I can't. I barely remember that whole night."

"Whatever," Morty said. "In any event, it doesn't sound like you got very much. Not to me, anyway."

"No?" I said. "Think about it. Isn't it possible that Madeline Vincent's suicide, probably caused by Tony Oakhurst, might be the motive for his murder?"

"That's kind of a stretch, isn't it?" Morty said.

"I don't think so. If I had a daughter who was raped, and then she killed herself because of it, I think I'd be pretty upset. Maybe upset enough to kill the guy who did it." I turned to Sarajane. "Is there anything else you can tell us?"

"Not much. I remember that she was a loner. After class most of us used to go for coffee and talk. Occasionally, but not often, she would join us."

"Anything else?"

"She was a pretty girl. Quiet. Hardly ever said anything. We felt sorry for her."

"What did everyone think when she killed herself?"

"We were shocked. It was horrible."

"I still think it's a stretch," Morty said. "Besides, wasn't that a long time ago? Why would the killer wait so long?"

"It was a little more than seven years ago. 1993. Enough time to build up a good deal of hate."

Morty had stopped pacing. I noticed his barrel chest had become a bit larger since I'd last seen him. He needed to cut back on his meat, potatoes, and dessert diet. Being a doctor he ought to know better.

He took the remaining chair. "Now I'll tell you my news. The police contacted me. They told me they've decided Sarajane's no longer a suspect. If she comes back and answers their questions, they'll drop the warrant they've put out for her arrest. What do you think of that?"

"I think it's great. But how sure of this are you?"

"I got a call from that detective in charge of the case. Nolan. She told me. So I went and talked to that lawyer we used before, Jeremiah Longwood. Remember him?"

I remembered the guy—tall, gloomy Gus. I nodded.

"He said it sounded kosher and probably the best thing to do. He offered to go along and be there with her for the questioning. Sarajane agreed. As long as you're okay with it."

I was surprised she wanted my okay. I'd been so sure she couldn't stand the sight of me. "You want my approval?"

She nodded. "I won't do it if you think it's not a good idea."

"I'm flattered. But here's what I think. On the surface it sounds fine. Still, I'm always skeptical when it comes to the police. Is there a hidden motive somewhere? I don't know. What I'd like is to hear it directly from the source."

"You can call her," Morty said.

I shook my head. "No good. It's got to be in person. I want to see her eyes when I talk to her. After that I can let you know how I feel. It's time for me to go back anyway. There's nothing more for me to do here."

Morty turned to his daughter. "What do you think?"

"I'm happy with that arrangement," Sarajane said.

"Then so am I," Morty said.

Thankfully, and uncharacteristically, Margo didn't say a word. I prayed it would continue and that she'd make no mention of the coke.

"What do you say we all go out and celebrate?" Morty said.

Sarajane smiled. I'd forgotten what a beautiful smile she had "Lets," she said.

CHAPTER 43

Something unexpected happened when I came back from London. The instant I walked into my house, Rosalind's presence enveloped me. I let my carry-on bag drop to the floor and stood there, immobilized. Tears came into my eyes. Rosalind's death had turned me into stone for a long time. There were periods when memories of her were so powerful they consumed me. I couldn't resist them. In fact, I didn't want to resist. With time and effort, I'd managed to return to a semblance of a human being. And I wanted to stay there. But there were ineluctable forces that continued to lurk. Depression was one. Like a cancer in remission, you believed it had been wiped out, that all the cells had been bombarded or chemo'ed and were cleaned out of your blood. And then one day you're surprised to notice a little lump on your side that had never been there before, and you go to the doctor and learn that what you thought was gone had returned.

As if that wasn't enough, there was grief. It would appear without warning, not a black cloud, but a gut-wrenching mass that swam in the bloodstream like a slimy parasite.

From the east to western Ind, No jewel is like Rosalind. Why, after more than a year, would it not go? I asked myself the question, already knowing the answer. It was because I didn't want it to. I didn't want to let her go.

At the same time, I knew I'd have to.

Two days passed. That helped me to get over jet lag but not with anything else. I wandered about the house, swilling vodka with the intense concentration of a newborn sucking his mother's tit. I'd been drinking again almost as much as after

Rosalind's sudden death. Morty had called and asked when I was going to see Sienna Nolan. I told him I'd get to it soon, trying to sound as if everything was under control. I didn't want him coming over and making speeches at me.

I called my father. I realized I hadn't given him a thought for a long time and felt suddenly bad about it. There'd been some trouble with Zeena, I remembered. She'd complained about his tomcatting. But he sounded exactly as he always did, full of energy, raring to go, and not laying any guilt on me because I hadn't called.

"So everything's okay with Zeena?" I said.

"Fabulous."

"You're not giving me any bull on this, are you, Dad?"

"Why would I lie to you? You're my son. And speaking of that, where've you been? I called your house and got your machine."

"You didn't leave a message, did you?"

"No. I didn't want to bother you."

"I was in London. Remember that chef who got murdered? I'm working on it."

"That's fantastic," he said. "I can't get over how good a detective you got to be."

"I'm trying, but it's a tough case."

"You want to talk about it? How about you come into the city and we have dinner together?"

"I'd love to, Dad. But right now, it's impossible."

"I understand, sonny. But I want to remind you of something, okay? Watch your back. I don't want to hear you're in a hospital, or worse yet, a morgue. Just remember what happened to you before when you got involved in a murder."

I thanked him for his concern, promised to be very careful, and also promised I'd call him soon.

I went into what I jokingly called my library. The joke was that the room was not much larger than a walk-in closet, about eight by ten, lined with bookshelves I'd built myself. The shelves were filled with most of the books I'd accumulated through the years. The overflow were scattered throughout the house. Every kind of book from spies and thrillers to the Russians, to Conrad, to the plays of O'Neill and Shaw, to Bellow and Mailer and Roth, and to, of course, Shakespeare, the master.

An old beat up recliner stood in a corner with a lamp next to it. I'd spent many hours reading and sometimes sleeping, in that chair.

I drained the vodka I'd been carrying and looked at the empty glass. Should I have another? Why? It filtered into my consciousness that I'd been feeling sorry for myself again. What would Shakespeare make of that? Would he compare me to Falstaff, the fat slob and drunk? Or maybe to the manic-depressive Hamlet, seeing ghosts? What did Hamlet say: *Words, words, words*?

I changed into a polo shirt, biking shorts, and sneakers, got my bike out of the shed, strapped on a helmet, and began riding. I was looking for a long ride, twenty or thirty miles. That wasn't going to be easy because I hadn't ridden in a long time. Good. I wanted it to be hard.

I began pedaling along Noyac Road and came to where it changed to Stoney Hill Road. This was a tough stretch because much of it was up a steep incline. My muscles began to ache with the effort, signaling how out of shape I was. I reached Scuttlehole Road and went East to the Bridgehampton-Sag Turnpike, then headed south. After a while, the leg action and the concentration on what was I was doing began to have an effect. I began to notice things: people in front of their houses, trees, shrubbery. I was aware of the perspiration on my body. It felt good to be sweating.

When I got to Bridgehampton, I had to wait at the light. I abruptly remembered the knife attack in the alley in Paris. I realized how lucky I was to be back home, on my bike, on the way to the ocean.

When I finally made it to the beach, I looked at the waves and listened to the sound of them crashing onto the shore. I inhaled the air, which smelled of the sea. As always, there were others doing the same thing. I thought of how many times Rosalind and I had walked on the East End beaches, how we'd held hands, and often stopped to kiss.

I don't know how long I stayed where I was without moving. All I knew was that I felt better for being there.

When I got back from the ride, I filled a tall glass with water and drank it in one gulp. The urge to drink anything stronger had left me. In my sweaty clothes, I went back into the library, sat in the recliner and thought about what I'd promised to do. I was supposed to get in touch with Sienna Nolan and verify that what Morty heard in regard to Sarajane was valid. In other words, that she could return to The Hamptons with complete impunity. I was skeptical about promises from authorities. They could lie, couldn't they? On the other hand, Jeremiah Longwood, Morty's lawyer, had already spoken with them. He'd assured Morty it was okay. So why was I worried? Habit, I supposed. Or was it that I was nervous about seeing Sienna again?

It was undeniable that when I thought of her, I got excited enough to feel a tremor in the loins. I put my hand on the front of my pants and felt myself harden. This was absurd. How could it happen when at almost at the same time I was still mourning Rosalind? I'd loved Rosalind more than anyone in the world. And now, as difficult as it was to comprehend, I had to reckon with it. It seemed more than likely that I was falling for that red haired detective.

CHAPTER 44

Sienna worked in the Detective division of the Suffolk County Police Department, or SCPD. It was located in the John L. Barry Police Headquarters building in Yaphank, more than an hour's drive from Sag Harbor. I had her office number on a card in my wallet. I called and got a male voice asking me how to direct my call. I told him and waited to see who would answer. In the past, on previous cases in which we'd both been involved, she'd rarely been available. I could feel the tension in my body as I waited.

"Hello?" It was actually Sienna.

"Hi." I let out my breath. "It's Jake Wanderman. How are you?"

"So you're back. How was your trip?"

"Very interesting. There's a lot I'd like to talk to you about."

"I'd like to talk to you, too, but I'm very busy. I'm working three cases. Two guys are out, one on vacation, one sick, so I have to help pick up the load."

"I understand. I can come there, if I have to. I don't expect you to drive all the way out here just to talk to me."

I heard a grunt. "Since when are you so accommodating?"

"Since always. You know I'm a pushover, don't you?"

"Uh oh," she said. "I smell a rat. What's this all about?"

"Too complicated to say on the phone. When do you have time for me?"

"I'll tell you what. I'm going to be very good to you. How about today? And I'll even save you part of your ride. I'll meet you for lunch at the diner in Bellport. 1 p.m. Lunch is on you."

"Deal," I said, then remembered her amazing appetite. "I'll bring two credit cards, just in case."

"I'll do my best to make you need them."

I was happy that she'd agreed to meet me so quickly. I hoped it was because she wanted to see me as much as I wanted to see her. Maybe she hadn't forgotten that enchanting and lengthy kiss at the duck pond, way back before the girls had fled East Hampton for London.

The parking lot at the diner was almost full. I looked for her red Mitsubishi Eclipse but didn't see it so I guessed I'd gotten there first. I was wrong. She was already there, standing just inside the entrance. As always, she was smartly dressed. She wore a light beige pantsuit, navy blouse, low-heeled shoes, earrings but no other jewelry. Also, as always, she was drop-dead gorgeous.

She didn't offer her hand, or her cheek, but she gave me a warm smile. "Hi."

I already felt myself melting. "Hi, yourself. I looked for your car but didn't see it."

"I traded it in for a Miata convertible."

"Red, of course."

"What else?"

We were taken to a booth and handed the usual diner menu, as thick as a phone book and slip-covered in plastic. Not quite the same ambiance or the same quality food as the little bistros I'd enjoyed in Paris. She read through several pages before deciding on a surprisingly light Caesar salad with grilled chicken. I'd expected her to go for a steak, at the very least. I opted for a BLT. We both ordered coffee that came immediately. Coffee was always served right away in diners, sometimes before you'd even looked at the menu.

"It's good to see you again," I said. "You look great."

"Could we skip the pleasantries and get to the chase? As I told you I've got a lot on my plate."

Whew! That quickly dissolved the warm glow of contentment I'd been basking in. I tried not to let it show by sipping a little coffee before answering. "Sure. I want to hear from you about the deal you offered Mr. Adler in regard to his daughter and her friend."

"No problem. I've been through everything we have on the case with the DA. He says there's not enough for an indictment. They're ready to drop the warrant for their arrest if they'll come in and talk to us."

"What about? You already have statements from them."

"The truth is we've come up with a blank. We haven't got a damn thing. I'm hoping if I go over everything with them again, maybe something'll show that I haven't thought of. It's a long shot, I know. But frankly, I'm desperate."

"Is your deal guaranteed?"

"For the outstanding charge? Yes. As for anything that may come up in our interviews or discoveries, no. Of course not. You have to know that."

"Then why should they come back?"

"Only if they want the ability to enter the United States again. If that isn't important, then they don't have to bother."

"You'll definitely drop the warrant if they agree to come back? It'll have to be dropped before they go through customs, otherwise they'll be arrested by immigration."

"Don't worry. If you tell me they agree to talk to us, I'll make sure they come into the country without a problem. In fact, we'll even meet them at the airport."

"In other words, you're going to grill them the minute they set foot on U.S. soil?"

Our order arrived. We held off speaking until the plates were set down in front of us and the coffee was refilled.

"Good," Sienna said, not answering me. "I'm starved." She began attacking her salad.

"I repeat my question. Is that what you're planning to do?"

She chewed for a while and nodded. "This is a good salad. Lots of flavor. What do you think? We're going to give up the warrant and then have them disappear on us again? Uh uh. We've got to protect our interests."

"I don't like it," I said. "They'll think they're being arrested."

"It's not like that at all. You can be there. Their lawyer can be there. Everything'll be on the up and up."

I began eating my BLT. "That might work."

While chomping on my sandwich I decided now was the time to tell her some of what I'd discovered in London and Paris. I had to be very careful to avoid any mention of drugs. I also had to be sure not to mention anything about SJ's involvement with the victim. If Sienna heard that, it'd be all over. What I emphasized was the story of Madeline Vincent's rape and suicide and how I'd found flowers on the grave. And then I summed it up. "I think it's more than possible that this girl's death may be connected to Oakhurst's murder."

She listened without saying a word. Her plate had only a speck of salad left on it. All the bread she'd been given was gone, as well. She drained her coffee and looked at me.

"Well?" I said.

"It's an interesting theory. But so what? You don't have any names. You don't even know if the person who left the flowers is a man or a woman. You have a ghost for a suspect. What is it you expect me to do with that theory? How would I investigate it?"

I shrugged. "That's your job, isn't it?"

"There might be information in Paris to substantiate your theory. But I have no resources there. There's nothing I can do."

"What about the people at the opening? Couldn't you check their backgrounds for ties to Paris?"

"We've already interviewed over one hundred and fifty people. That includes the guests and the workers."

"And you found nothing?"

"Nothing."

"But you weren't looking for this kind of information, were you?"

"No. But if you think I can get my boss to go down this road, you're living in dreamland." She gave me a dazzling smile. "How about dessert?"

CHAPTER 45

In the parking lot she held out her hand. I had no choice but to shake it. What I wanted was to hold on to it, squeeze it, pull her close, but of course, I did nothing of the kind.

"I hope you'll persuade Dr. Adler's daughter and her partner to come back," she said. "It'll clear their names, and hopefully, they can tell me something that will help with this case."

"I'll do my best."

I watched her climb into her Miata convertible and drive away with a wave.

I was more than frustrated. She hadn't given my theory any consideration. On a more personal level, she hadn't given any hint that she remembered our kiss at the duck pond, or that she might be the least bit interested in a repetition.

I got into my car and began to back out of the space when I realized something was wrong. It felt like a flat tire. I got out to take a look. A tire was flat, all right. But it wasn't an ordinary flat. The tire had been attacked with a sharp pointed tool of some kind. There were punctures all around the sidewall.

I immediately went to see about the other cars near me. Their tires were okay. Then I went to another part of the lot and checked the tires of the cars over there. They were all untouched. Only mine had been singled out. Fuck!

Who the hell did this? Obviously it wasn't random. So the next question was why? Was it to send me a message? To stop doing what I was doing? And what was that? All I'd done since I'd come home was to see Sienna Nolan.

Maybe that was enough.

I was about to change the tire myself then decided the hell with it. I called Triple A and got the usual response. It would be forty-five minutes to an hour until they could get to me. I thought about reporting this to the cops, but I knew the result would be only red tape and a waste of time. Calling Sienna might be the smarter thing to do but I decided against it. What would or could she do about it, anyway?

Nobody knew I was going to the diner except Morty. I couldn't think of anyone Morty might have told other than Sherri, his wife, and Longwood, his lawyer. Longwood was certainly not going to talk about it. Maybe Sherri, but who? I couldn't think of anybody. This meant that someone followed me, or else my phone was tapped. I hadn't given any thought to being tailed. Probably dumb, after what happened in Paris, but I was back home and had felt safe. As for the phone being tapped, I'd never considered it but maybe now I'd better.

After a wait of about an hour the Triple A guy arrived, made a few snarling remarks about how the world was going to the dogs and changed my tire. On the way back to Sag Harbor I kept checking my rearview mirror. I didn't see a tail but that didn't make me any less uncomfortable.

I stopped at the Southampton tire store and bought a new tire. On my way home I remembered that I'd wished I'd had a tape recorder when I was in Paris so I stopped at Radio Shack in Bridgehampton and bought one. The salesman told me I was better off getting a digital one. That way there would be no worry about using up the tape. I didn't have any specific plan for it but felt it might come in handy some time. It was late afternoon by the time I got home. I wasn't in any mood to talk to Morty about Sienna or the tire incident. So I changed into workout clothes and went down to the basement where I punched the bag viciously for fifteen minutes. After a shower it was getting close to five o'clock, the hour a friend of Rosalind's used to call "drinky-poo time." Okay, I thought, that special hour was fast approaching. But one drink only. After that, I'd give some thought to what I'd feel like having for dinner.

As I was heading toward the little bar I'd made out of an old cabinet, the phone rang. I wasn't going to answer it but then I reluctantly picked it up.

"Mr. Wanderman?"

The voice was vaguely familiar but not one I immediately recognized.

"Who is this?"

"Chantal Badeau. Do you remember? We spoke at my apartment in Paris not long ago."

Of course, I remembered. She was rich, attractive, and had not been of much help. "Yes. This is a surprise. How did you get my number?"

There was a moment's silence. "I believe you gave me your card, did you not?"

I'd given out a lot of cards, so that made sense. "Of course."

"I was in New York City. I was told I must go to see the famous Hamptons. Voilà!"

"You're here? In The Hamptons?"

"*Exactement.*"

"Are you here with your husband?"

"Alas, no. He had to remain in Paris. Business, you know. I am *toute seule*, quite alone."

What was this all about? "What can I do for you?"

"*J'espère*, I hope, you might wish to spend some time with a lonely visitor."

Come on lady, I thought. "What did you have in mind?"

"Perhaps you would take me to a tour of the local attractions. Would that be good?"

Local attractions. Was I one of them? "I could do that. Sure. It would be a pleasure. When would you like to get together?"

"Whenever it is a convenience to you. I am utterly available."

"How about tomorrow morning? I could pick you up at ten o'clock. Is that okay?"

"*Mais oui.* I'm staying at the Huntting Inn. I look forward to seeing you again. And many thanks."

I poured my usual Luksusowa vodka over ice. There was no doubt in my mind that Chantal Badeau's visit to The Hamptons was not what she'd suggested it was. A tour of local attractions? Get outta here. What did she really want?

I remembered that I still had to eat. I decided to take some shrimp from the freezer and make a scampi with a lot of garlic. Umm. My mouth began to water just thinking of it.

CHAPTER 46

Early next morning Morty called. "Did you talk to that lady cop?"

"Yeah." I told him what Sienna had said. I didn't mention Chantal Badeau.

"Then it's okay? Everything'll work out?"

"That's what she said, unless something turns up that implicates them."

"Great. I'll call and give them the good news."

"I'd tell them to act as quickly as possible before anything happens that might change their minds."

"Will do," Morty said.

The Huntting Inn was familiar territory. Aside from the numerous times I'd eaten at the Palm, a world class steak house located inside, it was where Sarajane and Margo had been staying at the time of Tony Oakhurst's murder. I parked in the lot and headed toward the entrance wondering if someone already knew about my coming here to meet Chantal Badeau. I was sure I hadn't been followed because I was now checking my rearview mirror almost constantly. If anyone knew, it would have to be because my phone was tapped. I realized I should have called Sienna and asked her how I could find out about that.

Chantal was seated in the lobby turning the pages of Elle. When she saw me come through the door, she put the magazine down and I got a good look at her. It came back to me that she had this theatrical presence, the kind of thing that makes you watch one particular actor when she's on stage or screen. She was not traditionally beautiful—it was more than that—everything about her was perfection, from the smoothness of her skin, to her makeup, her dress, her bearing. She was tall, slim, with dark eyes outlined in black, and an oval shaped face that belonged on a cameo. I vaguely remembered the outfit she'd worn in Paris, some kind of silky top with matching pants. Today she wore a light gray cashmere sweater with darker gray linen pants. The rubies she'd worn in Paris were nowhere in sight but I did notice a rather large sparkling rock on the ring finger of her left hand where there should have been a wedding ring. What might that mean?

I led her out to my car.

"I am delighted that you are doing this for me, *Monsieur* Wanderman. I am so looking forward to spending this time with you."

"My pleasure." I was determined to play the tour guide until she showed her hand.

I drove her around East Hampton village, pointing out some of the glamorous stores that had come into the town in recent years. I didn't bother to tell her they'd driven out the mom and pop stores that had been there for generations. Then I took her past the mansions where the people lived who supported those stores. Most of those mansions had driveways barred by gates, and were surrounded by hedges so high you couldn't see over them, but that was the point, wasn't it?

I took her to Main Beach where she could see the beauty of our white sand. I wasn't mean enough to point out the difference between our beach and the stony gray crud found on the Riviera. Then I drove her out to have a look at Montauk. All this time not a word was said about what she wanted from me. On the way back, I stopped for lunch at one of the clam shacks on the Napeague strip. We were the only ones there. It was warm enough to sit at an outside table.

As we dug into our fried clams, I decided I'd had enough. "Okay, Chantal. The tour is over. Why did you really call me?"

She didn't answer at first. Maybe she was considering how long she should keep up the charade. "You think I have a hidden motive?"

"Come on, babe. I don't believe for a minute you came from Paris to take a look at The Hamptons."

"*Voilà*! You are too clever for me."

"Please don't," I said.

"What?"

"Don't bullshit me. Just tell me what's on your mind."

She hesitated. "All right. I will tell you but it is difficult. It is complicated."

"I'm sure you'll figure it out," I said. "Just start."

"I am looking for something that is lost. We think you know where it can be found. Do you understand what I am saying?"

"I really don't."

She pushed some food around her plate. "I was afraid you were going to be difficult."

I reached across the table and took hold of her wrist to stop her playing with the food. "Listen to me. I don't have any idea what you're talking about."

She looked around even though we were alone. "Cocaine. That's what's I'm talking about. It's lost and we want it back."

I let go of her. "Wait a minute. You're in this thing, too?" I tried to get my head around what she'd just said. Cocaine? We? A dozen other questions rattled through my brain like an electric spark, important questions, like was she also connected to Haley Sanford and Shaved Head, and/or to Frenchie?

She nodded. "*Oui. C'est ça.*"

"You're a drug dealer? Why? I thought you were rich."

"Sometimes one appears to be rich, when in fact, one is not, or at least not as rich as one wishes to be."

"You said, *we*, a moment ago. Just who is this other person or persons you're talking about?"

"Did I say, *we*? A slip of the tongue, perhaps."

"Yeah, right. Okay, I suppose it's none of my business. But you've made a lot of assumptions. If I say to you I have no idea of the whereabouts of what you're looking for, what then?"

"Please, Mr. Wanderman. This is not a moment for games playing as you just said. We—I can explain to you how I know you are connected to this issue."

"Then why don't you do that? I'm intensely interested."

Her lips compressed tightly then relaxed. "*Trés bien.* Tony Oakhurst brought with him to New York a large quantity of coke. After he was murdered it was nowhere to be found. His residence out here as well as in the city were both searched. The last people to have seen him alive were Sarajane and Margo. I know all about Margo. Therefore, we believe it was taken by her with the help of Sarajane. Since you have been closely associated with them, it is reasonable to suppose you know where it is. And can therefore deliver it. We're not asking too much. It does belong to us, after all."

"You think you've got it all wrapped up, don't you? Suppose I tell you you're way off base. That you couldn't be more wrong?"

She shrugged as only the French can. "I would not believe you. Neither would my associates." Her voice changed and became hard and flat. "You told someone in London you had it. Unfortunately, we didn't believe him. And you had somewhat of a misadventure in Paris. Do you recall?"

"So you know about that? Why am I not surprised? And I suppose you know something about a tire on my car being slashed yesterday? Do you also happen to know a beautiful young woman with diamond studs in her ear?"

She shrugged again.

"If you think you can threaten me into doing something for you, you're wrong. It won't work." I knew if I showed fear, I was finished. I leaned back and smiled, to demonstrate to her how little I was worried.

"I have no desire to threaten you. I'm just trying to show you that I am serious. There is, however, something I can offer in exchange." She opened her purse, took out a pack of Marlboroughs and lit one with a gold lighter. "I can offer you a trade. Information for information."

"What information do you have to offer that I might want?"

"Back in Paris, when we first met, you said that you were investigating Tony Oakhurst's murder. I believe I can help you with that. I know a great deal about Tony Oakhurst. Things you don't know. Information that may help you with your investigation."

"What things?"

She pointed her cigarette at me. "Do your part, and I shall do mine."

"How do I know you have any real information?"

She thought a moment. "How does knowledge of a certain Madeline Vincent strike you?"

"It doesn't. The fact that you know her name doesn't mean a thing."

"I know much more than her name. You will have to trust me on that."

"Trust you? That's a good one."

"I promise that I have useful information. You can believe me. What do you say? A deal?" She held out her hand.

I didn't take it. I wanted to. It was crunch time but I was in a bind. I'd flushed the cocaine down a toilet in London. How could I make a deal? Then a glimmer of a way out hit me. Could I bluff her?

I stood up. "Let me think it over."

"I don't have much time," she said, putting out her cigarette by dropping it on the gravel and grinding it under her shoe.

"Why not? You've waited this long, haven't you? I'll let you know by tomorrow."

"*D'accord*. I will wait. But only until tomorrow. If not, remember there is another alternative."

I laughed, hoping it sounded real. "How could I forget?"

CHAPTER 47

Back home, after reflecting about what had happened, I knew Chantal and Haley were in the game together. I wondered why Chantal hadn't gotten to me in Paris when I remembered there hadn't been time. I'd left Paris immediately after I'd been attacked.

I called her that evening and agreed to her deal. I told her she'd have to give me a day to get it. I made it sound as if I had the stuff stashed in a distant location. I wanted to buy as much time as I could to make sure I made a fake good enough to get by the first glance. If she opened the package right away I was done for. I had a plan how to avoid that. I had to hope it was good enough to work.

I thought about when to tell Sienna. I was prepared to give her the whole story but I wasn't ready to go that route yet. I wanted to hear what Chantal had to say first. If the information she gave me was worthwhile, then I had a better chance of getting Sienna back into the case. In any event, I knew I'd eventually have to tell her because I was going to need her help once Chantal found out I'd tricked her. I'd need Sienna to make sure they didn't come after me. A visit from a cop with knowledge that Chantal and Haley were in the drug business should do it. The question was, did I need backup when I made the meet with Chantal, or could I handle it myself? I gave myself time to think about it.

In the interim, I set about making something that would look like a brick of cocaine. I'd read that people in the drug business used cornstarch to cut pure cocaine so I decided to use that. I went to the IGA and bought a big container. I filled a Ziploc bag with it but one bag wasn't enough so I filled another one. The two of them, held together with rubber bands, looked about right. I had some brown paper around to use for wrapping paper. I tied it with string and decided it looked enough like the original to pass inspection. Until she opened it, of course. I waited until late afternoon to call her again.

"Okay," I said. "I've got it. When do you want to get together?"

"*Immediatement*. I've been waiting all day to hear from you. By the way, how did you get the cocaine past the customs people?"

"That's my business. Where do you want to meet?"

"The beach. I think you called it Main Beach. You know, where you took me before."

"I don't think so. I'll be much more comfortable with people nearby."

"You still don't trust me?"

Like hello! Of course, I didn't trust her. "Let's just say I'll feel more comfortable if we can get together in public. We'll still be able to talk."

"All right. If that is your wish, I shall go along with it. Where do you suggest?"

"There's a little place called Rowdy Hall. It's only a few blocks from you. Ask at the desk. They'll tell you exactly where it is. I'll meet you there in an hour."

"*D'accord*. One hour."

I wasn't sure if I was doing the right thing, meeting her alone. Still, it was going to be in an open place with people around. There wasn't much she could do to me there. It was afterward I might have to worry. I'd call Sienna then. But what if she wasn't in? A strong possibility. I still didn't have her cell number. I decided to call her right away to make sure I could reach her.

Sure enough, she wasn't there. The cop I spoke to said he expected her back later. I left my name and cell number and a message for her to call me right away. All I could do was hope she'd call soon. But even if she didn't, I wasn't too worried. I had a good idea about how to handle this. When I got to the restaurant I'd put the package on the table. She certainly wouldn't open it there. I'd suggest she take the package to the bathroom to inspect it, after we had our little talk, and while she was away, I'd take off. Nothing she could do to me, at least not then. If she came after me later, by that time I'd have Sienna in the picture.

I'd told Chantal an hour even though it was only about a twenty minute drive. I wanted to get there first to make sure everything was kosher. Before leaving the house, I remembered my tape recorder. I put it in my shirt pocket. The recorded conversation might help convince Sienna to get involved. I double-checked the street for a parked car that shouldn't be there and then drove carefully, using the rearview mirror.

It was now well after Labor Day, which guaranteed parking spaces where none had been available before. Route 27, which led to East Hampton village, went past a pond that held some ducks and swans. The leaves on the trees surrounding the pond were beginning to turn color. They helped make the approach to the commercial part of the village even prettier than usual. I found a space near the movie theater, a half block from the restaurant.

I left the package under the floor mat and strolled along one side of Main Street looking for anybody or anything that was not normal. I was really searching for Frenchie. I had no idea if she was here, but some inner feeling told me she was. If I was right, I knew I had to be very careful.

Walking slowly I checked out every parked car to make sure she wasn't sitting in one. I crossed over and did the same on the other side of the street. Then I wandered up Newtown Lane pretending to be window-shopping. I glanced across the street and saw a young woman sitting alone in a parked car. My breath caught.

I crossed over to the other side of the street behind her. I walked slowly toward the car. As I approached I realized I was visible in the side view mirror. I put my hand over my face as if I were coughing until I was close enough to glance inside. It wasn't Frenchie. I breathed a little easier.

I went back to the car, got the package, and entered Rowdy Hall. I took a table near the front window with my back to the wall. The waitress came over and I told her someone was joining me. I held off on ordering a drink while waiting. I needed to be on high alert. I didn't want alcohol interfering with the workings of my brain.

I set the package down on the table and waited for Chantal.

CHAPTER 48

It wasn't long before she came in. The moment I saw her, I switched on the recorder.

Immaculate as usual, she raised her eyebrows at the package resting on the table, sat down, and said in almost a whisper, "Isn't that a bit conspicuous?"

I smiled. "We have nothing to hide. Just act as if it's a present for you."

"I had every intention of opening it to make sure it is what you say it is. Now it is not possible."

"I suppose I could let you take it to the ladies room, but I don't know that I'd ever see you again."

"So you are still not trusting me?"

"Well, you're not trusting me either, right? You're telling me you want to check it out."

She turned that over in her mind for a few seconds, then apparently having made up her mind, hung her quite large handbag on the back of her chair. "I think I'd like a drink."

I signaled for the waitress. Chantal ordered a gin and tonic. I ordered coffee.

"The only thing good ever to come out of the UK," she said.

I laughed. "Typical nasty comment from the French about the English."

"But I am French, of course. And I can be quite nasty at times."

"I'll remember that," I said. "Now how about getting to why we're here."

"Allow me to have my drink first."

I waited impatiently for the order to arrive and for Chantal to have her first sip. "Now?"

She smiled. "*Voilà.* Here's what I think you will be interested in. Tony Oakhurst and Madeline Vincent were lovers. But it was not a happy arrangement. Madeline also went with women and Tony did not like that."

"I already know that. Besides, wasn't Tony screwing every woman he could get his hands on?"

"*C'est vrai.* True enough. But that did not prevent him from being jealous. And one day, when she refused his advances, in a fit of rage, he raped her."

"How do you know this?"

"I heard it from someone."

"And who might that someone be?"

"Haley Sanford."

"How would she know?"

"She and Madeline were lovers, too."

"You're telling me what I already know. Haley told me herself that she and Madeline were lovers. True, she didn't tell me about the rape. I wonder why. But even so, what you're telling me is hardly worth what I'm giving you in trade."

"You're a demanding fellow, aren't you?" She smiled, a smile as counterfeit as a three dollar bill. "*Alors*, there is one more thing. Madeline told me something once, something she said she'd never told anyone."

"How come? You never said you were close to her. Were you one of her lovers, too?"

She shook her head. "*Pas du tout.* I prefer good looking men." She gave me a sort of half-smile. "You, for example. I find you quite attractive."

"And I find *you* quite attractive, *madame*, or is it *mademoiselle*?"

She lifted her glass. "*Madame* will do. Here's to being attractive to each other."

Yeah, like being attracted to a cobra. "So what was it Madeline spilled the beans about?"

"It happened one night after class. We'd all been out together and, as usual, there had been wine and drugs. Madeline could barely walk. I volunteered to get her home. When we were there she begged me to stay. She brought out some more wine. I didn't refuse. We were both rather gone when she began to talk about herself. I remember only parts of what she said because I was rather under the influence, *moi-même*. But what she said was so startling I could not ever forget it."

She stopped and took another pull at her gin and tonic.

I held off making a comment. I didn't want to break her concentration.

"She told me she'd been brought up in an orphanage. She'd been abandoned by her parents. She had no idea who they were or why they'd given her up. Some years before, she'd gotten the idea to try and find out something about them. She'd gone back to the orphanage but they wouldn't tell her anything or show her records. They told her the papers were confidential. One of the women in the office stopped her outside. 'I shouldn't tell you this,' she said, 'but your mother's name was Julia Vincent. No father was listed on the birth certificate.'

"She tried to find Julia Vincent. There were a few Vincent's in the phone book. She called them all. There was no Julia. One man hung up on her. She called him back. He hung up again. She felt there had to be a reason why he would not talk to her. She called again and again until at last he said something. 'You must be the bastard my brother conceived. He's dead. The bitch who gave birth to you took everything he had. Then she left him to go back to America. Don't call again!'"

Chantal stopped and reached for her drink. "I can never forget the sound of her voice when she told me that story. Despair! The crushing sound of despair!" She took a good swallow. "Does it help you? I sincerely wish that it does."

"I don't know. Maybe." Actually, it gave me something I didn't have before. The information that her mother was American. But I wasn't going to tell her that.

She took hold of the package. But instead of getting up and taking it with her, she reached for her handbag and tucked it inside. She took out a small pair of scissors that looked like manicuring scissors.

"What are you doing?" I said.

"Just making a little inspection."

"I thought you were going to do that in the bathroom."

"Why bother? I can do it right here."

Shit! My brilliant plan about getting away before she found out I'd tricked her was not going to work. Now what? All I could do was watch and try to think of something.

She poked around inside the bag. I couldn't see what she was doing but I could guess. After a while she put a finger in her mouth, then inside the pocketbook, then out again. Now she rubbed her gums with it and closed her mouth. It was clear she was running her tongue back and forth over her gums.

For a second or two I considered getting up and taking off anyway. But I knew I couldn't do that. Run away like a coward? No way. Besides, as I'd figured before, it seemed to me there wasn't much she could do about it right away. She'd just have to acknowledge that I'd beaten her at her own game. Later, of course, was another story. But hopefully I'd have Sienna's help by then.

I waited.

CHAPTER 49

She stopped doing what she was doing with her tongue and gave me a cold look. Then she removed the bundle from her purse and put it back on the table. "I don't know what is in the package, but I do know it is not what it is supposed to be. Just what are you playing at?"

"It's a little hard to explain."

"Do you really think you can get away with this?"

"I said it's hard to explain, but let me try."

"I will have another gin and tonic."

I raised my hand to catch the waitress's attention. When she looked at me I pointed to the glass and nodded. "It's coming," I said.

"I don't think you realize the depth of the trouble you are in."

"Maybe not. But the truth is, I don't have the coke. Nobody has it. I flushed it down a toilet."

"I find that impossible to believe."

"It's the truth."

"Why would you do that?"

"I said, it's complicated. Yes, I had the coke in London. I was going to give it to Shaved Head."

"Shaved Head? Who is that?"

"A man who was following me and Sarajane. A big guy. His head was shaved to the skull. That's what I called him. I think you know who I'm talking about." I waited for her to say she knew him but she didn't speak. "Anyhow, he was stalking the girls. I figured he was after the coke. So I made a deal with him. I would give him the coke and he would leave the girls alone. Everything was all set. But something happened. The day I was going to meet him he was killed. I'm pretty sure you know about that."

"Perhaps."

"*Perhaps*. Come on, you know exactly what I'm talking about."

"All right. His name was Victor Ivanov. We learned he had been stealing from us. He had to be eliminated."

"You did it at the wrong time for me. Try to understand the position I was in. What was I going to do with the coke? I wasn't about to give it back to Margo. I couldn't keep it. So I did what I thought was best. The toilet."

"Why didn't you tell me that in the first place?"

"I wanted to hear what you had to say about Madeline. I thought it might be important. I figured a little lie wouldn't hurt to get some information."

"If you thought that, you were wrong. Even if I were to believe you, it would not matter. I am not alone. There are others involved who will not believe your story. They will want something for their trouble. If you do not produce what they want, you will suffer the consequences."

"What kind of consequences?"

She shrugged.

"What kind of consequences?" I repeated.

"I'm not sure. Possibly they will kill you."

"What good would that do? It won't get them the coke back."

"That's not the way their minds work. If they don't get it back, at least they will have satisfied their taste for revenge."

"Just who are these others you're talking about? One of them wouldn't be Haley Sanford by any chance?"

She shrugged again, not answering. The waitress arrived with her gin and tonic. She lifted the glass and saluted me with it. "This will probably be the last time we see each other."

"What happens now?" I said.

"I will finish my drink and leave. As I said, I don't expect to ever see you again. I am sorry."

I watched as she emptied the glass in one long swallow, picked up her purse, pushed her chair back, and stood. She looked down at me and gave me a wan smile. "*Tant pis!* Too bad. It might have been quite pleasurable." Then she left.

Was she serious? Would they really try something like that? I tried to drink the dregs of the coffee but it was cold and bitter, like my insides. I flipped open my phone and called Sienna again. She still wasn't there. I told the cop it was urgent. I wanted to say I was in danger but why would he believe me? He had no idea who I was. I asked him to call her cell and have her call me back. "Please," I said. "I'm not some kook. This is really important. Sienna knows who I am."

"Okay, okay. Don't get your nuts twisted. I'll call her."

Then I suddenly remembered I *had her cell number from that time she'd called me.* I called it and was forwarded to a message system. Shit!

I ordered another cup of coffee. People came and sat near me. I could hear them. They were talking about movies, normal conversation. Did they know they were sitting near someone in danger of being killed? Of course not. How could they? I tried to drink the coffee but the taste was terrible. I looked at my watch. Five minutes had passed. Feeling desperate, I called the precinct again. A different cop answered. I asked if the other man was there I'd just spoken to.

"What other man?" he said.

I told him the same story. I pleaded with him to get in touch with Sienna.

"Okay, dude. I'll call her now. Hold the phone." After a while he came back on the line and said she wasn't answering. He said he left a message to call my number. I thanked him and hung up.

I couldn't sit there anymore. I paid the check, took the package, and went outside onto Main Street. I'd never had a gun or any kind of weapon. I'd never thought of having one. Now I wished I was Dirty Harry with a gun as big as a cannon.

I looked all ways. I didn't know who or what I was looking for but it was more or less the same thing I'd done before. Try to spot something that was out of place. A person or persons who didn't look as if they belonged.

I didn't see anything unusual. I began walking toward my car. I passed a garbage bin and tossed the package, glad to be rid of it. I walked quickly, hoping to get into the car before anyone could get to me. As I got nearer I pulled the key out of my pocket and hit the button to open the doors. The lights flashed and I heard the door locks pop. So far so good.

I reached the front of the car and stepped off the sidewalk to get to the driver's side. I opened the door quickly and got in. I was about to hit the lock button when the passenger door opened and someone slid into the seat opposite me.

"Nice to see you again, Mr. Wanderman," Frenchie said. She had a gun in her hand and it was pointed at me.

CHAPTER 50

Talk about feeling like an idiot! I hated to admit it but there was the fact, sitting right there. Was she smarter than me? Yes. So far. I had no choice but to play along and hope that at some point I might get myself out of this.

"Okay," I said. "What now?"

"Drive," she said.

"Where?"

"To your house."

"My house?"

"That's right."

"Why?"

"Because I say so. Just do as you're told."

I'd thought of her as Frenchie, but I'd never before heard her speak. There was no trace of a French accent. In fact, she sounded like an American.

I started the car, made a left turn onto Newton Lane where there were a lot of stores and restaurants as well as the Waldbaum's supermarket. I was hoping there'd be traffic but there wasn't. I drove slowly, looking for an opportunity to get into a minor accident that would bring the cops and hopefully my freedom.

I felt the gun thrust into my ribs. "Hey!" I said. "That hurt."

"Why are you driving so slow? You thinking of pulling something? Forget it. Drive normally."

I felt as if she were reading my mind.

I went onto Long Lane past the East Hampton High School until I got to Stephen Hand's Path then made a left to Route 114. From there it was a direct drive at the 45 MPH speed limit to

Jermain Avenue, where I made another left and continued on past Mashashimuet Park onto Noyack Road and to my house. I thought a few times about driving off the road into a tree but decided it wouldn't do anything except maybe kill the both of us. When we finally got to my house, I stopped the car in a part of the driveway where it could be seen through one of my neighbor's windows. All I could do was hope someone might be looking and see the gun in her hand.

"Don't move until I say so," she said.

She got out then walked quickly around to the driver's side and pulled open my door, all the time pointing the gun at me. It was a surprisingly small weapon but that didn't make me feel any better. I knew if she pulled the trigger, it wouldn't matter what size it was.

"Get out of the car."

I did as she said.

"Okay, now listen carefully. We're going inside. I know you have a security system. When you open the door, deactivate the system. Let me remind you not to do anything stupid."

I wanted to ask how she knew about my security scheme but thought it would be better to keep my mouth shut.

I opened the door, punched in the code, and disarmed the system. She closed the door and looked around. "It's not much of a house, is it?"

"Depends what you mean by much. I like it."

"How many rooms are there?"

"I never stopped to count them. There's a living room, a dining room, two bedrooms, one of which I made into an office. There's a kitchen, and a bathroom. Also a full basement. You want to know how many square feet?"

"Oh? You're a funny man, too?"

"A laugh a minute."

"Show me what you call your office."

"I also call it the library."

"Whatever," she said.

I took her in there.

"This will do," she said.

"Where did you learn to speak such good English? You have no accent."

"That's because I'm an American. Now empty your pockets."

I took everything out of my pants pockets including my cell phone but left the recorder in my shirt hoping she wouldn't notice it.

"Now turn around and put your hands behind your back."

I did that and felt handcuffs being snapped onto my wrists.

She took my arm and pushed me toward my recliner. "Sit."

I sat on the edge of the seat and looked up at her. She smiled, but it was a smile that left me chilled. With my hands behind my back I was more than uncomfortable. If she kept me in that position for a while, I'd start cramping.

This was really the first time I'd gotten a close look at her. I was surprised to see how young she was, early twenties at the most. She had the creamy skin of the young, fair complexion with a small nose, a hard mouth that was two straight lines of dark lipstick, eyes a pale blue, cold and penetrating. Altogether, the look of a man-eating shark. It was clear she could have my balls for breakfast without so much as a tremor.

"So you're an American citizen, but you live in Paris?" I said.

"That's right."

"And how'd you get into the drug business?"

She waved the gun back and forth. "Someday I'll tell you my life story, but right now I don't have the time. Slide back farther in the chair. As far as you can go."

I had to squirm but I managed it.

She pulled the lever that made the chair recline. It went all the way back so that I ended up with my legs higher than my head. I was as helpless as a trussed chicken in a roasting pan.

"That's better. Now I don't have to worry about you."

She put the gun on my desk, took the bag she wore off her shoulder, and rummaged through it. I watched as she took a syringe and a vial out of the bag. She stuck the needle into the vial and filled the syringe.

"What are you going to do?" I said. Was she about to finish me off? Chantal had said bad things would happen to me but I never thought they'd actually kill me.

"Don't worry. It won't hurt."

"Is this what you did to Shaved Head in front of the Tate? Stick a poisoned needle into him?"

She grimaced. "You're talking about Ivanov, I suppose. He had to die. In your case it may not be necessary. You'll fall asleep but you'll wake up fairly soon."

She came around to the side of the chair taking away any possibility of my kicking out at her. She pushed me forward a little and rolled up the sleeve of my left arm. She then wrapped something elastic around my bicep. It was just like getting a shot in the doctor's office.

"Good," she said. "You have excellent veins."

I felt her finger touching my *excellent vein*. Then I felt the sting as the needle went in. I closed my eyes and waited for whatever was going to happen. If it was death, so be it.

Death, as the psalmist saith, is certain to all: all shall die.

The next thing I knew my eyes were open and my eyeballs hurt. I realized I'd been unconscious but had no idea for how long. I wasn't dead, at least, but I did not feel good. I had a vicious headache and there was a taste in my mouth, like I'd eaten rotten onions. I thought I was going to vomit. "What the hell did you give me?"

"A harmless drug, similar to what used to be called truth serum."

"You mean, sodium pentathol? You're kidding me. I thought that was a lot of baloney."

"This is a little different. The Soviets have come up with an improvement. We'll see if it's baloney or not. I'm going to ask you questions. You'll answer them truthfully, I hope."

"I might throw up on you."

"You're welcome to throw up all you want. But unless you can vomit backward you won't get near me because I'm going to be behind you."

The light was hurting my eyes. I closed them. "Ask away."

"What is your name?"

"Jake Wanderman."

"Where were you born?"

"Brooklyn, New York."

"Where do you live now?"

"Sag Harbor, New York."

"Are you afraid of me?"

I was calm and felt fearless, yet at the same time I was afraid. I could have said I wasn't scared, but I didn't want to. "Yes."

"Why are you afraid?"

"Because you have power over me."

"Yes, I do. Now listen to me, Jake Wanderman. I promise you that you'll come to no harm if you tell me the truth. Do you believe me?"

I wanted to believe her. "Yes."

"Good. Now tell me about the cocaine. When and where did you get hold of it?"

I was feeling a little better. The headache had calmed down somewhat. It didn't bother me at all to tell her what she wanted to know. In fact, I wanted to tell her everything. "I got it in London. I'm not sure how long ago that was. I took it away from Margo."

"How did Margo get it?"

"It was there where Tony Oakhurst died. They found the body and Margo saw the coke and she grabbed it."

"Why did she give it to you?"

"She didn't want to. I told her she and Sarajane were not safe as long as they had it."

"Okay. Now you had the coke. What were you going to do with it?"

"I was going to give it to Shaved Head. I made a deal. But when I went to deliver it, he was dead."

"So what did you do with it after that?"

I had no hesitation telling her. "I flushed it down the toilet."

"You flushed it down the toilet?"

"That's what I said."

"You said you'd tell me the truth."

My eyeballs were still painful. They moved in their sockets like rusted ball bearings. I tried to turn around to look at her but I couldn't. "I'll say it again. I flushed it down the toilet."

"Where was this?"

"In the hotel in London."

"What was the name of the hotel?"

I tried to think but my memory was fuzzy. I couldn't come up with the name. "I can't remember."

"You're sure that you did this? You're not trying to fool me?"

"I had to get rid of it. Flushing it down the toilet seemed like the only thing I could do."

There was total silence for a while. Then I heard her get out of her seat and come around to the side of my chair. She stared long and hard into my eyes trying to read what was in my brain. I looked back at her, willing her to believe me.

She went over to the table where her pocketbook was and took out a cell phone. She dialed and walked out of the room. In a little while she came back and slapped me hard across the face. Then she slapped me again. "You fucking idiot! Do you know how much that was worth? A hundred and fifty grand. If you're telling the truth, you're going to pay for that. Believe me, buddy-boy, you're going to pay. Big time."

She went over to her bag again, reached inside, and took out a small rubber club. They called them saps in the old gangster movies. She tapped it against her palm a couple of times while she stared at me, probably contemplating the damage she was going to do.

"How will it help to beat me up?"

"It'll do me a lot of good. I'll feel a whole lot better knowing you're going to get what you deserve for sticking your nose into places it shouldn't go."

She came over and without warning whacked me on the side of my head. The pain was immediate. It felt like a lightning bolt. Then another blow got me on one cheek just under the eye. I closed my eyes and held my breath. I knew more was coming. Another crack on the head. It felt like she'd split it open. The pain was incredible.

I didn't know how much more of this I could take. Then came a shot to my arm, directly on the bicep. Once, twice, then the other arm. This was different from the throbbing in my head. It now felt like rivers of pain were flowing through my body. A wild cry came out of me. When I realized the sound was a scream, I did it again, as loud as I could, hoping someone would hear me.

"Go ahead," she said. "Yell some more, if it helps."

I could hear her breathing. The club hit my head again. A black pool appeared in front of me and I was glad to sink into its warm embrace.

CHAPTER 51

I opened my eyes. I was still in the recliner with my hands behind my back. I had no idea how long I'd been uncon- scious. The room was dark except for a small amount of light coming from a lamp on the desk. My arms and body were sore and my head was throbbing.

"I think you've done enough," I heard.

The voice was familiar. My eyesight was blurred but I managed to focus enough to make out that the voice I heard be- longed to Haley Sanford. She was looking down at me. Next to her was Frenchie, the sap still in her hand.

"I was told to do a number on him, right? I was just doing what I was told to do."

"That's right. And now I'm telling you to stop. Get him out of those handcuffs"

Frenchie took the key out of her bag and unlocked the cuffs. I took a deep breath. It was a relief to bring my arms back to a normal position.

"Okay. Now you can go."

"You want me to leave you alone with him?"

"Not to worry. He doesn't look like he could hurt a fly."

I had no doubt she was right about that. My headache was now like the screech of a hundred nails being dragged across a blackboard. My arms and shoulders were throbbing, All parts of my body seemed to have fused into one colossal wound.

She took Frenchie by the arm and they both went out of the room. I heard them talking but couldn't make out what was said. After a while I heard the front door close and Haley came back alone.

I pushed the lever and got the recliner to where I could sit up straight. "Thanks," I said. "It felt like I was turning into hamburger."

"She does have a way about her, doesn't she?"

"You might say that."

"I had to let her take your car. I hope you don't mind. But don't worry, we'll get it back to you."

"Sure. Whatever you want." I explored my head with my fingers, searching for cuts. There was something on the top of my head that felt like blood. My cheek hurt when I touched it but it wasn't bleeding. I squeezed one bicep where Frenchie had applied the sap and felt needles of pain slither through me, persuading me not to touch the other arm. "Your girl did quite a job on me. How come you stopped her?"

"Because what was done was done. I heard from Chantal about what you told her. Then Alice called me after she'd given you the sodium pentathol. Apparently you were telling the truth about flushing the cocaine down a toilet. So I decided that you didn't do what you did with malice and harming you wasn't going to bring the coke back. Alice didn't agree. In fact, she wanted to dispose of you altogether."

"Alice? Your girl's name is Alice?" I couldn't help smiling.

"What are you smiling about?"

"Hard to explain. I just pictured something more exotic, that's all." I tried to get up but my legs wouldn't support me. I sank back in the chair. "But you stopped her. How come?"

"Because it would've been stupid. It would have brought the police into it, and that's something we don't want."

"Whatever. Anyway, I thank you for stopping the slaughter."

"You're welcome. But there's something I want in return."

"Oh? And what's that?"

"I want you to find Julia Vincent."

"The mother? I thought you were finished with all that."

"I was. But I just heard what Chantal told you about Madeline's mother, something I'd never known before."

"You mean, that she was American?"

"That's right."

"How come she never told you?"

"It wasn't anything we ever talked about. Chantal and I became business partners. We had more important things to do than reminisce about old times."

I suddenly felt a weakness come over me. I rubbed my eyes. "Sorry. My brain is a little fuzzy. I didn't really take in what you said."

"It's understandable. Alice must've hurt you quite a lot. Can I get you anything? Maybe some water."

"Yeah. There's water in the fridge."

She went out and after a while came back with a bottle. I uncapped it and drank almost the whole thing. I hadn't realized how thirsty I was.

"Okay, tell me again. You said you want to find her. Why?"

"I have my reasons. They're personal."

"If you say so. But just how do you expect me to do it? She could be anywhere. She could've changed her name. She could've gotten married and have a new name. She could be dead. There are a thousand possibilities."

"Just so. But it's worth a try, isn't it? I'll even pay you for your time."

"What if I refuse?"

Her body stiffened. "That wouldn't be prudent, Besides, didn't I just save you from something worse than you already got? Show a little gratitude."

The last thing in the world I felt at that point was gratitude. What I wanted was to punch her out or at least shove a grapefruit in her face like Jimmy Cagney. "Did you kill Tony Oakhurst?"

"What kind of a question is that?"

"An important one." I couldn't work for her if she was a murderer.

"The answer is no."

"Did Chantal do it?"

"No."

"How about Frenchie? She's certainly capable."

"Who's Frenchie?"

"That's what I called Alice before I knew her real name."

"If she'd killed him, we'd have the cocaine, wouldn't we?"

"Unless she was scared off before she could take it."

"She didn't kill him."

"What about the woman in Tony's apartment in New York? The place was tossed and the woman was killed. Did Frenchie do that?"

"What difference does it make?"

"I like to know who I'm dealing with."

"She was only supposed to search the apartment. She wasn't told to kill anyone. Unfortunately, Alice has a tendency to violence."

"Tell me about it." The weakness came back. Along with it came a new wrinkle, nausea. The pain had grown into an enormous dull ache that went through my entire body. I fell back in the chair. Without consciously doing it, my eyes closed.

"Are you okay?" Haley said.

"I seem to have lost all my strength. I can't even keep my eyes open."

"Of course. It's a side effect of the drug Alice gave you. Why don't you rest a while? It will take some time to wear off."

Something was making noise. It was my cell phone on the table where I'd put it when I emptied my pockets. Then I remembered the tape recorder in my shirt pocket, I wondered if it was still working.

Haley picked up the phone and read the number to me. "Know who this is?"

"No idea," I said, although I was pretty sure it was Sienna. I tried to open my eyes, but couldn't. I managed to mumble some words before I felt myself sliding into the now familiar pool of warm blackness.

CHAPTER 52

When I came back to consciousness the room was dark. I was still sore but the headache had calmed down a little. I heard voices coming from the living room. It wasn't easy getting out of the chair but I managed it. I walked slowly into the other room and there they were, all of them: Haley, Frenchie (I still couldn't call her Alice), and Chantal. How could I not think of Macbeth's witches? *How now, you secret, black and midnight hags!*

The three of them looked at me with varying expressions on their faces. Chantal's look was neutral (she was good at that), Haley smiled, while Frenchie glared. I guessed she was still pissed at being deprived of giving me more of a working over.

"How are you feeling?" Haley said.

"Fantastic. Like I could do a triathlon."

"Why don't you join us? Would you like more water, or perhaps tea or coffee? Not alcohol. That wouldn't be good for you at this point in time."

Frenchie and Chantal were on my couch. Haley was on the love seat. I chose to sit on a chair away from them. "Water will be fine."

"There's some in the refrigerator. Get it for him, Alice, will you please?"

"Why me?" she muttered. But she went and got it.

"We've returned your car," Haley said. "Now let's get back to business. Are you going to do what I asked of you?"

"Do I have a choice?"

"I wish you wouldn't put it like that," she said.

"How else should I put it? You're putting the screws to me."

"I said I'd pay you, didn't I? That should count for something." She looked at the other women then back to me. "Let's not play any more games. You'll do the job. I'll pay any reasonable amount for your time. Will $500 a day cover it?"

Apparently, she was pressuring me and bribing me at the same time. As I saw it, I might as well accept the offer.

"Deal," I said. "But remember, the odds of my finding her are very much against us."

"Understood." She opened her purse and fished out a stack of bills. She counted out what she wanted and put the money on the coffee table in front of her. "There's two thousand for a start."

"How will I get in touch with you?" I said. "Are you going to be around here for a while?"

She took a small notebook out of her purse, wrote something, and handed it to me. "My cell phone number." They got up preparing to leave.

Before they went, I asked, "How long have the three of you been running this drug operation?"

"Why do you want to know?" Chantal said.

"It's none of your business," Frenchie said.

Haley laughed at them. "Idiots. You've already told him what he wanted to know. Clever, Mr. Wanderman. Now let's hope you can be just as clever at getting the information we're looking for."

CHAPTER 53

I didn't feel clever. My body felt as if bits and pieces inside were disconnected. I squeezed my eyes shut to try and quiet the throbbing in my head. I rewound the tape recorder and pressed the Play button. The voices were not clear. I knew that having it in my pocket was not the best way to record, but I hoped the recorder was good enough to overcome that. I could make out a lot of what Chantal had said, and Frenchie's voice was there, too. There was enough to help convince Sienna. That is, if she needed convincing. My thought was that it wouldn't be necessary once I told her what had happened.

It took all the energy I had left just to get into bed and pull the covers over me. I didn't get much rest because every time I moved a sharp pain woke me. I was glad when I finally saw the first pink glow in the sky that told me it was morning.

A long hot shower and strong coffee helped. My arms were swollen with an interesting patchwork of blue and purple markings. One side of my face had similar coloring. I gingerly explored the top of my scalp for cuts and swelling. It didn't seem too bad, but I felt pretty much a mess, a container full of aches and pains. Still, I was alive. And I expected to stay that way for a while since there was no longer any reason for them to do anything else to me.

In addition to that good news, I'd been given a job that I actually wanted to do. Now it was time to think clearly. Good idea, but my brain couldn't carry the ball. It was fuzzy and wouldn't cooperate. I was left with questions: What was it I had to do? What was it I could do?

The coffee table had the stack of bills on it to remind me of what had happened the night before, not that I needed reminding. I tossed the bills into a drawer in my desk just to get them out of sight. *What did I have to do? What was it I could do?* The questions tugged at me, nagging me. My cell phone was on the table, too. Sienna! I remembered the phone ringing and not being able to answer it. I opened it to see who'd made that last call. It was a number I didn't know. It had to be her. I should call her before she called me again. She'd want to know why I'd left those messages. But now I wasn't sure what to tell her. If I told her the truth, the worms in the can I'd open would run wild. I tried to think of a plausible story about why I might have been in danger and in need of her help without getting into everything else. What could that be? I tried to think but I couldn't manage it. Thinking about Sienna and a story to tell her only made my head hurt more.

As I stood there trying to think, the phone began ringing. I answered.

Of course, it was Sienna. "What was with those calls last night? You said it was urgent, but when I called you back you didn't even answer."

"I know, I know. I guess I was already asleep when you called back."

"Asleep? You were asleep at nine o'clock? If that's the case, what the hell was so urgent?"

"I always feel urgent when I talk to you."

"Cut the crap, Jake."

"All right, I'll tell you the truth." I closed my eyes and took a deep breath. Think of something, I thought. Think! "I wanted to talk to you. I wanted to hear your voice."

"George, the cop who called me, said you sounded very upset."

"Did I? I don't know how to say this. I'd been doing a bit of drinking. I'm ashamed, I really am. But I was feeling lonely. I thought of you. I think about you a lot."

"Jake, you have a way of pissing me off that's…Listen, if you ever do this to me again…never mind. Goodbye!"

She was gone. I felt bad about lying to her but at the same time I thought it still might be smarter to bite the bullet than tell her the truth about what was going on. Because that would mean I'd be asking for her help. I hated that idea for a lot of reasons, the most important being my pride. She'd saved my life once, wasn't that enough? Another reason was that it would mean I'd have to tell her everything. How would she react? I had a good idea—something like Mount Vesuvius going off. And since there was no longer any danger involved, I ought to be able to handle this on my own. I hadn't done a good job of it before but maybe this time would be different.

My brain was clearing up a little. I had to do something and the something was to do what the three witches had paid me for, investigate! Find Julia Vincent.

I was suddenly energized. I pulled on a jacket, locked up the house, making sure to set the alarm, and got into the Cabrio. I was on my way to see Valerie Venable. It struck me that she might have important information. She was close to Haley, wasn't she? Was it possible she was in on this drug business, too? Maybe yes, maybe no. My gut told me that either way there had to be some kind of connection.

Because it was a mild day I put the Cabrio's top down. I took Noyac Road to Jermain Avenue and then across to 114. I'd driven this way hundreds of times. It was a boring ride except for the sun and the breeze. It was also comforting that the rear-view mirror showed I was alone.

I couldn't help thinking about how Rosalind had always loved convertibles. When we finally had enough money for a second car, that was what she wanted. There weren't many days above freezing that she hadn't have it wide open to the air. "Don't you get cold?" I asked her more than once. "No. I love it. Besides I keep the heat on full blast."

Valerie's gallery was swarming with activity. It was filled with men and women dismantling SJ's installation. There was a lot of hammering and shouting of instructions. Dust clouded the air making my eyes sting. I wandered through the rooms trying to avoid getting hit by moving furniture as well as by the walls that were being taken down. I finally found Valerie and was surprised to see she was wearing jeans and a sweatshirt, not a hint of red anywhere. I guessed the red was for public occasions only.

She was cool, as usual, showing no surprise at my showing up suddenly. "Mr. Wanderman," she said. "I suppose you have a reason for being here?"

No pleasure either, it was plain to see.

"As a matter of fact, I do. I can see you're busy. Can you spare me a minute?"

"A minute, yes, but not much more than that."

"Thanks. I appreciate it. Could we go somewhere a little less noisy?"

She gestured for me to follow her. We went through a door into her private office. The room was small but showed that whoever decorated it had both style and elegance, as well as a lot of money. The walls were painted a dark plum color and were hung with paintings, some of whose names I recognized. I saw an Eric Fischl and a Warhol among them. Valerie moved behind am ornate walnut desk on which was, most certainly, an authentic Tiffany lamp. There was a small couch and a leather chair for the visitor. I sat in it and found it so comfortable I was all but tempted to close my eyes and take a nap.

Valerie sat in what seemed to be an even more luxurious leather chair and folded her hands together. "You look as if you had an encounter with a hard object. Nothing too serious, I hope."

"Right. Nothing too serious. Have you seen your friend Haley Sanford recently?"

"Yes. She's here on business. Why?"

"How about Chantal Badeau and Alice...I don't know her last name?"

"I have no idea who you're talking about."

"You don't know anyone named Chantal Badeau, or Alice, her diamond-studded friend?"

"No, I don't. And I don't like your tone, which suggests that I'm not telling you the truth." She began to push herself up. "I don't have to talk to you, you know."

"Please," I said. "Please sit down. I didn't mean to imply that you were lying or anything like that. If my tone suggested it, I apologize."

She sat down. "All right."

I tried a new approach. Frankly, I had no idea of what I was going to get out of this, but I hoped that by keeping the conversation going, something might happen. I felt like a detective on *Law & Order* trying to get the goods out of a reluctant witness. "Did you know Sarajane is coming back here?"

Her carefully plucked eyebrows lifted. "No. I didn't think she was able to come back."

"The cops have offered her some kind of immunity. All she has to do is submit to questioning about the murder."

"She's no longer a suspect?"

"That's what they say."

"That's very good news. I like Sarajane. I respect her as a person and as an artist."

"Did you know anything about her being involved with Tony Oakhurst?"

"Of course not. If I'd known that I would never have hired him."

"Did you know anything about Oakhurst at all?"

"Only that he was a celebrity chef who got a lot of publicity. He seemed the ideal choice for our opening."

"You mean, Haley never said anything to you about him? Ever?"

"What could she have said? Are you suggesting she knew something about him?"

"Only that he once had an affair with a woman she was in love with. And that he probably raped her as well."

She sat up straight, her eyes opening wide. "You mean he raped Haley?"

"No. He raped the woman Haley was in love with." I watched Valerie closely to see if there was any response to what I was going to say next. "Her name was Madeline Vincent. Have you ever heard that name before?"

Valerie's cool didn't desert her. "No. That name doesn't mean anything to me. I find this all very hard to believe. Where did you get this information?"

"From the horse's mouth. Haley herself."

She shook her head in apparent disbelief.

"How many years have you and Haley been doing business?"

A pause before she answered. "A long time. More than ten years, I should think."

"And you never talked about anything personal? All you ever talked about was business?"

"Of course not. We socialized a bit, but we never became close friends. Perhaps because our personalities were quite similar, I think. We're both Type A. We're entrepreneurs. We want to succeed. Talking about our personal lives was not what we did. It was just outside our focus."

"That's exactly what Haley said. How do you feel about that now? Don't you think she might've warned you about the kind of man you were dealing with?"

"Why would she? This show had nothing to do with Haley. I never discussed it with her."

"What about after Oakhurst was murdered? When you were in Paris?"

"You know. It never came up."

"Well, I have news for you. I think I can tell you why it never came up." I leaned forward to give my words emphasis. "Because Haley didn't want it to."

"And why was that?"

"Because your business associate, Haley Sanford is in more than the art business."

"I suppose you're now going to tell me she's a drug dealer."

She got me with that one. "You mean, you know she is?"

Without answering, Valerie opened a drawer in her desk and removed a small notebook. She turned pages for a while. "Ah. Here it is. This is my business diary. I made this note three years ago, in November of 1997. I saw some people in her gallery who didn't look as if they belonged there. I can't explain why. Haley was off in a corner with them and when I came in. She abruptly stopped talking and rushed toward me. They left immediately. Haley was not quite her usual composed self, at ease and in complete control. I sensed something was wrong. I asked her if everything was all right. She reassured me that everything was fine. Just a little problem with a supplier. Later that night, the scene stayed with me. I made this note. The note was a question. The question was, 'Is Haley doing drugs?'" She smiled at me. She had the satisfied look of someone who'd just swallowed something scrumptious.

"So you're pretty smart, aren't you? You suspected something that long ago?"

"I didn't really. I never looked at or thought about that note again." She stood up. "I must get back to work. All this won't help me get things right out there."

"Wait a minute. There's more."

She opened the door. "Not today, there isn't."

CHAPTER 54

Cool. That's what she was. And infuriating. Damned infuriating. I never got a chance to talk about Julia, Madeline's mother. She said the name Madeline Vincent didn't mean anything to her so I suppose she would've said the same thing about Julia Vincent. The thing is, that as cool as she was, I had no doubt she was holding out on me. I was sure there were things she knew that she wasn't willing to tell me. That left me disgruntled, because I had no idea how to pry anything more out of her. I'd hit her with the big one about Haley's drug business but she hadn't even blinked. She said she didn't know about it but went right to the note in her diary that all but says she did know.

I drove home with the top still down but didn't enjoy the ride. I was too busy feeling bitter and frustrated as well as aware of my aches and pains. What was I going to do next? When I got home, I reluctantly switched on the computer. I'd start my search for Julia Vincent there. The problem with that was that the computer was an unwelcome stranger in my house. I had it because I thought I ought to have it. But I hardly ever used it. Like the cell phone. I was not adept. If I needed information, I still had to go to the library.

I Googled Julia Vincent, the name Chantal had given me and got more than I bargained for. There were Julia Vincents all over the place, in all parts of the country. I immediately realized I had to add something to narrow it down. Of course, even if I did get some meaningful hits, it could still be a wrong way street. The woman could've married, could've changed her name, could have died. All distinct possibilities, but since I had nothing else I decided to keep plugging away. I tried "Julia Vincent France." That didn't do much. Then I found a sponsored site that traced people for money. The good thing was that even without payment they had photos, and more important, a list that included age. That was my first break. I could figure out her probable age based on when her daughter was born. Again, I had to make an assumption that Julia was somewhere between eighteen and twenty-five when she had the baby. I could see Madeline Vincent's gravesite and the gravestone as if I were standing right there. Madeline Vincent was born in 1974 and died in 1993. Assuming her mother was around twenty in 1974, that would mean she was born in 1954 or thereabouts. We were now in the year 2000 so the arithmetic narrowed Julia Vincent's current age to somewhere between forty-five and fifty.

I went back to the list and focused on those ages. There were too many to even try counting them. My frustration with the process was increasing by the minute. Besides, my eyes were having trouble reading the characters on the screen. I suddenly realized I was tired. I looked at my watch and noted with astonishment that I'd been at the computer for more than three hours. Abruptly, I was once again conscious of my body and how much I was hurting, courtesy of little Alice. It wasn't right that a vicious bitch like that should be named Alice. But what's in a name, right? *A rose by any other*...Some rose. A two-headed thorn was more like it. I wished I were the type to hunt her down so I could beat the shit out of her. But that wasn't me. If I found her in the act of doing something bad, then maybe I could do it. But I doubted it. I'd get more pleasure out of seeing her in jail.

I saved all the information I'd found in a file I named JuliaV, not very original, and switched off the computer. I thought about eating but I wasn't hungry enough to go to the trouble of cooking. I didn't even feel like having a drink. Wow! I didn't want to eat and I didn't want to drink. I was sure a long way from getting back to normal.

I searched the freezer and found a container of onion soup I'd made some time ago. I had no idea how old it was but didn't care. I had a baguette in there, too. I defrosted a piece of the baguette and heated the soup. When the soup was hot, I dropped the bread into it, added a few drops of extra virgin, sprinkled a little Parmesan on the surface, and found the dish more than satisfying. I hit the sack, hoping to get a better night's sleep than the one before.

In bed I had another idea. Sienna might be the answer to the search. All I had to do was convince her to get some computer nerd in her department to do the search for me. That ought to be a breeze, right? No problem. I think I was smiling at my own joke as I fell asleep.

CHAPTER 55

The next morning the phone rang showing a caller ID I didn't know. It turned out to be Haley Sanford, wanting to know how I was progressing.

"Slowly. But I'd like to know something. I asked Valerie Venable if the two of you had ever talked about Oakhurst's past and she said no. Is that true?"

"Entirely true."

"How come? You've known each other for years."

"The subject never came up. I certainly wasn't going to talk about him, especially when I learned she'd hired him to do the opening at her gallery."

"Of course. You were doing business with him. And Valerie knew nothing about your other activities?"

"Nothing. I don't think she'd have continued working with me if she'd known. She's very straight-laced."

"I've got what might be bad news for you, then."

"What's that?"

"I told Valerie about you."

Her sigh was loud enough for me to hear. "I suppose it was inevitable that she'd find out some day, it might as well be now. I'll have to call her and see how she's taking it. Chantal has gone back to Paris, by the way."

"How about little Alice? Did she go too?"

"No. Alice stays with me. She makes an excellent body-guard."

"Anything else she does for you?"

Her voice became harsh. "Don't be disgusting, Mr. Wanderman."

"Sorry, I'm the nosy type. Was she with you the last time you were here?"

"You already know the answer to that. Now I'd appreciate your not interrogating me. I'm paying you to do a job that has nothing to do with either Alice or me."

"I hope that's true. If it isn't, there's going to be a lot of trouble. Now, if you'll excuse me, I've got to get to work."

I hung up on her. The woman pissed me off. In fact, all the women in this case pissed me off. Except for Sienna, of course. In her case, I pissed *her* off, or so she said.

The phone rang again. Morty. Good, I needed a friend. I regretted that I hadn't paid enough attention to him since I'd been back. Sure, I'd been distracted, but he was the one who'd gotten me into this in the first place. I owed him contact, at least. "What's up?"

"Good morning to you, too, asshole," he said.

"What's your problem?"

"How about saying hello, or good morning, or how the hell are you?"

"You got me at a bad time, Morty."

"Never mind. I'm calling to tell you Sarajane and Margo are here. They're staying with us. We called the lawyer, what's-his-name, to set up an appointment with the cops. You want to be there, don't you?"

"Absolutely." A thought came to me. This gave me a good excuse to call Sienna and maybe get back into her good graces. "Tell you what. How about I call Detective Nolan? See if I can speed things up a little."

"Right. That good looking babe. Do I imagine it, or do you have the hots for that lady?"

I had no idea he had so much as an inkling. "What are you talking about?"

"Don't give me that bullshit. This is your old buddy you're talking to. You're different when she's around. You're as tight as a violin string. And I'll bet she knows it, too."

"All right, all right. I'm not denying it, but nothing's happening. We are definitely not an item. So don't tell the Post's Page Six. Okay?"

He didn't laugh at my feeble joke but he agreed to keep his thoughts to himself and we said we'd be in touch as soon as either of us heard anything from the law.

CHAPTER 56

I called Sienna, using the cell phone number I'd remembered to save. She answered on the first ring.

"How'd you get this number? Never mind. I know. I called you so it's on your phone. What do you want this time? Nothing urgent, I hope."

Her attitude was as bad as Morty's. I needed a suit of armor this morning. "I heard that Sarajane is back. I wanted to know when you're going to do her interview. I want to be there."

"I don't think so. Her lawyer is enough."

"Her father wants me there. That ought to count for something."

"Counts for *nada*, Jake. This is a murder investigation."

"But you already said you're not going to charge her with anything."

"I didn't say that. I said she was no longer a suspect unless something new turns up."

"What if her lawyer won't let her answer any questions?"

"She made a promise to answer questions, so that's not going to happen. If she tells all she knows, I'll be satisfied."

Ugh. What if Sarajane mentioned the dope? Would they try to get her on some kind of charge? Destruction of evidence? Obstruction? I had to speak to Morty and the lawyer about it. I mentally slapped myself. Why didn't I think of this before?

"Okay. I hear you," I said. "Now I've got a favor to ask."

"Aha! The real reason for your call."

"You're a cynic. I wish you wouldn't be, where I'm concerned." I hoped she heard what I was really trying to say. Then I explained about looking for Julia Vincent and what I'd done on the Internet. I told her who Julia Vincent was and that Haley Sanford was an art gallery owner whom I'd met in Paris and that I was working for her. "She wants to find this woman for personal reasons. I want to find her because I think it could help in learning who killed Tony Oakhurst."

"I don't see the connection."

"I could explain but it's complicated. Also, I don't want to have an argument with you about this. But at least go along with the idea that I may be right. I'm not good with the computer. I'm uncomfortable and slow as molasses. What I'm asking is that maybe you could get some computer maven cop to do this research. I'd really appreciate it."

"You're kidding, right? Get a cop to do your job?"

"It would take me forever. It would probably take him a few minutes."

"Jake, you don't know what you're asking. This is a busy cop shop. Nobody has time to fool around."

"Everybody has time to fool around. It's government, isn't it? Don't tell me you're all busy all the time. Not possible. What do you say? Do me this favor."

There was a pause. That was a good sign, I thought. At least, she wasn't instantly telling me to take a flying fuck.

"I'll see what I can do. What did you say that name was?"

I repeated Julia Vincent's name and the age bracket I was looking for, between forty-five and fifty-five.

"I don't know why I'm even considering doing this," she said. "If I get anywhere with it, I'll let you know."

"You're the sweetest thing alive," I said.

"Don't push it, Jake," she said, hanging up.

CHAPTER 57

I notified Morty that I was not going to be allowed at the interview. It was to be the girls and Jeremiah Longwood, the lawyer. Nobody else. Then I told him my concerns.

"Thanks for that, Jake. I'll bring it up with Longwood. He should know the whole picture."

"Let me know how it turns out."

My worries about Sarajane and the dope turned out to be unnecessary. There was no fall-out, at least as far as the law was concerned. Forensics had shown that Tony Oakhurst had a snootful of coke in him when he died. They'd also found traces of cocaine on Sarajane's and Margo's clothing, so it wasn't exactly a surprise for them to learn about Margo's theft. What they'd really wanted was confirmation of what they'd guessed all along. Sienna let them go with just a warning to stay out of trouble in the future.

Morty was okay with it, too. He understood my not telling him was for his state of mind and not just to keep him out of the loop.

But Sienna was not okay with it. Not one little bit. She appeared at my house with steam coming out of her ears. *What sudden anger's this? How have I reaped it?* I knew how I'd reaped it.

"You blindsided me, Jake. I'm so mad I can't see straight. And all along I thought you were working with me, not against me."

"I *was*. But I couldn't tell you about the dope. I had to protect Sarajane, didn't I?"

"You could've told me once the two of them were out of the country."

"Right. If I'd told you, what would you have done? You wouldn't have let them off the hook. They'd still be in London, afraid to ever come here again."

We were in my kitchen. The sun was coming in through the windows, bright and cheerful. I hoped it might change her attitude. Instead, she suddenly did a double take and looked closely at me.

"What's the matter with your face?"

"Oh that. It's nothing." I'd forgotten what I looked like. The swelling had gone down but of course, some of the color still showed.

"It looks bruised. What happened to you?"

I tried to avoid answering. "Want some coffee? Espresso?"

"Come on. It looks like you've been holding out on me in more ways than one." Those green eyes were burning a hole in me.

"I apologize. Sincerely."

I was on shaky ground. I wanted to be honest with her but I also wanted her on my side. Only I didn't know how to get her there. I ground some beans and poured them into the gizmo that fit into the espresso machine I'd picked up on sale at Target. I'd never given a thought to an espresso maker but no way could I resist a bargain.

"Am I going to hear an explanation, or not?" she said.

The machine began making hissing sounds and then gurgling. It was telling me to make up my mind. "Okay. You deserve to know everything. Have a seat."

I started at the beginning. I told her about London and Shaved Head and the deal I'd made with him. I told her about his murder. I told her about my interviews in Paris and what I'd learned. I told her about Haley and Chantal and Frenchie. I told her how I'd almost been killed in the Paris alley. And I told her about Chantal and Rowdy Hall and what had happened with Frenchie. I reached for the tape recorder intending to play it for her so she could more fully understand, but I changed my mind. She didn't need to hear any more.

Her gaze was directed down at the table. A single tear had escaped and trickled down her cheek. I reached out and smoothed it away with my finger. The espresso was ready. I poured it into cups and put one in front of her.

"They tortured you?"

"Nah. More like an old fashioned whupping."

She raised her cup and sipped from it. I wondered what she was thinking. Something was happening in the air around us. It suddenly felt as if we were at a crossroads. There would be a new direction, a new path. Our lives were going to change. I drank some coffee, enjoying the familiar bitter taste.

"I thought you were smart," she said. "But you're a fool."

"I know. *The common curse of mankind, folly and igno-rance.*"

"How could you let all this happen without saying a word? You could be dead and nobody would have a clue as to who did it and why. What in God's name is wrong with you?"

"That's what my Dad said when I lit a fire inside the pi-ano."

"You did what?"

"I was only four years old. I thought it was fun."

"Yeah, but it was a harbinger of things to come."

"You're wise beyond your years," I said.

"There was no way you should have done any of this alone."

"You're absolutely right."

"You could've been killed."

"But I wasn't."

"Pure luck. Not any of your doing. If I'd been there, I could've stopped them."

"I tried to get hold of you, remember?" I sipped the last dregs of coffee. "But you know, it may have worked out for the best. If you'd been there, they wouldn't have done anything. At least, not then. The way I figure it, now they have no reason to do me harm. They want me, they need me."

She held her cup with both hands. "I wonder about that, too. But maybe you're right. In any event, you're still a fool."

I leaned across the table. She allowed my lips to make contact with hers. Our lips touched, my body sang—aches, pains, disappearing as if by magic.

It seemed that only seconds had passed when she said, "I have to leave."

"Why?"

"I don't think I can handle this right now, Jake."

She stood up and headed toward the door. I followed and took hold of her arm. "Stay," I said.

Her eyes were still moist. "I can't." She reached into her purse and handed me some papers held together with a clip. "I almost forgot. This is what you were asking for."

I glanced at what she'd handed me. The worksheets for Julia Vincent.

CHAPTER 58

I watched her drive away. I stood in the doorway staring at the garden, noticed that a shrub had to be moved, then closed the door, and went back to the kitchen. I paid no attention to the papers she'd given me. Instead, I thought of how her lips had pressed back against mine. And how utterly delectable they tasted. There was *witchcraft* in those lips, *elegance in a sugar touch of them*. So much so they made me think vaguely of a future.

In spite of that kiss and my request, she hadn't stayed. It was clear she was troubled. I thought it might have something to do with her boyfriend, the one I'd seen her with the year before. A youngish guy, handsome, could've been a male model. She'd broken up with him but I remembered her saying they'd gotten back together again. Maybe he was the reason her cell phone had gone unanswered.

I looked again at the list she'd given me. There were fifteen Julia Vincents in the right age grouping. They were scattered all over the country. One in upstate New York, two in Florida. One each in Pennsylvania, Ohio, Oklahoma, North Dakota, Arkansas, Louisiana. California had three.

How could I find out if one of them was Madeline Vincent's mother? I had their addresses, their phone numbers, in some cases a brief note about careers, arrest records, marriage, children. There were even photos of some of them. Unfortunately, none of that information did me any good. The only thing I could think of was to call each one with a story that would make them give up that kind of information. I needed something to motivate them to open up.

That was the key. What was it that everybody wanted? Money, of course. But I couldn't just offer to pay them for that information. If I told them I'd pay, they could lie. I needed something to help me determine the truth, yet always bearing in mind that the Julia Vincent of Paris may no longer even exist.

I got up and paced around the house trying to come up with an idea. Nothing. It didn't help that my brain was cluttered with images of Sienna.

I needed a break. I got the bike out and pedaled around for a while, not going anywhere in particular, just letting the road take me wherever it wanted to go. Riding randomly like this, I often found neighborhoods and houses I'd never seen before, even though I'd biked in the area for so many years that it didn't seem possible I hadn't seen them all. But there they were. New houses springing up all the time where undeveloped land had been before. It hurt to see another part of the forest with its trees and evergreens disappear and, in its place, yet another overly large house surrounded by massive rows of manicured privet.

I was headed home, riding on a quiet street in North Haven. There were no bike paths here but the area had little traffic so there was no worry in that regard. I was pedaling at a moderate pace when I heard the sound of a car approaching. The sound got louder quickly. The driver was going fast, very fast, because in another second it sounded like it was right behind me. I turned my head and saw with horror that the front end of the car was headed right at me. I had no chance to get out of the way except to dive off the bike. I let go of the handlebars and hurled myself into the air. As I did the car flew by. I landed hard on a patch of weeds and grass and felt the breath go out of me. I rolled over on my back. My heart was banging away inside my chest and I was sucking air as fast as I could get it in. From a distance I heard a funny sound, like a thump, then a screech of tires. After a while my breathing began to slow down. I got up. I was shaking. My knees were wobbly. I was wearing biking shorts so my legs were exposed. There was blood oozing out of a cut on my right leg. My arms had scratches on them but other than feeling bruised all over, nothing felt broken. I always carried tissues and bandages in my bike bag. I got a tissue and pressed it hard against the cut. When I thought the bleeding had stopped I pasted on a Band-Aid.

I was okay but not my bike. The rear wheel had been run over and bent into more of an oval than a round. I stood it up. The wheel wobbled but it turned enough to be able to walk with it. I was about a mile from home. It would be a hike but not too bad.

The car had come and gone too fast for me to identify it. I thought from the very quick glance I'd had before jumping, that it was foreign, maybe a Mercedes or an Audi, but I couldn't be sure. The only thing I was sure of was that it was gray.

I stopped at the corner where the car had disappeared. Just inside the street and very close to the road was an oak tree with slashes on its trunk. The sound I'd heard must have been the car hitting the tree. The poor tree would survive but I imagined the car had a couple of scars. That ought to help in locating it, right? All I had to do was find a gray foreign make with scratches on the passenger side and I'd have the culprit. A breeze!

I began to continue walking when I saw what looked like a hubcap on the other side of the street. I crossed over. I had no way of knowing if it was from this car, or if it had been there for a long time, but when I picked it up and saw a Mercedes logo I felt it had to be from the car that tried to run me over. The hubcap must have come off from the jolt of hitting the tree. I put it in the bike basket and headed for home.

When I finally got there, I made sure all the doors were locked even though I knew it was only a gesture.

The fact was that someone had tried to kill me. It couldn't have been Haley and Frenchie again, could it? That didn't make sense. They'd just let me off the hook. Why would they go after me again? Then who? And why?

This time there was no hesitation about Sienna. I called her cell and told her what happened in detail, making sure she knew I wasn't hurt.

"Someone tried to run you down? Hit and run, you mean?"

"That's right. Someone tried to kill me."

"Just a minute. You don't know that. The car never touched you, right? It could've been a reckless driver."

"I'm telling you, he was heading straight at me."

"Or a drunk driver."

"Why don't you believe me?"

"I didn't say I don't believe you. But looking at it from a police perspective, this is what they say. You weren't hurt. You've got no plate number, no paint scratches, no ID, there's nothing to prove attempted murder or even assault. As for the hubcap as evidence, they wouldn't even invoice it. You can't even be sure it came from the same car."

"That's your perspective. Mine is, I know someone was out to kill me and I mean to find out who."

"And how are you going to do that?"

"Beats me. But a starting place might be trying to figure out the why."

"That's easy. You're dangerous."

"What are you talking about? I'm the sweetest, most lovable guy in the world. You're the only one who doesn't know that."

"This is no time for your so-called humor. Someone thinks you're a danger to him, or her. Think about that."

"Right now, the only thing I'm doing is trying to find this Parisian girl's mother. I told you about that. You think that might be the connection?"

"I don't know. Anything else you're involved in?"

"Well, there was all that stuff about the cocaine, but I thought that was over and done with."

"Maybe not. Maybe there's a thread that links to that."

"That's a big maybe. By the way, you said they wouldn't even look at the hubcap, but you could, right? Maybe you can at least tell me what year and model the car was."

"Maybe, I don't really know. But if you get it to me, I'll turn it over to the auto people and ask them about it."

"Okay. I'll drive it over right now. Are you in your office?"

"Yes, but I'll be at a meeting. Just leave it at the front entrance and mark it with my name."

"Will do."

I got a brown shopping bag and used a Sharpie to write Sienna's name on it with exclamation points. I was extra cautious leaving the house, driving to the Headquarters building where I left the hubcap as directed. I kept looking in the rearview mirror and at the cars alongside of me

While driving, I tried to think who might want me out of the way. There hadn't been that many people I'd been in contact with since this whole thing started. In Paris I'd thought it was Frenchie behind the knife attack. But there was no way she'd do anything on her own. She was working for Haley then and now. Could Haley have set her on me? But Haley had just hired me to find Madeline's mother, so even if she had, why would she send Frenchie after me again? That didn't make sense, unless her hiring me was a just a cover.

Could it be Chantal? Again, I couldn't see why. She'd given me real information. What about Valerie Venable? I'd pressed her a couple of times, in Paris and now here. Could she have a reason for not wanting me to find Madeline's mother? What about Morty's wife, Sherrie? Sherrie was no angel. She'd been involved with stolen Faberge eggs. And there was Margo? She certainly had no love for me, especially since I'd taken her candy away. Sarajane? Now I realized I was stumbling around like a man in a pitch-dark room. My best friend's daughter? His wife? Ridiculous. Or was it?

I needed to talk to someone. Who better than my best friend?

"How about a drink?" I said, when he answered the phone.

"Sure. When?"

"Now?"

"Give me an hour. I'll meet you at the American Hotel."

What could I do for an hour? I was wired and needed activity. The sheets of paper were lying in front of me. I looked at the names again. An idea suddenly popped into my head. I could call these women. I could pretend to be a lawyer with an inheritance to give away. The recipient would be Julia Vincent. I wouldn't have to say who was giving the money away. Just that it came from France, from Paris, specifically. All the real Julia Vincent had to do was convince me that she was in Paris in the early 1970's when Madeline was born.

It was a long shot, I knew, but why not try? I decided to use my cell phone so there'd be no ID they could trace to me, even though they'd have the phone number. I made up a name and a story and wrote it down so I wouldn't goof by forgetting who I was.

The first one I called was in North Dakota. The phone rang six times before someone answered. A quavering male voice said hello.

"May I speak to Julia Vincent?"

"Afraid not. She's dead. Died a while ago. Are you some kind of a weirdo?" Click.

Great start. Didn't even give me a chance to practice my routine.

I tried Pennsylvania next. This time a woman answered.

"I'm looking for Julia Vincent," I said. "My name is Martin Baron. I'm an attorney with the firm of Farrington and Hubbell, Attorneys-at-Law. Are you Julia Vincent?"

"Yes. What is this all about?"

"I've been retained by the estate of Madeline Vincent. There's an inheritance left to a Julia Vincent."

"An inheritance? How much is it?"

"Substantial. But obviously, it's vital that I determine you are a rightful heir before we can go any further. Do you have a relative named Madeline Vincent?"

"Well…I'm not sure. I have to think about that."

"What do you mean? Either you have one or you don't."

"Umm. Well, I guess I don't."

"Thanks for your honesty. Goodbye."

I looked at my watch. Those calls had taken only a couple of minutes. I had time for more.

Some of the people I called next were suspicious. "Is this some kind of scam?" I was asked. I did my best to convince them it wasn't but I wasn't always successful. I was hung up on, cursed a couple of times, the end result being that not one of those I called had any connection with a Madeline Vincent.

And then I came to one in California that seemed promising. A man answered the phone. When I asked for Julia Vincent he said she was out and wanted to know who I was and why I was calling. When I told him I could hear the excitement in his voice.

"How much is it?"

"Substantial. But there are many questions to be answered before I reveal any more."

"Sure," he said. "I understand. What do you want to know?"

"I think it would be more appropriate if I spoke to Ms. Vincent herself."

"I'm her brother, Miles Vincent. I know everything about her. What is it you want to know?"

"Did she have a relative named Madeline Vincent?"

"Yeah. Absolutely. We have a cousin named Madeline. My uncle's daughter."

"Has Julia Vincent ever been in Paris?"

"Paris, France?"

No, I wanted to say, Paris, Timbuktu. "Yes."

"She loves Paris. Goes there all the time."

"What about your cousin, Madeline? Does she go to Paris, too?"

"Madeline? Is that important?"

"Just answer the question."

"I think so. Yeah, sure. Madeline loves Paris, too."

"That's nice. When was Madeline there last?"

"A couple of years ago, I think."

"Wrong answer," I said.

A few minutes later, my cell phone rang. I saw that it was the number I'd just called. I answered, just for the hell of it.

"Fuck you!" he said.

I deserved it, I guess.

In the end I called every name on the list and got zip. For all that effort, I'd accomplished nothing. I was totally in the dark and out of ideas.

CHAPTER 59

The American Hotel is in Sag Harbor, on its Main Street, which consists of one block of stores, restaurants, and a movie theater on one side and two short blocks of stores, banks, and restaurants on the other. I set the alarm before I left the house and checked the rearview mirror as I drove, even though it was only a couple of miles to the village.

Sag Harbor and the hotel have a long history. The town was busy in Revolutionary times and thrived again in the 19th century when whaling was a major industry. When whaling died, the village went on hard times, reviving for a short period when the Bulova company opened a factory, only to go downhill again when the factory closed. The hotel had been there through the years, although it, too, went through good and bad times. Now it was an elegant inn with a great restaurant, bar, and one of the best wine cellars in the world.

Happy Hour was in full swing. The bar was noisy and crowded but I managed to squeeze in close enough to order a Stoli on the rocks. When Morty came in he got his usual Dewars. We found a place to sit away from the bar and clinked glasses.

"Hey," he said. "What happened to you? Looks like you ran into a building."

"Something like that. That's one of the reasons I wanted to see you. Can I tell you a story?"

I didn't wait for his answer. I told him what happened on the bike that day and then everything else. The telling took a long time.

"Holy shit! Are you okay now?"

I nodded.

"All I can say is you've been busy. But I'm pissed that you waited until now to let me in on this."

"There was a lot going on. I didn't have time to think."

"Yeah, yeah. Bullshit. But since you're my old buddy, it's water over the bridge, or is it under the bridge? Whatever. What are you going to do?"

"I wish I knew. Somebody's after me but I don't know who and I don't know why."

"The way it looks to me is that it's got to be tied up with this mother thing. Somebody doesn't want you getting into it."

"I think so, too."

Morty drank some of his scotch. "You know, about the car that hit the tree? I'm thinking that if it's local, maybe you can find it."

"How?"

"I don't know. Walk around the streets and look for a Mercedes with dents and also missing a hubcap."

"Say what? Are you out of your mind? What are the odds?"

"Not as high as you'd think. Assuming, of course, that it's a local car."

"Give me a break."

"What've you got to lose? Take a few hours and cruise around. You've got Sag, Bridgehampton, Wainscot, Water Mill, East Hampton, Southampton, Amagansett, maybe Montauk. You drive around the shopping areas. It's a long shot but it's worth a try, isn't it? If you want, I'll even help you out."

I couldn't help smiling and shaking my head. "You are a piece of work, old buddy. That's the craziest idea I ever heard."

Morty laughed, his jowls shaking a little. He really needed to lose some weight. "I'll drink to that."

We both did.

"I got another idea," he said.

"What? Rent a helicopter with a telescope?"

"Always the smartass. No. You said there was a relative in Paris. A brother of the girl who killed herself?"

"Not her brother, her mother's boyfriend's brother."

"Well how about getting in touch with him? He ought to know something. Something that might help."

"Like I just look in the phone book and find him? I don't think so." I swirled the ice around in my glass, thinking. "You know, you might have something there. But I'm not going back to Paris again. Besides, I don't speak enough French to get any-where, even if I found him."

"So..." Morty held out his hand as if inviting me to follow him into another room.

"Of course. Get the Parisians to do it. Did I ever tell you you're brilliant?"

"Dozens of times. But you can tell me again."

CHAPTER 60

When I reached Haley she was in the city. I told her what I wanted her to do in Paris. "When are you going back?"

"I'm leaving tonight."

"Good, the sooner the better. This man, the father's brother, may have information that could help us."

"Yes, it's possible. I can't guarantee that I'll be successful, but I'll certainly try. I'll start on it as soon as I get back."

"By the way, someone tried to run me over. You wouldn't know about that, would you?"

"Are you serious? Someone tried to kill you?"

"Exactly."

"Of course, I didn't have anything to do with that. Haven't I just hired you to work for me? And given you a couple of thousand dollars, as well?"

"Just asking."

"Why does someone want you out of the way?"

"I'm wondering the same thing."

I no sooner hung up when my cell rang. It was Sienna.

"I don't have much info for you on that hubcap. They told me that even though it has a Mercedes logo, it would fit on some other cars, too, that are not Mercedes. But if it is actually from a Mercedes, their best guess is that it's fairly new, that it probably came from an E class model. I don't know how much good that'll do you."

Just hearing her voice stirred up a lot of feelings. "Thanks. It may help. But there's something else on my mind. I need to talk to you."

"Jake—" She stopped.

"When you were here the other day, something happened. You know that."

"Yes. I do know."

"Then let's get together and talk about it. It won't do either of us any good to keep this buried."

"My life's very complicated right now. I don't need any more permutations and combinations."

"This is not a mathematical exercise. I'm talking about us. You and me. Something good might come out of this if you give it a chance."

"I'm not so sure about that."

"Can we at least talk about it? That's all I'm asking."

A long silence followed. I wanted to urge her to make a decision but felt the best thing to do was keep still and wait.

"All right," she said, at last. "All right. Should we meet at the diner again?"

I was almost lightheaded. "Anywhere you say. I don't care."

"It's convenient."

"When? Can you go now?" I checked my watch. "It's almost seven. How about 8:30?"

"Okay. But, Jake, I said we can talk. But that's it. Don't expect miracles, because there aren't any."

"Maybe not, but if not miracles, there are always dreams. *All days are nights to see till I see thee. And nights bright days when dreams do show thee me.*"

"Very pretty," she said.

CHAPTER 61

I took a shower and changed my clothes. What was I going to say to her? What would she say to me? I barely remembered to set the alarm when I left and had to force myself to check for a car following me while I drove. For these moments, at least, nothing else in the world mattered.

In spite of that, or maybe it was because of that, thoughts of Rosalind broke in. Was I doing a disservice to her memory? When my sister's husband died, she told me she couldn't think about another man in her life for years. In fact, it was fourteen years until she remarried. And after a friend of mine had been gone a few years I asked his widow if she was seeing anyone. She told me she had no intention of ever marrying again. "I can't bear the thought of another man touching me," she said.

I knew in my heart that Rosalind wouldn't want me to feel that way. We'd been very physical—touching, hand holding, kissing. After more than a year without a woman—except for that one brief encounter with Sienna, and a couple of mild flirtations with two others—I was more than ready. In fact, I knew the need was even stronger than I wanted to admit.

I pulled into the diner's parking lot, feeling nervous, anxious, unsure of myself. I'd forced her to meet me here and now I was at a complete loss about what to do or say.

When I stepped inside the entrance, I saw that she was already in a booth. She was staring out the window. The overhead light shone on her red hair. There was a feeling of sadness about the scene that reminded me of a Hopper painting. I sat down across from her and mumbled, "Thanks for coming."

She turned toward me, a look of concern on her face. "Are you okay? I know I didn't seem very sympathetic about what happened to you. But I really do care. You must be pretty shook up over the whole thing."

I forced a laugh. "Yeah. It's not every day a car gets to run over my bike."

"Thank God, it was only your bike."

"At least, it was a Mercedes that did it, not some cheap econobox."

"Sure. That's important. You weren't hurt at all?"

"A few scratches, that's all."

The waitress dropped menus on the table and we went through the ritual of looking at them. I had no appetite but felt I ought to have something. I was surprised when Sienna ordered only an English muffin and coffee. I ordered the same. If her ability to eat was impaired, that could only mean she was truly upset. Whether that would be good or bad for my cause, I didn't know.

When the coffee and muffins arrived, I avoided talking by fiddling with the package of marmalade, getting it open, and spreading it on the muffin. I hoped Sienna would say something first, thinking it would make it easier for me. But she was doing the same thing, in no hurry to get any kind of discussion going.

Finally, I said, "I really appreciate your coming tonight."

"You already said that."

I cleared my throat. "Right. Okay, let me tell you what's on my mind. You know my wife died some time ago. I was very much in love with her. For a long time I had no thoughts about another woman in my life. It was something I didn't, or couldn't, contemplate." Okay, I was lying. But just a little bit. "Then you came along. You know what happened. I've come to realize that I care a lot about you. I think you have feelings for me. Am I right or wrong about that?"

Her mouth was full at that moment so I had to wait until she swallowed before she could speak. "You're not wrong."

"I'm not wrong. Is that what you just said? Then what's the problem?"

She took a long deep breath. "I've had a long relationship with someone. It's been going on for almost five years."

"I know that. But now I'm guessing it's over."

"Yes, otherwise, I wouldn't be here. The thing is, this is not the first time we've broken up. It's happened a few times. But somehow we've always gotten back together."

"Only this time you won't."

"That's what I want now. But my problem is that he's always had this power over me."

"Power over you? Hard to believe."

"Maybe. I can only tell you there were times I wanted nothing more than to get away from him. And so I did. Then after a few months, he'd begin calling, sending me flowers, telling me how much he loved me, how he couldn't live without me. And it worked. I'd go back."

"Phew! And you're afraid it might happen again?"

"That's just it. I don't know. I think I'm over him. The problem is I'm not a hundred percent sure. I keep thinking, what if I start a new relationship and then have that old feeling again? It wouldn't be fair to you. Don't you see? I'm just not sure enough of myself to do that."

I reached across and took her hands in mine. "You can do it. I know you can do it. And if we're together, it ought to make it easier."

She shook her head. "Not yet. I can't do it yet. I'm just not sure enough of myself."

"What? Sienna Nolan? The tough lady cop? Not sure of herself?"

She managed a smile. "Not so tough, after all, as you can see."

I slid out of my side of the booth and moved over to hers. I kissed her. She kissed me back. We sort of smiled at each other.

"Now what?" I said.

"Give me time. That's all I ask."

"Of course. Take all the time you need. I wouldn't dream of putting pressure on you."

She squeezed my hand. "You're so sweet."

I squeezed back. *"The hand that hath made you fair made you good."*

She shook her head. "You do amaze me sometimes. But to change the subject, what are you going to do about what's been happening? I wish I could give you some help, but my hands are tied. All I can suggest is that you've got to seriously watch your back."

"I'm going to do more than that."

"What do you mean?"

"I'm going to find this guy, whoever he is."

"How are you going to do that?"

"I have an idea."

"What is it?

"I'll let you know when I've worked it all out."

"I hope it's a good one. Not the kind that gets you into more trouble."

"I'm with you, kiddo."

CHAPTER 62

I didn't sleep well. Not surprising with all the thought processes racing through my brain. I felt conflicted about Sienna. She seemed to respond to me but at the same time I had a sense of something uneasy emanating from her. I wondered if she was ever going to be able to break away from this guy. I sure hoped so. That was about all I could do about it.

On the other hand, the idea I'd mentioned was bugging me. I wondered why I hadn't thought of it before. The car that went after me had looked fairly new. It occurred to me the owner would want to get it repaired ASAP. A clean car shows no evidence and it also eliminates the need to explain how the car got damaged in the first place.

Right after my bagel and coffee, I got out the phone book and looked up the local auto body repair shops. There were fewer than a dozen locally. They were in Southampton, Water Mill and East Hampton. All I had to do was what I'd done before trying to find Julia Vincent. Only this time, instead of being a lawyer, I'd be a cop.

I decided to become Detective-Sergeant John Corcoran of Suffolk County PD. I'd tell them I was looking for a fairly new foreign car that had been in an accident. There would be some damage to one side. I was pretty sure it had to be the passenger side because the car had struck the tree on the right side of the road. I'd also tell them the car was gray and that it might be missing a hubcap. I had to say "might" because I still couldn't be sure the hubcap I'd found came from that car.

The body shop people bought my story of being a cop without question. It took four phone calls before I struck gold.

"Yeah, Detective. I got a new Mercedes in yesterday. A 2000 E-320 sedan, gray, just what you described. It's got scratches and dings on the passenger side and it's also missing a hubcap."

"Who brought it in?"

"A lady. I assume she's the owner."

"Can you give me her name?"

He didn't hesitate. "I'll get the paperwork. Just a minute." I waited until he came back. "The name is Valerie Venable."

I almost dropped the phone. "You're sure about that?"

"Yeah. I got a deposit with her credit card, so I'm sure."

"Did you start working on it yet?"

"Yeah. She said she was in a hurry."

"Too bad. How much did you do?"

"Most of it. Haven't gotten to the paint yet, though."

"All right. It would've been better if you hadn't touched it, but that can't be helped now. There's one more thing. It's very important you keep quiet about this phone call. The owner mustn't know and nobody else either. Understand?"

"Yeah. I get you."

"Okay. Thanks for everything. And don't forget what I said. Not a word to anyone."

Valerie Venable's car? Could it really have been her? I never saw the driver. Jesus! Now I had to do some serious thinking. Why would she want me out of the way? Why was I a threat to her? Could it have anything to do with the drugs? Unless everyone was lying, that wasn't it. Then it had to be connected with Madeline Vincent.

Madeline Vincent…her mother, Julia Vincent…could Valerie Venable be Julia Vincent? Wow! I had to give some thought to that. After a few minutes of running things through my head, it seemed to me that it was possible, even more than possible. The age was right. The daughter, Madeline was how old when she died? I hadn't forgotten the dates on the headstone. Born 1972 – died 1993. That made her twenty-one at her death. If Julia Vincent, the mother, was a student at the time, then she herself would have been in her late teens or early twenties. We were now in the year 2000, so that would make her around fifty. VV appeared to me to be in her fifties. It was Venable who hosted the show for Sarajane. It was Venable who made all the arrangements for Tony Oakhurst to come to her gallery. Why? To murder him, of course. If she was Julia Vincent, she had reason enough for murder. Revenge on Oakhurst for driving her daughter to suicide. It all fell into place, didn't it?

Excited now, I Googled Valerie Venable. There were pages of information about her but nothing that tied her to anyone named Vincent, nothing that tied her to Paris twenty-six years before. All I had was conjecture, not one element of proof. I needed Sienna more than ever. With all the information I now had, I was sure she'd want to get into this. She had a lot more experience than I had. Maybe she could come up with an idea.

Before I could get to Sienna there was a call from Haley.

"I made contact with this man. Or rather Chantal did. I thought it would be better for a Frenchwoman to handle the situation and I was right. She persuaded him, as only Chantal could, to tell her all that he knew. A few hundred euros helped, as well."

"What did he have to say?"

"Not much. His brother met a woman named Julia at the Sorbonne where they were both students. They were studying, among other things, art, and culture. They had an affair which resulted in the girl becoming pregnant. His brother wanted to marry her and keep the baby but Julia would have none of that. She broke up with him, refused to see him, but took money from him for support. Unfortunately, the brother was killed in a traffic accident. She had the baby, and the rest you know."

"So she put the father's last name on the birth certificate. Tell me a little more about you and Valerie Venable."

"Like what? I thought I'd made clear to you that she was not involved with my other business."

"That's not what I want to know. What I'm interested in knowing is whether she was aware of Madeline Vincent and what happened to her." Valerie Venable had been shocked when I'd told her about Oakhurst raping Madeline. I waited anxiously while she pondered my question.

"You know, I'm not sure. I might have told her the story at some point. Then again I might not. But you know, we did talk a lot about the old days in Paris. Wait a minute." Her voice became charged with excitement. "Now I remember. She told me she'd once studied art at the Sorbonne. My God. Do you think she could be Madeline's mother?"

"That's exactly what I'm thinking. But at the moment, I have no way of proving it."

"I can't believe it. Why wouldn't she have told me?"

"Maybe she had revenge on her mind."

"What are you saying?"

"I'm not saying anything."

"Are you suggesting Valerie killed Tony Oakhurst?"

"I have no proof of anything like that." I wanted to keep the information that Venable had tried to run me down to myself.

"Of course. We have no way of knowing if any of this is true. But it is something to think about, isn't it?"

"Yeah. In the meantime, mum's the word, right? We keep all this to ourselves. I'll let you know what, if anything, develops."

"Yes. Good work, Jake. Do you need more money? You've earned it."

"Money is not what I need right now. But thanks."

I was sure of everything now. Valerie Venable had studied at the Sorbonne when she was a girl. It couldn't be a coincidence. There'd been no mention of it in Google but that was because her name then was Julia whatever.

I called Sienna and happily, found her in the office. "Got to see you right away."

"Jake. I thought I made it clear last night that I needed time."

"This is not about us. I've got something serious to tell you and I don't want to use the phone."

"You want to come here?"

"Right. Stay where you are. I'm on my way."

CHAPTER 63

I drove directly to police headquarters in Yaphank. I'd been there before so I knew the drill. I announced myself to the cop behind a glass front. He picked up the phone and made a call. A few minutes passed before he called my name and I was buzzed into the main building.

Sienna was waiting for me. She was wearing a plain black pant suit that might have made her look forbidding, but for the pale yellow silk blouse underneath the jacket. She didn't smile or hold out her hand. Her eyes met mine for an instant before she looked away. "Follow me," she said.

We went down long corridors that eventually led to a stairway. We walked up a flight, down another long hall and finally entered a room with six desks and bright fluorescents overhead. Three of the desks were occupied by men too busy or not curious enough to look up. "Let's go into an interview room," she said.

The lighting in here was a little softer. It was a plain room with nothing in it but a table and chairs. "Gives us a little more privacy," she said.

We both sat, she on one side of the table, me on the other. She'd brought a notepad and a pen with her. "Okay, Jake. I'm listening."

I didn't go back to the beginning because she knew all that. But I told her again of the car trying to hit me and how I'd suspected it had collided with a tree when getting away from the scene. "So I called the local body shops, thinking the owner would want to have it repaired right away. And I found it."

"You found the car?"

"Right."

"How can you be sure it's the same car?"

"It has to be. I saw the color. I recognized that it was a foreign make and then I found the Mercedes hubcap. Remember?"

"I think I told you the last time, you couldn't be sure the hubcap necessarily came from that car."

"That's right. I wasn't sure. Except that the body shop told me the car they were repairing was missing a hubcap. Also it had scratches on the passenger side, the side that hit the tree. Come on. How much more do you need?"

"They told you the name of the owner?"

"Yes. And here is where it gets interesting. The owner of the car is Valerie Venable."

"The woman who owns the gallery? Why would she want to kill you?"

"Good question." I told her what Haley had said about Valerie going to school in Paris at the right time. "Here's the kicker. I'd bet the house that she's Julia Vincent, the mother of the girl who was raped by Tony Oakhurst."

"That a big bet."

"It has to be her. And that's why she wanted me out of the way. I told her I was looking for the mother."

"So what if she's the mother? How does that explain anything else?"

I was getting exasperated. Why couldn't Sienna see what I thought was so obvious? "Her daughter committed suicide after she was raped. Tony Oakhurst was the rapist. That makes it likely that she plotted to get revenge on Oakhurst for what he'd done."

"You're saying she's the one who murdered Tony Oakhurst?"

"Exactly. She enticed him here to the opening and then she killed him."

"Whoa," she said, holding up her hands. "You're jumping to a whole lot of conclusions. Didn't the rape happen a long time ago? If she wanted revenge, why would she wait so long?"

"I think it's because she wasn't aware of what had happened. In fact, she didn't know anything about her daughter. I think she found out through her association with Haley Sanford, the woman who owns the gallery in Paris."

"How would that work?"

"In the course of doing business together, she heard the whole story about this girl, all about her being abandoned by her mother, growing up in an orphanage. At some point, she must have made the connection and realized it was her daughter that Haley was talking about. I think she looked further into it and finally recognized the truth. I'm positive she visited the grave. There were flowers left there the same time she was in Paris. Why would she go to the grave if she didn't have anything to do with the girl?"

"How do you know that she was the one who went to the grave? And how do you know she left flowers there?"

"I don't know. I have no proof. But it makes sense to assume it. I went to the cemetery. Venable was doing business in Paris at the time. There were flowers on the grave. Fresh ones. I know Haley didn't put them there because I asked her. So who else could it've been?"

"Her family?"

"No way. They wanted nothing to do with the girl. Haley had her buried. And Haley also said that, except when she herself brought flowers, she'd never seen flowers there before."

"It's a good story, Jake. But it's all theoretical. And I mean highly theoretical. Off the charts, you might say. I don't mean to be negative but you have no proof of any kind."

"I know that. That's why I thought you could help. Maybe we can trap her in some way."

"Come on, Jake. You've been watching too many movies."

"Maybe. But as I see it, the only way to find out is by action. Listen to my idea before you say anything else. Okay?"

"I'm listening."

"My idea is that I go to see her and tell her I know everything. Meanwhile, I'm wired and you're listening to the whole thing. Maybe I can get her to talk."

"That's a big maybe. If she's smart enough to have pulled off this murder, with all the planning it took, why would she suddenly become dumb and tell you everything?"

"It's not a question of smart and dumb. It comes down to emotions. She's been carrying out this revenge plan for a long time. Who knows how long? Maybe years. It's been eating at her and eating at her. Finally, she gets it done. The rapist is dead. She did it. And she got away with it. But suddenly there's an insect in the soup. Jake Wanderman comes poking around, asking questions. She gets upset. She tries to kill him to keep herself safe. It doesn't work. Now here he is again. He walks in on her and tells her he knows everything. He describes her life to her in detail. Wow! He does know everything. She's blown away. She breaks down and confesses just to get the whole thing off her back." I looked at Sienna for a reaction. "Well? What do you think?"

She shook her head. "Too much conjecture. Not enough to go on."

"Give me a break. What've you got to lose? It won't cost you much, will it, to wire me?"

"You don't know what's involved, Jake. It isn't simply putting a wire on you. Actually, we don't even do that anymore. We've got a lot more sophisticated ways of recording. But to make the surveillance works in a court of law, we have to do things a certain way. And how do I get my boss to authorize it?

"Does he have to know?"

She shook her head. "You are too much."

"If you don't think he'll go for it, don't tell him."

"You want me to lose my job?"

"All right. Then convince him. It's a long shot, but if I turn out to be right, you've caught yourself a murderer. Isn't that worth a gamble?"

She doodled on her pad. It looked like flower petals. "Tell you what I'll do. I'll talk to my boss. I'll run the whole thing by him and see what he says. That's the best I can do."

"Fair enough," I said. "When can you do it? Like now?"

"No. He's not here. I expect he'll show up later today." She stood up and held out her hand. "I'll do my best, Jake. I promise."

I took her hand in mine and pressed it. At least I was touching her. "I know you will."

"I'll show you the way out," she said.

I didn't understand why she was being so formal. I wanted to put my arms around her. I wanted to tell her how wonderful she was but her coolness held me back. I walked quietly after her until we came to the exit. Then before she had a chance to object, I gave her a quick kiss. "Thanks for everything."

There wasn't anything else I could say.

CHAPTER 64

Two days went by without my hearing from Sienna. I knew it wouldn't be wise to call. I felt she was on my side and would do her best to help me. My pushing her wouldn't do any good. I passed the time cooking, riding my repaired bike, punching the bag, lifting weights, doing my Korean exercises, and of course, reading Shakespeare.

I opened a book of Shakespeare's sonnets. As always I went first to #116, one of the greatest poems in all literature.

> *Let me not to the marriage of true minds*
> *Admit impediments. Love is not love*
> *Which alters when it alteration finds,*
> *Or bends with the remover to remove:*
> *O, no! it is an ever-fixed mark,*
> *That looks on tempests and is never shaken;*
> *It is the star to every wandering bark,*
> *Whose worth's unknown, although his height be taken.*
> *Love's not Time's fool, though rosy lips and cheeks*
> *Within his bending sickle's compass come;*
> *Love alters not with his brief hours and weeks,*
> *But bears it out even to the edge of doom.*
> *If this be error and upon me proved,*
> *I never writ, nor no man ever loved.*

I didn't like leaving the house but when I did I was very careful to observe my surroundings. I made sure not to let myself do anything or go anywhere that might make me vulnerable. I didn't really expect another attack from VV. I had the feeling she was waiting for something to happen and then she'd figure out a way to respond.

The call from Sienna came at last.

"Well?" I said.

"I can be very persuasive when I want to be. It took a lot of arm twisting. But I finally got the go ahead."

"That's great," I said. "What comes next?"

"We have to set up a time and place. The place is very important. We've got to have a controlled environment."

"What does that mean?"

She laughed. "It means we want somebody watching to make sure nothing bad develops. It would be embarrassing if she managed to kill you while you were attempting to get her to talk. Not only that—"

I cut her off. "Wait a minute. It would be *embarrassing* if I got killed? That's a hell of a way to look at it. Think how I would feel?"

"Don't worry. We're not going to let that happen."

"I sure hope not."

"Anyway," she went on, "in order to make the evidence work in court we have to follow certain protocols. If I'm called on to testify, I have to be able explain what device or devices were used, how, when and where they were placed. Before we start, I put an introduction into the record. Like, *I am Detective Sienna Nolan of Suffolk County Homicide. Today is October 1, 2000. It is 4:35 p.m. and we are recording a conversation between Jake Wanderman and Valerie Venable at the Hole in the Wall Café.* After it's all over, I do the same stuff again, the idea being that I observed the conversation and am able to identify both parties."

"Okay, I get it. Where do you think we should do it?"

"A public place that's not too noisy."

"Why not her gallery then?"

"Umm…I suppose I could hang out there and look at the art work while you're taping her. But she might recognize me. I interviewed her right after the murder."

"You could change the way you look, couldn't you? Wear a wig, glasses, something like that?"

She gave the idea some thought. "I could do that. No problem."

"She has an office in the back. That's where I spoke to her last time."

"That's not so good. You'd be in a room with the door closed."

"Well, she'd hardly do anything drastic there, would she? Try to kill me in her own gallery?"

"Anything is possible. But wait, I have an idea. Maybe we can do it there, after all. I can set you up with a video device as well as a recorder. That way we'll be able to see what's going on as well as hear you. I'll just have to be careful."

"Yeah. I get you. But it's not that difficult, either. I can set up a meeting with her at her place. You can be in the gallery at the same time. You can be a potential customer. Right? Wouldn't that work?"

"I think it would."

"Okay then. Suppose I call her and set up a meeting. When's the best time for you?"

"Set it up for the middle of the day when it's likely people will be around. That'll make it safer."

"I'll get back to you," I said.

CHAPTER 65

I was excited. My heart was pumping so hard it made me dizzy. I called the gallery and was told she wasn't there. I asked when she'd be back. They didn't know. I waited an hour and phoned again. Still not there. I left a message for her to call me.

The afternoon dragged. I kept going into the kitchen to look at the clock. The second hand ticked as if it were struggling to advance. *And so from hour to hour, we ripe and ripe, And then from hour to hour, we rot and rot.*

The excitement I'd felt before wore off, replaced by lethargy. Then a sound from heaven, the trill of the phone. I grabbed at it and looked at the caller ID. It was my father. I couldn't help feeling disappointed. And then, of course, I felt, what else? Guilt. I'd promised to keep in touch with him and it had completely slipped my mind. Sure, there were good reasons for that, but when it came to my father, reason of any kind was out of the question.

"Well, sonny, what've you been up to?" He was too subtle to ever directly accuse me of being a terrible son. "Everything all right with you?"

"Hi, Dad," I said in the most upbeat voice I could produce. I was in advanced middle age but sometimes, where my father was concerned, I was fourteen again. "Yeah. Fine. How're things with you? And Zeena, of course. Everything smooth?"

"Why shouldn't they be?" He always answered a question with a question. "She's a wonderful gal. I don't know what I'd do without her."

"Indeed she is. I'm glad you recognize that."

"Of course, I recognize it. Do you think I'm some kind of an ignoramus? I know how old I am and I know how young she is. But she stays with me for a reason, doesn't she? And I can tell you it's not pity. I hold my own. I give her everything she wants. In every way, if you know what I mean. You can be sure of that."

"Okay, Dad. You don't need to spell it out for me."

"And what about you? Are you getting any?"

"It's none of your damned business. And the answer is no."

"That's not good. Not good for the body. Not good for the brain. A man needs to have sex on a regular basis, otherwise everything in him dries up. You hear what I'm saying?"

"Unfortunately, yes."

"So what's happening with that murder case? I keep looking in the papers and on the TV but there's been nothing about it anywhere."

"It's moving along, but slowly." I was tempted for a moment to say more but resisted the urge. The slightest wrong move could ruin everything. I didn't mind lying when it was important.

"That's good, in a way," he said. "At least, it means you're safe and I don't have to worry about you. At least, in that way."

"You got it, Dad. Not a thing to worry about."

"Good. Oh, by the way, did I tell you Zeena's pregnant? You're going to have a baby brother."

"What!"

He laughed. "I'm kidding. Just wanted to see if you're paying attention."

"When haven't I ever paid attention to you? I love you. You know that."

"I know. But it would be nice if you called me for a change. Take care of yourself. And don't forget to let me know if anything happens. Especially if a woman comes into the picture."

"I'll be sure to do that, Dad."

After we'd hung up, I still had the phone in my hand. I dialed the number for the gallery again. I got the same person on the phone I'd spoken to before. I identified myself. "Did you give Valerie the message I left?"

"Yes."

I got really angry. "Now listen to me. This is damned important. I want you to tell Valerie that this is not an idle phone call. She's in a lot of trouble. You tell her there'll be hell to pay if she doesn't get back to me. And I don't mean some time in the future. I mean right away. Got it?"

I cut off the call before she could answer. I was taking a chance talking about her being in trouble. But I felt I needed to do something to shake her up. If she wouldn't make contact with me, how could I set up a meeting? If no meeting, all the police gadgets in the world wouldn't matter.

I waited to hear from her but night came and nothing from Valerie. Why? Did she know something? Could the guy in the body shop have talked? I doubted it. I had to think of something else to get her to talk to me.

That night I double-checked every door and window before going to sleep. Because of the message I'd left, I wasn't taking any chances. Who knew if she might decide to try to finish me off one more time?

In the morning, I decided what I was going to do. I only hoped it would work and that Sienna wouldn't kill me if she heard about it. If it worked, she wouldn't have to hear about it.

I went to the gallery. Before anyone had a chance to stop me, I walked straight into her office. She looked at me from behind her desk without any change of expression. It was almost as if she'd been expecting me. She wasn't wearing her signature red. But she was fully made up, and as composed as always.

"You're becoming quite a nuisance, Mr. Wanderman. You keep pestering me with phone calls and if that isn't enough you're now here in person."

"You'll wish all I was doing was pestering you."

"What is that supposed to mean?"

"I know who you really are," I said. "And I think you know what that means."

I left immediately. I didn't want to have to say anything more. Certainly not without the benefit of Sienna and her wiretap.

I went home and waited to see if the strategy had paid off. I'd barely had time to make myself a cup of coffee when the phone rang.

"What did you mean when you said you know who I really am?" Valerie said. She sounded a little less cool than usual. "Are you playing some kind of game? What is it you want?"

"To talk."

"What do you want to talk about?"

"I think you know."

"I don't know anything. You're the one who thinks he knows something. So talk."

"Not on the phone. In person."

"All right. Where and when?"

"How about your office tomorrow at one o'clock?"

"Very well," she said. "Tomorrow at one."

I called Sienna and told her.

"I'll be at your house in the morning with all the equipment. We'll set everything up then."

CHAPTER 66

Sienna arrived wearing a long-haired, black wig and glasses. I was surprised at how different they made her look. Along with her was a young man she introduced as her partner. "This is Diego. Diego Palmer."

He shook my hand. Diego was a stocky kid in his late twenties, with dark curly hair and a powerful grip.

"Let's get to work," Sienna said. She opened her briefcase and took out what looked like a ballpoint pen. "Put this in your shirt pocket."

"Is this a tape recorder?"

"Right. It's digital. Tape is a thing of the past." She showed me a pair of ordinary-looking glasses. "Try these on. Let's see how they fit."

"What are these for?" Then it struck me. "Oh, I get it. Is there a video camera in it?"

"Bingo. There's one in the frame. We'll be able to see whatever you're looking at."

"They fit all right but they feel funny."

"Doesn't matter. They're plain glass. Like the ones I'm wearing"

"What if Venable notices them. She's never seen me wear glasses before."

"If she asks, just tell her you wear them occasionally. Like when your eyes are tired."

"I hope that works."

"It shouldn't be a problem. Lots of middle-aged people do that. No offence."

I held my tongue. "None taken."

"Now here's the plan," Sienna said. "Diego's going to be in the car, monitoring both the video and the sound. I'll be in the gallery with an earpiece. We'll both be able to hear you. If Diego sees something happening that I should know about, he'll alert me."

"Sounds good," I said.

"First, let's do a test. Speak a few words. And look to the right and to the left."

"*It is the cause*," I said. Why Othello's words came to me, I didn't know. "*It is the cause*."

Sienna nodded. "Good to go."

They followed me to Venable's gallery in East Hampton. As I drove, I recognized that something was going on inside my head. I was beginning to feel less sure of myself. The closer we got to the gallery the more my previous heroic-like feelings about this operation began to change. Here I was, an aging, retired teacher making out like I was Sam Spade. I was walking into the lion's den with my only protection a pair of video eyeglasses and a tape recorder. Was I nuts?

I parked and checked my watch. It was a few minutes to one o'clock. Just to be certain the gadgets worked, I spoke a few words out loud and looked back, getting a nod. I clamped my teeth together and took a deep breath.

I knocked once on the door to Valerie's office and walked in. A second after I sat down she said, "I never noticed you wearing glasses before. How come?"

Was she on to me already?

"You're very observant. I guess that comes from looking at art all the time." I gave her the answer we'd agreed upon and held my breath.

"Umm," she said, not indicating one way or the other whether she believed me or not. Tell me something," she went on. "Are you planning on taping this conversation?"

I tried my best to make my face look innocent of guile. "No. Of course not."

"I want to believe you. I really do. But just to make sure, empty your pockets."

"You're kidding."

"Most definitely not."

"You're a pretty suspicious person, aren't you?" I stood up, took everything out of my pockets and put them on her desk: wallet, handkerchief, coins. I added the pen, too.

"Good," she said. Now take off your shirt."

"Now you are kidding."

"Not one bit."

I took my shirt off, happy the cops were no longer using body wires.

"Now drop your pants."

"I think you're being ridiculous."

"Perhaps, but indulge me."

I let my pants down, and pointed to my underwear. "You want to see the rest?"

"No thanks."

"Your loss."

"There's something else I've decided," she said, after I was dressed again.

"What's that?"

"I've changed my mind about where we're going to have our little talk. We're going to talk in my car."

"You're something else. Do you think I bugged your office for God's sake? How could I do that?" I returned everything to my pockets and the pen to my shirt.

"I don't know and I don't care. We'll talk in my car or not at all."

This was just what I'd been worried about. Something un-expected screwing up the works. I hoped Sienna and Diego were getting all this. "Okay. You're the boss."

She stood up. "Come with me."

Now she pulled another surprise. We went out through the back of the gallery. I never knew there was an exit that way. I was sure Sienna didn't know either. What was going to happen now? I had to find a way to give them some clues.

There was a parking space behind her gallery. Sitting there like a gray ghost was the Mercedes she'd used when she'd tried to kill me. We got in and I said, "Where are we going?"

Without answering, she drove out onto Main Street and turned south.

"It looks like we're heading toward the ocean," I said, hoping Sienna was getting this.

Just past Guild Hall she turned left. I'd driven this road once or twice but never took notice of its name. Now I saw the street sign. "So this is Dunemere Lane," I said. "I've driven here before but never knew the name of it."

We passed part of a golf course. It was the Maidstone, of course, one of the most famous golf clubs in the world. She turned right and drove past some large homes that looked as if they were already closed for the winter. Millions and millions of dollars' worth of real estate sitting empty for months at a time waiting for their ultra-rich owners to return for the season.

"Are we heading for the beach?" I said.

Venable didn't answer.

After a few minutes we came to a small parking lot with spaces for a couple of dozen cars. None of the spaces were occupied. A sign had the name, "Wiborg Beach" on it along with a notice that parking there required a permit from May through September. The beach was there but you couldn't see it from the lot.

"Wiborg Beach," I said out loud. "Who was Wiborg?"

"Haven't a clue."

She shut off the engine. It was suddenly very quiet. I could hear the waves coming in to the shore. I understood now why she'd chosen this location. If she had killing in mind, this would be a good place to do it. We were completely alone. Nobody would see or hear a thing.

CHAPTER 67

"Okay," I said. "This is where you wanted to talk. So let's do it."

"Yes. Let's. But you go first. You're the one who initiated this."

I turned and faced her, hoping the video and the recorder were working. Looking at her this way, even though I knew she had murdered someone, I couldn't get myself to believe she would kill me in cold blood. Maybe that was wishful thinking.

"Okay, Valerie. Here it is. I know who you really are. I know all about you. Everything."

She laughed. "Everything? I doubt that."

"Well, let's start with one thing. I know that your name wasn't always Valerie Venable. That's right, isn't it?"

She was silent for a moment. "Suppose it is, what difference does that make?"

"Your name was Julia. Julia Venable, or something else?"

"It doesn't matter."

"Maybe not. But it was Julia. And you became Julia Vincent when you needed a name to put on a birth certificate."

"If this is what you have to say, then we're done. I'm not going to sit here and listen to this garbage."

"Don't bullshit me. You came out here because you wanted to find out what I know. Well, you're going to find out that I know a lot. For one thing, I know that you tried to kill me once. Maybe you have it mind to do it again."

"You're being ridiculous."

"Your car was in the repair shop recently. How come?"

"I had a slight accident."

"Right. You sideswiped a tree in North Haven, just after you tried to run me down on my bike."

"You are more fantastical by the minute. Somebody hit me in a parking lot."

"They hit you hard enough to dislodge a hubcap?"

"Of course not. I lost my hubcap some time ago when I hit a pothole. I'm sure you're aware of how many potholes there are out here."

"Yes. Lots of potholes. So maybe I can't prove you tried to kill me but I can tell you why you could have a motive."

"Go on. This might be entertaining."

"You realized I was snooping around when I interviewed you. You became afraid that I'd learn the truth about you and Madeline Vincent."

"Who is Madeline Vincent?"

"You're cool," I said. I glanced out the window. The sun was bouncing off the asphalt of the parking lot like shards of glass. "Madeline Vincent was your daughter."

"I don't have any children."

"When you were a girl you were a student at the Sorbonne. You were called Julia then. You had an affair. You became pregnant and had a child, a girl. You named her Madeline. You put your name on the birth certificate as Julia Vincent because the father's name was Vincent. But you didn't want the baby. You abandoned both her and the father. Then you came back here and began a new life as Valerie Venable." I looked closely at her. "How am I doing?"

"You should write science fiction. You have a feverish imagination."

"There's more. You knew nothing of Madeline. You thought she was out of your life forever. But your work took you to Paris where you began doing business with Haley Sanford. Somehow, perhaps in conversations, you learned about Haley and a girl she'd been in love with. Her name was Madeline Vincent. You'd abandoned her and never expected to know of her again. Now you heard about her and about her death." I paused. "Am I right so far?"

Valerie said nothing.

"You went to the cemetery, to her grave. You put flowers there. And then you learned more details. You heard about Oakhurst and what he'd done to Madeline. To your *daughter*. You felt he caused her to kill herself. You hated him for it. Of course, you hated him. It was an entirely human reaction."

I looked at Valerie to see how she was reacting. I couldn't tell because her face was turned away from me. But I felt I was getting to her.

I went on. "There he was, king of his world, in spite of what he'd done. If only there were a way to make him pay for his crime. There should be a way, shouldn't there? You thought about it. For how long, I don't know, but eventually you came up with your grand idea."

Valerie had slumped in her seat. She was still looking away from me. The waves were still murmuring. She seemed to be lost in memory.

"You investigated him," I said. "You learned everything you could about him. You found out he was a doper and guessed he was involved with Haley. You came up with a brilliant plan. Hire him to be a celebrity chef at your gallery opening. He would be in your gallery at all hours of the day and night. All you'd have to do is wait for the right moment, perhaps when he was high. It wouldn't be difficult for you to arrange things to get him alone. And once that happened, you'd have your revenge. Ah, how sweet that must have been when the time finally came."

A sound came from her. It was a groan that seemed to have all the sorrows of the world in it. She continued to stare out the window.

Then she spoke: "Yes, that was the plan. What I hadn't expected though, was to find him leaning against the kitchen counter, dazed, and bleeding from a cut on his head. I asked him what had happened. He began cursing Sarajane. 'She attacked me,' he said. 'And what the hell are you doing here, bitch?'

"At first I didn't answer him. I saw the knife on the floor and picked it up. In that split second, that actual moment when I took hold of the knife—I hadn't been sure I could go through with it—but then I knew I could. I said, 'For all the women you abused, but especially for my daughter, you're going to die.' He looked confused. 'What?' He held up his hand as I went toward him. Then he turned and tried to run away. I used all the strength that was in me—that was the most exhilarating moment of my life." She closed her eyes for an instant.

"But a few seconds later I was horrified by it. I thought he'd be dead but he wasn't. He'd fallen down, blood was spurting all over. He was making horrible noises. Grunting, groaning, unintelligible words coming out of him. It was all I could do to keep from screaming." She shivered. "At that point, all I wanted to do was get out of there. I didn't care whether he lived or died. But I knew enough to protect myself. I wiped the handle of the knife, made sure I didn't step into any blood, and ran out as fast as I could. I wasn't worried about the night watchman. I knew he was a rummy. I'd given him a bottle of rye as a present and put knockout drops in it, too."

"Then what did you do?"

"I went home. It wasn't until the next day that I heard what happened."

"When you found out they'd arrested Sarajane, weren't you concerned about her? Didn't that bother you?"

"Not really. I felt it was only a matter of time before they learned she was innocent. Actually, I was sorry Haley hadn't stayed. If she hadn't gone back to the city, she might have been a suspect."

"You are a cold piece of work," I said.

"Perhaps." She opened her handbag. "So now you know you were right. Does it make you happy?"

"Not a bit," I said.

She took a gun out of her purse. It was a sweet little thing, like a toy, pink with a black barrel. She pointed it at me.

"Very pretty," I said, trying to act cool. "I've never seen a pink gun before. What kind is it?"

"It's a Taurus 738. I joined a gun club after I bought it. I've gotten quite good at shooting."

"I don't doubt it. But if you're planning on killing me, you'd be making a big mistake."

"Why? You're the only one who knows anything. Am I right?"

"No. You think I came here on my own? The cops are right behind us."

"Is that so? Then where are they?"

"They're coming. They'll be here any minute. If they find me dead, you're finished. But with the kind of rat Oakhurst was, and a trial, you've got a good chance of getting off. Who knows what a jury would do?"

"Actually, I wasn't planning on killing you."

"Then what?" I suddenly got it. She was going to take her own life, not mine. "No, Valerie. That would really be stupid. Don't do it. I'm telling you, you've got a great chance if there's a trial."

"Get out of the car," she said.

"Okay, I will. But tell me something first. When you started doing business in Paris, did you ever think of trying to find your daughter?"

"Do you really want to know or are you just stalling, hoping something will happen?"

"Both."

"An honest man. How unusual. But I'll answer your question. I thought about my daughter a lot. I wondered how she'd grown up, what she was like, what she was doing. I even paid a visit to the convent where I'd left her. They wouldn't tell me anything. They said the records were sealed."

"What about the father? Why didn't you marry him and keep the baby?"

"Please. He was a child himself. Beautiful but spoiled, vain. He would have been hopeless as a father. I knew I couldn't bring her back to The States with me. There'd never be a chance for a career. I left her at the orphanage with the birth certificate. I listed the mother's name as Julia Vincent. I went straight from there to the airport. When I got home I changed my name to Valerie Venable. I thought it had a nice ring to it."

"When you found out about your daughter, did you think about telling Haley you were the mother?"

"Of course not. You don't go broadcasting the rotten things you've done in your life. Besides, what would've been the point? I was so shocked by the news of Madeline's death I had to give myself time to think about it."

She was looking at the gun and fondling it. I wondered if I could snatch it from her. She must have read my mind. "Whatever you're thinking, forget it. I have my finger on the trigger."

"Okay, I won't do anything."

Suddenly a car came into the lot at high speed and braked to a screeching stop. The doors opened.

Valerie tried to put the gun in her mouth but I grabbed hold of it and pulled it away from her.

"Why did you do that?" she said. Her composure suddenly left. Her face crumpled and she began crying. Tears streamed down her cheeks and her body shook. "Why did you do that?"

"I had to," I said. "And someday you're going to thank me for it."

She howled. "In prison? In disgrace?"

"It's better than being dead, isn't it?"

Through her tears, she said, haltingly, "I—don't—think—so."

Sienna was out of the police car, running toward us, the long hair of her wig tumbling around her face. She pulled open Valerie's door and pointed a gun at her. "Put your hands on your head." she said.

Valerie raised her hands.

"It's okay," I said. "Everything's okay."

Sienna paid no attention to me. Her voice was harsh. "Step out of the car. Now! Her voice rose. "I said, now!"

"Hey," I said. "Take it easy. I've got her gun. Everything's under control."

"Keep out of this."

Valerie tried to move, but it was difficult with her hands on her head. "Is it all right if I lower my hands?" she asked.

"Just do what I say," Sienna said. "Step out of the car."

Valerie finally managed to get out and I did, too. I was still holding her pink pistol. Diego was there by then. He held his hand out. "I'll take that."

I was glad to give it to him.

CHAPTER 68

Valerie Venable's arrest was news. A murder by a well-known gallery owner not only brought local headlines but also was immediately picked up by the major media. And the fact that it happened in the glamorous Hamptons generated even more interest. The story was featured on all the New York and Long Island TV channels.

Valerie connected with a celebrity lawyer who knew exactly what to do. She got VV out on bail, whereupon Valerie then went back to running her gallery. The grapevine buzz was that because of all the publicity she was doing more business than ever.

Her lawyer worked the media like the master she was. She painted Oakhurst as a serial rapist, an altogether nogoodnik who deserved everything he got. After watching a few of her performances on TV, I was ready to concede that no jury in the world was going to convict Valerie Venable of anything but doing a good deed for mankind.

I didn't care. I wasn't about to moralize about Valerie being a murderer. Life was full of bad people who deserved to die. In fact, some people might argue she did the world a favor. I wasn't one of them, but at the same time I didn't feel I had the right to judge her.

As for the rest of it, even though Frenchie got away without consequences, I'd helped Morty and Sarajane, the people most important to me. And I'd fulfilled my obligation to Haley Sanford. In spite of a few detours, I'd managed to get to the truth. I thought I'd done a first-rate job, and I'd more than proven I could do what cops and professional private eyes do. Maybe even better. Move over, Sam Spade.

The phone rang a lot. Friends, acquaintances, the local papers, some people I didn't even know. Of course, my Dad was one of the first to call.

"I am so proud of you, sonny. I can't tell you how much. Zeena is too, of course."

"Thanks, Dad." It didn't matter that I was getting old. He was still my father. His praise meant a lot.

Where Sienna was concerned everything was up in the air. After the arrest, she claimed she was too busy to see me. I tried calling but didn't get anywhere. What I got was the *I'm sorry Jake, it'll have to wait* reply. I saw her on TV news programs. She came across well, so well, that I thought some smart producer might offer her a contract.

Not seeing her was frustrating, but because she was who she was, I felt that pushing her might backfire. So I held back and waited. My hope was that by being patient, something good might happen.

Morty came over to tell me that he'd taken Sarajane and Margo to JFK. I gave him a beer.

"They're on their way back to London," he said. "They both asked me to say goodbye for them and to thank you for everything."

"That's nice. I'm sorry I didn't get to see them before they left."

"They said they'll be back for a visit every once in a while. Isn't that great? I guess my daughter likes me."

"Why wouldn't she? You're a good guy."

"Thanks. So what's doing with the lady detective?"

I shrugged, not really wanting to talk about it. "I haven't seen Sienna since the arrest."

"How come? I know you're hot for her."

"I don't know what I am. But it doesn't matter. She's too busy. Doesn't have time for me."

"That's not you, Jake," Morty said. "Make her have time. If you let her push you around now, what kind of a relationship will you end up with?"

I laughed. "You are truly funny. We don't have a relationship. That's the whole point. Sienna is not the kind of person you tell what to do. That's one of the things I admire about her."

"What kind of bullshit is that? You don't admire a woman. You love her or you don't."

After he left, I began thinking. How *did* I feel about her? Did I really love her, or did I just want to fuck her? The truth was I wasn't sure. But I needed to know.

The next morning I called her, I didn't waste any time with small talk. "I have to see you. I don't give a damn if you're the busiest cop in the universe. I need to see you right away."

"Hey," she said. "What's got into you?"

"I've been trying to see you for weeks and all I ever hear when I call is that you're too busy. I'm not a life insurance salesman. Stop putting me off."

"I have been busy. That's not a lie."

"I'll take your word for it. Meet me for lunch. One o'clock. I know a really good restaurant in Patchogue. They've got great food."

"I'm not sure I can do that, Jake."

"You can do it."

There was a pause. "All right, I'll do what you ask. But I don't have time for a fancy lunch. I'll meet you where we met before, the diner in Bellport."

"Agreed."

CHAPTER 69

I drove all the way in a state of nervous anticipation. I had no clue as to what to say to her. I knew I had to get the guts of what I wanted out on the table. The trouble was that I didn't know what it was I wanted.

I pulled into the familiar parking lot and abruptly remembered what happened the time I met her there when I was trying to find out why the cops were willing to have Sarajane come back to The States. As usual, she'd been giving me a hard time. The frustrating conversation was compounded afterward by my finding my tires slashed. What a fun day that had been.

Her red Miata wasn't there so I went inside and got a booth for us. I told the waitress there'd be two. She brought the settings, menus, and two glasses of water. I'd invited Sienna to have lunch but not only was I not hungry, the thought of eating was impossible. My stomach was all but groaning. I could always watch Sienna do it, though. Her appetite was one of the most remarkable things about her. To watch her eat would be any Jewish mother's delight. I lifted the glass of water and saw Sienna come into the restaurant.

I stopped breathing. The sight of her did it. I now knew why I was there. There were several reasons. The wonderful color of her hair and the way it formed a perfect complement to her face. The startling green eyes. I couldn't see their color from that distance but I didn't need to. Her lovely body, partly concealed by clothing, this time not a suit but a sweater and skirt. She looked ultra-feminine and I immediately remembered what she looked and felt like underneath the clothes.

She began walking toward me. Her body moved with a smooth, fluid motion that made me giddy. When she got to the booth, I stood up, feeling an urgent desire to hold her. I wanted to feel her body against mine. I wanted to kiss her and have her kiss me back.

But I didn't. Instead, I said, "Hey! I'm so glad you're here."

She leaned toward me and barely touched my lips with hers. "I'm glad you're glad."

She slid into the booth across from me and put her handbag on the seat beside her. The waitress came over and asked if we were ready to order.

"I'm not very hungry," she said. "I'll just have coffee."

"What?" I couldn't help saying.

"I'm not hungry."

"Are you sick? Is something the matter?"

Sienna's eyes went cold. "Why don't you order? The young lady doesn't have all day."

"I'm not hungry either. Just coffee for me, too."

"Two coffees," the waitress said, grumpily. She was clearly distressed that the tip would be small.

I knew I'd put my foot in it again. Why did I have to be such an asshole and make a fuss about the food?

"Okay," I said. "Let's begin all over. I'm very glad you're here. I'm very glad to see you."

"You already said that."

"So I did. How are things going with the case?"

"Everything is in the DA's hands now. I've done all my paper work, given them all the information. I'm back on the job and dealing with other issues. Valerie Venable is no longer my concern."

"You don't mean that."

She raised a hand in protest. "I do and I don't. I do in the sense that I'm finished with the case until the trial. Then I'll be called on to testify, of course. But yes, I do think about her and her child and what she did."

"Sure," I said. "I'm glad it's over, too. But it resonates. I have to admit that."

The waitress put two cups of coffee on the table and left.

I suddenly blurted out. "Sienna, I think about you all the time."

She gave me a kind of blank look but didn't say anything.

"I think about you because I'm in love with you. I wasn't sure about it until now. The minute you walked in and I saw you, I knew. I knew beyond a doubt it was real."

Sienna looked down at the table. She still didn't speak.

"Do you hear what I'm saying?"

I reached across the table for her hand. She let me take it.

She raised her head and looked at me. Her beautiful eyes were full of tears.

"Darling girl," I said. "Why are you crying?"

She squeezed my hand then withdrew it. "Jake...I don't know what to say."

"It should be easy. Say you love me, too."

"I do," she said. "I do, but..."

"But? What does that mean, but?"

She took a deep breath. "There's someone else in my life."

"The guy you were with before? The guy you said you were addicted to?"

She hesitated. "Actually no. It's someone else. Someone new."

"What?" I couldn't believe what I was hearing. "When did this happen?"

"We met only a short while ago."

"That's pretty fast, isn't it?"

"I'm sorry. It just happened. He's so—"

"Stop," I said. "I don't want to hear it. You tell me you love me but you go off with someone else. What am I supposed to say? What am I supposed to think?"

"I know it sounds crazy but I do love you. You're so sweet, so funny. You're good, too. The best person I've ever known. That's why I came here today. I didn't want to tell you on the phone. I wanted you to hear it from me, in person."

"Damn thoughtful of you," I said.

"There's no explanation I can give you that's any good." She leaned forward and touched my cheek with the tips of her fingers. "It's just the way it is."

I felt as if I'd been punched silly.

We sat there, not speaking, letting the coffee grow cold.

"I'd better go," she said.

I didn't say anything.

She slid out of the booth.

I stared at the table, not looking up. I don't remember how much time passed. Eventually, I pushed myself up, put a ten dollar bill under the saucer, and left.

When I got out into the parking lot, the sun was high and bright, the air cool. It meant nothing. The last thing I cared about was nature. I was in pain and filled with pity for myself. I got into my car, started it up, and backed out of my space. As I did I felt a thump underneath the wheel. Was something wrong with the car? Not again! Now, when I needed to get out of there as fast as I could? I bowed my head and hit the steering wheel with the palms of my hands.

I opened the car door, got out, walked around to the back, and saw what had caused the thumping sound.

The rear left tire was on the asphalt. Unequivocally flat! I looked closer. There were no slashes. It was just a plain, old, dumb flat tire.

I stood there for a while, feeling as flat and low as the tire, when a thought suddenly struck me. What in the world was I down in the dumps about? Life, that's all this was. One more moment in the unpredictability of everything and anything we do. We can no more control our destiny than we can predict the weather. What it came down to was that life was a blast. That was all there was to it.

William, as usual, had the potent comment: *What fates impose, that men must needs abide. It boots not to resist both wind and tide.*

Okay, I thought, exit the stage, laughing.

The End

About the Author

Many fiction writers have long been urged to get out of their ivory towers and research the real world for their material. Robert Boris Riskin did better than that. He went out and actually worked for a living. A Brooklyn native, he traveled the world. He supported himself and family at a variety of jobs—from dishwasher to factory worker, busboy to a hawker of low-price, high-fashion garments for women—all the while experiencing firsthand the stuff of the human condition that feeds his writing.

Riskin's work has appeared over the years in a variety of literary magazines, including The New Yorker. Long an avid reader of mystery-thrillers, he decided to try his hand at it. The crackling results were *Scrambled Eggs* and *Deadly Bones* which introduced a salty, new, reluctant sleuth and Shakespeare maven, called Jake Wanderman. *Deadly Secrets* is the third book in the series.

Riskin now lives and writes in Sag Harbor, at the eastern end of New York's Long Island, where, he says, the bay and ocean are close enough to touch, and the air is alive with stories.